A KNIFE FOR HARRY DODD
AN INSPECTOR LITTLEJOHN MYSTERY

GEORGE BELLAIRS

ABOUT THE AUTHOR

George Bellairs was the pseudonym of Harold Blundell (1902—1982). He was, by day, a Manchester bank manager with close connections to the University of Manchester. He is often referred to as the English Simenon, as his detective stories combine wicked crimes and classic police procedurals set in quaint villages.

He was born in Lancashire and married Gladys Mabel Roberts in 1930. He was a devoted Francophile and travelled there frequently, writing for English newspapers and magazines and weaving French towns into his fiction.

Bellairs' first mystery, *Littlejohn on Leave* (1941), introduced his series detective, Detective Inspector Thomas Littlejohn. Full of scandal and intrigue, the series peeks inside small towns in the mid twentieth century, and Littlejohn is injected with humour, intelligence and compassion.

He died on the Isle of Man in April 1982 just before his eightieth birthday.

ALSO BY GEORGE BELLAIRS

Littlejohn on Leave
The Four Unfaithful Servants
Death of a Busybody
The Dead Shall be Raised
Death Stops the Frolic
The Murder of a Quack
He'd Rather be Dead
Calamity at Harwood
Death in the Night Watches
The Crime at Halfpenny Bridge
The Case of the Scared Rabbits
Death on the Last Train
The Case of the Seven Whistlers
The Case of the Famished Parson
Outrage on Gallows Hill
The Case of the Demented Spiv
Death Brings in the New Year
Dead March for Penelope Blow
Death in Dark Glasses
Crime in Lepers' Hollow
A Knife for Harry Dodd
Half-Mast for the Deemster
The Cursing Stones Murder
Death in Room Five
Death Treads Softly

Death Drops the Pilot

Death in High Provence

Death Sends for the Doctor

Corpse at the Carnival

Murder Makes Mistakes

Bones in the Wilderness

Toll the Bell for Murder

Corpses in Enderby

Death in the Fearful Night

Death in Despair

Death of a Tin God

The Body in the Dumb River

Death Before Breakfast

The Tormentors

Death in the Wasteland

Surfeit of Suspects

Death of a Shadow

Death Spins the Wheel

Intruder in the Dark

Strangers Among the Dead

Death in Desolation

Single Ticket to Death

Fatal Alibi

Murder Gone Mad

Tycoon's Deathbed

The Night They Killed Joss Varran

Pomeroy, Deceased

Murder Adrift

Devious Murder

Fear Round About

Close All Roads to Sospel

The Downhill Ride of Leeman Popple

An Old Man Dies

A Knife for Harry Dodd

GEORGE BELLAIRS

This edition published in 2019 by Agora Books

First published in 1953 in Great Britain by John Gifford

Agora Books is a division of Peters Fraser + Dunlop Ltd

55 New Oxford Street, London WC1A 1BS

Copyright © George Bellairs, 1953

All rights reserved

You may not copy, distribute, transmit, reproduce or otherwise make available this publication (or any part of it) in any form, or by any means (including without limitation electronic, digital, optical, mechanical, photocopying, printing, recording or otherwise), without the prior written permission of the publisher. Any person who does any unauthorised act in relation to this publication may be liable to criminal prosecution and civil claims for damages.

To
Nell, Duncan and Pam

Cut off even in the blossoms of my sin,
Unhousel'd, disappointed, unaneled;
No reckoning made, but sent to my account
With all my imperfections on my head:
O, horrible!

— HAMLET. ACT I. SCENE V.

1
TROUBLE AT MON ABRI

Two women were sitting in the drawing-room of *Mon Abri*, a small bungalow on the main road between Helstonbury and Brande. The lights were on and you could see inside. They never drew the curtains, thus giving a peep-show for passers-by.

They were obviously mother and daughter. By looking at the old one you could tell what the young one would be like in twenty years' time. They sat there among a lot of modern furniture, pink silk cushions with pink parchment lampshades to match, illuminated by a lot of little lamps instead of one from the ceiling. The old woman was knitting, her back straight, her lips moving, counting the stitches. The younger one was reading a novelette. She had her legs tucked under her in the large chair, and from time to time she helped herself from a box of chocolates on a little table nearby. In the hearth an electric fire glowed; two hot bars and beneath them a lot of illuminated cardboard coal and a fan revolving to make it flicker.

The younger of the two still bore traces of good looks in a lush kind of way. She was small, with large eyes and yellow dyed hair. Her face was round, good-natured and self-indulgent, her figure full and rather attractive for those who liked them that way. A smell of cheap powder hung around her. The way she was sitting showed a good five inches of pink flesh above the top of her stocking. The old woman leaned forward and, with a tightening of the lips, decently adjusted her daughter's dress.

Mrs Nicholls, the old one, was the thinner of the two, a worried-looking woman with a mass of white bobbed hair and always dressed in black. She wore rimless spectacles and seemed to be ever on the alert, as though expecting something to happen at any minute. She knitted interminably. Scarves, jumpers, stockings, gloves, caps. It kept her arthritic finger-joints from stiffening and found her something to do to while away the time.

The radio was going at full blast. A smart comedian cracking jokes and pausing for laughter, which came regularly like a roar created by some monotonous machine. Neither woman heeded the wireless. It provided a background of noise; otherwise it might just as well not have been on.

'Is that the telephone?'

The old woman cocked an ear in the direction of the door. Above the chatter of the comic they could just hear the rhythmic noise of the bell.

'Shut that thing off…'

The younger woman lazily turned and flicked up the knob. The bell kept ringing.

'Hello…'

The old woman's voice grew affected.

'Hello…'

She listened, gingerly laid down the instrument, and returned to the room.

'It's Dodd. He wants you… Quickly, he says…'

She always called him Dodd when he wasn't there. It was her way of showing lack of respect for him. Her daughter, Dorothy, had worked in Dodd's office in Cambridge until six years ago. Then the pair of them had run away together. A terrible scandal, because Dodd had a wife and grown-up children.

The old woman turned her ear in the direction of the hall, trying to hear what was going on.

Dodd hadn't wanted his wife to divorce him, but the family had pushed it through. His son took over the business in which the bulk of his mother's money was invested. He made it pay better than his father did. Harry Dodd was a funny, lackadaisical sort, who liked knocking around in old clothes, free-and-easy, talking and drinking with common people. His family pushed him off in spite of their mother, and the price at which they bought out his shares in the firm was quite enough to keep him.

And then Dodd hadn't married Dorothy Nicholls at all. He'd bought *Mon Abri* in Brande, taken her and her mother to live with him, and started a *ménage à trois*. Dorothy called herself Mrs Dodd in the village. Dodd never objected, but he slept in his own room, a sort of cockloft over the bungalow, and treated his two women like relatives. Dorothy didn't seem to object. Dodd kept her well in funds and was polite to both of them. The old woman felt her presence there gave the union a kind of respectability...

'But you know I can't, yet...'

Dorothy sounded scared.

'All right then... If it's that important. I'll get it out...'

She hung up the receiver and almost ran into the room, her bosom heaving as if she were ready to have a good cry.

'He wants me to take the car and meet him in the village...'

'But...'

'He says he's ill and can't get up the hill. I'll have to try. He sounds bad. I could hardly hear him at the end.'

'But you'll smash it up. You never were any good at it. Didn't you stop learning because you hadn't confidence...?'

'I'll have to try. He might die. I don't know how I'm going to turn round, once we get there...'

'I'm coming with you.'

They hurried to the garage at the side of the house. In the

confusion it took them twice as long to get the door open and light up the drive.

'Where is he?'

'In the phone box at the bottom of the hill.'

Every night Dodd walked down the hill for a drink at the village pub; then he walked back. Sometimes he got in very late, but the women left his supper and went to bed if he wasn't in by eleven. Now it was just after ten.

'I've forgotten how to start it…'

The old woman never tired of talking about when her father had a carriage and pair, but she knew nothing of motor vehicles.

'I've forgotten the ignition key…'

She ran indoors, rummaged in a drawer, found the key, and this time got the engine turning over.

'Don't you have to put the lights on?'

She fumbled with the dashboard again and this time illuminated the whole of the car, inside and out. The headlights shone full and fair into the road, with moths flitting about in the beams.

Dorothy went through the drill, like a child practising something. It was nearly two years since she had tried to learn to drive. Dodd used the car quite a lot himself and took the women with him now and then. Dorothy had once taken a fancy to driving but could never pass the tests. Finally, she had abandoned it.

'What if you're caught? You haven't got a licence. It's not fair of Dodd…'

Clutch out, gear in, brake off, accelerate, clutch in… Dorothy ran through the routine and then tried it out.

'I say, it's not fair of Dodd. What if…?'

'Oh, shut up, Mother. It's bad enough…'

The car leapt forward, down the drive and into the road with a wide sweep. It was a good job nothing was coming in the other direction. Dorothy was scared about changing gears. She decided to run downhill in bottom. They progressed uncertainly down to the village, Dorothy clinging tightly to the wheel, keeping unsteadily to the left.

The headlamps blinded oncoming traffic and cars began to signal frantically. Dorothy didn't know what it was all about…

Then, near the bottom of the hill, they saw Dodd. He was not a tall man, but now he looked like a little hunchback. His arms swung limply in front of him, his head was bowed, his shoulders sagging. He could hardly put one foot after the other.

Dorothy frenziedly tried to remember how to stop. But before she could act, Dodd had fallen on his face in the road, his arms spread out above his head, his hat in the dust. More by good luck than good management, Dorothy stalled the engine and found the brake in time.

It was only when they picked him up that the pair of them discovered that Dodd had been stabbed in the back. Whimpering, they struggled to get him to his feet, and then they found the blood. All they could think about was how to get him in the car. He was a heavy little man, and they tussled and dragged him between them and finally sat him on the floor. Not another vehicle passed, or else it might have been a different tale. As it was, Dorothy contrived to get the car home by taking a loop road instead of turning, and when they got Dodd to his own fireside, he was dead.

Although the Nicholls women drove Dodd home just before eleven, it wasn't until hours later that they finally did something about it. PC Wilberforce Buckley had long been in bed and was annoyed when they roused him. Dr Vinter, the police surgeon from Helstonbury, who had just retired after a rather hectic night at the Medical Ball, was even more annoyed.

'Why did you put it off till now, Mrs Nicholls?' asked Willie Buckley.

Willie was a young officer whose father had been in the force before him. He was a tall, heavy, red-faced constable, with the beginnings of quite a formidable moustache on his top lip, and heavy black eyebrows, which looked like little moustaches as well. He had a comfortable wife and four children. The youngest had started to howl when the telephone rang, and Buckley had left him yelling his head off.

'We didn't realise he was dead… We didn't quite know what to do… It was so sudden, like…'

Frantically Mrs Nicholls tried to find excuses, whilst her daughter, alternately scared by the situation and anxious about the future, wandered from room to room, weeping now and then, with a wet handkerchief screwed tight in a ball in the palm of her hand.

At first, the women hadn't believed Dodd was dead. They had put him in his pyjamas, fixed up his wound with plaster and lint, and put him to bed. Then, they'd realised he had died quietly whilst in their hands. It troubled them, not so much out of affection, although, in a way, it was nice to have him about the place. What bothered them was what was going to happen to them now that supplies were cut off.

Harry Dodd had been a genial enough man, but very self-contained. He never mentioned his family, they never visited him, and the Nicholls pair didn't even know their address, except that it was somewhere in a suburb in Cambridge. He had an only brother, too, somebody well known in politics. Dodd had betrayed that once when Dorothy had found his brother's picture in the paper and had asked Dodd if he were any relation. He had been the image of the man in the paper; you would have said it was Dodd himself. Harry Dodd had grown annoyed and impatient whenever asked about his personal affairs, but Dorothy had looked it up in the reference books at the library, and as Harry and William Dodd were both from Cambridge and had both gone to the same school, she had put two and two together.

The Nicholls women were anxious to know if Harry had left a will. If he hadn't, it meant they would soon be out of *Mon Abri* without a cent.

'It's not good enough,' said the old woman. 'Here he's died and made no provision for you. And you as good as his wife, and more good to him than his beastly family...'

They started to turn the place upside down to find any documents Dodd might have left behind. He seemed to have had no private papers. A cheque-book — all stubs and no forms — a lot of old sweepstake and lottery tickets, some seed catalogues and a few paid bills were all they could find in his desk, and when they forced open the only locked drawer, they found it full of home-made dry-flies for Dodd's fishing trips. In the loft it was the same, except that there they found a locked trunk which resisted all efforts to open it.

'He's done it on us proper, the rogue,' panted Mrs Nicholls after their fruitless exertions.

'He was good to us while he was with us, Mother...'

'Good to us! I like that. Do you know you'll have to find a job again...'

And she started to pace the room muttering, 'I can't believe it', until finally her voice rose to a hysterical shriek and she began to beat the walls in temper.

To tell the truth, Dorothy was standing it better than her mother. At first, taking a man from his wife and family had seemed quite a conquest, especially when he was rich and decent. Somehow, she had imagined in those days a life of elegant ease, servants at her beck and call, cruises and the Riviera... All the stuff she read about in the novelettes she gobbled up. But it hadn't turned out that way. How was she to know that Dodd's business really ran on his wife's money? Or that Dodd still loved his wife after his lapse, in spite of the fact that his family wanted to get rid of him and pushed through a divorce? And then Dodd had said nothing about marriage but taken her on as a kind of housekeeper at *Mon Abri*, where he retired from the world. He'd even suggested she bring her mother along for company!

Dorothy had long been fed-up with it. Dodd had never been

her idea of a romantic lover, but after the divorce, he'd behaved like someone who had done wrong and was anxious to make amends to his former wife. He'd started to treat Dorothy, too, as if he'd wronged *her*! He'd given her all she needed in the way of money, never put anything in the way of her enjoying herself, but had retired with his personal secrets to his bed in the cockloft. It had suffocated Dorothy sitting at *Mon Abri* with her mother when Dodd was out in the evening with his vulgar pals at the local pub, or away for a day or two, fishing somewhere with nobody knew whom. Dorothy was still under forty, romantic, passionate, and comely. She wanted a taste of life before she grew like her mother, bitter, querulous, and parsimonious. Sooner or later she wouldn't be able to stand the hothouse imprisonment of *Mon Abri*, and Dodd and her mother… She'd kick over the traces and go… Now she was free again, although the way she'd secured her release made her weep for poor Harry Dodd.

'What are we going to do? There's only ten pounds in his wallet. He must have put his remittance in the bank. We can't get that out…'

'Oh, shut up, Mother. We can work. I can get a job. I'm not too old…'

'Well, I'm not taking any more lodgers in to please you or anybody else. It's a dirty, mean trick life's played…'

'What are we going to do?'

'What do you mean…?'

'With him… With Harry…?'

They had been too busy wondering how the affair was going to affect them to get in a panic. Now they faced each other in fear.

'He's been stabbed by somebody. Likely as not by one of them Dodds, his family. They always hated him. And here we are, holding the body. It's not fair.'

'We'd better get a doctor, Mother.'

'What's the use? He's dead. It's a police job, my girl. But before we get the police in here messing about, we've got to think things out.'

'Police!'

Dorothy hadn't thought of that. She started to cry noisily, tears like glass peas running down her cheeks.

'Shut up! I've got to think.'

The old woman's face was as hard as a rock. She'd had plenty of troubles of her own in her time, and it needed a lot to put her out. Dorothy had inherited her father's amorous propensities. He'd had two girls in the family way on his hands at the same time, and then drowned himself in the canal. There wasn't much Mrs Nicholls didn't know after Nicholls had finished with her.

They turned the house upside down again, looking for the will, but nothing more came to light except a little diary with a list of investments from which Dodd seemed to derive his income. And they were in the hands of a firm of London solicitors! Mrs Nicholls solemnly took the photograph of Dodd which stood in a silver frame, beaming on Dorothy's bed, flung it across the room, and then followed it and ground it under her heel.

'The swine!'

'We ought to do something... The police ought to know...'

It was three in the morning, Dodd was lying dead in the old woman's bed, and they weren't a bit nearer getting his money.

'Has it dawned on you, my girl, the police might think we did it?'

Dorothy's mouth opened wide and she emitted a loud, high-pitched scream.

'No... No... They know we wouldn't... Besides, why should we?'

'You never know, when the police get about, what they find out, and if they don't find out, they make up. However, there doesn't seem any way out. If we bury him in the garden and keep on drawing his income, it'll mean getting round the bank and them solicitors. It just wouldn't work. And if we ran off, they'd find us, you being too dumb to drive even the car. No, better get in the police. We've done nothin' wrong. They can't say we did it. Who's goin' to do it, you or me? What shall we tell Buckley when he gets here? He'll want to know what we've been doin' all this time with the body.'

'I can't think…'

'You never could. I'd better ring them, and we'll say we didn't know he was dead or the formalities in cases like this. We'll just act dumb. And that won't be difficult for you, my girl. You're never any help…'

But Dorothy didn't seem to hear. She was actually smiling a kind of smug, feline smile at her own thoughts. Freedom and adventure again…

'Well…? What are you smilin' at? Go and phone Buckley at the police station. Just tell him Mr Dodd died suddenly and will he come up. Don't say any more. You hear me? Not another word. Now get goin'…'

Dorothy undulated to the hall. There was a new provocative swing of her hips and her lethargy was gone. Mrs Nicholls suddenly changed her mind and took up the phone before her daughter could get to it. She never knew what Dorothy would say with a man at the other end! She dialled a number, after looking it up in the book. At the police house in Brande the bell began to ring, the dog barked, PC Buckley turned and grunted, and Charles Buckley, aged ten months, awoke and started to howl.

2

BIG GUNS

Littlejohn wouldn't have been in the case at all but for Willie Dodd. The Midshire County Police, under whose jurisdiction the village of Brande fell, had a CID of their own and up-to-date forensic laboratories which they boasted were as good as those of the Metropolitan Police, any day. But that wasn't good enough for William Dodd, MP, who had his eyes set on the premiership and was now a prominent member of the cabinet.

And just as the Prime Minister was hinting about a dissolution and a general election, the black sheep of the family, Harry, Willie's younger brother, got himself murdered. A loafer, living with a woman not his wife, Harry looked like becoming the centre of a lot of dirty linen and unsavoury publicity. Willie Dodd wanted a quick solution and an end to his brother's publicity, before the political news broke. Harry's name must not only be out of the headlines but chased right out of print before the party manifestos appeared. Willie depended, for his large majority, on Methodist and Catholic votes, in an industrial constituency. Loafing and living in sin wouldn't go down well with them at all…

The news of Dodd's death broke early. The police informed his family in Cambridge before nine o'clock, and Harry's son, Peter, at once let Uncle Willie know. Before ten-thirty Willie Dodd had spoken to the Home Office, the Midshire Police, and the Commissioner at Scotland Yard. Littlejohn and Cromwell arrived at Brande by police car at just after two.

'It's a top level job. The big guns are going off...'

There was a wry smile on the Deputy Commissioner's face as he sent his men about their business.

It looked like an auction sale or a car rally outside *Mon Abri* when the detectives got there.

'What are all this lot?' said Cromwell, picking a spot in which to park the car. At the end of the row of cars stood Uncle Fred's bicycle.

Uncle Fred was Mrs Nicholls' brother, and she had sent for him at once to represent her and her daughter against the power of the Dodds. He was a retired lawyer's clerk and thought no end of himself. When Littlejohn entered the house, the county police were working silently, but Uncle Fred, whose surname was Binns, was arguing with Peter Dodd, who had also turned up to represent the family.

'Pending a proper settlement, you ought to make it a thousand, without prejudice...'

Peter Dodd had offered the Nicholls women five hundred pounds to clear out and leave the bungalow and the dead man to the Dodd family for attention. When they were trying to settle matters as decently and quickly as possible, it was a humbug having Father's mistress and her mother hanging round.

'Make it seven-fifty then...'

The photographers had done their work, the finger-print men had given it up as a bad job, the body was in the morgue at Helstonbury, and Superintendent Judkin was waiting to talk the matter over with Littlejohn as soon as he arrived.

Uncle Fred mistook Littlejohn for the family lawyer and wrung him by the hand.

'I've just been suggestin' that we fix a sum of seven hundred and fifty for the expenses of my sister and niece, *pendente lite*...'

He was a little man with a boozy face and watery eyes, the sort you fear might have a stroke any minute. His nose glowed, and he smelled of whisky already.

The attendant constable was getting rattled.

'We can't do with either of you about here now. You'll have to settle your private matters elsewhere...'

And he manoeuvred Peter Dodd and Uncle Fred out of the room, like two wandering geese, one to his opulent car and the other to his bicycle.

Superintendent Judkin was in plain clothes. Thanks to the pressure of William Dodd and the Home Office, he'd been hastily recalled from holidays at the seaside. He welcomed Littlejohn cordially, and started to grumble right away.

'I'm glad you've come, though I don't know what for, really. It looks like an ordinary sordid little murder to me, and one we needn't have troubled you with. But the heat's on because Dodd happens to be well-connected...'

Judkin was a small, hatchet-faced officer, with a tanned skin and clear blue eyes. He seemed amused at something.

'I can't help laughing. The black sheep of the family gets himself murdered and all the respectable ones start to shiver in their shoes because there looks like being a scandal. They've been at it since ten o'clock trying to hush it all up. They stand a poor chance. The Coroner in charge is a mustard-pot. The very fact that they want it kept dark is enough to make him pull out all the stops...'

And he briefly outlined the case as far as it went.

'I've got the two women here in the lounge in case you'd like a first-hand account of what happened, or what they *say* happened. When I got here, there was a relative of theirs who says he's a lawyer, insisted on advising them, but I soon told him where he got off. That's the fellow in the road there arguing with young Dodd...'

Uncle Fred, in his tweeds and shoes with crêpe soles an inch thick, and young Dodd in his business suit with a pearl grey tie, were arguing still, and Uncle Fred was thumping the bonnet of young Dodd's car.

Littlejohn looked round the room in which they were waiting. It was furnished in cheap oak; a dining suite and table and a sideboard, and a lot of silly little pink table lamps, cushions, and modern porcelain figures. There was a smell of stale, greasy cooking about the place, with a trace of face powder and cats.

'Perhaps you don't mind if we have a word with Mrs Nicholls and her daughter. By the way, what do you call the daughter…?'

'She poses as Mrs Dodd, but she isn't, you know. I call her Miss Nicholls…'

Judkin went to muster the women from the sitting-room, where they appeared to be waiting in state for official business.

Littlejohn stood on the hearthrug trying to absorb the atmosphere of the place. It was sordid, without a doubt. Dodd, in a fit of middle-aged foolishness, had gone off the rails with his typist. Left to his own devices, he'd soon have found out on which side his bread was buttered and returned to his wife like a naughty boy. And doubtless she'd have forgiven him. But his family intervened, pushed their mother out of the way, and engineered a divorce. From what must have been a comfortable, middle-class home, Dodd had been driven to this…

Littlejohn looked around again. The stuffy atmosphere, the little pink-shaded lamps, the dreadful watercolours on the walls, which looked as if Mrs Nicholls, Dorothy or Uncle Fred had copied them from picture postcards… No wonder Dodd went to the village inn and drank with the local ne'er-do-wells and cadgers. He'd lost his job and become a remittance-man, too. All day with nothing to do! Nothing, except listen to Mrs Nicholls and Dorothy…

So much Littlejohn had gathered from the files. Now here

were Mrs Nicholls and Dorothy, Dodd's two women, to put their point of view.

'May I offer you anything?'

Mrs Nicholls addressed the three police officers and indicated a decanter and a lot of little pink cocktail glasses. The kind of thing you won at hoop-la or on shooting-ranges at a fair. The bottle was half-full of what looked like sherry.

'May I offer you anything?'

They didn't want to hurt her feelings, so explained that it was against the regulations to drink on duty.

Dorothy was quite in the background. Her mother and Uncle Fred had told her they knew best what was good for her.

'Could you tell me what happened last night…? What time did Mr Dodd leave?'

'Won't you sit down?'

Mrs Nicholls indicated the chairs and they all settled in them.

'Mr Dodd left about seven, didn't he, Dorothy?'

'Yes… The news was just starting on the wireless. He usually went out about that time.'

'Where did he go? Right to the village inn?'

Mrs Nicholls nodded without answering.

'Are you sure, Mrs Nicholls? How do you know?'

'Well…'

The old woman looked a bit bewildered. She'd never followed Dodd out on his nightly jaunts. She'd taken his word that he was going to the village for a drink and left it at that. He might have gone anywhere for all she knew.

'He always *said* he was going for his drink. I never followed him. We'd no reason to doubt him.'

Hadn't they? Littlejohn was surprised and wondered if Mrs Dodd had ever said the same thing before he ran off with Dorothy!

'Did he never take you or Miss Nicholls out with him in the evenings?'

Mrs Nicholls straightened herself up.

'We aren't in the habit of frequenting public houses, Inspector. We stayed in most nights. One night a week, usually on Wednesday, we went to the pictures in Helstonbury, together, and now and then Mr Dodd took Dorothy when there was something good. He wasn't very fond of pictures…'

'What did he do with his time?'

'He did a bit in the garden… went off fishing now and then… took us for a ride in the car about once a week, and then we'd end up in Helstonbury for shopping or the pictures…'

Littlejohn waited, but there was no more.

What a life! One slip, and Dodd was condemned to boredom for the rest of his existence. Unless he found diversions unknown to the two women.

'Did he ever stay away from home?'

'Now and then. He'd go away on fishing trips, or perhaps a weekend with an old friend. He always told us, and we always knew it would be all right.'

'He didn't carry on any business?'

'No. He had money of his own. But for his family takin' advantage of him, he'd have had a lot more.'

'Did he make a will, do you know?'

The effect on the two women was the same. Tension, anxiety, and a bit of resentment.

'He never told us. He never mentioned his private money affairs and, of course, we didn't pump him…'

I'll bet you didn't, thought Littlejohn.

'Coming to the night he died… last night. You say he rang up on the telephone and asked you to come to the village to pick him up.'

Dorothy now took the stage. She shouted her mother down. Littlejohn felt a bit relieved. Mrs Nicholls, with her chatter, was a prize bore, and her affected voice and efforts to make a ladylike impression were pathetic.

'Mother answered the phone. I can't drive properly. I can't pass the driving test and I suppose I did wrong to take out the car, but I didn't know what to do. We met him on the road, trying to get home.'

She blubbered a minute and then burst into tears and howled.

'It's not good enough, a good man like Harry to get that done to him. He never did anybody any wrong...'

She sniffed and dried her tears on a handkerchief which was damp already. Presumably she'd been having a private weep now and then whenever she could shake off her mother.

'I must confess that when I answered the phone, I thought Harry was drunk...'

'Mother! You never said a word...'

'No, but I had my own thoughts.'

'Did he often come home drunk, Mrs Nicholls?' asked Littlejohn.

'Now and then, if he met one of his pals at *The Bear*... that's the village inn. Sometimes he'd have a bout. We didn't say anything to him about it. After all, Inspector, one has to be broad-minded...'

Yes, one had. Especially when Dodd held the purse-strings.

'...He was always a gentleman, even when he'd taken too much.'

'How did his money come?'

'I believe it was paid to the bank regularly, every quarter. He always gave Dorothy her allowance when it came. Always a quarter's housekeeping, etcetera, in cash, when his remittance came... I don't know what we're going to do now. There's this house and a lot of bills...'

'Could you tell me if he seemed worried or content of late?'

The two women looked at one another rather surprised. The elder one, as usual, spoke first.

'He seemed comfortable enough. We looked well after him and he never complained.'

'Did he read much?'

Littlejohn had been looking round. There were plenty of paper-backed novelettes scattered about, but nothing a man might read.

'Oh, yes. He read quite a lot. He was a member of a library in Helstonbury, and he got books from a book club as well. He always had his breakfast in bed. We took it up with the morning paper, and then after he'd read the paper, he'd read his book a bit...'

Judkin and Cromwell exchanged glances and smiled at one another. Cromwell's smile was a bit self-satisfied. Littlejohn was teaching Judkin a thing or two. All about Dodd...

'What time did he get up as a rule?'

'About eleven...'

'Tell me this, Mrs Nicholls... Did Mr Dodd shave every day... or had his existence as a retired man made him a bit free and easy...? Did he miss a day or two shaving...?'

'Oh, dear, no... He shaved every day. As soon as he got up, we'd hear his electric shaver going. He might have looked a bit free and easy in his dress, but that was always his way. His things were good, and he was clean and neat. He never went to seed, as they say.'

Littlejohn turned to the Inspector.

'We'll be going down the village to *The Bear* later...'

'Yes... I fixed dinner there for you, and if you want rooms, they'll manage that too.'

'Thanks. Did they say, Superintendent, whether or not Mr Dodd left in his usual health and spirits last night...?'

'Yes. He had a few drinks with his pals and then said goodnight about ten o'clock and went off. Whether or not somebody attacked him for his money and then got fright... His wallet and cash and his watch were all on his person. His keys, too...'

The women exchanged covert glances.

'And instead of going back to the inn for help, he telephoned home and wanted to get back there. So much so that he started to walk... It might be that he hoped to hush up the attack, or that he didn't want a fuss...'

'Could we look over the house before we go? I'm sorry to trouble you, but you quite understand...'

'Of course. The police have been over it already. They've disturbed things a bit. We're house-proud, Dorothy and me, and we always made Dodd comfortable, though I say it myself... Come this way...'

The little procession started.

The place hadn't been built for Dodd, and he didn't seem to have effected many improvements when he took over. There was a line of clothes pegs attached to a bracket in the hall, which made the place look a bit like a waiting-room. Raincoats, overcoats, and two women's fur coats hung on the pegs. A chair, a bamboo table and a chest on which stood a cheap chromium salver made up the rest.

To the right, a door into the dining-room in which they had just been sitting and, beyond that, a scullery with a bright new electric stove, a porcelain sink and a little pantry and china-cupboard.

'I did all the cooking and Dorothy kept the house straight. We had a woman from the village once a week...'

'Who was she?'

Mrs Nicholls raised her thick eyebrows. She looked ready to tell Littlejohn to mind his own business, and then recovered. 'Mrs Mattock. She lives in the cottages by the bridge.'

'Thank you...'

Cromwell made a note and they passed on.

They went to the sitting-room, a stuffy little place, with a fire-place of hideous dark-green tiles. A cheap suite in moquette, a lot of little tables, and more table lamps... Little else. Littlejohn bet to himself that Dodd didn't sit in state there very often. Instead he preferred *The Bear* and his disreputable pals...

'These are our rooms... Dorothy's and mine...'

Mrs Nicholls said it with an effort to be casual, but it was obvious that showing their bedrooms to a trio of men was making her a bit self-conscious. Dorothy was more than that. She looked positively coy, as if inviting them to sinful thoughts at least.

The police officers just peeped in and out, to get the lie of the land. Both rooms smelled stuffy; Dorothy's heavily laden with cheap scents, her mother's with a herbal smell, as though she applied potions or drank decoctions. The windows were closed…

That was all except for the bathroom.

'Where did Mr Dodd sleep?'

'Up there… We had to put him in my room after he died…'

'Up there' was a trapdoor in the ceiling of the passage, with a ring protruding. Mrs Nicholls took a long pole with a hook on one end and slipped it through the ring in the trapdoor, which gave way and let down a metal ladder.

Littlejohn and Cromwell climbed up.

'I've been up there already,' said Judkin, but the old woman followed. She wasn't going to miss anything.

It was a room made under the tiles… a kind of box of plaster-boarding. A camp-bed, a chest of drawers, a reading-lamp, a large tin box with a lock, a bedside table. All as neat, simple, and clean as a sailor's cabin. There were bookshelves along one side. Plenty of fiction, a lot of travel books, and some sea stories… Voyages round the world, across the Pacific, the Atlantic in a fishing smack… Dodd making voyages round the world from his camp-bed…

'Sometimes he used to draw up his ladder and fasten himself up when the mood took him…'

Yes; Littlejohn was beginning to understand that, too. When Dodd got bored or fed-up with the women, he severed communications and sat in isolation, reading travel tales or else rummaging in his tin box.

'Have we got Mr Dodd's keys, Superintendent? I'm just wondering about this tin box.'

Littlejohn called down through the hole in the floor.

'We haven't got so far yet, although I've got the keys here. I suggest, though, in the circumstances, that we get his lawyer before we open the box. He's a Helstonbury solicitor...'

'We'll do as you suggest. I'm coming down now.'

Mrs Nicholls was fascinated by the box.

'He never opened it when we were about. I'd like to know what's in it.' And she kicked it spitefully.

'We'll be dealing with it later, Mrs Nicholls. We'll be back this evening...'

They got ready to go. Outside, Uncle Fred and Peter Dodd were still arguing. They seemed to be killing time, haggling about a lump sum for the Nicholls women. The constable at the door wouldn't let them in the house until Judkin said the word.

'I've got the keys here. We emptied Dodd's pockets before they took the body away. There wasn't much.'

Judkin indicated a pile of odds and ends on the sideboard, and began to put them, one by one, in his brief-case. Keys, two handkerchiefs, pipe and tobacco, matches, cigarettes, some small change, a wallet containing ten pounds in notes, some papers and a driving licence, a pen, a pencil, and a penknife. Finally, a silly little oddment. It was the top of a beer bottle. A serrated cap of tin forced from the bottle by an opener.

Why Dodd had pocketed it, nobody knew. It was shining and metallic on one side, and on the other, red, with the name of the brewery in black. Hoods' Unicorn...

Judkin spun the metal disk in the air, caught it, and slipped it in his pocket.

'*The Bear* isn't one of Hoods' houses. The Unicorn Brewery is in Leicester, over thirty miles away, and their nearest house is in Coltby, eleven miles from here. So it looks as if Dodd did a bit of travelling now and then...'

3
WHAT HAPPENED TO HARRY DODD?

'It's nice to get back in the fresh air,' said Cromwell as he, Littlejohn, and Judkin left *Mon Abri*. 'And why do people always call shanties like this by French names? *Mon Abri*! What's it mean, anyway…?'

'My Shelter,' replied Littlejohn.

'H'm. A bit ironical, isn't it? Especially with those two sheltering as well…'

They climbed in the police car. Mrs Nicholls watched them off, and then you could see her call in Uncle Fred and Peter Dodd for more arguing and negotiating.

'We'd better drop you at *The Bear* in the village, Cromwell. See if you can find out all Dodd's movements last night until he left to go home, and if there were strangers about. I'll get along with Judkin to Helstonbury to talk things over…'

'I'll send a car out for you in an hour, sergeant. That do?' said Judkin.

'Fine, sir…'

The village inn was a cool old place, with low, beamed ceilings and a sanded stone floor. The door was open but there was nobody visible. In a room behind, somebody was talking angrily, and then the door opened to emit the landlord, a stocky, bald-headed man of middle age, with a grey moustache. He eyed Cromwell up and down, as if trying to assess something about him.

'How do you pronounce bosom, sir?' he asked.

Cromwell was taken aback but replied on the rebound.

'Buzzum,' he answered.

'I said so. That's what I said...'

The landlord looked very pleased with Cromwell for his concurrence, and then shouted through the door of the back room. 'Buzzum... There's an educated gentleman 'ere who agrees with me. Buzzum. Perhaps you'll not contradict me agen, Mister Clever...'

The landlord, 'John Richard Mallard, licensed to sell intoxicating liquors', according to the sign over the door, turned to Cromwell and explained the mystery.

'It's my grandson doin' his shorthand homework. Of course, he *knows* it all. Says it's pronounced Boozum. What does he know about it at thirteen? But then there ain't much you can teach 'em at that age nowadays. It makes me wonder what the world's comin' to. What can I do for you, sir?'

'My name's Cromwell. Are you the landlord?'

'That's me. Mallard's the name. And you're one of the two police gentlemen who's aimin' at staying here. We'll do our best, sir. 'Omely, that's what we aim at bein'. Nothin' posh. Jest 'omely. What'll you take to drink, sir?'

'Pint of mild, please. Perhaps you'll join me, Mr Mallard. I was wanting a little chat with you. It's about Mr Dodd's movements last night.'

Mr Mallard drew two pints and took them in a small room labelled 'Snug', and invited Cromwell to follow.

'It's a bit cosier here, sir, and there's a fire. Although the sun's nice outside, it's coolish for autumn, and this place is always cool... The stone floors, I reckon. Now about pore Mr Dodd.

What can I do? Nice gentleman; big pity. Jest excuse me a second…'

You could hear Mr Mallard dealing with his shorthand-learning grandson in the room behind and threatening him with various penalties if he didn't get on with his work.

'It's his half-day from school, an' as he wants to take wot they call "Commercial Course", he's got to do shorthand. I'm fond o' that lad, but he thinks he knows it all before he starts… Where were we, sir?'

'I believe Mr Dodd was a man of regular habits in the evening. He called here for a nightcap every night, didn't he?'

'As often as not, sir, yes.'

'What time did he usually arrive, Mr Mallard?'

'Round half-past seven. And he usually left as the clock struck ten.'

As if to inform Cromwell of its existence, the clock thereupon struck three quarters.

'Had he always plenty of money?'

'He always stood his corner, paid his dues, and never tried to dodge his round when it came.'

'Had he plenty of friends here?'

'Yes. 'E was a nice, sociable, genial sort, was Mr Dodd. Didn't talk a lot, but jest enjoyed himself and sort of glowed with sociability after a drink or two.'

'Any particular pals?'

'Well… There was a little crowd of 'em drank in this here Snug. Mr Gambles, the joiner; Mr Shadwell, the garage man; Mr Henry Hooper and Mr Charles Hooper, twin brothers, who run a nursery; and Cresswell, the clerk at the sub-office of the bank in the village. They always come in this room…'

'They formed a little exclusive party?'

'Yes.'

'Were they all together last night, Mr Mallard?'

Mr Mallard drank his beer solemnly, drew his moustache between his lips to dry it, and thought.

'Yes... They was all here. Mr Dodd went first, and the rest drank up and followed.'

'They went out as he did?'

'No... They bade him goodnight and stopped behind to finish their drinks. They hadn't the hill to climb like Mr Dodd, and he was usually the first man to leave. A man of very fixed 'abits, was Mr Dodd. On the first stroke of ten by the clock... up he gets...'

'Did anything unusual happen last night, before or after Mr Dodd left?'

'No. I can definitely say no, sir. It was just as usual...'

'Yet no sooner has Dodd put his nose out of the door of your inn, landlord, than somebody stabs him in the back...'

'That's the funny part about it. Who would have wanted to do it? I feel I could kill whoever did it to Mr Dodd with my own hands. You won't find any decent body in this village who'll say a wrong word about him, in spite of the rumours that go round. Those two women are a different cup o' tea... Nobody likes them. Them, with their airs and graces... Anybody can see what they are. I can't think how Mr Dodd came to be mixed up with them, or how he put up with 'em...'

'Has anything unusual happened of late in connection with Dodd...?'

'How do you mean, sir?'

'Any strangers about the village, or anybody asking about him?'

'Now you mention it, there was. About ten days ago... yes, ten days... a little chap like a bookie walks in here and asks for a drink. I didn't like the looks of 'im. The sort who asks for a drink and then tries to sell you somethin' or beg or borrow a fiver.'

'He asked about Dodd?'

'Yes, he did. "Is there a chap called Harry Dodd lives in the village?" asked the feller. "Yes," I says, and nothing else. But that wasn't enough. He tries to pump me about him. "Retired wealthy man?" "I don't know anythin' about his means," I sez, intendin' to dry the chap up. But he asks where Dodd lives. I told him, seein' anybody else could 'ave done the same. With that, he drinks up his beer and offs. I see him later goin' in the post office. I guess he was nosin' there as well. I never saw any more of him.'

'So all his friends thought well of Dodd?'

'Of course they did. He was one of the best…'

'Did he ever get drunk?'

'Not really. He knew when he'd had enough. Sometimes they'd get a bit merry, but never over the line. Mr Dodd and his friends was a very nice lot.'

Mr Mallard said it defiantly, like a challenge.

'I gathered from the Nicholls women that Mr Dodd came home tight now and then, and that he did his drinking with vulgar pals.'

Mr Mallard grew red with indignation.

'That's a ruddy lie. Because he didn't spend his evenin's in their company and wouldn't bring them here — which, by the way, wasn't respectable enough for them — they made out he was a bit beneath them. If that was the case, why didn't they pack up an' go? I'll tell you why they didn't. They was on a good mark. They'd battened themselves on an easy-goin' chap with money to spare, and wasn't givin' up a good livin'. That's what their ladyships was at! A pair of no-good tramps, that's what I'd call 'em.'

Mr Mallard tiptoed to investigate the ominous silence of the room behind the bar parlour. He returned looking very put out.

'He's gone off by the back way. Played Truant, he has, the young varmint. Not that I didn't do the same myself when I was a lad. All the same, that's different… Where were we…?'

'Did Dodd call here every night?'

'Now and then he'd go off fishin' for a bit. He said he met an old friend somewhere up north, and they'd spend a day or two in his pal's fishing hut. He didn't take any of his friends from the village. It was a sort of little trip on his own.'

'You're sure it was fishing he went for?'

'That's what he used to say. Whether he meant it serious or called it his fishin' trip as a joke, I can't say. He might have just been takin' off a bit of time from his two women...'

'Have Hoods' Brewery any houses round here?'

'Hoods? No. I used to keep one myself farther up north, at Kirby Muxloe. They're a Leicester company. Their nearest pub's miles from here. Why?'

'We found one of the caps from a Hoods' beer bottle in Mr Dodd's pocket, as if he might have been drinking Hoods' Ale and accidentally slipped it in...'

'Funny that... Hoods' is quite a small company. They own about twenty-five houses in and around Leicester. What can Mr Dodd have been doin' there?'

'That's what we want to find out. They haven't any, by chance, in or near Cambridge?'

'Hardly so far. My old place at Kirby was in the Southwest direction. Most of their houses are on the south side. I've a pal as keeps one of Hoods' places at Husband's Bosworth. Anythin' I can do to help?'

'Not just yet, thanks, Mr Mallard, but there may be later. You've given me an idea...'

'By the way, do you happen to have seen the feller who says he's related to the Nicholls women? He was in here for a few drinks this mornin'. Boastin', he was, that he'd see right done by them.'

'Yes. Fred, he's called. Fred Binns, I believe. He's Miss Nicholls' uncle...'

'That's the one. Well... I can see him makin' a bee-line for my front door now. Want his company? Because if you do, see he stands his corner. He's a one for free drinks, if you ask me. If you want to talk to him, I'll show him in here. Otherwise, I'll keep him at the bar.'

'I'll just have a word with him, I think. Yes; show him in here when he comes.'

Uncle Fred's eyes lit up when he saw Cromwell. He crossed the floor on eager feet.

'Hullo! You here? You're the police officer on the Dodd case, aren't you? I'm uncle to Mrs… ahem… Mrs Dodd.'

'You mean Miss Nicholls, don't you?'

'Yes, to be precise. Dodd didn't do the right thing by Dorothy. She gave up everything for him, and he ought to have married her. Didn't even settle anythin' on her. I've spent nearly all day tryin' to get Dodd's family to realise their responsibilities for their father's misdoin's, but no use. I used to be a lawyer's clerk. A good job they've got me to look after their affairs…'

'I thought you said you hadn't been able to…' Mr Binns turned purple.

'You tryin' to be offensive? No need to think the police impress or intimidate me. I've done plenty of court work in my time…'

Cromwell fixed Mr Binns with a steely eye.

'Are you wanting to pick a quarrel, Mr Binns? Here I was, peacefully enjoying a drink, until you came. Either let me stand you one, or leave me in peace…'

Mr Binns buried the hatchet at once.

'No offence. Mine's a double whisky, thanks.'

Cromwell thought, with comfort, of his expenses-sheet.

When the drinks came, they settled down.

'How long has Mr Dodd been living with the Nicholls ladies?'

Uncle Fred scratched his chin.

"Bout six years, I reckon. Ought to 'ave married Dorothy. Not fair, the way he did.'

'Cambridge they came from, wasn't it?'

'Yes. His office was there, and he was a lot older than Dorothy. Led her properly astray and then didn't do the right thing by her.'

'What line was Dodd in?'

'Engineering, I believe. They did say he'd a good brain for inventin' things. I've heard Dorothy say how clever he was with his brain, but he was a poor business man. Proper lackadaisical... Sort o' chap who'd disappear for days at a time when they'd important work to do at the shops, and then he'd come back and say he'd been off for a few days' fishin' with a pal... Dorothy was a little trump-card to him in those days, lookin' after him and seein' he kept his appointments and so on... He took advantage of her, and now he's left 'er in the lurch.'

'How do you know he's left her in the lurch? He might have remembered her in his will. Most likely has. It's not been read yet, has it?'

'No, but I don't expect he's done the right and proper thing by her. He shied off marryin' her, he'll likely as not...'

'You're a cheerful bloke and no mistake.'

Uncle's Fred's nose glowed as he upended his glass.

'Seen too much of life to be any other.'

He eyed his empty glass.

'Same again?' said Cromwell.

Uncle Fred agreed quickly before Cromwell changed his mind.

'Did you know Dodd apart from his relations with your niece and sister?'

'Yes. He was prominent in the Cambridge neighbourhood when I was a solicitor's clerk there. I knew him well. Funny, I thought it, when he went off the rails with Dorothy. Mind you, though I say it of my own flesh and blood, she was a smasher when she was his secretary. Yes, I remember Dodd. His family hounded him out of the city, good and proper, after his little affair with Dot... That's my pet name for Dorothy. I must confess that in my long experience I never knew children so vindictive against their parent. You see, they fancied themselves. Two of them married well and the other boy was in the legal profession, like me.'

'How many children had Dodd?'

'Three. Two boys an' a girl. One boy was in the business and fancied himself no end. You see, it was Mrs Dodd's family business, left to her by her father, and Dodd himself was one of the officials, sort of managing engineer, who married his boss's daughter. When old Sedgwick died, his only daughter inherited the lot. When the children grew up, they got a bit fed up with their father's ways. He just wouldn't behave like the big boss. He'd rather take a drink with his workmen, or play in a bowling match with them, than put on his white tie an' tails and go out with the family among the toffs.'

Cromwell wished Littlejohn was there. This was right up his chief's street. Dodd a disgrace to his family and pushed off at the first opportunity!

'Dodd's daughter married a brewer's son who inherited a baronetcy when his father died. She became Lady Hosea… Funny name. Ever hear of Hosea's Ales…?'

Mr Binns' nose glowed at the very mention of them!

'The eldest son went in the works with his father. He'd been to college and thought he knew it all. They'd some good technical men there, of course, and all it wanted was a bit of drive. Winfield Dodd provided that. Not 'arf. He used it on his dad, too, when the scandal broke. It's said that Lady Hosea and Winfield, between them, bullied their mother into a divorce. Of course I was glad at the time, because, after all, I expected he'd marry Dot…'

'Who was the man you were haggling with at *Mon Abri?*'

'Peter Dodd, that was. His mother seems to have sent him along to try and see things was done decent by his dad. Peter's a solicitor, but I wouldn't say much of one. Winfield seems to have got all the guts and drive. Peter's more like Harry Dodd, a bit slow. All the same, he says he can't commit himself about looking after Dot till he's consulted the family. Which is all to the good. I can't see her Ladyship and Winfield lettin' this scandal break. It's rumoured that Winfield's due for a knighthood on the next list. And there's another, too, who'll not relish publicity. That's Willie Dodd, Harry's brother. You know Willie, I suppose. Read his speech last Saturday night? He's heading for Prime Minister one day, or I'm a Dutchman. Look well, wouldn't it? "Minister's Brother Dies in Love Nest." Can't you see it? No; if she plays her cards right, Dot should come out of this okay.'

Uncle Fred was so pleased with his prognostications that he asked Cromwell to join him in a drink, and he was surprised to find that the sergeant wasn't half-way through his first pint

'Come on!' he said, by way of a taunt. 'Same agen for me, landlord. A double...'

'What sort of a woman is Mrs Dodd? Do you know her?'

'I shouldn't really say this, bein' Dot's uncle, but the old lady's one of the best. A perfect lady of the old school. Real gentility. A bit too docile, though, if you know what I mean. When Harry went off the rails, she let the family completely take things in hand. It was said at the time she'd have forgiven Dodd and taken him back, but the family wouldn't let 'er. She must have still been fond of 'im. Don't tell my sister or Dot that I told you. Among men, we can talk like this. Women just don't understand. I've always been broad-minded. Life in the Law makes you that way. Guess it's the same in the Force. Broad-minded... Well... Guess I'd better be on my way. Cycled from Cambridge this mornin', and I've got to get back before dark. Cycling's my 'obby. Keeps me young an' fit...'

Uncle Fred fixed his cycling stockings and looked ready for action. Cromwell wondered however he did it, in his condition and with so many pubs to pass on the way home.

'How many miles will it be?'

'Nearly forty...'

'Good going! All the best.'

'All the best. I'll have to come back in a day or two, so I'll be seein' you...'

He pedalled unsteadily past the window, took to the road, and was soon gone.

Uncle Fred had no sooner disappeared than the sports car of Peter Dodd roared down the village street and pulled up with a squeal in front of the inn.

'Wot, another?' said Mr Mallard, putting his head in at the door of the Snug. 'Pore old Harry Dodd's bringing 'em like flies round a 'oney pot...'

Peter Dodd had entered behind him. He ordered a pint of mild and appeared, carrying his drink, in the doorway of the room where Cromwell was sitting.

'Umph!' said Peter and took his drink away with him.

He was tall, slim, swarthy, and curly haired, and his small, turned-up nose gave him a faint look of perpetual disgust. His thin, dark moustache accentuated this.

Young Dodd suddenly changed his mind and returned to the Snug. He put his beer down on a table, flung himself on a bench, and crossed his legs. He wore his business clothes; black jacket, grey trousers, and he carried a black soft hat.

'You from the police...?'

Cromwell took a drink of his beer and did not answer. Dodd was about twenty-six; Cromwell was old enough to be his father, and more. It was the insolent, affected drawl which got Cromwell's back up.

'I was speaking to you...'

'And I'll answer when you remember your manners...' Cromwell took another drink, and then started to fill his pipe, the one like Littlejohn's.

Peter Dodd flushed and looked ready to jump up and start a row.

Then he suddenly cooled off.

'I'm bloody mad,' he said. 'People like those two women and their blasted Uncle Fred make me see red.'

He drank half his beer and came up for air.

'Been having a bit of trouble, Mr Dodd?'

'Yes. I came to see what I could do to help make the old man's end a bit decent. What do I find? A lot of hangers-on trying to improve the shining hour by screwing as much cash out of the family as they can. Blackmail, that's what it is. Unless we pay 'em off, they'll bleat to all the newspapers, and the Sunday readers'll all have a field-day.'

'You want to keep it quiet?'

'Of course. Why the hell do you think I'm here?'

'Now, now.' Cromwell's voice was sharp with rebuke. 'If you want any help from me, moderate your language and your tone...'

'Well, of all the...'

Then he started to grin. It completely altered his appearance. He looked boyish and quite charming.

'Sorry, old man. But it's got my goat.'

'Who sent you, if I may ask?'

'Oh, ask anythin'. Quite okay by me. I came at Mother's request. She's not well and I try to humour her. In spite of the filthy way he treated her, Mother always had a soft spot for Father. I was too young to interfere when it all happened, but I'll tell you straight, it's added years to Mother. Strictly between us two, they ought to have left her to deal with it all herself. Instead...'

He shrugged and drank his beer.

'You're your mother's boy, then, aren't you?'

Peter Dodd flushed again.

'Bein' a bit offensive?'

'No. Sorry to put it that way. Just trying to get at the truth. This is murder, you know. And, believe me, background, not clues, provides most solutions to crimes like this...'

Cromwell wished Littlejohn could have heard that! It was just the chief's method and idea, and he would have approved his pupil for the lesson he'd learned!

'Indeed! This is interestin'. And what background is going to help clear up this mess, may I ask? A lot of rooting and grubbing in our family history. Because I'll warn you from the start…'

'Don't start threatening. If you won't provide it quietly, there are plenty more who'll revel in washing a lot of dirty linen in public. The more help we get in a quiet way from the likes of you, sir, the easier it'll be for everybody.'

'What are you after?'

'A little information, if you can give it. Did you know your father well?'

Peter Dodd began to look a bit uneasy.

'Better than the rest of the family,' he said at length, rather sulkily.

'Why?'

'It's nothing to do with the case.'

'Hasn't it? Let me make a guess, then. I said you were your mother's boy… Now, now, now; hear me out. Your mother was still fond of your father. If she'd had her way, there'd never have been a divorce. She'd have forgiven him…'

'Well? He didn't damn well deserve it, but my mother was more charitable than the rest of the family.'

'And because you think the world of your mother, you're just a little bit inclined to be the same. In fact, you met the old man now and then, for your mother's sake. Am I right?'

'Yes. You may as well know. Mother's a mild and gentle sort. She's completely under the thumb of my elder brother and sister and my father's brother William… you know, the MP. She once talked of taking Father back… When she learned he hadn't married that awful Nicholls woman… There was such a shemozzle that it made her ill and she never raised it again. But she wrote to Father and he wrote back, and then they got meeting one another. That's where I came in. I used to take her for a run in the country, and we'd meet dad at a quiet pub for an hour or two. It was awful, really. Sort of underhand… And for somebody like my mother to have to do it. All the same, she looked forward to it so much, that I said nothing about it. And Dad was so happy about it, and so... so... so damned humble. If I'd only had the guts, I'd have told the rest of the family to go to hell and insisted on bringing them together again to finish their days out. Instead of which... Father gets killed in a sordid sort of way, and Mother's as stricken as if they'd been a perfect Darby and Joan all their lives. It's a bloody shame, and I don't know what to do about it. Can I get the body and give him a decent funeral, without those two awful hens to follow the coffin?'

'After all, you're his family and the Nicholls women have no claim on him. At best, they were only his housekeepers. He seems to have lived with them because he'd nobody else. You'll be able to set things right, as far as decency goes, after the inquest.'

'That's a relief, anyhow. I can't bear to think of Mother...'

'I'll do what I can. Look here, my chief's in Helstonbury with the police there. Let's drive over and talk to him. He's one of the best and I'll answer for him giving a helping hand for your mother's sake, at least.'

'It's damned decent of you. Let's have a drink before we go, just to drown my cheek when I first met you.'

'Right... Beer for me, please.'

Cromwell took a drink.

'By the way, where were your mother and father in the habit of meeting, Mr Dodd?'

'Mostly in one of the half-way villages. Hurford, Shopton, Stowsley.'

'Did you meet at inns or hotels?'

'Yes. Mostly at a quiet little place or other for lunch, and even tea later. It pleased them to be together. I'd have encouraged them to run away and start all over again, but you can't do that at their age. You see, Mother had an operation a year or two ago. She's not strong. And my brother controls the purse-strings now. Absolutely crawling with complications.'

'But did they have in mind starting again?'

'I used to leave them together for a while. Lord knows what they talked about, but I know Father wanted it. I wouldn't have been surprised if they'd decided it one day, in spite of all the obstacles.'

'Did you ever call at any pubs owned by Hoods' Brewery?'

'No. They haven't any places in the locality. Why do you ask?'

'Funny thing, your dad had the cap of one of their beer bottles in his pocket when he died. They haven't any houses near here...'

'I can't make it out.'

'Don't bother. What were your father's arrangements when he met your mother? I mean, what did he tell the two women at the bungalow?'

'He never mentioned them to Mother, of course. But he once told me, kind of jocularly, that he called the meetings with Mother his fishing trips. He often stayed the night before we were due to arrive and was there to meet us.'

'Had he plenty of money?'

'He wasn't rolling. The settlement was about six hundred a year. He wouldn't have got that but for Mother. It was paid to his bank in Helstonbury.'

'Did he ever tell you about his other friends, the men he might have associated with when he went away for spells? He must have been in the region of Leicester some time, because Hoods' houses are sprinkled round there.'

'No. We didn't talk much... He and Mother had so much to say. I made myself a bit scarce.'

Cromwell studied Peter Dodd carefully.

'You rather liked your father, didn't you?'

Dodd flushed again.

'Yes, I did. Mother ought to have had him around, instead of being a perpetual widow and eating out her heart all these years. He was so kind and considerate to her. It wasn't much fun for him, either, even if he did start it all, to be condemned for life to live in that stuffy, silly little shanty with that awful blonde and her mother. He actually slept in the attic to get away from them, and I believe he used to fasten himself in to get a bit of privacy… It's terrible. I could go berserk and wreck things.'

'Do the rest of your family… your sister and brother and your uncle Willie, MP know you're here?'

'No. They'll have a fit when they find out. I suppose they hope to bury or cremate him quietly here and keep it as dark as they can. But Mother wants him to come home and be buried in the family grave with a young brother who died, and I'll damn well see she gets her own way, or I'll kick up such a stink that'll make the Sunday papers look pale pink beside it. My blood's up. It ought to have been up long ago. This wouldn't have happened if only I'd shown some guts. But I'll see that Mother gets what she wants in this, if I've to blast the whole tale wide open. They'll not let it get so far…'

'Is the family lawyer coming down?'

'I dare say. I'm a lawyer, you know, but not a very good one. However, I stuck out against Uncle Fred, who was trying to work out the pay-off, with the body not yet cold. I packed him off in a huff. A drunken old scrounger, on the cadge… Why do you ask about the family lawyer?'

'There'll be the inquest, you know, and if it's to be kept as quiet as possible, it ought to be in expert hands.'

'Yes. I don't feel up to it myself. Aspinall, our lawyer, is the man. I'd better get him along…'

'Better see my chief first. Let's drive to the police station in Helstonbury. He's expecting me, I know…'

'Right…'

They got in Peter Dodd's racer, and it seemed as though the young man couldn't get there fast enough.

'I'm a married man with children,' protested Cromwell on the way.

'Don't worry, I'm insured,' answered Dodd above the noise of rushing air and clattering machinery.

4

THE FRIGHTENED MAN

With the advent of new industries, the overspill from large cities, and a natural increase in the size of its families, the population of the once quaint old county town of Helstonbury had almost trebled itself in ten years. This had called for a larger police force and police station. At the time Harry Dodd got himself murdered, the force was housed in temporary premises in an old house in the main square, whilst workmen pulled down their original headquarters and put them together again. It was originally estimated it would cost £10,000 and take six months to do. That was eighteen months ago, and they'd already spent £23,000. The jolly workmen on the new police station were still busy brewing tea, putting up and pulling down, brewing more tea, picking a few winners, and taking an odd afternoon off, now and then, to watch the local football team.

Superintendent Judkin took Littlejohn into his office on the ground floor. It had been the sitting-room of the house, and on the faded green wallpaper you could see the shapes of the sideboard, the bookshelves, and the pictures, in the original shade before the sun got at it. The back window overlooked a cobbled yard, stables and coach-house. Through the open door of the latter a policeman with his shirt-sleeves rolled up and his neckband turned in was sousing himself under a tap. Two more policemen were feeding three lost dogs in a wire-netting cage, and five more, dressed in full panoply, were drilling under a sergeant. It was like a Keystone comic!

Judkin looked through one window at the new headquarters and then through the other at the contents of the stable yard.

'The county police,' he said to Littlejohn and started to laugh as though they didn't belong to him at all. He sat down wearily at his desk, indicated a spare chair to Littlejohn, and started to rummage among a lot of files.

'Let me see... Harry Dodd... Here we are.'

There wasn't much in the folder. The statements of the Nicholls women, reports from finger-print men and their photographic handiwork. And then a lot of grisly photographs of Harry Dodd, taken in Mrs Nicholls' bedroom at *Mon Abri* and in the morgue at the police station.

'The body's across the yard,' he said. 'We've even got a temporary mortuary. Like to see it?'

'Not after these,' said Littlejohn, handing back the pictures of Harry's body. Why couldn't they make a more artistic job of post-mortem photographs? A little more light and shade, and perhaps a few sepia tints! These were stark black-and-white, done under a glaring light. Harry Dodd's family, who thought a good deal of themselves from all accounts, would have had a fit if they'd seen their poor father, stark naked on the slate slab of the temporary morgue, exhibit number one in the murder of himself.

'Excuse me...'

A polite young constable entered with a tray of tea things. Judkin, still fumbling with his file, introduced the policeman as his secretary, PC Drane. Drane, with the air of a professional waiter, set out the cups, applied sugar and milk, poured out the tea, and distributed it. He was very polite.

'Excuse me...'

He said it every time he passed in front of Littlejohn.

'Where's the doctor's report, Drane?'

'Allow me...'

Drane laid his hand on it right away. Judkin read it out to Littlejohn. It was simple and straightforward. Dodd had been stabbed and had died from internal haemorrhage. Everybody knew the time of death as eleven o'clock the night before, but the doctor had, for some reason, thought fit to deduce it by scientific observation.

'I would say the time of death was about four hours before I first examined the body...'

'What time is the inquest, Drane?'

'Eleven o'clock in the morning, sir. Mr Dommett has been to see the body...'

'Oh, hell! Is *he* back?'

Judkin turned to Littlejohn and made a wry face.

'That's Sebastian Dommett, the Coroner. He's been away on holiday, and I hoped he'd stay away till this was over. The Deputy's easy and gets things done in half the time. With Dommett, it'll be a real picnic...'

Drane sniggered and then started to choke.

'Excuse me... Excuse me...'

'Get a drink of tea, man...'

Littlejohn sat there waiting for something to start or turn up. He lit his pipe and sipped his tea, and thought how nice it would be, for a change, to be head of a county constabulary. Outside, the five constables were running round and round the yard, and another was emerging from the mortuary with a man, obviously an undertaker, who'd been measuring the body for a coffin.

'Have any of Dodd's relatives been here yet, Judkin?'

'Yes. Young Peter Dodd called this morning and identified his father. He seemed fond of the old boy. Broke down when he saw him. I rather like that lad. He's not tarred with the same brush as the rest of the family, and I think he'll prove useful to us. I asked him to come on here after he'd finished haggling with Uncle Fred, as they called him. I think Fred was trying to *sell* the body, or something.'

Having satisfied himself that the file was as it should be, Judkin handed it over to Littlejohn.

'I'm afraid it means starting from scratch,' he said cheerfully. 'There's not a thing to guide us. The knife wasn't found, as you'll see, although our men are on the look-out for it if it happened to be thrown away.'

'It won't be the first time we've started with nothing,' said Littlejohn.

'Well... I don't want you to think I'm washing my hands of all this. Far from it. But we've got top-level instruction that you're to run the case, and anything I can do to help, call on me.'

Peter Dodd's fast car drew up with a screech of brakes, and the owner and Cromwell emerged. Cromwell's bowler hat was wedged tightly on his head, and he had a relieved expression on his face. He followed Dodd unsteadily into the police station, a look of comic puzzlement taking the place of relief, as he tried to make out where he was being led.

'Is this the police station...?'

'Temporary premises...'

'Excuse me...'

It was PC Drane waiting in the hall to show them to the Superintendent's office.

'I really ought not to be here,' said Peter Dodd, after introductions had been gone through. 'But I wanted to clear matters up about the inquest. I hope there'll be no fuss.'

Judkin raised his eyebrows.

'No fuss! Your father was murdered, Mr Dodd. That's not the kind of thing that can be hushed up, you know. The press'll be round here like bees tomorrow.'

'All I mean is, can we get Father's body quietly away, and buried in the family vault. We don't want the Nicholls women...'

'No fear of that. They've no standing. But you'll have to await the Coroner's pleasure, of course.'

'I know that…'

Peter Dodd was like a schoolboy trying to see clearly through a problem. You wouldn't have thought he was a lawyer.

'Shall I go and see the Coroner, then?'

'That's a good idea. His office is the first on the left, round the corner of this building. You'll see it on the window. His name's Mr Dommett, and he's just back from holidays. If you could start the conversation by saying you like Sidmouth, you'll find it eases things a bit. He goes there every year, and it's good policy always to agree with his views.'

'Right; I'll remember. Well, thanks. I'll be down for the inquest tomorrow.'

Alone at last, the three police officers began to compare notes. Cromwell's information added considerably to the file on the Superintendent's desk.

'The motive could be anything,' said Littlejohn at length. 'It could be a case of sordid crime of passion. We've only got the word of the two women as to what they did last night. On the other hand, it might be a family affair. If Harry Dodd was likely to make things up with his wife, the family fortunes might suffer. The sons and daughter might find the money they expected to inherit diverted elsewhere by the return of father. Furthermore, the return of the reprobate might be a blow to them socially. Also Willie Dodd, faced with a General Election, might find a skeleton in the cupboard, like his brother, suddenly released on his constituents at the right time, would, to say the least of it, considerably reduce his majority.'

'But why now? Willie Dodd got in at the last election, in spite of the fact that his brother was, what his Nonconformist supporters would call "Living in sin" with another woman.'

'I was just thinking about the little chap like a bookie, mentioned to Cromwell by the landlord. He might have been a creditor of Dodd's, or a divorce detective, or he might have been a snooper, sent by Willie's political opponents to open up a scandal, just before the election. Willie isn't just an ordinary MP, remember. He's one of the big noises of the party now and has great aspirations. A reprobate brother, at a time like this, might not suit his book at all.'

'What do you suggest we do, then, Littlejohn?'

Cromwell was watching the drilling constables with wide eyes. An Inspector had just entered the yard, and was giving the sergeant some instructions. The bobbies continued running round at the double, like a watch wound up. Then Peter Dodd appeared with a tall, thin, stooping elderly man, with a dark waxed moustache and a flannel suit and a light-grey hat. Two chubby little men in bowlers accompanied the tall man.

'By the way, Peter Dodd seems to have talked old Dommett round pretty quickly. I see they're going to the mortuary to look at the body. That's Dommett, the tall chap…'

Judkin indicated the group in the yard. The policemen kept on cantering round and round.

'In the first place, I think we ought to get to know more about the little man who looked like a bookie. What was he after? We'll try to find out when and where he came from, and if he stayed anywhere. Then there's this metal cap from the beer bottle. What was Dodd doing in the region of Leicester? Is there some rendezvous he keeps with a friend or associate, and if so, what's it all about?'

'I'll put some men on it…'

'I'd be glad if you'd leave that to Cromwell and me. It might kill two birds with one stone if we saw the background of what was going on, instead of just getting a report. We'll start right away, although I'd like to be at the inquest tomorrow as well.'

'Of course. Anything else?'

Judkin closed the file and put it away.

'I'd like to know what happens to Harry Dodd's body, and

when the funeral's taking place. I think one of us ought to be there.'

Cromwell looked up hopefully.

'Excuse me…'

It was Drane again, polite as ever.

'Excuse me, sir. It's Mr Dommett. He wants to see you, Superintendent. He's just been to view the body and says he wants to tell you something.'

'Well, show him in then.'

Mr Dommett entered, accompanied by his two tubby men, like a bodyguard. Peter Dodd was hanging on the fringe.

'Good morning, sir. Had a good holiday?'

Mr Dommett's pale, cadaverous face looked as though another vacation and some sunshine would do him good.

'Very good, thanks. Very little sun and some rain, but I always say Sidmouth's good, in any weather…'

He looked round to see if anybody was going to challenge his statement. He was a bad-tempered man, especially in the presence of policemen. His daughter had eloped with a constable, and the sight of uniforms brought back unpleasant memories. There had been reconciliations, of course, but it had been the first time in his life that he'd said no and been defied.

'This is Inspector Littlejohn…'

'We've met a time or two before… How do you do…?'

He extended a bony hand to Littlejohn and Cromwell.

'I called to tell you that I've seen the dead man before.'

'No doubt you have, sir. He lived in Brande, of course, and came to Helstonbury regularly,' smiled Judkin.

'No, no, no…'

Mr Dommett rolled his head from side to side with impatience

'I don't mean that. I mean at an inquest, somewhere, recently. I'm just trying to think, if you'll only let me…'

He held up his hand for silence. They all stood spellbound, whilst Mr Dommett's apparatus of recollection started to function. Drane coughed apologetically behind his hand. Life was, to him, one long, polite apology.

'I've got it...'

That broke the spell. Everybody looked relieved, and the two tubby men, the bodyguard, beamed with delight. Their pleasure was short-lived, for Mr Dommett turned on them.

'*You two were there.* Why didn't you help me? What's the use of keeping a dog and barking yourself...?'

The bodyguard reeled back a pace, as though Mr Dommett had struck them across their mouths.

'It was at the inquest on that fellow... what was his name...? Conflict, was it? *You were both there...* The man who was killed in a car at Wayland Cross...'

'Comfort,' said both the tubby men at once.

'Comfort. That's it. Dodd was a witness at the inquest.'

'Did he see the accident, Mr Dommett?' asked Littlejohn, anxious to be getting on with it.

'No. He was in it. *Don't you two remember?* Dodd and Comfort were in a car together, and it overturned. Dodd got away with a scratch or two and a bit of concussion. But Comfort, who was driving, had the wheel driven into his organs and died...'

'Accidental death, sir?'

Mr Dommett looked annoyed at this attempt to hustle him.

'All in good time... It was *not* accidental death. An open verdict... They were driven from the road by a high-speed car travelling in the same direction. The police at Geldby, that's the Wayland Cross area, tried to trace the car without success. They did, however, find out the circumstances of the accident, or the murder, if you wish to call it such...'

Mr Dommett paused peevishly for dramatic effect. He liked making people wait.

Hitherto, Mr Dommett's bodyguard, like Tweedledum and Tweedledee, had stood there, silently concurring by nods and smiles. Now, however, Tweedledum could bear it no longer.

'Mr Dommett always thought that Mr Henry Dodd was terrified at the inquest,' he burst out in a high-pitched tenor voice.

Mr Dommett turned angrily.

'Did anybody ask you, Blackadder?' he snapped acidly, and he screwed his eyebrows up until they met in an angry line above his nose.

'Shhhh!' said Tweedledee to his partner, who blushed, apologised, and stepped back a pace to hide his confusion.

'As I was saying when I was interrupted... Let us get it straight and in sequence!'

Littlejohn didn't know whether to be angry or amused. Behind Dommett's back, Cromwell was making faces of resignation.

'...Dodd was badly shaken by the accident and pretended he didn't know how it happened. But the police, by tracing the lines on the tarmacadam, suspected things weren't quite straight. They broadcast for anyone who was on the road at that hour. Two men came forward. We had them at the inquest. They stated they noticed Comfort's car moving at quite a reasonable speed. Thirty miles an hour, I think it was. Wasn't it, Blackadder?'

'Yes, sir,' whispered Tweedledum.

'Both the witnesses testified to passing Comfort's car, and also stated that another large car appeared to be tailing it. They overtook both and each noticed the strange behaviour of the larger car. They thought the two cars were out for a run together...'

'I see,' said Littlejohn, more to encourage Mr Dommett than anything else. Cromwell was watching the cobbled yard in which the constables had now finished their drills and were entering what looked like a shower-bath in an outbuilding...

'The Geldby police carefully examined the road and saw that the Comfort car had been crowded off at a particularly dangerous gradient and corner, had crashed through a hedge, and toppled down an incline and overturned.'

'And Dodd was virtually unhurt?'

'I said so. The police and the BBC have done all they can to trace the car responsible, but it seems to have vanished. At the inquest, Dodd was obviously afraid of something.'

'Yes. He said he remembered nothing. He pleaded he was confused and suffering from shock. He stated he didn't notice the car crowding them off. He said it all happened in a second and before he realised it.'

'What makes you think he was afraid?' asked Littlejohn.

Mr Dommett's eyebrows drew together. He wasn't used to having his opinions challenged.

'I've been Coroner for nearly thirty years, and I reckon I can size-up witnesses, Mr Inspector. Dodd was afraid. Shock! Confusion! Rubbish! He knew what had happened, I'll be bound, but was shielding someone of whom he must have been afraid. In other words, all the circumstances pointed to the fact that somebody tried to kill either Dodd or Comfort. It was a deliberate attempt to overturn the car and slay the occupants.'

'Would it be possible to see the records of the inquest, sir? It might help us considerably if we could go over the ground again.'

Tweedledee and Tweedledum gasped, for the records were very sacred to Mr Dommett. But Mr Dommett had just returned from holidays and, as yet, his nerves were tolerably good.

'I'll send them round...'

'Shall I go for them now, sir?' asked Blackadder ingratiatingly.

'What's the hurry?' asked Mr Dommett. 'I'll let you have them in court tomorrow. The inquest will be at 10.30. And now I'll bid you good-day...'

Gathering his bodyguard, he left them. The room seemed empty after the little army had gone.

'He's a very awkward man to get on with,' said Littlejohn. 'Which makes more work for us. Who, I wonder, was Mr Comfort? What were he and Dodd doing together, and of whom was Dodd afraid? Also, was it Dodd or Comfort they were after?'

Judkin sighed.

'It's always the same. Dommett dislikes policemen. I'll just ring up Geldby and see what they've got to say.' He took up the phone and put through a call.

'They've promised to send the file with all the details of the case. It's fifteen miles away, and the stuff will be here in less than half an hour. Is there anything we can do in the meantime?'

'Yes,' said Littlejohn. 'Dodd was in the habit of visiting Helstonbury. Did any of your constables know him? If not by name, then let them see the body, and tell you if any of them know him and if they've seen him around town doing anything.'

'I'll do that right away.'

Judkin rang the bell and Drane entered.

'Excuse me,' he said as he passed Cromwell.

'Certainly...'

Judkin told Drane what he wanted.

'Excuse me, sir, but we all knew Mr Dodd. We all knew his old car and his two women. Bit of a joke, sir, if you'll pardon me.'

'For Pete's sake, Drane, don't make life one long excuse! What do you know of Dodd?'

'I can go fully into it with the men as they come in, but we were only talking about them in the canteen this morning. They usually went to the pictures when they arrived on market day. And we were smiling about the women trailing him round Woolworths'... a man like Dodd.'

'Go on...'

'He was as regular as clockwork. They'd get in after ten, the women would do their shopping and Dodd would go for a drink to *The Dog and Partridge*. PC Abbott is generally there on duty because of the cars going in and out the car park at *The Dog*. Dodd would have his drink and a yarn or two with the farmers and such. Then he'd go and meet the women and they'd have lunch at the Anne Boleyn tearooms. After that, the women would go to a *matinée* at the movies. If it was any good, Dodd would go too. If not, he'd walk round town, have another drink, meet them out, and take them home.'

'He seems to have been an exemplary lodger,' said Judkin. Drane tittered and exploded.

'Excuse me... Lodger... That's a good one.'

Judkin glared at him.

'What would you call him?'

'Sorry, sir.'

'Nothing else then, Drane?'

'One thing, but it's nothing really. Abbott said that he always went into the shop in Sheep Street, the one where they sell birds, white mice, and suchlike, and bought a packet of parrot seed. Funny Abbott remembering that, but he said it was one of those things...'

Judkin looked at Littlejohn.

'Did you see any parrots at what was it called...?'

'*Mon Abri*? No, I didn't. Now what would he want with bird seed?'

'Perhaps he ate it himself,' put in Cromwell.

Drane seemed unable to take a joke or laugh without choking. He made a speedy exit, coughing and spluttering and shouting 'Excuse me...'

Outside, a black police car drove up, and a road scout in police uniform jumped out and hurried in the police station carrying a briefcase.

'This'll be from Geldby...'

They had sent over the scout who had conducted the road enquiry after the accident. An intelligent and brisk young man, who knew what he was talking about. He gave them a full account of the investigation, but it amounted to little more than Mr Dommett had already told them.

The file was another matter, however. It contained good photographs of the overturned car, and the victim, Comfort, had been taken dressed and undressed, on the spot where the accident occurred and in the morgue. He was a medium-sized, slender man with a grey moustache and thin grey hair brushed from a bald forehead. He wore a check suit.

'The landlord of the inn at Brande said there was a man who looked like a bookie and enquired about Dodd. I wonder if this might be him. I'll borrow this, if you don't mind, and try it out on Mallard,' asked Cromwell.

'The Chief said to keep the file till you'd finished with it,' said the patrol officer.

No need for Dommett's record of evidence on the following day; it was all here in the Geldby police file. Dodd's evasiveness, and a pencil note at the side by someone, that Dodd had seemed uneasy and afraid, as though he might know more than he said he did. Details of the offending car, such as they were — grey, Letchworth saloon, number unknown, two occupants — had been widely circulated without any results.

Comfort's wife had given evidence of identification. He was a publican. They kept *The Bell* at Cold Kirby, not far from Market Harborough. Mrs Comfort knew Mr Dodd quite well. He came to the village to fish in the mere there. He and her husband were friends. Sometimes, when things were slack, they'd go for a jaunt together. She didn't know where they'd been when Comfort met his death. Dodd had called in the morning of the day of the accident, and they'd gone off. They had both seemed very cheerful and were in good form… They were both quite sober when they left and both were steady men…

Then followed details of police findings and a practically certain case against somebody who had hustled Comfort's car off the road and into the ditch. Nothing else of use at the time.

'Just one thing more,' said Littlejohn. 'Is *The Bell*, at Cold Kirby, a Hoods' house?'

'Yes,' said Judkin, after ringing up another police station in the vicinity.

But there was a disappointment for Littlejohn and Cromwell when they returned to their inn at Brande.

The landlord, Mallard, studied the gruesome photographs of Comfort and then shook his head.

'No, that's not the chap who called here. He had a little moustache and was smaller and thick-set. No... Besides, I remember Mr Dodd having the accident. It was after Comfort got killed that the bookie fellow called here. I recollect one thing about the accident, too. Dodd's friends here couldn't get him to talk about it after it happened. You know how men are over their beer. They tried to pump him for details. But Dodd stayed mum. Ask me, he got proper scared by that accident...'

5
DODD'S BOX

'Just two more little points before we go back to Brande,' said Littlejohn. 'Where did Dodd get his parrot seed, and who was his lawyer?'

Superintendent Judkin smiled. No accounting for the ways of these Scotland Yard chaps! Bothering about bird seed... He could understand a man wanting to know about the victim's lawyer, but bird seed... Judkin even forgot his manners in his surprise.

'Drane!' he shouted, instead of ringing the bell. 'Drane!'

The attendant constable thrust in a scared face.

'Yes, sir.'

He looked round the room to see if anybody were ill or being attacked.

'Come here, Drane...'

'Yes, sir... Excuse me.'

He thrust himself past Cromwell and stood before the boss at attention.

'Who was the shopkeeper you said Dodd bought his bird seed from? The parrot seed.'

'Lott, sir. Ishmael Lott. Just down Sheep Street. Shall I show you the way, sir?'

'No. The Inspector was asking...'

'I beg pardon. Shall I...?'

'Point it out through the window, please, Drane.'

The bobby with eloquent hands showed Littlejohn just where Mr Ishmael Lott kept his corn stores.

'And the lawyer...?'

'Archer and Pharaoh, just over the way, I believe. At least, that's what the Nicholls women said,' answered Judkin.

'I'll call on them both before we leave town, then...'

There was a batch of very good shops in Sheep Street, the main thoroughfare of Helstonbury, then a tile-fronted picture house, and, after that, the property became shabby and gradually petered out into slum quarters with fish and chip restaurants, greengrocers with their wares spread out on trestles outside their shops, pawnbrokers, old-clothes dealers... At the end of the second-rate batch stood a large corn stores with sacks of meal, hen-food, oyster shells, and bird seed in one window; in the other, white mice, canaries, guinea-pigs, and all kinds of things, from bird-baths and cages, to packets of egg producer and poultry spice. As Littlejohn turned to enter the premises, a large dog took a dog biscuit from a sack near the door and then lifted his leg in disrespect for the rest. This brought out the proprietor.

Mr Ishmael Lott was a small man with a hatchet face and a big domed head almost bald. At the crown of his head stood a large shining cyst, like another little dome growing from the main one. He wore a shaggy moustache, from beneath which protruded his little rabbit teeth, and he had a large white apron and bib over his clothes, the coat of which was missing. He emerged peering angrily for the dog through his gold-framed glasses.

'Yarrooo... Gerroff... Dirtylilldevil...'

He halted, panting, face to face with Littlejohn.

'Who put those there?' he asked Littlejohn, pointing to the sack of dog biscuits, and then, deciding that the Inspector knew nothing about it and that the offending dog wasn't his, he ran indoors and shouted upstairs.

'Haven't I told you not to put biscuits at the door? All the dogs of the neighbourhood are at 'em again...'

The answer came pat from above.

'Oh, put a sock in it!'

Mr Ishmael Lott wrestled with his feelings for a minute or two, overcame them, and turned to Littlejohn.

'I don't know why I stand it!' he said, almost in tears. 'I ought to retire and get out of it. I can afford it, but... well...'

He didn't finish the sentence, for it was interrupted by the heavy descent of a thin, peevish-faced woman, carrying a string bag and wearing a moulting sealskin coat and a hideous black hat.

'I'm goin' 'ome, Ishmael, now. Don't be late for yer tea. An' stop bullyin' Clara... shoutin' about the place. With customers in... I'm surprised at you...'

Her lips snapped as she uttered each phrase and she looked at Littlejohn, smiled acidly to appease him for her partner's outburst of temper, and then sailed through the shop.

'Call at the butcher's for the meat — such as it is! — on yer way up, Ishmael... And bring a lettuce from the fruit shop. I'll miss my bus if I do it meself... Remember, don't be late fer tea. I want them chops...'

She fired these parting shots on the way to the door and finished what she was saying half-way down the street. She was still talking as she vanished from sight.

'My wife, sir.'

Littlejohn understood Lott's reluctance to retire and stay at home all day!

'What can I do for you?'

'It's about Mr Harry Dodd, Mr Lott.'

Mr Ishmael Lott brightened up. He was a great gossip when his wife allowed him to get a word in edgeways. There wasn't much that went on in Helstonbury and twenty miles round that

Mr Lott didn't know. His corn lorries went all over the neighbouring countryside, and their drivers collected all the tit-bits and retailed them to the boss after every round.

'Poor Harry...'

Mr Lott sighed but smiled at the same time.

'A good customer here, in a small way, sir.'

'Parrot seed?'

'Yes... How do you know, and who are you?' Littlejohn explained and showed his card.

Mr Lott rubbed his hands.

'Come into my office,' he said, like the spider to the fly.

He indicated a trapdoor in the floor and led the way to the nether regions. As he stepped down the first step, he yelled upstairs.

'Clara! CLARA! SHOP!'

'All right, all right,' came from above, and the new guardian of the place descended with shuffling feet to take charge. She was a younger replica of her mother, with Mr Lott's rabbit teeth betraying his share in her progeniture. She frowned at her father's face, which was just above ground by then, and flashed the teeth at Littlejohn to show he didn't share her displeasure. She carried a paper novelette, with a picture on the back showing a cowboy embracing a girl as naked as the publishers dared to allow, and she set about it as soon as she had found a chair. Her teeth as well as her eyes devoured the pages, like the antennae of a strange insect.

Below ground, Littlejohn had never seen such a place. It baffled him at first. The floor was of concrete and the walls were of smooth white plaster. In the middle of the vast cellar stood a roll-top desk, two chairs, a waste-paper basket full to the brim, and a large filing cabinet. Part of the floor was covered in worn coconut matting.

But it was the walls which attracted Littlejohn. They were decorated from floor to ceiling, and their entire length and breadth, with wavy lines, some regular, some erratic, made in black crayon or charcoal. Mr Lott seemed pleased that Littlejohn had noticed them.

'Wot are they?' he asked proudly.

'Graphs,' replied the Inspector.

Mr Lott nodded his head and smiled with satisfaction.

'Wot of?'

That became obvious. The lines were in sections; about seven horizontal lots from floor to ceiling and eight or nine vertical divisions on each of the four walls. Each graph had its own name. From floor to roof were Consols, various categories of War Loan, and Colonial stocks. *Funds*, said the heading. Then, *Banks, Insurance, Textiles, Mines, Oils, Rubber*, and *Tea*, and a lot more all came in for their ups and downs.

'My system,' said Mr Lott with pride. 'Weekly averages in graphs form. I've got now, after working this so long, that I know when something's going up, and when down. I've made a nice little packet out o' this lot. Scientific, isn't it? I'm on Freifontein, just at present...'

He indicated a descending graph and rubbed his hands.

'If that goes on goin' down for another week, I'se buy, and then I'll foller it, scientifically, and sell when the records says so.'

'Do you ever make or lose much...?'

Mr Lott ran his hand through his thin, dusty hair and looked bewildered.

'I only do it for a hobby. I put the results down in a book, and I reckon if I'd actually done properly what I've done as a sort o' game, I'd have made, to date, two hundred thousand...'

His eyes popped, and his little teeth shot out in a grin of delight. He was as pleased with his imaginary investments as if he'd really made them, like somebody playing poker for dried beans and winning a pocketful.

He turned his pathetic face to Littlejohn.

'Between you and me, I never had the money to start. Else I'd have broken the bank at Monte Carlo good and proper. But since I went bankrupt six years ago, the business and all my assets have been in the wife's hands and I can't get her to see that there's better things can be done than selling corn and bird seed, when you know how…'

He was making for his filing cabinet to show the Inspector how it was all done, but Littlejohn had to call a halt. 'Shall we talk about Mr Dodd?'

It was like changing records on a gramophone. Mr Lott was eager to be starting. Upstairs, you could hear Clara, shuffling round, attending to a customer, the clink of change, then silence as she gobbled up her paperback again.

'Who did Harry Dodd buy bird seed for?'

'I never knew.'

That apparently was the end of it.

'…I know he hadn't a parrot of his own. It was a present for somebody else's bird. A bird he called Cora…'

'Cora? And did he never mention whose?'

'No. I tried to pump him, but he was mum. A bit of a close fish was Harry. He'd had a few more drinks than usual when he even mentioned Cora; but he wasn't too far gone to stop there.'

'He called regularly?'

'Every market day. Always a packet of parrot seed. That was all. Bit of an oddity was Harry. How he got mixed up with such like as the Nichollses beats me. He was a gentleman, was Harry.'

'Do you sell fishing tackle, bait, and the like, Mr Lott?'

'Yes; and I'm a bit of a fisherman myself, too. Why? Do you fish?'

'Yes… But I wondered if Harry Dodd ever bought gear from you.'

'No… Come to think of it, we once did talk of fishin'. He liked a yarn, did Harry, when he'd a bit of time to spare. He never did any fly-fishin'. He used to fish for coarse stuff, in some mere or other near where a pal of his lived. But that was all. I recollect him once havin' his little joke about fishin'. Said it covered a multitude of sins…'

Mr Lott cackled, as if he was a sinner of the same kind.

'…I think he made it an excuse to get away, when those two Nicholls women got on his nerves. Why he stopped with 'em, beats me.'

Funny thing. Here was a man in probably a worse pickle than Dodd, who did come and go as he liked. Poor Lott seemed completely hag-ridden by his wife.

'Dad!' shouted his offspring from upstairs. 'Dad, it's closin'-time. Mum said…'

'All right, all right. Mum said… I know wot she said…'

They climbed aloft again, and Littlejohn said goodbye and made for the lawyer's.

'Good luck,' said Mr Lott, baring his teeth. 'If you stay here long, let me know, and I'll take you fishin'…'

Mr Pharaoh, Harry Dodd's lawyer, was annoyed with Harry for getting himself killed when he did. Mr Pharaoh owned a nice little yacht, and travelled to Lowestoft nearly every week to make the most of her. Harry Dodd had inconsiderately caused him a lost weekend, as far as sailing went.

'This is an awful nuisance,' said Mr Pharaoh to the Inspector. 'My partner's on holiday and I'm really too busy to deal with the mess…'

He had the figure of a penguin, a livid round face, a fringe of grey hair, a button nose, and shining black eyes like shoe buttons. He dressed as nearly nautical as his profession would allow: reefer coat in navy blue, black tie, and white linen. On Fridays when he was off sailing, he left the office in his yachting cap.

Mr Pharaoh opened a cupboard and brought out a bottle of Schnapps, which he had smuggled from Holland on one of his pleasure trips. He invited Littlejohn to partake.

'If you'll excuse me, sir, I'm on duty. I came to ask if you could throw a little light on Mr Harry Dodd's affairs…'

The lawyer took a good glass of his potent liquor and leaned back in his chair.

'If you'll do me a favour in turn, I will. I'm due off to compete in a yacht race tomorrow. It means a lot to me. And now Harry Dodd goes and gets murdered. I'm his sole executor, and I ought to be at hand... What am I to do? If you can get me out of this for four days, I'll be eternally grateful.'

He took another dose of Schnapps and cast his eyes distastefully round his study. They came to rest on a model of a yacht in a glass case on the mantelpiece, and Mr Pharaoh seemed to buck up at the very sight of it.

'I ought never to have been a lawyer, but one has to work to pay for one's fun. I met Dodd yachting, years ago, before he went off the rails, and we started a friendship which improved with time. When he got himself into his matrimonial mess, he came to me, and I did what I could, including finding a place for him to live in with his two women. Silly business! Harry, if he'd known what this race meant to me, would have waited a few days to get himself murdered...'

Mr Pharaoh raised his glass. 'To Harry, God rest him...' And he drank a toast to his absent friend.

'I think it could be arranged, sir. Harry Dodd's youngest son is a lawyer, though he says he's a poor one...'

'Young Peter?'

'Yes. I gather he and the family solicitor will be here for tomorrow's inquest. That ought to be enough. But if you're going away for a time, I think you ought to tell the police, in confidence, what's in the will, how much, if you can, and also, if you can spare the time, go through Dodd's things with us at the bungalow. Is that possible?'

'You're a deep 'un, Inspector. You know as well as I do, that what you suggest is highly irregular...'

'All the same, sir, if you're away, and we have to wait for the slow wheels of the law to turn, the culprit might slip through our fingers.'

'Very well. What do you want to know, and then we'll go to that bungalow place with the silly French name and see what we can find. Sure you won't have a drink? No? Well, go on, then.'

'Had Mr Dodd any private money of his own to leave to anybody?'

'Very little. You'll find a few hundreds in the bank, and that's all. Even that didn't really belong to him. He borrowed it from his wife, his divorced wife…'

'I thought the family settled money on him…'

'They did. His elder son and daughter had great ambitions. All they wanted was Father out of the way, because they didn't approve of his mode of life. Harry Dodd was a homely sort. The kind you'd find pottering round the garden in his shirt-sleeves or inviting men from the works — artisan engineers and such — over to his home for a drink. He liked friendly folk. His children, with the exception of Peter, couldn't stand it. When they had their fancy friends round for tennis, Father would suddenly appear in old clothes, like a scarecrow, wheeling a barrow-load of manure for his roses, and when they held house-parties, he'd sit in the kitchen playing nap with a foreman or two from the works and suddenly appear seeking a fresh bottle of whisky. As soon as Harry Dodd slipped up with that awful Nicholls woman, they were on him, and they made a remittance-man of him. I suppose it was either a good bust-up and get it over, or putting up with Father's plebeian ways for ever, so they chose the bust-up. Before Mrs Dodd knew where she was, divorce papers were filed, and Harry was in *Mon Abri*…'

'Mrs Dodd was completely under her children's thumb?'

'Wait till you meet 'em. You'll understand. Once pa was out of the way, the elder boy took over in the works for his mother's sake. He's a go-getter and has prospered. He's not an engineer, though. He's strictly executive… And how!'

'We were talking about Harry Dodd's money...'

Mr Pharaoh nodded, took another drink, and then put his feet on his desk.

'Mrs Dodd wasn't a bit vindictive. I had the arrangements to make, and she was completely bewildered. It ended by a divorce without alimony. In fact, an allowance was made to Harry Dodd, on condition that he kept his distance. He was the family remittance-man and got several hundred a year paid into his bank in town here. He saved money — a few thousand — and bought Dorothy Nicholls an annuity. His will's a simple one; after a legacy or two, he leaves his love and all he has to his wife, Helena Dodd, with the exception of *Mon Abri*, which goes to Miss Nicholls.'

'Simple enough. But why do you say there's some of Mrs Dodd's money in the bank?'

'That's just it. The funny part. Over the years, Harry and Helena got together again. In fact, they never ought to have parted. They loved one another all the time. Just imagine the agony of Harry... the Nicholls pair! However, he paid for his little fling, good and proper. Full measure, pressed down, and overflowing, as the Good Book has it...'

Mr Pharaoh thereupon took out a large handkerchief and trumpeted in it, presumably from emotion.

'They used to meet. Harry told me that, quite plainly. He asked my opinion on the legal aspect. He was anxious not to bring his wife into any trouble. I reassured him. They met like old friends, and I wouldn't have been surprised, had Harry lived, to see 'em together again, husband and wife, whatever his high and mighty kids thought of it.'

'Did Mrs Dodd make up her husband's income, then?'

'Not exactly. He wanted capital and she lent him some. It was this way...'

The talk was interrupted by the entry of a dark girl, with a good figure and a most attractive face. She wore heavy-black-framed spectacles, as though trying to hide her good looks.

'It's six o'clock, Mr Pharaoh. Have you, ahem, decided…?'

'Yes, Joan… I'm finishing tonight. This is Inspector Littlejohn of Scotland Yard. He says I can go…'

Littlejohn smiled at the girl, and she smiled back at him. There flashed between them a glance of understanding for Mr Pharaoh, who cared not about his law practice, Harry Dodd, his murder, or Joan's sparkling beauty. His heart was set on the *Betsy Jane*, his true love, waiting for him at Lowestoft.

'So you can go, Joan, and look after things while I'm away. Open my letters and read 'em, and don't bother me about anything. You know where you can find me, but don't for heaven's sake, do. And as for the law, if anythin' crops up, take it over to Corncrake and get him to help. That's all, Joan. Goodbye…'

Mr Pharaoh shook hands with Joan, as though they were parting forever, and she cast upon him a look of the utmost maternal affection, the kind which many of the young men of Helstonbury would have given all they'd got to receive.

'Nice girl, Joan. Knows more about the law than I do. Got her LLB… Where were we…? Yes, Harry needed capital. You see, he was an engineer when he married Helena. It was in his blood. Do you know what his company do?'

'No, sir.'

'They make machine tools. I went through the place once, before Harry's troubles started. You know the cutting-tools they use on lathes, jigs and the like. Well, it's only the edge of 'em that's really hard, what they call, I think, high-power steel. The rest is cheap, soft stuff… a sort of handle to hold the really hard face of the tool. Well, Dodd's firm makes tools, the principal process being the fixing of the hard steel to the soft shaft or handle. Harry Dodd was the patentee of that process. Damn' good at processes, but no good at selling either himself or his products. That's where his elder son shone…'

'And after he left his wife and home, did Dodd keep on with his experiments?'

'That's it. He spent two or three days a week at a little workshop he'd fixed up at a place called Cold Kirby, not very far from here. He took me once. A little asbestos garage arrangement, with a furnace and a few machines running electrically. He played about there. It was in a field at the back of the village pub, and the landlord, a chap called Comfort, himself an engineer until his health broke and he turned to the village inn life, gave him a hand. Well... his wife found the money for the little set-up and financed some of Harry's experiments.'

'Did he have any success...?'

'Yes. That's just it. He told me he was in the act of perfecting a formula for the welding of tools. You know, joining the hard to the soft steel — which would cut overheads, at the present rate, in two.'

'And he died before he could perfect it?'

'Yes. See what that meant? Harry Dodd would have been back in circulation again with a fortune in his pocket. If his children didn't behave, he'd just to sell his formula, or whatever it was, to a rival, and put 'em out of business.'

'That's motive, good and proper, sir.'

'Yes, but I don't fancy the idea of his own flesh and blood stabbing him in the back because they were ashamed of him...'

'They did worse than that in the divorce matter.'

'Yes. But they aren't the sort who'd stab anybody in the back with a knife...'

'Might they try engineering a motor accident?'

'So you've heard of that, have you? This isn't the movies, though. However, that's up to you. Is there anything else I can tell you?'

'Nothing that won't wait, Mr Pharaoh. Shall we go and look over the bungalow at Brande?'

'Yes. I'll run you over there. By the way, where are you staying whilst you're here?'

'The inn in Brande.'

'That's all right. Plain but very comfortable. It's usually known as *The Bear*, though its full name's *The Bear with the Ragged Staff*. You'll be all right…'

Mr Pharaoh brought out a nice little fast coupé and they were drawing up at *Mon Abri* very soon afterwards. There was a bicycle standing at the gate, a lady's model, with high handlebars and a huge oil-lamp on the front.

Mrs Nicholls opened the door in answer to their ring. She flushed with pleasure at the sight of Mr Pharaoh, presumably thinking he'd called already to put everything right for them.

'Dorothy, my dear, it's Mr Pharaoh…'

She evidently didn't think Littlejohn of enough consequence to merit formal announcement. She preened herself, talking in a high-pitched, affected, nasal voice, and throwing aitches about in her emotion.

All the blinds had been drawn and Mrs Nicholls was in deep black.

'You'll have to h'excuse us, Mr Pharaoh… The dressmaker has just called from the village to measure us for mourning. Poor 'Arry. This is a terrible shock, Mr Pharaoh… terrible…'

She sniffed in a handkerchief, and led them to the living-room, after a lot of scuttering had indicated that the dressmaking session had moved itself from thence to one of the bedrooms.

'No need to disturb yourself, Mrs Nicholls. We've just called to look over Mr Dodd's things…'

He was quite tetchy about it.

'Harry's things? But surely they aren't going to be moved away! They were h'all 'is. That is, unless he's left them to us in his will.'

'Miss Nicholls is provided for… But you'll have to wait for that. Where *is* Miss Nicholls?'

'I'll get her…'

The old woman scampered off, tottering on her high heels, her overly tight skirt emphasising her heavy rear. They got a sight of a thin, anxious woman, with a mouthful of pins, and a tape-measure round her neck, rushing from room to room, as Mrs Nicholls sought a few private words with her daughter before letting her loose on the visitors.

'Don't sign anything... Better 'ave your Uncle Fred here if anything wants signin'...'

Dorothy entered, doing her best to look stricken and bereaved. Mr Pharaoh expressed no sympathy.

'You needn't worry about this place. My client left it to you and all that's in it. And now, may we look at his private things?'

'You mean... You mean the loft...'

'Did he keep his personal things in the loft?'

'It was his bedroom. We weren't allowed up there.'

'What did he keep there?'

'His bed, his clothes and things, and his private papers locked up in a big tin box.'

'I thought you weren't allowed up...'

Dorothy made no reply. She was putting on airs like her mother. Trying to impress them that she was as good as Dodd and his family.

'We got a notice to go to the inquest. Will we need a lawyer?'

Mrs Nicholls, who had been listening, thought it well to intervene and marched in the room, apparently looking for something.

'Dorothy's Uncle Fred, who's a lawyer himself, is coming to look h'after our affairs. He'll be with us at the h'inquest.'

'We'd like to look in the loft, please...'

The two women pulled down the disappearing metal ladder, and the trapdoor of the room opened automatically at the same time. The aperture appeared too small to admit Littlejohn's shoulders or Mr Pharaoh's paunch, but they managed it. It was a larger hole than it looked.

There was nothing much in any of the furniture. The latter

had evidently, at some time, been hoisted in through the roof light, a large window, hinged outwards, and consisted of a simple iron bed, a chest of drawers, a table with a mirror on it, and a single wardrobe. They came at length to the trunk.

Mr Pharaoh looked at it and then shouted down the hole in the floor.

'Who's been at this tin box?'

He showed Littlejohn, who'd already seen them, fresh marks which glinted against the background of black enamel.

'Eh?'

'Have you been trying to open this box?'

'No...'

'Who's been at it, then?'

'Must 'ave been Uncle Fred. He was up. Said he was looking for the will.'

'Well, tell him to keep his hands off in future. I'm executor, and I won't have...'

Mr Pharaoh left it unfinished, for Littlejohn, who had brought along Harry's keys from the Helstonbury police station, had flung back the lid of the box.

It was empty.

6

THE BELL AT COLD KIRBY

'Who's been at this box?'

Mr Pharaoh bawled down the trap in a voice that brought both women to the foot of the ladder.

'Eh?'

'You heard me. Who's been at this box?'

The protagonists were in the most impossible positions for carrying on a battle of words for long; Mr Pharaoh's round livid face, set in the frame of the hole in the ceiling, glaring down at Mrs Nicholls, and the old woman twisting her head and body in horrible contortions, the better to face him and argue.

'You needn't look at me as if I'd emptied it...'

'How did you know it was empty?'

'I lifted it and shook it... I 'ad to dust the place, didn't I?'

'Have you tried the keys in it?'

Dorothy's face and the gasp she gave were enough to give her mother away.

'No...'

'Don't tell me that tale. I'm coming down. I can't stand here shouting and arguing...'

Mr Pharaoh began to descend the narrow ladder, missed his

footing, hung on the framework of the trapdoor for a second to recover his balance, and then made an undignified finish of the journey. Littlejohn followed, after locking the box, an old tin trunk, with HD on the lid in white paint.

'I understood from you earlier in the day, that you hadn't used the keys...'

Littlejohn looked Dorothy in the eyes, and she lowered them.

'We... we... we thought he kept brandy in it and we wanted some for him...'

Mr Pharaoh stamped his feet and waved his hands.

'Pah! I never heard such a tale! Well; it's a criminal offence, that's all. It's theft...'

Mrs Nicholls' hands flew to her hips and she leaned towards Mr Pharaoh, thrusting her face close to his own.

'And what do you mean by that? Haven't we said there was nothin' in it. That's how we found it when we h'opened it. There was nothin' in it. Last time I was up there, a fortnight ago, it was heavy and there was things in it. I couldn't open it because Dodd had the key. When we did open it, as my daughter h'observed, to get the brandy, which he always locked up, it was empty. That's the truth and before I say another word, I want my lawyer 'ere... my brother Fred.'

'Damn your brother Fred! Don't you realise there may have been valuable papers, a will or something, in it? What did you do with them?'

Mrs Nicholls closed her eyes and screwed up her mouth, intent on keeping the vow of silence which only Uncle Fred could cause her to break.

'It *was* empty...'

It came from Dorothy in such a thin, frightened voice that both men believed it. Littlejohn was a bit sorry for Dorothy. She seemed an honest enough girl, a bit stupid, but quite without guile. Without her hag of a mother perpetually prodding her and nagging her, she'd probably have parted company with Dodd long ago.

'Has anyone been up there lately...? Anyone who could have stolen the contents...?'

Mrs Nicholls stood there with her eyes shut and her lips tight, like somebody asking the gods for strength.

'No, sir. Till Harry died, nobody went up there, except him or one of us. You can see, sir, it would have been a bit difficult for anybody to get the ladder down without us knowing.'

'All the same, the contents of the box have gone!' shouted Mr Pharaoh, interrupting Dorothy and laying emphasis on each word. 'You! What do *you* know about it?'

The old woman shook her head but did not speak.

'You old fool!'

Mrs Nicholls squeaked, but still didn't break the vow of silence.

'I think Harry took his things away, bit by bit...'

Dorothy began to gulp and sniff.

'I think he was getting ready to leave us.'

Tears came, and she started to howl.

Mr Pharaoh made gestures of despair.

'One struck dumb and the other... well...'

Littlejohn passed his handkerchief to Dorothy. She took it with a grateful, swimming look and started to mop up.

'Now, Miss Nicholls, what made you think that?'

'I just felt it. I think Harry had got tired of this life. Something certainly had happened to change him. He was away more and, well... instead of bein' bored, he seemed interested and excited about something...'

She was handing back Littlejohn's handkerchief. This was too much for Mrs Nicholls' respectability.

'Give that 'ere,' she said, snatching it from her daughter. 'One would think you'd been brought up in the gutter. That'll want washin' before you give it back to the Inspector...'

'That's all right, Mrs Nicholls. I've another here…'

'I h'insist! Such manners! And as for Dodd bein' bored, excited, interested in somethin', it's all her imagination. She reads too many novels… Imagination, miss.'

Having broken silence, Mrs Nicholls was getting ready for a full spate again. Mr Pharaoh wasn't having any more of it.

'We'll be going now, but you'll hear from me again. I'm not satisfied…'

He hustled Littlejohn out of the place before Mrs Nicholls could recover her breath.

'Did you say you wanted to go to *The Bell*, at Cold Kirby? Because, if you do, I'll run you there before I go to dinner…'

Mr Pharaoh had recovered his good spirits very quickly with the thought that, on the morrow, he would be with the *Betsy Jane*, thanks to Littlejohn.

'…You can order dinner at *The Bear* and we'll be back before half-past seven…'

Mr Pharaoh pursued a breathless career to Cold Kirby, and they were there in less than half an hour. Mrs Comfort, a buxom, bonny woman of middle-age, was busy in the bar, but turned over the work to the casual waiter when the two visitors arrived.

The Bell was merely an ale-house.

'We only sell draught beer here,' said the landlady.

It was a very old-fashioned house, lying in a hollow just off the main road, with creeper and roses climbing over its whitewashed walls. The rooms were low and the windows narrow. Outside, there was a gravel square for cars to draw up in, and a pond with white ducks swimming here and there and larking in the mud. Behind, a large vegetable garden, with a white sectional shed of concrete rising incongruously in the middle of it. The evening was still, and smoke from the chimneys rose straight upwards and vanished in the blue.

Inside, there was only one public room of the typical country-inn variety. There weren't even beer-pumps, and the barrels, with wooden taps, stood on trestles just inside a little alcove which served as a bar. The noise of a crowd of jolly country voices rose from the taproom, where things were moderately busy.

Mr Pharaoh told Mrs Comfort they wanted a word with her about Harry Dodd and her late husband. She led them into a quiet little living-room which was her private quarters, bade them be seated, and burst into tears.

'I can't get used to being without Comfort. I keep thinkin' he'll come back one day… and then I remember he won't… ever…'

It was one of those situations which made Littlejohn's blood boil. A wanton murder by a callous killer, with no thought of what it might imply to anybody but himself.

'Had your husband any enemies, Mrs Comfort?'

'What… Arnold…? No… He was everybody's friend. Too much so sometimes…'

Her voice grew resentful.

'Why?'

'I think I'll just go and get me a drink,' interrupted Mr Pharaoh. He was being tactful. And, besides, tomorrow… He'd got the holiday mood.

'Why, did you say, sir? Well, look at Mr Dodd. He got to know that Arnold had been an engineer before we took this place. So nothing would do but that they should start tinkering in the shed they put up in the back there. He was always here, and Arnold got properly took-up with it, too. The reason we took this public was that my husband's health wasn't too good and the doctor said… Oh, what does it matter now…?'

She began to sob bitterly again.

Littlejohn went to the window and looked out until she grew calm. A pretty garden, a few hens and ducks, a little pub with a nice little lot of friendly customers who caused no trouble. A good wife and peaceful existence, with no man his enemy. That was Arnold Comfort. Then along came Harry Dodd…

'Did you like Dodd?'

'No. I told Arnold so, too. But Arnold laughed. He was that way. Trusted everybody…'

'Why didn't you take to Dodd, Mrs Comfort?'

'Instinct, more than anythin' else. There was somethin' about him… You never got to know him or what he was after. Why come here with his experimentin' and his workshop? Disturbed the whole happy atmosphere and upset my husband, too.'

'Upset?'

'Yes. Arnold was on good pay when we left Sheffield. The doctors said, if he didn't give up engineering and the worry of management, he wouldn't last long. He'd to take things easy and quietly. We had a little bit saved… just enough to make ends meet with the little we take here. I do a bit of catering as well. We screwed down our expenditure to rock-bottom and we found we could do nicely… Then, along comes Dodd and persuades Arnold that with the new process or something he's got in mind, they can make their fortunes. What do they do but put up that white concrete place in the garden, there, fit in machines and lathes and such, and start a sort of engineering laboratory of their own. Arnold got so completely wrapped up in it that his health began to give again. I carried on at him, but he just laughed. "We're going to be rich soon, old gal, and then no more working your fingers to the bone. We'll get a nice little house by the sea, and end our days in peace with all we want…"'

She grew angry.

'What did it get him? A grave… Driving about the country with Dodd and, from what I hear, somebody deliberately killed my Arnold. Some of Dodd's fine friends…'

She wept again.

'What did they do in the workshop?'

She dried her eyes.

'Would you like to see it?'

It was a spacious shed. Much larger than it looked from the road. The base was of concrete, and there were a lathe and a drill screwed down to the floor. In one corner, a small furnace. Then, a bench with bags of powder on it and bottles of acid and other coloured chemicals. There was dust over everything, and the machinery was going rusty.

'I don't know what it was all about, but there it is. I hate it all...'

As far as papers went, the place had been cleared. No books, bills, formulae... nothing. Just the bare necessities for the practical work.

'Did Dodd ever stay here overnight, Mrs Comfort?'

'No. They knocked off pretty early, and they'd have a meal, and Dodd would go then.'

'How often did he come?'

'About three times a week. Then they'd come across here, and you'd hear the machinery going... They had a motor in the little shed behind.'

Littlejohn looked in. A small, efficient-looking electric motor provided the power for the machines.

'And there were just two of them at it?'

'Yes. My son, Andrew, helped them now and then. Andrew's in the forces doing his National Service with the RAF...'

'How long did your son give them a hand?'

'Quite a lot. He was goin' in for engineering. In fact, he's taking an engineering degree when he finishes his service.'

'Where is he now, Mrs Comfort?'

She rose and took a letter from behind a jug on the mantelpiece.

145632 A/C Comfort, Andrew,
Lidbury,
Yorks.

She read out the address, and Littlejohn made a note of it.

'Andrew knows more of what it's all about than I do. He got

compassionate leave when his father died, and he's coming home this weekend to clear up the workshop. If you call again...'

'I'll do that, thanks. He may be a great help. Meantime, did Dodd do anything else when he came here?'

'Nothing special. He was so taken up with what they were making in the workshop. That's one of the things I didn't like about him. He seemed all on fire to finish what they were doing just to get his own back on his family.'

'You mean, he bore them a grudge for what they'd done to him?'

'That's it...'

'But from what I gather, he was an easy going, mild sort of man.'

'He used to be at first when he started coming... about three years since. But he changed. From not caring a thing about his family, he seemed to grow to hate them. Whether they'd done something to him to make him that way, I can't say.'

'He was out for revenge?'

'That's what it seemed to me...'

Mr Pharaoh's beaming, livid face appeared at the door. Littlejohn thought he'd have to drive back to Helstonbury himself, but Mr Pharaoh crossed the floor with steady steps.

'You two finished? It's time I made my way. I've things to do before I set out for Lowestoft.'

Littlejohn took the red beer-bottle cap from his pocket.

'Yours is a Hoods' house, isn't it, Mrs Comfort?' he said.

'Yes. But we don't sell bottled beers. Our customers like draught ale, and we don't turn over enough to casuals to keep bottled stuff. If Mr Dodd drank bottled beer and had that cap in his pocket, as you say, he must have been somewhere else for it. There's quite a lot of bigger houses of Hoods' sell it. You're going to have a job finding out, Mr Littlejohn.'

'It looks like it. Just one more thing, Mrs Comfort. Did Dodd ever bring parcels of stuff or store anything here?'

'No. What kind of things?'

'I hardly know. But he had a big tin trunk affair at his bungalow. It was full once, I believe. Now it's empty. He seems to have moved it somewhere.'

'No. It wasn't here, sir.'

'As regards your husband's accident. Where had they been when it happened?'

'Just a run to Helstonbury for materials, they said. They'd a case of tools they'd called for at the railway office.'

'You remember the details at the inquest, Mrs Comfort?'

'Shall I ever forget them…? I was in a daze at the time, but they seemed impressed on my mind for ever after. Why?'

'I was wondering if you ever saw the grey car which caused the accident, before. Did you see anyone hanging round the place, or was anybody in asking questions?'

'Funny you should ask that, Inspector. There was a man here enquiring for Harry Dodd not long after it happened. He called casually for a drink and asked about him. I always wondered what he wanted and if he was connected with that accident.'

'What did he want?'

'He asked if Harry Dodd lived in the village. I told him no. Then he wanted to know if I knew him, and if he was a customer of our place. There didn't seem much point in denying it. Everybody here knew Harry. I just said he came sometimes. With that, I had to go and see to something, and when I'd finished, the man was gone.'

'What did he look like, Mrs Comfort? Would you recognise him again?'

'Yes, I think I would. Tallish, well-built, wore a sporty suit, looked a bit like a bookie…'

'Had he a car?'

'I didn't see one. But he might have parked it anywhere on the road. What I did notice about him was the ring he wore. If I met him again, I'd look for it and recognise him. It was a silver one.

Like a snake. It looked so out of place because he was smartly dressed. A man like that ought to have worn a gold ring. But, then, sometimes things like that are keepsakes and people wear them for that...'

* * *

In Brande, Cromwell had fixed their bedrooms, ordered and approved their evening meal, and had a pint of beer. Now he found himself with time on his hands till Littlejohn got back.

'Is there anybody handy I could have a bit of a talk with about Harry Dodd till the chief gets in?' he asked Mr Mallard, who had taken off his coat and was peeling potatoes in the kitchen.

The landlord looked up a bit sheepishly. He slipped the potato he had been rotating in his fingers back in the bucket.

'Got to give the missus a 'and now and then. It's the maid's day off,' he said apologetically. 'Yes. You're just in time. You ought to have a word with Mrs Mattock. That's the woman that does for the Nichollses up at the bungalow. She also cleans the little village bank, and as it's been open today... open two days a week... she'll just be moppin' about now. That's the bank across the way.'

He rose and took Cromwell to the door. Over the road stood a small, neat, timbered building with the Home Counties Bank plate on the door, which was closed.

'Knock hard. She'll come.'

Cromwell crossed and followed instructions.

'We close at three...'

The woman who peeped out evidently regarded herself as one of the bank's staff. She was a tubby little thing of sixty or thereabouts, with white hair, a button nose, and little fat arms with sleeves rolled past her elbows. She was holding a mop.

'Mrs Mattock? Can I come in and have a word with you?'

The little woman did not yield an inch. She must have thought

Cromwell was a bank robber. Her hand tightened on the mop and she looked a bit scared and ready to scream for help.

'It's about Mr Dodd… I'm from the police…'

She didn't ask for his credentials, but swung back the door, taking, however, the precaution of fastening it open with a wedge used for the purpose.

'Pore Mr Dodds. It is a sad affair. Nice man, Mr Dodds. Never a wrong word in all the time I was doin' up there. Not that I thought anythin' about them Nicholls women. Jumped-up 'uns, they are. But Mr Dodds… well… A proper gentleman, he was…'

She continued to reel off testimonials until Cromwell thought it well to butt in.

'I wonder who would want to kill Mr Dodd. Can you think?'

'I can't, unless it was those two women. Deep 'uns, they was. That Missis Nicholls… Well… I've given me notice.'

She tightened her lips expressively.

'Why should they want to kill him? He was the goose that laid the golden eggs, wasn't he?'

'Goose? You've hit it there, mister. He was a proper goose ever takin' up with sich trash. Missis Dodds, she used ter call 'erself. I never called 'er by it. Always Miss Nicholls. Like it or not, that's what she got. An' that's all she deserved. Tryin' to come it over the likes o' me as has their marriage-lines proper…!'

'But they wouldn't want to kill Dodd, would they?'

'If he left 'em in his will, they would. Proper old grabbers. Tried to beat me down to two shilling an hour. Me… as does for a bank, if you please. I soon told 'em.'

'But they didn't know about any will.'

'So they say. Deep 'uns. Specially that Mrs Nicholls. Eyes at the back of 'er head, that one. *And* Dodds knew it.'

'Why?'

'He hid things from 'em. Locked 'em all in his big box and kept the key himself. Then he emptied it and took the things away somewhere…'

'Did you see him?'

'Of course. Mr Dodds and me got on well. He'd let me up to do his attic. He slep' there out of the way of them two. I never see him sleep in any of the beds downstairs…'

Mrs Mattock coughed behind her hand to indicate that she had modest feelings and couldn't speak more plainly of the obvious.

'What is all this about taking his things away?'

Mrs Mattock indicated that she was busy by thrusting her mop in a pail of dirty water and, with a deft gesture, flinging a flood of it over the tiled floor. Then she dried her mop by wringing it in a device like a sieve on the top of the bucket and began to slop up and down as she talked.

'As I was sayin', Mr Dodds tuck away his things bit by bit. There was papers and books in the box. I saw 'em…'

She paused to push back a wisp of hair and then started again, to and fro, to and fro… Mrs Mattock wore a large black hat which bobbed in time with her thrusting and pulling at the mop. It almost hypnotised Cromwell.

'He took out a big handful, put 'em straight, and then popped them in his raincoat pocket. He thought I wasn't lookin'…'

There was a small counter, a mahogany screen behind it, and leaded lights on the top of the screen. A pair of bright brass banker's balances and a pile of weights beside them, with a brass shovel; all to remind you of days when gold sovereigns were shovelled and weighed out like packets of tea. A clock on the wall ticked with the sound of a bouncing ping-pong ball. There were notices on the counter and walls. *Bankers' Notice to the public… Buy Defence Bonds… £5 Is All You Can Take Abroad With You In Cash…* And Mrs Mattock busy mopping and slopping about in the midst of it all.

'If you ask me, Mr Dodds was gettin' ready to do a bunk… to run off an' leave them women…'

Mrs Mattock paused to emphasise this by soaking her mop in

the bucket and discharging its dirty water again over the tiles. There was a pause. Pink-ponk, pink-ponk, ponk, pink. Every now and then the clock seemed to miss a beat. Someone had been eating monkey-nuts in the manager's room, and Cromwell could see a pile of empty shells on the floor round the waste-paper basket.

'...He was packin' up.'

'Whatever for?'

Mrs Mattock put her mop down in the bucket.

'It's my belief he'd got fed up. He was takin' his belongin's away, bit by bit. Somethin' had happened and he wanted to get away.'

'What was it?'

Mrs Mattock had all the answers. What she didn't know she guessed at or made up.

'One day I was cleanin' his attic and he was rootin' in his box, an' sudden-like I turns, and there he is lookin' at a woman's photo...'

She paused for effect, thrust back her hat from her brow, and nodded for emphasis.

'And it wasn't what you think...'

Cromwell wasn't thinking at all. He was waiting for the sequel.

'It wasn't a young 'un. It was an old-fashioned picture. In my opinion... in my opinion it was the photo of his first wife from who he was parted. He looked at it fondly, and then when he sees me lookin' put it away agen, bashful-like.'

'And what might that have meant?'

'He was pinin' for his old missus. He was sorry he'd left 'er.'

Mrs Mattock sniffed, tightened her upper lip to prevent the flow of tears, and resumed her mopping.

'So you think he was sneaking off to go back to Mrs Dodd again.'

'Yes. An' that's not all. My friend Missis Cleethorpes, who does for Mr Henry 'Ooper and Mr Charlie 'Ooper, bachelors both, heard 'em talkin' together one day. They was Mr Dodds' pals... She heard 'em sayin' to one another that Mr Dodds 'ad got friendly with Mrs D agen. "Good thing, too," sez Mr Charlie. "Time he give them Nichollses the go-by..." What do you think o' that?'

'Did you ever see anybody hanging about the bungalow whilst you were there, Mrs Mattock?'

'Meanin' 'oo?'

'Strangers, up to no good, say.'

'That Uncle Fred, or 'ooever he is, called a time or two. Drunken old gasbag, that's what 'e is. I don't recollect anybody else particular.'

'You think Mr Dodd was afraid to make a clean break with the two women and was going to sneak off?'

'Yes. He was afraid of the 'ullaballoo the old woman would kick up if she knew he was goin'.'

'A bit of a terror, was she?'

'More than a bit. The young 'un would never 'ave stayed on there but for her mother nagging 'er. Dorothy's a bit too flighty, when she's allowed to be, to want to bury 'erself alive in a quiet spot like that. But her mother saw to it that she behaved proper. She knew when she was on a good thing, did ole Nicholls. I wouldn't put it past 'er to stick a knife in Dodds if she thought he was plannin' to leave 'em 'igh and dry.'

'Did any of Mr Dodd's family ever call at the bungalow?'

'Not that I'd know. And now, if it's all the same to you, I'd better be finishin' me work. If anybody tells the bank manager that I was 'ere at this time talkin' in the bank, 'e'd carry on 'orrible...'

So Cromwell had to thank her, tell her goodbye, and leave her to her job.

Back at the inn, Mr Mallard was waiting impatiently for Cromwell.

'Helstonbury police have just been on the phone wantin' you,

Sergeant. It was Mr Judkin and 'e said it was important. Shall I get 'em again?'

He looked eager to do anything to please his guests. 'If you don't mind.'

'The Inspector's not back yet, then?' said Judkin at the other end of the line. 'Will you tell him, when he gets back, that my men have found the knife that killed Dodd. The man on duty at the bungalow thought the earth under one of the azaleas looked disturbed and got a fork to it. The knife was buried there. It's got young Dorothy's finger-prints on it, and it's the Nichollses' breadknife.'

'I'm glad you've found it…'

'Glad? Why, it makes it an open and shut case. Dorothy did it out of jealousy. She knew Dodd was fed up and wanted to get away.'

'Did she? So she knifed him with the breadknife, left her prints on it, hid it where it was sure to be found, and then confessed…'

'She hasn't confessed. My men are just off to bring the pair of them in. I'd like the Inspector and you to come over when he gets back. And don't you back-answer me that way, Sergeant. I'm in charge here and…'

'I'm sorry, sir. I didn't mean to be insulting. But really, Dorothy Nicholls couldn't kill a fly. I'll be very surprised…'

'I don't want to argue with you. Tell the Inspector I want to see him when he gets back. That's all…'

Cromwell hung up the instrument with a puzzled frown on his face. He took a step or two in the direction of the bar and then returned to the telephone and addressed it, as though Judkin himself were in its place.

'Silly damn' fool!'

And then he went off for a drink to soothe his feelings.

7

THE RED CAP

Judkin nodded and smiled at Cromwell, as he and Littlejohn entered the temporary police offices at Helstonbury. It was obvious he'd had second thoughts on his outburst over the telephone and wanted to be friends again. It was the nearest to an apology he could give. Cromwell smiled back, and that ended it.

'Shall I hold them on suspicion?' said Judkin to Littlejohn after he had told him about the discovery of the breadknife.

It was dark, and outside, gas lamps lit up the deserted town square. In the distance the neon signs of the picture house glowed a diabolical red, and now and then the stentorian bellow of the braided commissionaire assured the town in general that there were seats in all parts.

There had not been electricity in the old house now occupied temporarily and, expecting to be out of it quickly, the police hadn't had it wired. Gas jets threw a clear white light over everything. The night patrol was getting ready for duty, and there was a lot of tramping and shuffling about in the constables' common-room at the back. PC Drane, the polite policeman, was off duty and had been replaced by a uniformed attendant in new boots. He kept creaking about self-consciously, now tiptoeing, now walking on the sides of the soles, in a frantic effort to stop their squeaking.

'I think we'd better talk to the pair of them first, Judkin. There really doesn't seem much point in locking them up. We can always get them if we want them; they can't go far…'

'Bring in the two women, Saxilby. And for heaven's sake get those shoes oiled. They get on my nerves…'

'Yes, sir.'

PC Saxilby, very red about the ears, made a silent exit, walking on his heels.

'I won't say a thing without my lawyer. I want my brother Fred…'

You could hear the old woman protesting as they led her in. They were both got up in their best black clothes. Dorothy had been careful about her make-up, too, and brought the scent of cheap perfume along with her. She was quite self-possessed and looked ashamed of her mother. Mrs Nicholls was wearing a sealskin cape and carried a large black plastic hand-bag. Both hands were clasped over the handle of the bag, and she was upright with indignation. She made a beeline for Littlejohn.

'I won't say a word without my lawyer, Fred. This is an h'outrage…'

'Please sit down, Mrs Nicholls.'

Littlejohn and Cromwell rose to give the women their seats. There was a lot of scuffling and creaking as Saxilby scoured the building for more chairs. At length all was quiet again.

'There's no need to get excited, Mrs Nicholls. You're not being arrested.'

'Well, what did Mr Judkin want hauling us all the way from Brande to here at this time of night? He could have asked what he wanted to h'ask at the 'ouse.'

Funny, Mrs Nicholls always started to talk affectedly when addressing Littlejohn, as though assuming he was a cut above the local police and she could rise to it.

'I understand the police have found the weapon which killed Mr Dodd, Mrs Nicholls.'

Dorothy made a noise between a gasp and a sob, but the old lady was unmoved.

'I saw them diggin' in the garden. Then there was considerable h'excitement. They didn't say what they'd found. I think we might 'ave been told.'

She sniffed and threw back her head like one whose dignity has been affronted.

'Here it is, Mrs Nicholls,' interposed Judkin, and with a dramatic gesture he placed the knife carefully on the table. 'Is this yours?'

'Yes, it is. But I haven't used it for years. I use a knife from a carvin' set for bread. That knife was in the garage. Mr Dodd took it there and put it with his tools. If you're thinking I used it, or Dorothy, or my brother Fred… you're mistaken. I'd forgot it even existed.'

'So, somebody took it from the garage and later killed Mr Dodd with it?' Judkin had a note of sarcasm in his voice for some reason. It was not lost on the old woman.

'I want my lawyer.'

Judkin was getting mad.

'How are we going to get your brother Fred here at this hour. He lives in Cambridge, doesn't he? For the Lord's sake be a bit more helpful…'

'No need to blaspheme. We was just getting along well enough, till you interrupted…'

She indicated Littlejohn to show whom she meant. She was wearing knitted black string gloves.

Judkin passed his hand through his thin hair and shrugged his shoulders at Littlejohn.

'They could easily have killed Dodd at home with that knife and made up all the tale about going up and down the hill in the car…'

'But we didn't, and what you say's libel…'

'Slander,' corrected Judkin, hardly knowing what he was doing.

'I don't care what you call it, but you're making up a pack of lies. I'll…'

Littlejohn leaned forward.

'Mrs Nicholls, please try to get to the point. We want your help, that's all.'

'Funny way of asking for help. What did you want to know?'

Her tone changed towards Littlejohn, as though she might have been speaking to an equal after dealing with inferiors. After all, her father had ridden around in a carriage and pair! Dorothy sat by, not saying a word. There was a faint coquettish smile on her lips, and she finally rolled her eyes at Cromwell, who blushed and looked through the window at the red neon sign along the street…

'Was the garage always kept locked when the car was in or out?'

'Not always. If Dodd was going out in it on his own, he'd leave the doors open, the two of us bein' at home.'

'You could see all that went on there, then?'

'Well, hardly. The garage is at the side of the house, and there's a little window overlooks it, but we weren't always lookin' out of it.'

'So, someone might have slipped in and taken the knife when you weren't looking?'

'Quite right. They could.'

'When did you last see the old breadknife, Mrs Nicholls?'

'About a fortnight since.'

'What were you doing with it?'

It was Judkin intervening again. The old woman turned on him.

'Was you speakin' to *me*?'

'Of course I was. Who else?'

'Well, I went for the pliers in Dodd's tool-box about a fortnight since. A parcel came wired up, and I wanted to cut the wire. The knife was in the box with the pliers then. Are you satisfied?'

Judkin grunted. He indicated by a gesture of his hands that the floor was all Littlejohn's again.

'Have you noticed anybody hanging about the house of late. Say, during the last fortnight, Mrs Nicholls?'

'There's always callers. Tradesmen, 'awkers, and such-like. I can't remember anybody in particular.'

'Think hard…'

Mrs Nicholls started to think, screwing up her face and gazing into space through the window.

'Yes… A man called askin' if we'd any old gold. They do come round, you know. I sent him off.'

'Was that all?'

'Do you remember anythin', Dorothy?'

'Eh?'

Dorothy was waking from her daydreams. The presence of a lot of presentable men had stimulated her to thoughts of her new freedom. She patted her hair under her chic little black hat.

'I said, do you remember any strange callers over the last two weeks, besides the man with the old gold…'

'The one that asked if Mr Henry Dodd lived there?'

Littlejohn swung round.

'Did he ask that? Was he after Mr Dodd?'

Dorothy smiled seductively.

'Yes. He seemed to have a list of likely places to call at for his gold. He ticked it off after we'd told him he was right.'

'And he went off right away?'

Mrs Nicholls now took over.

'No, he didn't exac'ly. He asked if we could tell him where he could get a cup o' tea. He seemed respectable enough and as the pot was on the table, we gave him a drink and some biscuits, didn't we, Dorothy?'

'Yes, we did, didn't we?'

'That's right.'

Judkin made a gesture of resignation and himself stared out of the window dejectedly, watching the red sign. EMP RE. One of the letters wasn't illuminated…Why couldn't they get it put right!

Littlejohn persevered.

'Did he drink his tea with you both?'

'Yes. We gave him some chocolate biscuits, too. He seemed tired. Who wouldn't be with a job like that?'

'He was a nice man…' added Dorothy, the expert in erotic matters.

'What did he look like?'

It was evident that the stranger had been a bright spot in Dorothy's bored imprisonment. She'd taken him in to the full and could remember every detail.

'About forty or thereabouts… Nice manners. A proper gentleman. What he was doin' on a sort of pedlar's job like that, I don't know…'

'Had he any gold with him, or scales, or anything else to show his trade?'

'No. Of course he didn't turn out his pockets…' Dorothy giggled, her mother glared at her, and Judkin raised his prominent eyes to heaven praying for endurance.

'Go on with your description, then, Miss Nicholls.'

'He wore sporty tweeds… sort of grey check…'

'Grey check!'

Cromwell said it as if to himself.

'Yes. Very dark; almost Spanish, as you might say. And beeeootiful manners…'

Mrs Nicholls eyed her daughter suspiciously, as though during her absence for cups of tea, the pair of them had been making passes at each other.

'You mentioned 'is manners before, Dorothy,' she snapped, in tones of rebuke.

'Did I?'

'How tall would he be?'

'I'd say… I'd say, perhaps two inches less than you. Well set-up, he was.'

'Did he wear a ring?'

Dorothy's eyes glowed with admiration. So did those of Cromwell, if it came to that.

'How did you know?'

'What kind was it?'

'I remember it was a funny ring… The kind a gentleman like him wouldn't hardly wear… Silver it was…'

Littlejohn nodded.

'What shape?'

'It was like a serpent… Sort of snake, coiled round and eating its tail…'

'You wot?'

Mrs Nicholls was getting a bit ashamed of her daughter's frivolity.

'That's all right, Mrs Nicholls. What Miss Nicholls says is true. Would you both recognise this man again?'

'Oh, yes…'

It came eagerly from Dorothy. The flashy, and probably bogus, gold-hunter must have made a great impression. A rare bird in the way of callers and a challenge to Dorothy's charms.

'Did he talk much… or ask questions?'

'He said about his job. There was less and less gold about. Yes… And he asked about Harry. Did we all three live there? He said he once knew a Harry Dodd. Perhaps it was the same man…'

Mrs Nicholls interposed heavily.

'When it came to a stranger probin' into private affairs, we didn't h'encourage it. We didn't answer his questions, did we, Dorothy?'

'No…'

Dorothy hesitated.

'Was he alone with you for a bit?'

Littlejohn asked it blandly of Dorothy, and Mrs Nicholls sat like a cat watching a mouse.

'Just while Mother was getting a cup and some biscuits.'

'Did he ask you anything then?'

'If I spent all my time there... and what I did with my spare time.'

'Well!! You didn't tell me that.'

'What was there to tell...?'

The old woman's jaws champed together; there was a further inquest in store for her daughter when they got back home!

'Did he ask any other questions, Miss Nicholls? This is very important.'

Dorothy began to agitate such brains as she'd got and, in the end, looked quite pleased with herself.

'Yes, he did. He said he thought Harry was the one he knew. And then he said a funny thing. "How's the old man?" he says. "How's the old man? Seen him lately?"'

Mrs Nicholls couldn't control herself.

'And 'oo might the old man have been? You never told me all this.'

'It was only casual talk. It wasn't important. The old man was Harry's father. I said I didn't know Harry had a father, and he must have got the wrong Dodd. In any case, I told him I'd never seen his father. He'd never been here. And he must be mistaken.'

She looked very happy to get all this rigmarole out of her system.

'And with that, he left?'

'No. He had his tea and biscuits and then he went.'

'Was the garage open?'

'Yes... Harry was out in the car and hadn't closed the doors. He never did when he was coming back the same day.'

'Did the man in the check suit go in the garage?'

'He could have. It was there and open. Why should he do that?'

Mrs Nicholls was hot and dishevelled with anger. Her hat had gone awry and her nose had started to glow. She looked like Widow Twankey.

'Because he might 'ave stolen the knife. Can't you see?'

She said it slowly, loudly, and with simulated patience, as though addressing a small, backward child, or like a music-hall Smart Alec educating his stooge.

'Why, yes…' Dorothy looked pleased about something. 'You mean the knife they found under the azaleas. I put it there. I'd been using it to thin the roots. I forgot to bring it in…'

Judkin could stand no more. 'Why the hell…?' he said, and bit off the rest of the question. 'Weren't you aware that that knife was the reason we brought you here? We thought Dodd was killed with it…'

'No…'

Judkin looked as if he didn't know whether to laugh or cry. He rang the bell. 'Take 'em home, Saxilby,' he said without suggesting the form of conveyance, and the two women were led off.

'I hope he murders them on the way. Of all the dumb fools, that Nicholls girl beats the band!'

Next day they were to learn more about old man Dodd.

Early the following morning the Leicester police came on in reply to enquiries. They'd got a list of Hoods' Brewery houses which sold Red Cap Ale, but the brewers, it seemed, also supplied clubs and private customers locally.

'They only deliver within five miles, privately, however,' went on Leicester. 'Not that they restrict the radius particularly, but Red Cap's only well-known and popular in and near Leicester. Farther afield it mainly goes to Hoods' public houses.'

'Have you got the list of the public houses you mention? We might try them on the off-chance. Even then, it's almost certain they won't remember a casual caller. We'll have to risk it. Will you read them out, please?'

Littlejohn took pencil and paper and jotted them down.

The Barley Mow, Kilby.
The Bleeding Wolf, Kegworth.
The Ring of Bells, Shipton Magna.
The Laughing Cat, Galby.
The Herald Angels, Husband's Bosworth.
The Lollards' Arms, Lutterworth…

and so on. Twenty-six public houses with the usual picturesque names. Cromwell read them over as he finished his breakfast. He smacked his lips over the names and the marmalade.

'It 'ud be interestin' to write a book on how pubs get their names, sir. Take this, fr' instance. What's a Lollard…?'

'A Lollard, my dear chap, was one of the followers of John Wyclif, who was once vicar of Lutterworth…'

'Didn't I tell you, sir?! Now that's terribly interesting. I do believe…'

Cromwell's eyes began to glow as he pondered another hobby. Bird-watching, Yoga, photography, window-box gardening, singing in the police choir, they'd all had their day. Now it was the history of pubs…

'I'll save this paper for you when we've solved the case, Cromwell. A very useful index for your thesis. There's one other name on it which will no doubt interest you…'

'Yes?' said Cromwell in tones which implied he could hardly wait.

'The County Asylum, Gayford. There is also a pub called *The Marquis of Granby* which they supply in the same village.'

'But why the asylum?'

'The Inspector at Leicester says Hoods' don't serve private people far afield, but Gayford is a special case. It seems the inmates tasted Red Cap at *The Marquis of Granby* in their village. Since then they'll drink no other! Well, hardly that. You see, one of the Hoods is on the Board of Management at the asylum and they support, you might say, home industries.'

'Well, well. With pubs and loony-bins we're going to have quite a day.'

'You are, Cromwell. I shan't be with you. I'm off to Cambridge to see Mrs Harry Dodd. She's been out of the picture far too long. I'm sure she can help us, if only she's that way inclined.'

'So I've more than a score of pubs to call at. Do I buy a drink at each one, sir? Because, if I do…'

'No. I suggest you start at the ones nearest here. We'll get a road map and plan your itinerary, and you can gradually close in on Leicester. Mind you, I don't promise you success. This might be a wild-goose chase. It most likely will be. But it'll keep you out of mischief while I'm away.'

'Do I *walk* it?'

'Our friend Judkin, who, by the way, told me last night he'd been rather rude to you over the telephone and regretted it, has promised to lend you one of his natty little police cars. Which means you can't even try a Red Cap on your travels.'

Cromwell had been poring over a map on the wall.

'Here's Gayford… It's ten miles from here, on the main road from Leicester to Cambridge.'

'Then I suggest you get rid of the asylum first. You can enquire if Harry Dodd was interested in any of the inmates and if they drank Hoods' Red Cap together.'

Gayford Asylum had been a large private residence until the owner died in 1936. Unfortunately, his uncle, from whom he had inherited it with just enough to keep it up, had only died two months before, and the Treasury had been adamant about not letting off the estate with single death duties. So to pay double, the place was sold to the County. Gayford Hall stood in many acres of ground. Cromwell zigzagged his car along the mile-long drive, through a belt of trees, past a large lovely sweep of lawn, and then to the front of a spacious Georgian house which, in its day, had boasted fifty bedrooms, now converted into over two hundred cubicles.

It was a pleasant day and many of the inmates were enjoying the open air. They might have been holidaymakers taking pleasure in one another's company, talking quietly in knots, strolling, gardening, playing croquet. On a cricket pitch a match was in progress between rival teams of inmates. Here only it was that Cromwell saw any signs of abnormality. The fast bowling was of a type he wouldn't have cared to stand up to himself, and the mightiness of the batting showed more zest than caution.

He asked a man working in a rock garden near the main door where he could find the medical superintendent. The man asked Cromwell if he had called to join the party, warned him not to touch him, as he was made of glass, and then lucidly directed the sergeant to the proper place.

Dr Fenniscowles, the superintendent, was seated in a large room which had once been the morning-room of the mansion. The place was full to capacity with filing cabinets, as though there he kept the records of all the unfortunate mental cases of the British Isles. He was a tall, stooping man, with cadaverous jaws, large cruel teeth and a huge dome of a head fringed in grey hair. He wore a flannel suit and an open-necked green shirt with a black tie fastened round his bare neck and tucked down the shirt.

'You are Mr Grappenhull,' he said, fingering a card from the cabinets. 'You have discovered a way of reducing taxation and your doctor has sent you along to discuss it with me... Well, Mr Grappenhull, I shall be very interested to hear about it.'

Dr Fenniscowles thereupon put on a pair of large, round gold-framed glasses, drew a pad and pencil towards him, and indicated that he was ready to hear about Income Tax.

A pretty nurse, sitting at a table nearby, thereupon crossed the floor and whispered at length with the doctor.

'Well, why wasn't I told? Where is Grappenhull, anyway? He ought to have been here hours ago. Tomorrow? Well, who put his appointment down for today? *I* did? *I did not*... Oh, very well. What is the use of arguing. Everybody denies what I say. Yes, Mr

Cromwell? What can we do for you? Not another offer of a male-voice choir, country dancing, or theatrical performance to inflict on my poor flock! No?'

Cromwell patiently told the doctor what he was after and produced the red beer-bottle cap and the picture of Harry Dodd, borrowed from the bedside of Dorothy Nicholls.

Dr Fenniscowles regarded the red cap blankly.

'Beer? Where do we get our beer, Miss Clarke?'

'I think it is made by Hoods', Doctor. I see the bottles in the canteen. That looks like one of the caps.'

'So it is. How interesting it would be to form a collection of these small, corrugated metal disks, eh? One from each of the breweries of England! People have collected more stupid things, I can assure you, sir. We have in this institution, for example, men who collect match-boxes, moths, cigarette cards, eggs, stamps, matches and transparent paper. I myself collect National Savings Certificates…'

He roared at his joke and then suddenly cut off his laughter like turning off a tap.

'Who is this?'

He indicated the photograph.

'A Mr Harry Dodd, of Brande, sir. He was murdered two days ago, and we found that red cap in his pocket.'

'He is an obvious extrovert…'

And the doctor then began to analyse poor Harry Dodd's make-up in terms which were double-Dutch to Cromwell, who felt that if he didn't get away pretty soon, he would go mad himself and have to be detained. It was a nightmare. He looked at the pretty Miss Clarke for relief. She smiled at him.

'The officer has just called to ask if Mr Dodd ever came here whilst he was alive. I think we can help him, Doctor.'

Dr Fenniscowles suddenly leapt to his feet as if someone had thrust hot needles in his flesh.

'*Dodd*, did you say? Dodd? My dear Inspector, have you called to say you have him? Is the long search, the long agony over? Is he safely back in the fold?'

Miss Clarke joined them at the desk.

'Mr Dodd escaped recently. He was an inmate and got away. He seems to have vanished. We feared some accident had happened to him. There are disused mineshafts around here. We have searched everywhere…'

Dr Fenniscowles raised his hands above his head and then brought them down to his hair, which he tore in frenzy.

'We have never lost an inmate before, sir. If they have tried to get away, we have found them and brought them home. This one has baffled us, evaded our every effort.'

Cromwell looked from one to the other of them.

'Was he called Dodd?'

'Of course he was called Dodd, Inspector. Why else would I be so agitated? Had he been called Webb, Bolter, Widdows, or Bookbinder, I wouldn't have minded, for we have no inmates of that name, but his name was Dodd and that is the man you also seem interested in.'

'Harry Dodd?'

'Harry? Certainly *not*! Walter! Walter Dodd. It haunts me in my dreams. I hear it called aloud. Walter Dodd. All night long.'

'It isn't the same man. Our man is Harry Dodd.'

Miss Clarke thought it well to intervene.

'Our patient was Walter Dodd. He was an old gentleman, precise age seventy-eight. His son, Harry Dodd, called to see him regularly. He was well known to us. He must have drunk the beer here with his father. The old man liked a bottle of beer as often as he could get one. Harry Dodd called a little over a fortnight ago. The following day his father escaped and has not been seen or heard of since.'

The doctor sat at his desk looking wildly ahead, whilst the nurse finished her recital. Suddenly a light appeared in his eyes and he bared his cruel teeth in a smile.

'I am so glad you have taken up the case, Inspector. We always hesitate to call in the police, but now our reputation is at stake. Never before have we been beaten. We mustn't be beaten this time, Inspector, must we?'

Cromwell, clutching at straws, agreed. He also said he was a sergeant, not an inspector, but Fenniscowles waved that aside, as if he knew best.

The doctor rose to his full height and was at Cromwell's side in two long strides. Taking the sergeant's hand in a grip of iron, he pumped it convulsively up and down.

'On then! On to victory! Good luck and God speed.'

He flung Cromwell's hand away and rang the bell for the next caller.

Outside, the man who thought he was made of glass was still hanging about. He'd been admiring the bright little new car with 'Police' in a sign which you could illuminate, on the top of it. He sidled up to Cromwell.

'Got a cigarette? Don't touch me. I'm fragile. Made of glass, you know.'

Cromwell gingerly passed his packet across.

'Thanks. My name's Glass. Fragile, with Care. What's yours?'

'Cromwell.'

The man cackled and looked sly. He was used to that kind of thing. One of the inmates, his special buddy, said he was Guy Fawkes, and there was another, George Washington, who always attacked a fellow called George the Third whenever he met him.

'Pleased to meet yer.'

Mr Glass drew at his cigarette hungrily.

'You here about Walter Dodd escapin'?'

'Yes. How did you know?'

'Well... You see, Oliver, there ain't much goes on here I don't know. Walter's been gone quite a while now, and I know Big Head... that's what we call the doctor... Big Head's very worried about it. I thought, as there's nothin' else for a policeman to call about, you might have…'

He waved the cigarette airily above his head, trying to assemble his wandering thoughts.

'They'll never get Walter here again.'

'Why, Mr Glass?'

'No…Walter has too many friends outside. He's up to his neck in intrigue, if you know what I mean.'

Cromwell didn't. He felt to be getting more and more out of his depth.

'Well… Quite often Walter would walk down to the gates and there would be a nice little car waitin' to take him for a drive. Off he'd go in it with his pals, and his friends here would pretend he was somewhere about in the grounds. He wasn't supposed to go out, you know. He was kept in here by the Big People…'

Mr Glass winked one eye and said Big People as if they really were Big and Cromwell knew them all.

'Who are *they*?'

'Don't tell me you don't know. Don't try foxing me or I'll have one of me awkward dos and throw stones at you. Walter was kept in here by the Big Ones…'

'Did he tell you?'

'No. But he told others I know, and they told me. But, now and then, he'd play hookey and go for his ride. Listen…'

Mr Glass, as he called himself, looked around to see if anyone was looking, and then spoke without moving his mouth.

'The last time Walter was out, he came back in a terrible state. Good job it wasn't me. I'd have been smashed to smithereens. He'd been in a motor accident.'

'He'd what?'

'He'd been in a motor accident. And he'd run back here all the way. All dirty and cut, he was. He told the doctor he'd fallen down in the wood, there, and hadn't been able to get back for his tea. They'd been huntin' for him, you see.'

'Did he tell you that?'

'No. He told George, who passed it on to me. You see, Walter wanted to see a newspaper to find out if anybody got hurt. George the Third's allowed newspapers. Some of us aren't. We get too excited by the things that go on outside. George says they're all mad outside, so he isn't affected much by what they do. It seems the man who was driving Walter in the car was killed. The Big Ones held a sort of inquest on him, and who do you think said he was with the dead driver when it happened? *Harry* Dodd, Walter's son. He must have said it was him as was there, to save his old dad, who'd have got into shocking trouble if the Big Ones had known he was out. Got another cigarette?'

'Did Walter say any more about the accident?'

'Not a thing. Next we knew, he'd run away. George said Walter was frightened... If you're turnin' that car, I'm off. One little slip and... well... I'll get badly chipped, if you don't break me altogether...'

Mr Glass thereupon took gingerly to his heels and was gone.

'I wonder how much of that is true?' said Cromwell to himself.

In the distance he could see Mr Glass pointing him out to one of his friends and they started to laugh together.

Not far from the gates stood a telephone box. Cromwell entered and rang up the Cambridge police. Littlejohn had told him where to find him if he needed him. The Inspector was in the police station, as it happened, and they talked together for a long time.

8

THE OLD HOME

Harry Dodd's old home was several miles out of Cambridge, but with police directions to guide him, Littlejohn found it easily. Mrs Dodd still lived there, with Peter, the unmarried son, and several old servants.

The house was an ugly, square edifice built in red and yellow brick. The long drive was dark and gloomy, with old neglected rhododendrons and poplars fringing it. Then it opened out on a large, well-kept lawn with formal flower-beds and a rose garden. It had been a family house, and the rotting arbours and out-houses testified that it was now too big for the present occupants. Littlejohn felt the melancholy of its decayed splendours and its silence meet him as he faced it. He climbed the five stone steps to the large door with its glass panels decorated with stars and rang the bell.

An elderly maid in cap and apron took his card. Inside, the house was well kept. The hall furniture was heavy and Victorian, and there was thick Turkish carpet on the floor. At the far end another door led to a conservatory.

'Mrs Dodd will see you.'

He followed the maid through a door on the right into a large room which overlooked the front lawn. There was too much furniture, and it was stuffy, for, in spite of the warm weather, a good fire burned in the old-fashioned grate. The sideboard, the easy fireside chairs, the tables and the cabinets were of mahogany and all outsize by modern standards. They seemed to tower over the occupants of the room.

An old lady rose to meet Littlejohn. She was tall, erect and frail, with a pink enamelled-looking complexion and delicate, long, thin hands. She put down a piece of embroidery as she rose.

To associate Harry Dodd and his two Nichollses with this woman seemed absurd. She had all the graciousness of a queen mother, all the breeding and kindness of a great lady. A Pekingese dog, sitting on a cushion, rose as quickly as his fat little old body would allow, and began to yap savagely at Littlejohn. The Inspector extended a friendly hand and the dog thereupon fastened his sharp teeth in his forefinger and drew blood. Mrs Dodd quickly pressed the dog back on his cushion and turned to the Inspector.

'I'm terribly sorry, Inspector,' she said, after rebuking the animal, which settled quietly down, still growling. 'Rab isn't very well. He's old and a bit off colour, like his mistress. Let me see the bite...'

She examined the finger, and in spite of Littlejohn's making light of it, showed him the way to a small washroom near the main door, told him to wash it well, and then herself dressed it with lint and iodine. Littlejohn admired her calm and poise. She had about her an air of invulnerability. She was wearing a black dress, presumably out of mourning for her husband. In the confusion of his entry and the affair with the dog, Littlejohn had quite forgotten Mrs Dodd's bereavement.

'I'm very sorry about Mr Dodd, madam,' he said to her. 'I called to ask if you could help us in investigating the matter of his death. If you don't care to talk about it just at present, however, it can wait, although time is rather precious in a case like this.'

'I quite agree, Inspector. I wish to help you all I can. The circumstances are rather unique, one must admit. Our marriage was dissolved long ago, but I feel the loss of my husband just as much as if it hadn't been. We had remained good friends...'

Her voice grew husky, and she was on the verge of tears. She was silent for a minute and then went on.

'What is there I can tell you?'

She bade him be seated and then rang the bell.

'You'll take coffee with me. I was just about to have it when you called. That is, if you care for my sort of coffee. The real thing doesn't agree with me at all. But my doctor recommended a kind of powdered stuff... *Coffex*, and it's very nice. Rab likes it, too, but I'm afraid he's not going to get any for his behaviour...'

'Don't worry about that, Mrs Dodd. If he's out of sorts...'

'Real coffee affects him the same way as his mistress. He's fond of it, too, and always has his drink with me. We were both very seedy after dinner the other evening. I got better the quicker of the pair of us. I'm very fond of Rab. He's old, but Harry bought him for me years ago...'

The maid arrived with the synthetic brew, and Littlejohn confessed he liked it as well as the real thing.

'I was wondering, Mrs Dodd,' he said at length, 'if you could tell me some of the circumstances of your separation from Mr Dodd and the subsequent friendship which developed between you...'

'I don't mind at all, really, and I'll tell you right away, that had this monstrous thing not happened, we had planned to remarry. The whole affair was a misfortune and ought never to have been. I was as much to blame as my husband.'

'You mean in the matter of the divorce?'

'Yes. I spent far too much time on social life in those days. Harry, my husband, wasn't that sort at all. He was a very plain man of simple tastes, and at the time that unpleasant event occurred, was just reaching the age when he wanted his fireside with his wife, his pipe, and his slippers. Instead, this house was always overflowing with people. The children had grown up and were launching out, and though they are my own, I must admit they moved, and still do, in a circle quite above that their father found comfortable. Mind you, they'll never be as good as their father was…'

It was pathetic. The old woman, surrounded by memories of Harry Dodd; his picture on the mantelpiece, his dog on a cushion, living in the past and on recollections of their days together. Mrs Dodd seemed to read his thoughts.

'You must think the whole business was a mad one. I thought differently of it in those days. I was younger then, more proud and self-willed, full of pride. I couldn't forgive him. The shock was so great…'

'And your children didn't help you?'

She gave him a keen glance.

'Who told you that, Inspector?'

'I've seen your son, Peter…'

She smiled.

'Peter, of course, was in the forces then. He was fond of his father and took his side more than the others. Yes… I must confess the other children took it badly. They both moved in rather snobbish company at the time and… well… they were a bit ashamed of their father. In the confusion of events they rather rushed me into a divorce. In that they were assisted by the family solicitor, Aspinall. No sooner had the decree been granted than I bitterly regretted it. For my husband, confused and anxious to do the right thing, bought a house and took the woman in the case and her mother to live with him. His transgression had been to spend a weekend at Brighton with his secretary. He told me afterwards… long afterwards, that he was lonely and simply fleeing from the discomfort of his home. He certainly chose the wrong person to flee with and, unfortunately for him… and for me, as it turned out later, he walked right into my sister and her husband at breakfast the following morning. Poor Harry... He didn't even defend the suit. My sister, who has since died, came straight to me, of course, told me everything and, with a kind of avuncular protectiveness, her husband, who has married again, by the way, told my eldest son, Winfield, what had happened. Winfield, of course, brought in Aspinall without even consulting me. I suppose the chance of disposing of his father was too good to miss. I cannot think he did what he did out of consideration for me...'

She spoke harshly.

'Your son, Winfield, must have disliked his father very much...'

'He did. They were opposites. Besides, it gave Winfield a chance to get control of the works, which he did very quickly after his father went. I fear I helped him to do so. Looking back on the panorama of the past, one sees things with different eyes.'

'You met your husband afterwards?'

'Not until comparatively recently. A little more than two years ago, he wrote to me. He had left the Dodd family Bible here and wanted some particulars of the family... It was all written out on the fly-leaves. He asked if I would send it. I had thought kindly of him as I grew older. He never married Miss Nicholls, he was a bit of an outcast, and he was the father of my children. I told him I would bring the book. We met at a hotel between here and where he was living. The condition of my husband filled me with compassion. He had grown flabby, neglected-looking, lonely and so very, very humble. All his pride had gone. We enjoyed our meeting, once the ice had been broken. Peter drove me there and back and, after that, we met quite regularly. Some time ago I took the bull by the horns. "Harry," I said to him. "This is rather ridiculous. Here we are meeting like a couple of young people carrying on a clandestine courtship. You may come home, if you wish." For answer he broke down and cried. "Life's been a hell since I left you," he said. "If you'll have me, I'll come back, and I won't get in the way..."'

This time Mrs Dodd was weeping openly. Littlejohn let her calm down.

'I told him I would welcome his return,' she said at length. 'I suggested to him that we should remarry. I also told him that we had our lives to live, that we needed each other, and that the children were old enough to fend for themselves. In any case, if they didn't like it, they would have to put up with it. We told Peter and asked him to keep it a secret…'

'When did you plan to get married again, Mrs Dodd?'

'We hadn't fixed it. Harry said he had one or two things to settle and provision to make for Miss Nicholls. He said it would take him a short time to arrange matters…'

'And only your son, Peter, knew of the remarriage?'

'I understand so. You must ask him whether or not he let out the secret.'

'Does Mr Peter live here?'

'He has a flat in town, but many of his things are here. He has gone with Aspinall to the inquest today.'

'So he told me. By the way, did you know, Mrs Dodd, of some new steel process in which your husband was interested?'

'Yes. He told me of it most enthusiastically. It seems that he and a friend had been doing some research in a little workshop they'd fitted up. I said that when he came back, he could take it down to the works, if he wished…'

'You still control them?'

'Nominally. They were my father's, of course. I retained the nominal controlling interest, although Winfield is my nominee. He is chairman and has made the business prosper. Still, if Harry had discovered means of improving processes, he ought to have the right to use them for the benefit of the family concern…'

'Did Mr Winfield Dodd know of this?'

'Of course not. He wouldn't have taken kindly to it. Harry talked of floating a rival company of his own, but if he had returned to me, I'm sure he would have reconsidered it.'

'Do you keep in touch with Mr Dodd's brother, madam?'

'William, you mean? No. William, as you will doubtless know, if you read his speeches, despises people like me, the parasites, the grinders-down of the suffering poor. I also despise William. Not because he wants the money of the rich to give to the poor, but because he is an office-seeker, a time-server. He doesn't want our money. All he wants is to shout about it to earn himself votes. We never agreed.'

'Did Harry and William get on well?'

'No. When Harry and I married, William was astounded. He never thought Harry would marry his employer's daughter and enter the firm. Harry always rather laughed at his brother's ways. Froth and hot air, he used to call them. When the divorce occurred, however, it was William's turn to look down on Harry. You see, William was, by then, a rising politician. He was elected for a manufacturing town in the North, where rigid nonconformity on one side and strong Roman Catholicism on the other, get the candidate in. Harry, from being the despised owner of capital, became the skeleton in the Dodd closet, the spectre which, by his public appearance in the columns of the more disreputable newspapers, as a libertine and divorced person, might cost William many votes. William was furious. He even came here and tried to patch it up. He and Harry quarrelled and, I believe, never met again.'

'Mr Dodd's father is alive?'

Mrs Dodd looked Littlejohn in the face.

'Yes. That is another family scandal. He is in an asylum!'

'Why a scandal, Mrs Dodd?'

'Because he is not mad.'

'Who put him there, then?'

'William. I grant Harry's father was a bit eccentric. Harry got many of his traits from his father. His love of working-men and their company; his genuine modesty and humility; his inability to tolerate snobbishness and cant. That was what made Mr Walter

Dodd, Harry's father, follow William around, heckling him at meetings.'

Littlejohn could not repress a smile.

'Yes, it is funny, isn't it, Inspector? Father heckling son. But, until he took to politics, William was the idle-Jack of the family. He was a lazy-bones who caused his parents a lot of trouble and heart-burning. His mother even had to go out cleaning, because William wouldn't work when his father was ill. Harry, of course, was the younger and was at school at the time. He gave up and got a job... Then William got in politics. He had the gift of the gab, of course, and that went a long way. It was then that his father proved a great stumbling-block. Far from being proud of his son, he disliked his politics, his party, and his efforts to get something for nothing. He finally took to heckling William at meetings. When William talked of workers, his father would ask him what he knew about work. In the middle of a heart-rending harangue about the toiling masses, a voice William was now getting to know well would ask what William was doing whilst his dead mother was toiling... The old man had grown to hate his elder son. It became a battle between them, and William won. He used his influence to have his father certified insane and put away in a quiet asylum in the country.'

'And your husband used to sneak him out and take him off for little outings in his car...'

'How did you know?'

'We found out at the asylum. Did Mr Dodd tell you of it?'

'Yes. When he returned here, Harry was going to get his father out and offer him a home with us. Meanwhile, until he was declared sane again, he wasn't allowed out of the asylum. But Harry, in his rather adventurous way, used to sneak the old man out and give him a treat.'

'And one day, when Mr Walter Dodd, Harry, and a friend called Comfort, who owned the car they were driving in, were on one of their jaunts, the car was driven from the road. Comfort was killed, Mr Walter, badly shaken, ran back to the asylum, and Mr Harry pretended that he and Comfort alone were the passengers.'

'He told me. Harry was sure that accident was deliberately done. He didn't know whether it was he, his father, or Mr Comfort they were after, but he gave his father money to get a taxi and get back to the asylum at once. He was afraid someone might be after his father, and felt he would be safer in the asylum...'

'But who could be after him?'

'Shall we say William?'

'William, who looks like being in high office if his party gets in at the next election and whose father, if he got around his meetings might, to say the least of it, affect his majority at the polls?'

'Yes. That might be it.'

'Do you know that Mr Walter Dodd has escaped from Gayford Asylum and is at large?'

Mrs Dodd rose and clutched her throat. Her pale complexion grew the colour of parchment.

'No! He is at large?'

'Yes. Are you sure he *is* sane, because, if he isn't, might he not have something to do with his son's death?'

'He was never violent. A most peaceful man...'

'Until upset by people like his son, William?'

'That is so...'

'And then, he'd do queer things?'

'But not kill... Not Harry... He loved Harry. Harry was his only friend.'

'Hadn't he even his grandchildren to turn to... or you?'

'He and I got on very well. Not intimately, though. The children had little to do with him. He grew out of their lives very early in our marriage. Harry kept in touch.'

'Where did Mr Walter live?'

'Not far from here. Gale Cottage, Helton. It's the house of a former tanner, but the tanyard has gone and only the house remains. It's empty now, since Mr Dodd went to the asylum. His furniture was left there… You don't mean he might…?'

'I certainly do. Where else could he go?'

'Then someone ought to go there. He might be ill, or…'

'Or in danger? Why should he be in danger?'

'I can't think. Surely William would not harm him.'

'I don't know. We must see. By the way, did Mr Harry say why he wanted the family Bible?'

'No… I think he was so excited at our meeting again that it slipped his mind. Why?'

'Was there something between Harry and his father that might make him want the family tree, or something?'

'I can't say.'

'Where is the Bible? Did you get it back?'

'Yes. He handed it back to me. I put it in its old place. Would you like to see it, Inspector?'

She rose and left the room before Littlejohn could answer, and returned carrying a large volume, leather bound, with the backs old and faded and dog-eared.

'Here it is. I haven't looked at it since I brought it back.'

Littlejohn took the book and opened it.

The fly-leaves had been all removed.

'But someone's torn out all the entries! Why should Harry do that?'

'Are you sure he *did* do it?'

'Who else?'

She looked anxiously in Littlejohn's face. She was worn out and bewildered by the course of events.

'Did you examine it when it came back?'

'I'm sorry… I didn't…'

'Do you remember any of the entries?'

'I did once, but it's so long since.'

'How long did Harry Dodd keep this?'

'About a week. I took it one week and he returned it the next.'
'And he didn't say anything about tearing portions of it out?'
'No.'
'Well, I think I must be going now, Mrs Dodd. Thank you for being so helpful. I'll have to call again, probably, to see Mr Peter. My colleague is driving to Cambridge to meet me, and we'll call at Helton and take a look at Gale Cottage…'

It was dusk when Littlejohn and Cromwell met at the Cambridge police station. The sergeant had brought the car.

'Helton? Where's that, please?'

They told Littlejohn how to get there. It was on the way back to Helstonbury. They had little difficulty in finding it.

Gale Cottage stood, as Mrs Dodd had said, on the site of an old country tannery. The house was ringed by tall dark trees, obviously at one time planted to shield it from the works behind. Now, gloomy and overgrown, they made complete night of the late dusk. The car ran up the neglected drive and drew up at the front door. The building stood four-square in its plot of elms and poplars. The door was heavy beneath a semi-circular canopy; the large sash windows were dirty, and inside shutters covered all on the ground floor. The whole place was tumbledown and neglected, probably awaiting the demolishers when the local authorities would let them begin.

Littlejohn beat on the door with his fist. The sound echoed through the house.

Cromwell, sitting at the wheel, felt his spine crawl. In the Metropolitan Police Choir, of which he was an enthusiastic if indifferent baritone member, they were just polishing up a new piece called *The Listeners*, a poem by Walter de la Mare.

> *But only a host of phantom listeners*
> *That dwelt in the lone house then*
> *Stood listening in the quiet of the moonlight*
> *To that voice from the world of men…*

Cromwell looked through the dark foliage of the trees. A half-moon seemed to be struggling through them to get at him.

Littlejohn's blows on the door made him leap in his seat.

'Nobody at home?' he asked, and then thought what a silly question it was.

'I don't like it…'

Littlejohn stood back and looked at the upper windows.

'Is that a light up there?'

Cromwell climbed out of the car. The moon was making a silver reflection on the windows overhead, but, it seemed, one of them was illuminated from behind.

'Let's force the door. It shouldn't be much of a job. The wood's old and rotten, and the lock'll most likely give.'

They put their shoulders to the door and, after three heaves, it flew open with a harsh, tearing sound. Not only the lock, but a bolt and a chain ripped the wood off their screws and clattered behind the panels.

The hall was dusty and damp, and the furniture, just visible in the gloom, stood heavy and sombre at the foot of the stairs. At the end of the passage, a door, agitated by the draught of the open one at the front, began to swing on its hinges, creaking and banging. Cromwell switched on a torch and they could see where someone had entered or gone, leaving the door off the latch.

'Let's go up…'

Their feet rattled on the uncarpeted stairs. At the top, a dark landing with open doors giving upon it, and, through some of the openings, moonlight was shining. The door on the left hand at the front, that of the illuminated room, was closed. Hastily they opened it and entered.

It had probably, at one time, been the best bedroom, but was now cold and damp, with the furniture shabby and grey from neglect. A large four-poster stood in the middle, with disordered bedclothes, soiled and in holes from lack of use. A bare electric bulb glowed down full on the bed, illuminating its contents mercilessly.

'There's… there's…'

Cromwell stood speechless on the threshold.

'Yes. There's someone in it…'

Littlejohn took a step, seized the pillows with both hands, and flung them aside. Beneath, with wide-open eyes and livid lips, stared a bearded face. It was utterly transformed by terror, but it sufficiently resembled the other victim of the case to be identified.

It was old Walter Dodd, and somebody had smothered him with the pillows of his own bed!

9

THE BENEVOLENT PARROT

Helton was under the county police, and they were soon on the spot. The sergeant who arrived in response to Cromwell's alarm from a call-box, was quite overcome to find two Scotland Yard men there.

'What had I better do first?' he asked deferentially, like a general practitioner who, having opened up a body on the operating-table, suddenly finds a renowned surgeon at his elbow.

Littlejohn and Cromwell had already been through the house and found little to help them. It had apparently been deserted since Walter Dodd had been certified insane and removed to the asylum. It looked as if nobody had cared to take any other trouble than to lock it up and leave the contents to moulder away.

The furniture was old and dirty, and there were moths in the curtains and upholstery. Dust lay over everything, except the solitary bedroom occupied by the old man since his escape. He had unearthed blankets and pillows and made himself a shake-down in his hiding-place. The kitchen, too, had been used. Tins of food, fresh bread and margarine, tea and sugar; even milk and daily newspapers.

'Somebody must have been looking after him,' said Cromwell.

'I wonder who it was. Mrs Harry Dodd was surprised when she knew he'd escaped...'

'But who could have wanted to kill an old, harmless buffer like Walter Dodd, sir?'

'The same applies to Harry Dodd as well, Cromwell. They were somebody's unlucky pair. Old Walter must have been here since he fled from the asylum.'

There was nothing in the drawers of any help. The papers had all been cleared away by someone, and most of them were empty.

Lastly, Littlejohn turned over Walter Dodd's clothes.

The old man was lying in his shirt and trousers, as though expecting an alarm, even in the night. He had placed a few bits of silver and some coppers on the table at the side of the bed; the forlorn contents of his trousers' pockets. His coat and vest were draped over the back of the only chair in the room. The Inspector went through the pockets. There was little in them. A pipe and a pathetically empty pouch. Matches. A knife with two broken blades. A wallet with a pound note in it and a picture of a woman taken long ago; presumably Walter Dodd's wife. Finally, two penny stamps and a piece of paper torn from a notebook with an address scribbled on it.

The Aching Man Inn, Helton, Midshire.

Littlejohn instructed the local sergeant, and left him in charge after asking him about *The Aching Man*.

'It's on the main road, sir. Turn right from here, follow the lane to the high road. It's what you might call a secondary road now, sir, though once it was the highway to Bath. That's why the pub's called *The Aching Man*, on account of invalids on their ways to Bath stoppin' there for a rest...'

The sergeant paused for breath after his recital.

'Very interesting, Sergeant. Who runs the inn?'

'A chap called Boone... Sid Boone, and his sister, Margaret, known locally as Peg. A queer couple they are, and we keep an eye on them. We once suspected they were up to the neck in the black market, but we could never bring it home. Too clever, they are...'

'Is it their own place?'

'No; they're tenants. Hoods, of Leicester, own it.'

Littlejohn and Cromwell exchanged glances.

'We'd better make a call there.'

'You don't suspect those two, sir?'

'No, Sergeant. I'm a bit curious about them.'

They found *The Aching Man* as described by the sergeant. On the gable of stone, the name shone from a sign made of reflectors which caught the headlamps of the car.

THE ACHING MAN.
HOODS' PRIME ALES.

There were one or two cars parked outside, and lights shone from the two rooms on the front. The detectives entered.

There was nothing pretentious about the inn. A small porch, a glass door, followed by a dark corridor from which the stairs rose. On each side of the passage a door, glass panelled. Voices sounded in both rooms; shouting and a lot of laughing. Littlejohn opened the door on the right. It was a large room with a bar at one end and a leather upholstered seat running round the walls. A few iron tables with marble tops and some cane chairs. The place was brightly lit. A number of countrymen were sitting and chatting, and at one end four men were playing darts. They all looked up at the newcomers and then froze, almost instinctively recognising them as police.

Behind the bar, a handsome woman was standing talking to a customer who hung over the counter. She was tall, well-built and full-breasted, with black hair and an oval, pale face. The hair was worn long and gathered in a bun in the nape of the neck. A slender neck, with the head held proudly. The dark eyes were wide-set, the nose aquiline and delicately chiselled. The mouth large and shapely, with full, sensual lips. All the men in the room were terribly aware of her presence, like a pack of rivals, anxious to please her, bragging to gain her attention and favours, and her calm self-possession rebuffed them all. She looked with contempt at the man she was serving, who couldn't take his eyes from her face. Her eyes sought those of Littlejohn and held them for a minute. It was as if she had been waiting for something, and now it had arrived. They understood one another immediately.

Peg Boone took the money for the whisky from the toper and slid it in the till without so much as a look at it. Then she raised the flap of the counter and emerged straight for Littlejohn.

'You were wanting me?'

It was a question and an answer at the same time.

'Yes. I want a talk with you. You are Miss Boone?'

'Yes. Wait here till I get the barmaid…'

She left the room with the graceful poise of an Eastern woman whose gait is full of lovely rhythm from carrying water-vessels on her head. As she closed the door, all the eyes which had been upon her lost their interest, the darts flew, men drank deeply and relaxed. Danger had left them for a respite.

A little peroxide blonde entered, followed by Peg Boone, who made her look cheap and insignificant in contrast.

'Come this way.'

It was an order.

They followed her into a small den, made like a cocktail bar, with a red and black counter, chromium and leather stools, and red upholstered seats in alcoves.

'This is closed tonight. We haven't many customers…'

They all sat down.

'Drink?'

'No, thanks…' said Littlejohn, and Cromwell smiled and shook his head.

'You're police, aren't you?'

Her self-possession was amazing. She hadn't the slightest doubt about her looks, her make-up, or her impact on her visitors. She didn't move a hand to adjust her hair or dress. She was sure of everything.

'Yes, Miss Boone. We're police. Scotland Yard, to be exact.'

'Scotland Yard? So it's not about the road accident?'

'No. Has there been one?'

'Yes. A motor-cyclist was killed right in front of here this afternoon. I saw it happen. I made a statement, but I thought you were after more information.'

'No. Do you know a man named Walter Dodd?'

Her eyes held those of Littlejohn. Nothing about her seemed to change, not even a tell-tale frown or a twitch.

'No.'

Littlejohn knew she was lying.

'He seems to have known you, or of this place, at least. He had a slip of paper in his wallet bearing your address. Can you explain that?'

'Easily. Somebody must have recommended us, and he made a note of it. One day he'll be turning up for a drink.'

'No, he won't. He was murdered earlier this evening about a mile or so away from here. Do you know Gale Cottage?'

'Gale Tannery place, you mean?'

'Yes. He was found dead there. Smothered in bed. And with the name of this hotel in his pocket.'

'I can't help that, Inspector. I certainly didn't smother him and leave my address. It must have been as I said.'

'Do you know any of the Dodd family?'

'Which Dodds?'

'Steel people in Cambridge, I think. William Dodd is a well-known MP and Cabinet Minister.'

'I've heard of Willie Dodd. He's always having his picture in the papers.'

'Yes, I know. But I'm asking about the Dodds who live quite

near here. Two or three miles on the main Cambridge road, I'd guess.'

'Why should I know them?'

'I'm not interested in the *why* for the time being; I want to know if you *know* them.'

'I don't. I can't see where this is getting us. I've got work to do, and I'll be obliged if…'

Littlejohn ignored the hint but passed over the slip of paper bearing the address. 'Do you recognise the handwriting?'

Peg Boone scrutinised the paper and returned it.

'No.'

'Sure?'

'Of course I'm sure.'

Her eyes flashed, and the tips of her well-shaped ears grew red, as though her anger were somehow concentrated there.

She was growing a bit exasperated at the two stolid men sitting facing her. As a rule, the sternest melted under her charms and smoothed away difficulties. With this pair, it was like beating against a stone wall.

'Have you finished?'

Peg Boone rose slowly, like a cat uncurling from a chair.

'Not yet, Miss Boone. Is your brother in?'

'He won't be able to help, either. Look here, I've tried to be civil and given you a hearing, although we're very busy…'

'You don't seem so, Miss Boone. And I don't think you're helping at all.'

Littlejohn met her angry glance with a bland smile.

'The handwriting on this slip is, unless I'm mistaken, that of *Harry* Dodd. He was the son of the murdered man and was himself murdered the other day. Does that strike any chord?'

Peg Boone leaned against the counter, her shapely legs stretched straight, and her back wedged against the woodwork. She was quietly dressed in a jumper and tailor-made skirt, both of which emphasised her splendid figure.

'I've read about it in the paper.'

'Is that all?'

'What do you mean?'

Littlejohn took out his pipe and began to fill it.

'I think I'll have a drink after all. Do you keep Hoods' bottled beer?'

'Yes. Will you come in the public room?'

'No, thanks. I want to talk to you here…'

'I've nothing more to tell you.'

Cromwell sensed tension in the air and wondered how Littlejohn was going to find an excuse for keeping up this fruitless interview.

'All the same, please serve us here. My friend will have the same.'

She walked round the deserted counter, took out two bottles from behind it, and forcing off the red caps with an opener fixed on the shelf, emptied their contents in two glasses.

'Will you have a drink with us, Miss Boone?'

'Very well. I'll have a bottled beer, too.'

She filled a glass for herself. There were three empty bottles and three red caps on the counter. Littlejohn felt in his vest pocket, took out the red cap found on Harry Dodd's body, and placed it beside them. Peg Boone looked at the cap and then at Littlejohn. Their eyes met again.

'Well,' she said.

'That makes four, doesn't it? The fourth was found in the pocket of Harry Dodd after he died.'

'Was it? There must be hundreds taken off bottles in a day in this locality.'

Littlejohn lit his pipe and pocketed his clue. Cromwell found himself hanging on his chief's words and, judging from the tensing of Peg Boone's hands, she, too, was feeling the strain a bit.

The Inspector seemed settled for the night. He crossed his legs and smiled gently at Peg Boone again. She might have been a little girl interviewing the doctor or a schoolmaster, instead of a lovely and attractive woman using all her powers to get out of a difficulty.

There was a difficulty somewhere, for the woman's poise was weakening. She was afraid of something yet hoping to break down her adversary before she herself gave way.

'Yes… Harry Dodd had been spending the night with his friends in a place a bit like this; a country pub. He'd had a drink or two and perhaps he felt as we do, that it's a good way of passing an evening to be with good company in a cosy, hospitable inn…'

'I'm glad you feel that way, but I have work to do.'

'Not much longer, Miss Boone. Just till we finish our drinks. Harry Dodd had been drinking in one of Hoods' places earlier in the day. He'd carried off a red cap from his beer bottle. It was in his pocket when he died. Did I tell you that, Miss Boone?'

'Yes…'

'Harry Dodd rose as the clock struck ten. He bade his pals goodnight, because that was the time he usually left. He'd a fair walk uphill, you see. No sooner had he got in the dark village street than somebody stabbed him in the back with a knife!'

There was a pause. You could hear the distant voices in the public rooms and, behind a door in the far corner of the cocktail bar, somebody was moving about quietly, as if it might have been one of the family pottering around in their personal quarters.

Littlejohn indicated the door.

'Is that your and your brother's private room?'

'Yes. What's that got to do with it?'

From the tone of her voice it was evident that Peg Boone was immersed in Littlejohn's tale and resented the interruption as an irrelevancy.

'Harry Dodd wasn't killed outright. He'd just the strength to get to a call-box, and from there he telephoned home for the women who lived with him to bring the car and pick him up…'

Peg Boone caught her breath in a noise like a dry sob. Littlejohn didn't seem to hear it. He took a sip of his beer.

'…Then he tried to walk home. He fell in the road just as…'

'Stop it!'

It was wrung out of Peg Boone against her will. Her breath came noisily, and her breast rose and fell in agitation. 'Why are you telling me this…? I… I…'

She gulped and stopped for words.

'You knew Harry Dodd, didn't you? He used to come here. He gave his father the address, in case he needed a friend, didn't he? You knew about Walter Dodd, and how they put him away in the asylum because he was a family nuisance, and that Harry Dodd helped him to get away to somewhere where he hoped the old man would be happier…'

'He was fond of his father. He said he was the only friend he had when he was in trouble.'

'You knew Dodd, then?'

'Yes, I did. Now that I've told you what you wanted to know, leave me alone.'

'How well did you know him?'

'He called now and then for a drink. It was on his way to wherever he was living. He knew these parts. His old home was nearby. Gale Cottage, where his father died.'

'He called frequently, didn't he?'

'Now and then,' she persisted.

'But he was very familiar with the place?'

'What do you mean by that?'

'He'd come in and help himself to a bottled beer, wouldn't he? He'd go round the counter, get a bottle, take off the cap himself… And perhaps pocket the cap he'd got in his hand if he was talking or got excited or found something you had to tell him interesting?'

'Plenty of our customers help themselves. It's a free and easy place. We're all friends together.'

Cromwell remembered the roomful of customers next door. All friends together! If being drawn by the fascination of this woman was a form of being friends together, well and good. But he doubted it...

'Harry Dodd must have frequented one or two places where he got red-cap ale. The asylum, for instance, where he met his father sometimes. But, in such places, they open the beer and then bring it to the tables. The same with most other pubs where you don't help yourself. The bar-man, or whoever it is, takes off the cap at the bar because there's a fixture there for doing it, like the one over there. You don't pocket the cap then... Of course, I may be wrong...'

Peg Boone showed no more resistance. They might have been discussing a dear friend. In fact, the atmosphere had changed as though their mutual knowledge of the dead Harry Dodd had become a bond between them.

'So Harry Dodd was one of the party of all friends together. He called here now and then for a drink on his way to Helstonbury, helped himself, and then went off.'

'That's right.'

'Nothing more?'

'I don't understand, Inspector?'

She was on her guard again now.

'If Harry Dodd was just like the rest, why should he entrust his father to you...? An escaped lunatic, officially...'

'He wasn't a lunatic!'

'You knew him, then?'

'No. But Harry Dodd said so, and Harry wouldn't tell a lie about that.'

'It was arranged that the old man should come here?'

'Yes... I said we'd keep him safe till Harry could make other arrangements. It's quiet here and he'd be undisturbed.'

'Why didn't he come, then? Why did he hide himself in the old home, all alone? He escaped a fortnight ago and must have been there since then. He'd not long been murdered when we got there. An hour or so before we arrived.'

Peg Boone rose and walked up and down in distress.

'He didn't want to come here, he said. He'd stay in his old place. I said that was the very spot they'd go looking for him. But he said it would be all right. He'd call here for food and things after dark and keep a look-out in the day. Harry was making arrangements to get him free from the asylum, so there wasn't much danger. Only the old man didn't want to go back for the time Harry took to see things through for him. We had to humour him.'

'So you were friendly enough with Harry Dodd to do that for him?'

'Look here, Mister. I've got to be a bit hard in a place like this, but I'm not that hard against a poor old man. When Dodd suggested that his father… Well… I said we'd take him in and mind him for a bit. Anybody would have done the same for the poor old chap.'

'And that's all you have to tell me. You knew nothing else about Harry Dodd?'

'What is there to know?'

'You're very distressed about his death… However, I'd better have a word with your brother. Is he in?'

'Yes, but…'

She was interrupted in the midst of making excuses for her brother, Sid, by the entry of the very man. The door at the end of the cocktail bar opened and he appeared.

'Look here, Peg. The place is full and…'

He stopped in the middle of his complaint and eyed the two police officers.

They eyed him, too, for he was of medium build, well set-up, as dark as his sister, with a little black moustache, and he wore a check suit, like a bookie. He had a silver ring, fashioned like a coiled snake, on his little finger.

Sid Boone stood at the open door, hesitating.

'This is my brother, Sid. These are two officers from Scotland Yard...'

She didn't get any further, for from the room behind the man in the check suit came an unctuous, benevolent voice.

'Cora! Pretty Cora! Pretty Pol... Pretty Cora...'

Sid Boone stepped back a pace as if to stem the tide of parrot talk stimulated by the sound of voices, but he was a second too late.

'Pretty Cora! I'm wild about Harry, and Harry's wild about me!'

10

THE ACHING MAN

'You may as well come in our room,' said Peg Boone wearily. There was a note of despair in her voice, as though fate had let her down and shown all the cards in her hand.

'It's cosier in our room and there's no sense sitting here wasting light and getting chilled. You look like being here for some time...'

Littlejohn gave her a glance of agreement. She ushered them in their private quarters and even gave Littlejohn's shoulder an affectionate pat as he entered them. It was a gesture made out of trust or admiration for a new friend. The Inspector had come across such sentiments before after keen cross-questioning. Instead of growing resentment, there was often forged a bond of queer friendship between antagonists in a duel of wits. His wife, who attended university extension lectures in psychology, had once told him of similar relations between the parties in psychoanalysis, but he didn't know much about such things...

Sid Boone followed and shut the door.

'Cora's Harry's sweetheart... Where's Harry Dodd?'

The parrot kept shouting from its cage. It looked a very old and wily bird, but its expression was a benevolent one, that of an old lady who wishes nobody any harm.

'So this is Cora...'

Littlejohn tapped the gilded wires of the cage, and the parrot gave him a gentle, unwinking glance and with a lightning gesture seized the bandage Mrs Harry Dodd had put on his finger and whipped it off. That done, she lost interest in it, dropped it and slowly closed her eyes, the lids falling like little metallic shutters.

'Cora... That's me. Harry's girl...'

'She seems very fond of Harry Dodd,' said Littlejohn, rescuing his bandage. Peg Boone hurried to fix it for him. Her brother anxiously seized a large baize cloth and covered the cage.

'Please leave her uncovered. She might have something more to say.'

'What do you want?'

Sid was sulky and a bit truculent. He kept glancing suspiciously at his sister, fearing she might have betrayed something.

'Sit down, everybody.'

Peg Boone had ceased fencing and seemed ready to talk. The two detectives sat in chairs by the fire. The room was small and cosy, with armchairs by the hearth, a desk covered with papers in one corner, family photographs on the walls, and a standard lamp casting a cosy glow over everything. Sid remained standing by the parrot, whose cage hung from a hook on a chromium stand.

'There's quite a lot I'd like to know,' said Littlejohn. He bent and picked up a coloured rubber ball, tossed it upwards and caught it. Then he handed it to Peg Boone.

'Harry Dodd's child?' he asked, on an impulse.

'Yes. What of it?' Peg Boone replied automatically.

'You stupid little fool! Why keep playing into their hands? They've nothing on us, and the sooner we get rid of them the better.'

Sid was convulsed with rage and looked ready to hit his sister.

'Sit down, Sid,' said Littlejohn. 'On the result of our further talk tonight, will depend whether or not I arrest you on suspicion of murdering Harry Dodd...'

'Here! You can't pin this on me...'

'Sit down, Sid, and be sensible. I've told the Inspector quite a lot. I realised pretty soon that unless we tell the truth, we're likely to get in a spot of real trouble. It was bound to come out sooner or later.'

'Well, we've done nothing wrong.'

There was a minute's silence, as if somebody was making up his mind where to start. A little clock raced on the mantelpiece and then struck ten in thin tones.

'Closing time. I'll have to go and see to...'

'Don't be long, then.'

Sid left the room and Peg went into the cocktail bar and returned with more bottled beer. It might have been the start of a cosy little social gathering round the fire.

'Did Harry Dodd bring the parrot?'

'Yes. He gave it to Nancy... That's the little girl. She's asleep upstairs.'

'You're her mother?'

'Yes. I expect that seems queer to you. Especially if I tell you that I knew all about him. His divorce, his living with the Nicholls women, the way his family turned against him.'

'You were in love with him?'

'Yes. And he loved me, too. He was a lonely man and started coming here soon after they drove him from home. His affair with the Nicholls woman was just a flash in the pan. He kept coming here...'

'How old is the child?'

'Four last birthday.'

It was amazing! This attractive woman, admired, desired and courted, probably by most men in the countryside, fell for the blandishments of Harry Dodd!

'Harry Dodd! Where's Harry?'

The parrot, suddenly roused, began to shout for the man she had liked. The man who every week bought her a lot of seed from little rabbit-faced Ishmael Lott in Helstonbury.

'He wanted me to marry him when the child was coming, but I wouldn't. He'd made a big enough fool of himself as it was. This was no place for him, and he'd enough to do with his money. I wanted to see him a gentleman again, like he used to be, when first I knew him.'

'How long have you known him?'

'Since I was a girl. He used to call here for a drink when my mother kept the place. He'd been a customer since before he married. He was always so kind and polite and, when I first remember him, he was good looking. He always treated me, even as a little girl, as though I was a great lady. Then we heard about the divorce. I was well in my twenties by then, and I hadn't seen him for quite a time. We heard that his family had kicked him out. One day he arrived here for a drink. We got talking. He said he wished the old days were back again when I was a little girl and him pretending I was royalty. He'd got in a queer groove with the woman he'd run away with. She was never his kind, he said. It was a mistake…'

'I think he told you the truth, Miss Boone,' said Littlejohn. 'From what we can gather, he was a mere lodger with the Nicholls pair.'

'He said so, Inspector. Sid was in at the time, too. He just said casually that if ever Harry got bored, he'd always be welcome here. Harry took him at his word. He used to come and stay here, and fish in the river and shoot a bit with Sid's gun…'

'And the pair of you were attracted to each other again?'

'We fell in love!'

She snapped it vehemently.

'We fell in love. He was lonely, and well… He was different from the rest who come here. They always look at you in a certain way, try to paw you, make suggestions, and get fresh. Harry was never that way. It's funny… He gave a man a good hiding for trying to rough-handle me once in the bar. He got a black eye and a swollen cheek himself, and, looking at the mess the other man had made of him, I realised how I felt about him.'

Sid returned, very business-like, dropped in a chair, and glared around.

'Have you nearly finished?'

'We've hardly started yet, Sid. What were you doing in Brande recently, asking for Harry Dodd?'

'Who? Me? I don't know anything… I never…'

'Come, come, Sid. I know all about your enquiries at Brande, at the pub there, *and* at the Nicholls women's bungalow pretending to be a dealer in old gold. And then at Cold Kirby… You were very anxious about Harry Dodd. Why?'

Peg Boone was on her feet, her eyes blazing, standing over her brother.

'You never told me. What were you after, hanging round there?'

Sid was cornered, and at that minute the parrot decided to shout again for Harry Dodd. He hastily rose and flung the baize cloth over the cage.

'Shut up! We've had enough about Harry Dodd. To hell with Harry Dodd!'

Peg persisted.

'What were you after?'

'It's no business of yours.'

'But it's my business, Boone,' added Littlejohn. 'You'll tell me what you were after. Did you get to know that Dodd was going back to his wife, and did you go for revenge for your sister?'

Sid Boone flung back his head and laughed mirthlessly.

'Revenge. That's a good one! Tell him, Peg. Tell him all about it. Revenge? Why, it was her who persuaded Dodd to go crawling back to his wife. She wanted Nancy's father to be a gentleman, instead of the lodger of a motley pair like the Nicholls women.'

'Is that so, Peg?'

Littlejohn turned to her paternally. He was finding out more and more about Peg Boone, and what he knew he liked.

'Yes. I wasn't having him hanging round this cheap pub going to seed and becoming a sort of potman and, by the same token, he wasn't staying with the pretty pair he lived with at Brande. He'd told me that his wife wanted him back and would give him his old home and place again. She'd made up her mind that if he'd go back, he'd get his share of the works and her personal fortune if she died first. That was what I wanted. Even if Nancy wasn't legitimate, I wanted her with a gentleman for a father. Harry said he'd tell his wife about Nancy and they'd adopt her.'

'Silly fool!'

Sid spat it out and sat back growling.

'You hold your tongue! It was like Harry Dodd. A bit naive... I told him he'd do nothing of the kind. That would ruin it all. His wife certainly wouldn't take to the idea, and what did he think his grown-up children would do if a child of four was suddenly brought on the scene? I made him promise to say nothing about our child. One day he came and said he'd just got the family Bible and put Nancy's name in it. Of all the silly things to do! Just an impulse he said, and he was so fond of her. I tore out the pages...'

'So that was it. I saw the Bible with the missing pages.'

'That was a long time ago. I told him to give it back to his wife. It belonged at home.'

Littlejohn turned to Sid Boone.

'But that doesn't answer the question I asked you, Boone, about your enquiries in Brande and Cold Kirby. What did you want with Dodd?'

'It was a private matter.'

Sid was sulky and curt.

'You were after money, weren't you?'

'Sid... You didn't go cadging from Harry, did you?' Peg Boone was standing angrily over her brother again. He sprang to his feet and thrust his face close to hers.

'What if I was? He owed it to me, didn't he? What did I get out of all this Harry Dodd business? A sister on my hands with a bastard...'

Quick as a flash, Peg Boone slapped his face.

'Don't you dare use that word again. You know you're as fond of the kid as I am. But you just can't stop your betting and drinking, can you? You went to Harry for money?'

'Well? What of it? He made you an allowance for the kid... and it was a good one. Where did I come in? I never got a bean out of it. And then he started talking of going back to his wife. Do you think I was going to stand by and let him do that to my sister...?'

'You've suddenly grown very solicitous about me, Sid. Don't be silly, now. Although Harry's made a settlement for Nancy, I'm alone, now he's dead, in looking after her. I'm not having you mixed up in a murder rap, so you'd better talk and tell the Inspector what it's all about. You were trying a bit of blackmail, Sid. You were going to say you'd tell Mrs Dodd about him and me, weren't you...? Weren't you?'

'Well? You'd got the settlement. I'd got damn all. If he could afford to give you five thousand for Nancy...'

'How do you know?'

'Seen your bank-book...'

He looked pleased with himself and leered cleverly at her.

'And where did Harry Dodd get all that money from?' continued Sid. 'If he'd so much, he could get a bit more for me. You never let on where he lived, so I had to go and hunt around. I heard him talking about Brande and Cold Kirby, so I went. Unlucky, though, I was. He was away. Before I could get him again, he was dead.'

'Where were you the night he was murdered, Boone?' Sid Boone laughed at Littlejohn.

'Here. I've been here all night tonight, too. You can't pin it on me. A score or more of my customers'll give me a watertight alibi. I might be a bit of a gambler and, as my loving sister says, try to touch a friend now and then for a sweetener, but I don't rise to stabbing folks in the back. You'll have to try again, Inspector.'

'It's quite true, Inspector. My brother was here all night till well after closing time.'

'About the settlement, Miss Boone...Did Harry Dodd tell you where he got it?'

'No; and I didn't ask him. It was properly done. His solicitor, a Mr Pharaoh, I think he called him, attended to it.'

'Did the lawyer come here?'

'Yes. I know it seemed funny bringing him all that way, but he and Harry were personal friends. They'd been at school together, and Harry trusted him.'

'And did Harry tell you that his wife had agreed to take him back and... I want you to be sure of this... and *give him back his place in the works and his share of her fortune if she died first?*'

'Yes. That's quite true.'

There were sounds from overhead, and Peg Boone, after excusing herself, left to attend to the child.

'Peg's a BF,' said Sid Boone sagely. He'd been drinking and was getting sleepy.

'Peg's a BF. Loveliest girl in this county, bar none. Should have married into a County family... engaged to one of the Lumley boys at the manor, just by here. Nice fellah. Got himself killed though in the Battle of Britain. Plenty others wanted her since, but nobody else would do. She took it hard. Started drinking a bit too much. Then... along comes Harry Dodd. Well... I ask you... Harry Dodd! I wanted to show the fellah the door right away. Didn't like the looks of him and said so. But what I say's of no account here. An' after all, she's all I've got, is li'l Peg. All I've got in the world... I ought've looked better after her... Poor old Peg...'

He started to cry, full of beery self-pity.

'You'd better go up to bed, if you've been taken that way again,

Sid,' said his sister, returning. 'Is it the poor old Peg story, Sid? Don't worry. I can look after myself and the kid. And we won't turn you out in the snow. So get up to bed and sleep it off.'

Sid had grown very docile. He drank up his beer, took off his shoes, laid them in the hearth, and retired in his stockinged feet.

'Goo' night... No ill feelin's... Goo' ni'...' Shortly afterwards Peg Boone let the two detectives out. Littlejohn shook hands with her in the porch.

'Keep your spirits up, Peg.'

'Thanks. It's funny. One day it was all arranged. The next, Harry's dead. I can't go to his funeral. I can lay no claim whatever to him. He's just gone... And yet, I was the one he loved...'

She started to sob, and hustling the pair of them out, she closed the door on them.

11

DEAD END

When the two detectives arrived home at *The Bear* in Brande at midnight, Mr Mallard rubbed his hands and welcomed them to an extensive supper. He was prepared to overlook the eccentricities of their comings and goings or strange conduct. Had they got up in the small hours and started conducting an investigation, he would have been delighted. It was something to tell his customers about. The news that he was entertaining Scotland Yard at his lowly pub had spread far and wide, and tonight there had been a record house and bumper takings.

'Come in, gents,' said Mr Mallard, opening the door to them. 'There's a nice bit o' cold supper for you in the Snug. Don't 'urry. The night's yet young…'

The following morning the Inspector, leaving Cromwell to call for any news at the police station in Helstonbury, ran over in the car to Cold Kirby, where he expected to find Andrew Comfort, home on compassionate leave from the RAF to help his mother square up his late father's estate.

Andrew was a nice lad. Tall, well set-up, and a bit gauche and shy, he hung protectively around his mother when the Inspector called for a talk.

'It's time somebody took an interest in my father's death,' said Andrew. His shock of black, uncontrollable curly hair rose high on his head and gave him a surprised look. 'They never found out who caused the accident, but I think it was deliberate.'

His mother tried to restrain him, anxious that he should show a bit of respect for the police, but Littlejohn was curious.

'Why?'

'It came out that somebody crowded them off the road intentionally. Why? My father had no enemies. It must have been somebody after Mr Dodd. Why don't the police try to...?'

'We'll do our best. I'm sure your father's tragedy is mixed up with the later death of Harry Dodd. I want you to help if you can.'

Outside, the daily bus to town was drawing up at the stop in front of *The Bell*. A number of country women carrying shopping baskets mounted it, followed by one or two girls who eyed the inn anxiously, for word had gone forth that Andy Comfort was home, and not a few of the local beauties had designs on him. They couldn't leave him alone.

'Come on. Get in...'

The conductor was getting out of patience, hustled them aboard, rang the bell, and the party vanished in a lot of dust and noise.

'How can I help...?'

'Tell me what your father and Mr Dodd were doing in their little workshop. Was it anything likely to attract trouble?'

Andrew Comfort seemed amused. He grinned, showing his strong white teeth.

'Trouble? Why, it was the most harmless thing in the world. I know Dodd kept saying they'd make a fortune one day if they could only strike a formula that would beat the existing ones for welding; but they never did. I know Mr Dodd was feverish to do it and get one back on his family, but when he died he'd not done it. If they'd both lived, they'd have found out something or other of use. Two good brains like theirs, two good engineers like dad and Mr Dodd might have pulled it off. They didn't have long enough.'

'Are you sure?'

'Of course I'm sure, sir. I helped them till I joined up, and only the weekend before I left for the RAF, dad was down in the dumps about it. He'd hoped to be in the money with Dodd, you see, but they'd tried one formula after another and one process after another, but never had been able to beat existing methods.'

'So it wasn't anything in that line that attracted dangerous enemies to them?'

Young Comfort looked bewildered.

'You mean spies or such like?'

'No. Just family trouble from the Dodd angle.'

'Oh, no. Not that. There was nothing to threaten the Dodd family set-up.'

'You've no other ideas as to who might have had it in for Dodd or your father?'

'No, sir. It's a mystery to me...'

So that was a dead end! And yet Harry Dodd had tried to make out to his wife that he was on the way, by his researches, to threatening the family business and putting it off the map. It looked as if Harry hadn't been the straightforward type everybody thought he was. He'd talked of going back to his wife, yet he'd told her a fairy tale about his researches in steel, and he'd said nothing at all about his mistress and the little girl at *The Aching Man*. They were back where they'd started; in fact, the whole thing was much more obscure.

On the way to Helstonbury, Littlejohn had the road almost to himself and pondered the case.

It might be a crime of sordid love, or revenge, or just to put a nuisance out of the way. It looked as if Harry Dodd and his father shared some secret which made them dangerous to someone.

Walter Dodd had, after all, been his son's closest friend after Harry's family had cast him off. He might have given his father information which condemned him to death as surely as it had condemned Harry himself. It seemed absurd for Willie Dodd, the rising politician, to kill his father and brother simply to protect his majority at the polls. They might have made him seem a bit ridiculous — Harry with his shady amours and his father with his heckling and reaping up Willie's past weaknesses — but was Willie likely to risk total ruin by a murder?

Harry's ambitious family, Winfield Dodd and Lady Hosea, were hardly likely either to murder their parent and grandparent simply because they were a couple of common fellows who kept seedy company and behaved with little discretion.

But what of Peter Dodd, who was closely attached to his mother? Suppose, after Harry's borrowing from Mrs Dodd on a sort of confidence trick and settling thousands of pounds on Peg Boone and the child she'd borne Harry, young Peter Dodd had found it all out. He'd not only feel a fool himself but hate his father for the dirty tricks he'd played on his mother. And after stabbing his father, had he suddenly come up against his grandfather, who might have accused and threatened him?

That was the only sensible theory Littlejohn could concoct for the time being.

On the High Street in Helstonbury, he passed Mr Sebastian Dommett, who ignored his friendly wave. Mr Dommett had taken umbrage because the Scotland Yard officers had not, on the previous day, attended his court for Harry Dodd's inquest. It had been adjourned, of course, but Mr Dommett was sensitive to every form of disrespect.

At the police station, however, Littlejohn had no chance to talk about Mr Dommett and his foibles, for there he found Mr Pharaoh's pretty clerk, Joan, sitting in the Superintendent's room, crying her eyes out. Judkin and Cromwell were there looking helpless and letting her have her fill of tears.

'Mr Pharaoh's dead... Body washed up at Lowestoft this morning. Miss Jump here has just heard from the Lowestoft police. I'm trying to get them now over the wire.'

Joan Jump, although a barrister, was highly emotional where Mr Pharaoh was concerned.

'What has he done to deserve it, Inspector?' she asked through her sobs, as though somehow Littlejohn had in his possession some explanation concerning the rights and wrongs of her employer's decease. 'He wouldn't have hurt a fly...'

Littlejohn wasn't inclined to talk about the just and the unjust. He patted Miss Jump's comely bowed head, which made her cry all the more.

'How did it happen?'

Outside, in the courtyard, a policeman was showing a little girl the way to the wire-netting cage in which the lost dogs were impounded, and she recognised her own erring pet right away. It was a touching scene as they took him from among the rest, to see his joy; touching, too, to see the ones left unclaimed behind, pawing the wire to get free. Another policeman in the wash-house had soap in his eyes and was groping for the towel like a blind man.

'He must have been caught by the swinging boom or something. They found him washed up on the beach and the boat was miles out at sea. A fishing vessel towed it in; it was drifting, unmanned...'

'Was he drowned or...?'

'The Superintendent is just going to find out. They rang me up right away to check who it was. They found his card in his pocket... I... I...'

Miss Jump couldn't go on any further. Her eyes were all red and swollen and she kept taking off her spectacles and putting them on again in pathetic little gestures.

'He was so happy going off on his little trip...'

The telephone broke in on her reminiscences. It was

Lowestoft police for Judkin. They did all the talking. Judkin hardly said a word; just kept grunting and saying 'ah'.

'Indeed!' he said at length, in surprise. 'Yes, I'll arrange it.'

He hung up thoughtfully.

'There'll be an inquest, of course, and they want somebody to identify him,' he said.

Miss Jump gulped.

'It'll have to be me. He had no family except a sister in Canada. He lived with a housekeeper…'

Judkin thumbed his chin and scraped his stiff whiskers with a grating sound.

'That's not all, though… The Lowestoft police say that he must have been dead when he hit the water. The doctor says there's a bad fracture of the skull… In a place where they can't see how the boom could have caught him. A long narrow wound which might have been made by a piece of lead piping instead of a massive object like a boom… They think it might be foul play. They'll let us know…'

Joan Jump was on her feet instantly.

'I'm sure it's to do with Harry Dodd! When will it end? Dodd, his father, and now Mr Pharaoh…'

'Was he closely connected with Dodd?'

'They were friends and Dodd had been in and out a lot of late. Mr Pharaoh did his legal work.'

'Did you know what it was about…? I mean, why did Dodd keep calling?'

'There was a settlement on the Nicholls woman. You know about that.'

'Yes. Do you know Peg Boone, Miss Jump?'

Joan Jump's eyes opened wide behind her spectacles.

'Yes, I do. How did you come to know her, Inspector?'

'*The Aching Man* was an address found in the pocket of the late Walter Dodd, Harry's father. I went there and found Miss Boone. She told me quite a lot of things about Harry Dodd.'

'I'm sure she did, Inspector. Mr Pharaoh arranged a settlement for her from Dodd as well, not long ago.'

'Where did all this money come from? He surely didn't borrow it all from his divorced wife. I know he borrowed some for what he called research in metallurgy, but borrowing to settle incomes on his various women hardly seems right coming from Mrs Dodd, does it?'

'No, Inspector. I think Mr Pharaoh arranged it for him some way. It was between them, and I didn't enter into it at all.'

'You mean Dodd had some other source of capital; other than his wife and his own income?'

'He must have had. He raised over ten thousand pounds, from what I know, to settle on the Nicholls and the Boone women.'

There was a silence as if they were playing a guessing game and trying to think where Harry Dodd had got all his money from. Outside, the sun was shining, and shoppers were beginning to fill the streets. Clerks crossed the road to a coffee shop for their morning break, a bank porter was going the round of the banks changing cheques, and over the Conservative Club the flag slowly rose to half-mast, broke, and fluttered in the breeze. People looked up and turned to one another questioningly. The news of Mr Pharaoh's death had reached Helstonbury.

'Excuse me… Excuse me…'

Drane, the polite constable, was on duty again, bringing in tea in large, thick cups. He was more mannerly than ever on account of Miss Jump's presence there. He blushed.

'Might I offer you a cup of tea…?'

They all thanked him, except Judkin, who wished he'd make less fuss, and started to sip the hot, strong brew.

'Excuse me…'

Drane made a confused exit with his tin tray over Cromwell's outstretched boots.

'Are you going to carry on Mr Pharaoh's practice, Miss Jump?'

'Yes. We were just arranging for me to enter as junior partner.

Now, I'll take his place, because he said he'd left his half of the practice to me in his will. I'd rather he were alive…'

The pretty lawyer thereupon broke down and cried again.

'Perhaps you may be able to help us when you come to go through Mr Pharaoh's private papers. There may be some clue to all these crimes there…'

'I'll only be too willing, Inspector. The sooner the better. I have an emergency key for his private safe. I'll go right back and open it.'

'Do you mind if I go with you? From all appearances, someone has taken fright badly and is beside himself… or herself… to wipe out all traces, including people, of the reason for Harry Dodd's death. It might be safer if I came along…'

Joan Jump smiled for the first time.

'It's very nice of you, Inspector, but the staff are in the office and will protect me, I'm sure. If you care to come and look through the papers, you're very welcome, though.'

They crossed to Sheep Street and into the offices over one of the banks there. Up the familiar stairs and into Mr Pharaoh's room. There was an atmosphere about it as though the little fat lawyer had just slipped across the road and would soon be returning. The ship on the mantelpiece, the pen on the pad where its owner had hastily laid it down as he rushed to join the *Betsy Jane*, the homburg on the hat-stand which Mr Pharaoh had left behind when he put on his yachting cap, and the half-smoked pipe he'd forgotten in his hurry…

'Did he come back to his rooms after he left me, when we'd been to Cold Kirby together, Miss Jump?'

'Yes, he did. You remember he said he was just off and left everything to me. He phoned me later to say he'd been in the office to look up some papers about Harry Dodd. He also put a conveyance in the safe and told me where to find it.'

'Harry Dodd again, eh? Well, well. Shall we open the safe?'

It was a simple, but strong, personal safe, opened with a single key. Miss Jump took this from an envelope in her pocket.

'We kept it at the bank and I'm authorised to take it out in case of extreme need. This is such a case.'

She inserted the key and swung open the door. Someone had been there already! The papers were strewn all over the inside of the coffer, tossed here and there, pink tape cut, bundles torn and rifled...

'Someone's beaten us to it, Miss Jump. Someone who took your chief's keys from his dead body, by the looks of it.'

He stopped and picked up from the floor a ring full of keys.

'Those were Mr Pharaoh's. He carried them everywhere.'

'So it's murder, then. Don't touch anything. There may be fingerprints on that stuff, though I doubt it...'

Littlejohn was right. When the papers were tested by the experts, there wasn't an alien print to be found.

'Did Mr Pharaoh keep other private papers at home or at the bank?'

'I couldn't say. I'll keep in touch with you. And now, if you don't mind, I'd like to straighten things out a bit...'

Joan Jump's upper lip was beginning to tremble and Littlejohn, knowing she wanted to be alone to have another good weep, left her in peace.

Back at the police station, Judkin had received more news from Lowestoft.

Mr Pharaoh had apparently arrived there well past dark. The man who looked after his boat had seen him safely on board. Then the landlord and a number of his nautical friends at the *Albion Inn* on the quayside stated he had joined them in his yachting cap, and they had spent half an hour together, having a drink and a yarn. You'd never have thought Mr Pharaoh was a legal high-up; he was so free and easy. A proper gentleman...

It was late, and soon Pharaoh had bidden them goodnight, after telling them he was sailing on the morrow and competing in the race in the afternoon. They heard him strolling back to bed on his boat, and that was the last they'd seen or heard of him, until one of them found him dead on the tide-line early in the morning.

Later, a fishing boat had towed in the *Betsy Jane*. She had been drifting about three miles out. When they came to examine her, they found the boom was made fast. It couldn't have been that which knocked out Mr Pharaoh. The police had been all over the boat and could find no traces of intrusion. Mr Pharaoh's supper, a bottle of beer and some pork pie, was on the table. The berth hadn't been slept in. It looked very much as if somebody had lain in wait on the boat for the little lawyer and then struck him down when he came aboard.

Then the murderer had thrown Mr Pharaoh's body overboard, and the ebb-tide had taken it out, only to bring it back on the flood. A clumsy attempt had been made to make it look like an accident. As though the owner of the *Betsy Jane* had fallen overboard. Only the killer had forgotten to unlash the boom.

Judkin had made copious notes and recited his piece carefully in a monotonous voice, like somebody reading an incantation. He put down his papers.

'Well? Looks worse than ever. Who'll be the next? That's what I'm wondering. There's a mad killer loose.'

'Not mad. Just frightened out of his wits. He's taken panic, and now we're going to get him.'

'If he doesn't get us first.'

'Eh?'

Cromwell uttered it involuntarily. After all the dangers he'd been through, he was disgusted at the thought of anybody 'getting' Littlejohn in a small, one-horse town like Helstonbury.

Before they could answer him, the telephone bell rang again.

'Good Lord!' said Judkin in answer to the voice at the other end of the line. And then to Littlejohn and Cromwell:

'That's the constable at Brande. Somebody's burned down *Mon Abri*... the Nichollses' bungalow!'

When they arrived on the spot in the police car, PC Buckley and an assistant he'd collected from somewhere were having a busy time. A crowd had gathered, the village fire brigade were struggling with a large hand pump, there was furniture on the roadside, as though somebody had been evicted, and Uncle Fred was laid out under the hedge in a state of collapse.

Mrs Nicholls ran to Littlejohn, to whom she was accustomed to address herself, for she regarded him as an equal and ignored Judkin.

'Somebody's set the place on fire… We just got home from Helstonbury and found all this mess. It was deliberate…'

Dorothy didn't seem very upset. She was with the firemen, rolling her eyes at them and urging them on, although they had by now put out the fire. All that was left was a brick shell. Everybody was talking at once.

'Somebody set it alight with petrol. They've found the tin…'

'The gent in the hedge-bottom there found it. 'E telephoned for the fire brigade and police, and then started to shift the furniture…'

Littlejohn looked at Uncle Fred's handiwork. Chairs, tables, beds… The little lamps with pink shades and the pink cushions. He'd even got the sideboard out on the lawn.

''E'd got the pianner as far as the door, and then it stuck. He struggled so 'ard with it, he give himself a twist and collapsed.'

Uncle Fred was coming round under the ministrations of the district nurse, who had appeared from somewhere, fully uniformed. His waxed moustache was now Z-shaped, one point up and the other down. His bicycle was among the salvage, and he still wore his cycling-clips gathering his pants round his thin projecting ankles.

'Have they got the piano out?' were his first coherent words as he came to.

The nurse sighed and sadly eyed the smoking mass of wood and wires still wedged in the charred doorway. Uncle Fred was very attached to it and, in better days, had played *Melody in F* and *A Little Love a Little Kiss* on it, by ear, when he called.

'Did they get 'im?'

'Who?' asked Littlejohn.

Uncle Fred raised himself on hearing Littlejohn's voice.

'I'm glad you're 'ere, Inspector. The local police are no good on a job like this. Delib'rate arson, that's what it is. I saw 'im runnin' into the wood behind the house as I got here on my bike. Wish I'd been here two minutes sooner. I'd have murdered him…'

He collapsed again with emotion, and the nurse made as if to give him another dose of sal volatile.

'Try this,' said Littlejohn, handing over his brandy flask. It acted like magic. Uncle Fred rose to his feet like a giant refreshed, and they had to restrain him until he saw the wrecked piano. Then they had to give him the remaining contents of the flask.

A crowd gathered round him. He was the hero of the day.

'What did he look like?'

'I couldn't see his face. Middle built. Wore a check suit and he ran like a hare. Poured petrol on the place and lit it. It was a sheet o' flames in no time.'

He eyed the ruin with smoke-ringed eyes. How he'd got so much stuff out of the holocaust was a mystery!

'I'm proud of you, Fred. I don't know what I'd do without you. I'm 'omeless now, Fred…'

The old lady was worked up and putting on an emotional scene. Some people patted Uncle Fred proudly on the back, and others tried to comfort Mrs Nicholls. There was talk of passing the hat round on the spot.

Cromwell suggested that Uncle Fred might be better accommodated at the village pub than on the roadside, and that they take him down in the car. Uncle Fred accepted the offer with alacrity, and Mrs Nicholls having been helped to a neighbour's house, Dorothy, torn from the company of the firemen, was persuaded to follow her. The smoking ruins were left to the firemen and village police.

'I'll have to report to the insurance. Dodd told my sister it was covered... well covered... so I'll have to see to the claim...'

The excitement of drawing the insurance money acted adversely on Uncle Fred, and he started to talk to himself deliriously. They had to calm him down with more stimulants when they reached *The Bear*.

'The drinks are on me,' said Mr Mallard. 'I've 'eard of yore gallant conduct, sir. Allow me to shake you by the 'and. Proud to know you, sir.'

He pumped the bewildered hero's arm up and down.

Uncle Fred paused and then spoke gravely.

'He was after somethin'. Who could he be?'

Littlejohn removed his pipe.

'What was he after?'

'Well, for one thing, that tin box up in the loft where 'Arry slept. He'd smashed it open. I saw it. I tried to get the oddments down but couldn't get 'em through the trapdoor. There was the box, broken open. It's been melted since by the 'eat...'

'It was empty when we looked at it the other evening.'

'But *he* didn't know it. Can't have been an ordinary burglar. Why should he pour a can of petrol over the place and set fire to it, if he was just after robbery? I don't know what you gentlemen of the police think, but it's my view he was after documents, secret papers, or something. Something he badly wanted. Somethin' incriminatin', if you follow me. And when he couldn't find where they was hidden, he burnt the place down in the hopes of destroyin' them...'

Uncle Fred thereupon started to babble again, and Mr Mallard ran for more brandy.

'That's enough of that,' said Cromwell firmly. He was a member of Scotland Yard Ambulance Brigade. 'Brew him some tea and sugar it well...'

'Tea?' said Uncle Fred feebly. 'Tea?'

'Yes; tea,' replied the sergeant.

It was Harry Dodd's funeral that afternoon and the detectives were anxious to get away. They therefore resigned Uncle Fred in the care of Mr Mallard, who, making him comfortable, insisted on his removing his raincoat. This revealed that beneath it, Uncle Fred was wearing his mourning suit, the sight of which excited him again.

'My hat. I've lost my billycock in the fire. Whatever shall I do? I've a funeral…'

They left him trying on Mr Mallard's, which, with a bit of stuffing under the lining, fitted in a fashion. Packed from within, it looked to hang in mid-air close to his head without, however, touching it.

12

GOODBYE, HARRY DODD

Littlejohn attended Harry Dodd's funeral at Cambridge. It seemed the right thing to do, apart from any light it might throw on the murder. Littlejohn had lived so much with Harry Dodd and learned so much of him since he arrived on the case, that it was like witnessing the rites of an old pal. With the personal impression, created by the photograph he'd taken from Dorothy Nicholls' bedroom, he could picture in his mind's eye the chubby, little, sloppily dressed man hanging around *Mon Abri*, avoiding his two women when he locked himself in his attic, trudging home from a session at *The Bear* with his buddies, tinkering in the shed at *The Bell*, turning up at *The Aching Man* and being polite and kind to Peg Boone and playing with their child… A pub-crawler with a purpose.

Mrs Dodd was a strong-minded woman, and the real matriarch of the family whose father had been driven out for a single silly indiscretion. She had, presumably, ordered a gathering of the whole clan and they all turned up at the cemetery. They arrived in their expensive cars to meet the hearse which was bringing the deposed head of the family from the undertaker's.

Mrs Dodd and Peter were in an ageing barouche. The widow

was dressed in billowing black and the son in a black suit and bowler. There was a parson with them; a solemn dignitary with a large, round, flat face, Roman nose, and undershot jaw. Littlejohn was more interested in the rest of the party, for he had not met them before.

A chauffeur driving a black saloon with a crest on the door, dismounted, trotted round, and handed out a queer pair, who must have been Sir Bernard and Lady Hosea. A tall, lean, bored man, who looked as if he ought to have arrived in a horse-cab, for he was an anachronism. He was about sixty, with baggy, tired eyes, a long drooping grey moustache, and elegant but old-fashioned dress. A frock-coat, top hat, pointed boots of patent leather, and spats. He looked in the grip of a bad cold and shivered, even though the sun was shining. He glanced around at the rows of elaborate and costly marble vaults, tombstones and artificial flowers under globes, as though he had suddenly found himself in heaven and couldn't understand why. He slowly thrust his hand in the doorway of the car and helped out a lady at least twenty years his junior. Straight as a ramrod, haughty, tall, and dark, she was dressed in an expensive black fur coat, with a small hat to match it. She took his arm, and this queerly assorted pair walked straight to the open grave and stood there, greeting nobody, waiting, like two strange gothic characters, for their cues in the scene which slowly unfolded. They were followed by an even more expensive car, which slid into place, was opened by another uniformed flunkey, and which emitted a pompous younger replica of Harry Dodd himself. Winfield Dodd was a walking memorial to his father, except that he was about three inches taller and lacked his father's humility, humour, and kindliness. He blinked at the sunshine and the right side of his face twitched, for he had a perpetual tic.

Winfield Dodd helped his wife to descend. Littlejohn had a shock, for she was a blonde beauty; fair-haired, elegant, a bit flighty-looking, and evidence that her husband, at some time or other, had displayed his humanity and an eye for a good-looking woman. She had been a prominent actress in her time, and Winfield Dodd had, until he possessed her, done his share of dancing attendance and competing with younger and more eligible, if less wealthy, suitors. She looked bored and in a hurry to get things over...

And then, dead on the minute, Willie Dodd... working-class Willie, in a car more expensive than all the rest, driven by an official driver.

Littlejohn had not met the Rt. Hon. William Dodd in the flesh before. He rather took to Willie. A vigorous, bounding man, who seemed to radiate a strange magnetism, which he used to the full on political platforms. Obviously, he'd no need to fear discredit from Harry's peccadilloes or his father's heckling. He could brush such things aside with a gesture and, with a word and a flash of wit, turn the tables on his antagonists. He joined the rest with hasty, energetic steps and greeted them all genially. He didn't get a good reception, for the family looked like puppets miming a piece. With stilted steps they formed a little avenue, and the undertaker and his men, a leader in shabby black and a quartet of paid bearers, carried the coffin to the graveside, with shuffling, tottering feet.

Littlejohn stood some distance away, leaning his back against a large tombstone like a table on four legs. On the table top the names of one after another of a family called Cluttermule, fathers, sons, husbands, daughters, wives; dead and gone between 1823 and 1899. That was long ago, the monument was dirty and neglected, and those it attempted to keep in the memory of men, forgotten.

Harry Dodd was decently committed and the earth, automatically flung on his coffin according to ritual by those he had left behind, rattled on the hollow-sounding casket...

A taxi had drawn up outside the mortuary chapel a distance away, and three black-clad figures sneaked along, posted themselves beside a tomb like a small Albert Memorial, and stood watching the ceremony at the grave like three cockroaches. Littlejohn smiled faintly. Mrs Nicholls, Dorothy and Uncle Fred! The women's weeds had been burned in the fire and they'd had hastily to improvise and borrow. Pinned up and tacked, the old woman's clothes fitted where they touched; but Dorothy managed to look fresh and chic. Both were sniffing into handkerchiefs; Uncle Fred, not yet recovered from his feats with pianos and sideboards, looked short of stuffing and sagged at the knees as he stood with his borrowed billy-cock in his hand.

'Who's that lot? Not...?'

Willie Dodd, his eyes everywhere, full of zest, had spotted the Nicholls family, and it tickled him. He took a malevolent relish in pointing them out to his starchy companions, and his unfinished question was eloquent and faded away in chuckles. The rest of the party walked on, sought their conveyances, and pretended not to see Harry Dodd's companions in exile. As she turned, however, Mrs Dodd noticed Littlejohn and spoke quickly to Peter, who, letting her arm fall from his, hurried to join the Inspector.

'My mother thinks you might like to take this opportunity of speaking to the family, if you wish. We're all going home. Would you care to... to join my mother and me in the car... or...?'

He didn't quite know how to put it. He was conscious of all eyes on him, of the rest of the family anxious to get away and leave the erring member to be forgotten with his sins in the place of the dead. Lady Hosea and Winfield were whispering together.

'Who is it...? Have you seen those women...? Of all the impertinence...'

Their black figures bristled with affronted pride.

'I have a car here, sir. I'll follow in a little while. Please thank your mother for her help and consideration. I appreciate it at a time like this... If you'd rather...'

'By all means come. To the rest, this is no time for niceties. My mother forced them… Except Uncle William, who seems to think there's something funny about it all. We'll expect you.'

He almost ran back to his mother, and the family party scattered to their cars and drove away, stiff in mourning, like a lot of waxwork dummies.

The Nicholls family approached the open grave like a furtive crew of body-snatchers. Dorothy and her mother each carried a small wreath, and Uncle Fred had bought a kind of laurel crown which dangled from his hand. They paused a moment, looked in the grave, and softly threw handfuls of soil in it. The women blew their noses and wiped their eyes, Uncle Fred unsteadily placed the floral and laurel tributes on the heap of earth nearby, and then they slowly wound back to the waiting taxi. It was then that Littlejohn realised that Uncle Fred was half-drunk! Probably he'd taken it as medicine…!

The undertaker's men started to unload the wreaths from the hearse. Whether or not the family had seen them, Littlejohn did not know, but he himself was interested in them. He let the attendant mutes go their way and then emerged and looked at the flowers, reading the black-edged cards wired on them. There were about twenty all told, mainly roses, early chrysanthemums and carnations. The family wreaths were elaborate and formal, with visiting cards attached without comment from Sir Bernard Hosea and his lady, and from Winfield and his wife. 'From Peter.' 'To Harry with love from Helena.' 'From his old colleagues of the Sedgwick Engineering Company.' Then came the comic element, the 'tributes' brought by the Nicholls party. 'With Deepest Love and Sympathy from Dot.' And Mrs Nicholls' effort, with a sting of poetry in the tail.

> *With sympathy for Harry, from Emily.*
> *His virtues were many,*
> *His faults were few.*
> *He never deserved*

What he went through.

Uncle Fred's obituary outburst was attached to the laurels, which looked to have been filched from another grave.'In Memory of a Pal. Fred Binns.' Then, 'From his Friends in The Snug at *The Bear*, Brande', and a mysterious one from 'Charley, Sid and Joe.'

Littlejohn wasn't surprised at the glum looks of the family. Harry Dodd, with his pals, Fred, Sid, Joe and Charley! The homely vulgarity of his life seemed to persist in the cemetery. The Dodds had been anxious to get away, perhaps before Charley, Sid, Joe and a lot more arrived. One after another, Littlejohn looked at the cards, seeking out Harry Dodd's friends and connections. There was a large wreath in the middle of the lot. Littlejohn had to lift it to read the card which had got underneath it. It was an ornamental, printed affair, with strange symbols on it and, in the centre at the top, a picture of an all-seeing eye.

ANCIENT ORDER OF FREE FISHERS
HELSTONBURY BRANCH

*To the Memory of Brother Harry V Dodd
with Profound Condolences*

Littlejohn read it again. Harry V Dodd? He didn't know Harry Dodd had another name, one he kept dark from all except the secret society of which he must have been a member. No doubt they were a lot of fishermen, or maybe just a crowd of pals meeting for a night out now and then under cover of a cabbalistic name and a bit of homely mumbo-jumbo. He made a note of it.

Littlejohn drove into Cambridge and out to the Dodd home. The family seemed to expect him, and he felt himself rather at a loss about them. Peter was very helpful and led him to a small morning-room furnished with a table, two chairs, a lot of books, and a small sideboard.

'If you'd like to talk to any of us, you'll be able to do it in private here,' he said.

'I'd like a word with you, first of all. I do hope this isn't unseemly. Your father's only just been buried, you know.'

'Don't mention it. They're glad to see the last of him. If you don't get what you want to know from them now, you'll have a job seeing them together like this again. This is your big chance.'

Peter seemed in no mood for sorrow, either. He looked relieved, almost jocular, at the thought of his pompous family being subject to official questioning.

'Any need for Mother? She's lying down. But she told the rest to wait for you. You wanted to see them, she said. Winfield is blazing, Uncle Willie's a bit amused, and Bernard and Cynthia are offended at the thought that anybody could suspect them...'

'What were you doing on the night your father died, sir?'

Peter Dodd started as if found in guilty thoughts.

'Why? Am I suspect, then?'

'No. Just a formality. You seem to expect me to put the others through it. You ought to take your medicine, too, like a sport.'

Peter grinned.

'Oh, I don't mind. My mother was a bit off-colour that night and I went to the doctors for some powders. I'm afraid it was my fault. Coffee doesn't agree with her, and she has a special sort of stuff which is all right. The maid went out after dinner and I said I'd make some coffee. I'd no more sense than to use the real stuff. It made Mother very seedy. I realised what it was, when she started to be ill... She went to bed and I went for the powders. It would be ten, or thereabouts, when I got back. I'd been in to dinner. I'm sure Dr Macfarlane, just along the road, will remember. It'll be in his day-book, I guess...'

It was just the same all round. The family all had alibis. Willie, for example, hurried in next and told Littlejohn that he'd a train to catch to address a meeting in distant parts that night. He'd better be quick if he wanted to talk with him.

At close quarters, Willie Dodd closely resembled Harry. A rough-hewn sort. In fact, a bit more rough and ready than his brother. He had been a widower for years, there were faint rumours of his associations with dancers, wanton aristocrats, foreign princesses, and a celebrated actress. The usual legends which pursue prominent men. Black hair on the backs of his hands and sprouting from his nostrils and ears. He was full of energy and a quick and incisive thinker in matters concerning his own well-being.

'I saw to it that you were called in on this. Whatever his blessed family thought of my brother, I was fond of him, in a way. He wasn't like me. No fight in him and no guile. Do you think I'd have let that lot pack me off into exile like they did Harry? Not likely! What do you want to know…?'

'Did you see much of your brother, sir?'

'No. I'm a busy man and he never sought my company. As youngsters, we'd little in common. We drifted apart. That doesn't mean I didn't like him, though.'

'What about your father, sir?'

'What about him? He's to be quietly cremated tomorrow, without any fuss. The coroner's inquest was adjourned…'

'I know that. But I understand you were mainly responsible for his being certified insane and shut up.'

Littlejohn looked Willie straight in the eyes. Willie didn't flinch.

'Yes, I did. He'd got persecution mania, was a nuisance to himself and everybody else and, as I knew a place where they'd look after him and he'd be happy, I took the necessary steps.'

'Is it true he heckled you at meetings?'

'So you've heard that, too. Yes, he did. It didn't upset me, but it was a nuisance when my time was limited, getting involved in arguments and squabbles in the body of the hall, caused by my own father. You may smile, but that's not why I had him seen to. His brain was going and that was the best thing for him.'

'Where were you, sir, the night your brother died?'

Willie's bushy grey eyebrows rose. There were bags under his tired eyes. He was at full stretch, almost to breaking point, from the strain of his ambitions and his tireless flogging of himself in his political duties.

'I hope you're not thinking I killed Harry, *or* my father. Why should I? Oh, I know it'd look well in the headlines. Cabinet Minister murders father and brother! If you could pin it on me, you'd make an international reputation. But you can't this time, Littlejohn. My department was under fire in the House at the time Harry met his death. There was an all-night sitting and I was there, in my place, till seven in the morning. You can consult *Hansard* or, if you don't believe that, ask the Prime Minister. He was next but one to me all the while. The night dad died, I spoke at the Economic and Political Alliance dinner... Anything else you'd like to know...?'

He smiled and bared his strong white teeth. He stood on the hearthrug, his legs apart. Just the way he stood on platforms or in the House when he was assailed. Littlejohn felt that if he pressed any point, he'd be engulfed in a spate of the eloquence for which Willie Dodd was famous. Willie consulted a large gold watch on a chain slung across his paunch.

'Anything more?'

Willie Dodd had relaxed now. He was smiling a dangerous smile. He prodded Littlejohn familiarly on the chest.

'If I were you, I wouldn't waste much time on Harry's family. Helena's been a brick to him. The rest are milk and water. Winfield and his sister are just nonentities, however much they might try to be big shots. Winfield's entirely dependent on his hirelings for whatever he does in business; his sister's sold herself to old Bernard Hosea, a moneyed nitwit, for the sake of the title.

Neither of them has the guts to kill a fly, let alone Harry. Especially with a breadknife...'

'Breadknife? Who said it was with a breadknife?'

'Now don't try to catch me out, Littlejohn. Every morning there's placed on my desk at the Ministry a report from Scotland Yard on my brother's affair. I asked the Home Secretary to keep me posted. I heard about the breadknife being found... There's not much I don't know, you see.'

'Yes... But the breadknife wasn't the fatal weapon, sir!'

Littlejohn slowly filled his pipe.

He wasn't thinking of Willie or what a grand man he was. He was turning over the name in his mind. Harry V Dodd...

'Your brother had a second name, I gather, sir.'

'Who told you that? He always kept it dark. It was Villiers. He thought it didn't suit him at all. How Mother thought of it, I can't think. Probably the name of a hero in some novel she read before Harry was born. Yes; Harry Villiers Dodd. That was him.'

'And he never used his second name?'

'Except in legal documents when he was forced into it. He was a bit sensitive about it. He'd been laughed at when he was a boy for carrying such a high-sounding name and at the same time having the seat of his pants in holes. We were poor in those days, you know. Well, I must be off. Call and see me at the House one day when all this is over. I'd like to hear how it ends. But don't spend too much time on the family. Look into Harry's shady friends and perhaps some of the women he was mixed up with... Goodbye...'

He bustled off and he must have sent in for Winfield on his way to the door.

Winfield's tic was going twenty to the dozen. He was put out at the idea of being questioned by the police.

'Look here, Inspector, I can't see why...'

'I just wanted a formal word with you, sir. Have you seen your father or grandfather lately?'

'No, I haven't, and I didn't want to. They were impossible people. They were men who tried in every way they could think of to degrade their family and shame my mother. I don't see how I can help at all in finding out who murdered them. I gather that's what you're here for.'

His poached eyes sought Littlejohn's face anxiously. There was something funny about Winfield; something mentally unhealthy and unwholesome. He was a little sneak, a little prig, and lived in the rarefied atmosphere of his own conceit. Someone had told him that, having married him for his money and wrung a satisfactory settlement from him, his wife was carrying on with his secretary. Winfield had cut his informer dead ever since and refused to investigate it. It couldn't happen to him. Winfield Dodd, shortly to become Sir Winfield... he hoped.

'I can't help you.'

'Where were you on the night your father died, sir?'

'Eh?'

So that was it! He *was* suspect.

'Let me tell you...!'

Winfield's bald head grew pink with temper. He frothed at the mouth and cast up spray as he spoke.

'I won't stand for it.'

'A mere formality, sir. I've just asked your uncle the same question and he answered quite civilly.'

'I don't care what Uncle William did. I dislike him, I despise him. As to your insinuation that I murdered my... my... my...'

He couldn't get it out. To call Harry Dodd 'father' might have choked him.

'...My... Harry Dodd... to say that I murdered Harry Dodd, it's preposterous. Why, I was in Lille, France, when it happened. I was at a meeting of steel masters there. Ask anybody. My wife, my secretary... anybody.'

His wife, his secretary. Yes, they'd tell him! They knew it well.

Whilst the cat was away in Lille, the mice had played in his London flat...

'Is there anything more?'

'Did you agree that your grandfather was insane?'

'Of course. If I'd had my way, both of them would have been put in an asylum. Public nuisances! They've made our lives one long misery for years. I'm glad they're dead.'

His face jerked, and he started to pull his fingers and make the joints crack.

'Did you wish them dead before they were murdered?'

The full horror of it smote Winfield.

'Look here! I'll make you sit up if you dare to suggest that I... that I... Well... I'll make it hot for you. I have friends. Very influential friends... They could break you.'

Littlejohn stared Winfield out of countenance. He suddenly had a vision of Winfield as a small, fat, unwholesome boy, pulling the wings from flies and torturing his sister.

'That's all...'

'I beg your pardon?'

'That's all for the present, thanks. May I see your sister, please, and that will be the end?'

Somehow Winfield couldn't gather his dignity together and make a proper exit. He went out like a boy who had had six of the cane, walking sideways, eyeing Littlejohn, as though the Inspector might kick him in the pants to speed him on his way.

Sir Bernard Hosea brought in his wife.

'Look here, my man. People don't as a rule send for me or my wife. *I* send for 'em, or else they come to me...'

'Thank you for coming, then. I only wanted to ask Lady Hosea if she had seen her father or her grandfather recently, before they were murdered.'

Lady Hosea's complexion was pale like ivory. She used no cosmetics and her skin was clear and flawless. Littlejohn realised that he was going to have a job getting anything from this queer pair, for they hadn't a whole intellect between them. She looked at her husband.

'Does he mean...?'

Sir Bernard stroked his long moustache and looked baffled. 'Think he means the Dodd fellahs. Walter and Harry... or was his name Henry? Can't think.'

He turned to Littlejohn.

'My wife and I don't recognise the Dodd men as relations by blood or by marriage. In case you don't know it, my man, there was a divorce many years ago, since when neither of 'em's been part of the family. Hope you understand.'

'Yes, sir. I understand. And your wife and you haven't seen them lately?'

'Why should we? You haven't come across 'em, have you, my dear?'

'No, my love.'

She shook her head from side to side, and the little bells which made her earrings chimed faintly.

'H'm.'

They looked blankly at each other. They were a most affectionate pair, always together, self-contained, resenting intrusion, two perfect simpletons. It was said that until she married, Miss Dodd had been a statuesque beauty, much sought after for her charm and wit. Now, after fifteen years of married life with Hosea, she still had a kind of charm, but her wits had atrophied.

'Were you at home when the murders occurred, sir?'

'Oh, yes. Oh, yes. Yes, at home in our villa in Nice. We flew over for this gathering. Mrs Dodd needed us, she said. We came. We return at weekend. Is there anything else, my man? You can write to my London address, if there is. My secretary'll answer. My wife's not very strong... Don't want her botherin'...'

Lady Hosea had never had an illness in her life, but it was her husband's way of excusing his tender solicitude. He took her arm.

'Come along, my love...'

They were like a couple playing a part on the stage. They made a graceful exit and you might have expected applause as they reached the wings.

'Finished? Like a drink?'

Peter Dodd was back. He carried a bottle and glasses. Littlejohn felt like a refresher. Getting information out of this queer lot had been like crawling about on a fly-paper. 'Thank you. Just a small one.'

Peter found a syphon and filled up the whisky.

'Anything else you need?'

'Your father's second name...'

'Villiers. He hated it and kept it dark. Why?'

'He'd have to use it in legal documents, of course...'

'Yes. But only then. He hated it with an obsessive hatred. Mother once told me, he was ragged about it when he was a boy and it sort of made a phobia, if you understand.'

'Was he likely to have told it to his pals, say, the members of a friendly society of which he was a member?'

'Good Lord, no! They'd be the last people. Can't you see, they'd sort of be the grown-up counterparts of the boys who ragged him.'

Peter was the brightest of the bunch of Dodds Littlejohn had just interviewed!

'Did you see the wreath from the Free Fishers, sir?'

'Did I see it! Did I see them all! They kept arriving this morning. I thought Winfield was going to put his hat on and clear off. He seemed to think all dad's disreputable pals were going to foregather at the cemetery and disgrace us. Charley, Dot, Sid, Joc, Emily and Fred, whoever they might have been! And my sister kept repeating, "I can't understand it. I can't understand what Father was thinking of." And every time she called him Father, Hosea corrected her and reminded her that he hadn't been her father for years. As if, suddenly, it had come out that she'd been born on the wrong side of the blanket!'

Littlejohn eyed Peter Dodd. It was evident he'd had one or two drinks before. His eyes were sparkling, but his talk was mirthless and bitter.

'You don't like your family, do you?'

'With the exception of Mother, no. I hate them. Think of it; thanks to them Dad died in the gutter and Grandfather, a decent old bird really, hid himself, terrified, in the old home and was smothered by whoever was after him. It's a bloody shame! There ought to be some way of avenging the pair of them...'

He raised his glass and tottered a little.

'To the memory of Harry Dodd and Walter Dodd. May the earth rest lightly on my poor old dad...'

And tears mingled with his whisky as he drank it.

13

ALL PALS TOGETHER

'There's one last question before I go, sir. How much did your mother give or lend your father, in all, after they were reconciled?'

Peter Dodd soon composed himself after his sentimental outburst about his father, and he faced Littlejohn calmly again.

'I'll have to go up and ask her…'

'Don't disturb her. I'll telephone later.'

Peter shook his head.

'She'll be most annoyed if I don't tell her now. Her main thought is to see the murderer of my father brought to justice. I won't be long.'

He hurried out. In the hall, Littlejohn could hear the mourners departing.

'Where's Helena? I'd better say goodbye…'

Willie Dodd, jocular, forceful, was bustling Winfield and the maid around.

'Here I am…'

Mrs Dodd was down seeing them off. Voices muttered, and, above all, you could hear Willie boisterously telling his sister-in-law to find plenty to do to take her mind off her troubles. Cars drew up, there were more goodbyes, and the house fell silent.

'Good afternoon, Inspector...'

Mrs Dodd was pale and looked more frail than ever after her ordeal of the day. She was glad to be rid of the mourners who didn't care a hang about Harry Dodd. Now she knew the end of him and could resign herself.

'Peter tells me you want to know the total amount which I gave my husband since we met again. Five hundred pounds.'

Littlejohn's eyes opened wide.

'Five hundred! But from our knowledge he must have handled ten thousand at least, Mrs Dodd.'

She sat down, groping for the arms of the chair, and looked utterly at a loss.

'You're surely mistaken. After the divorce, the trust provided him with enough to buy the house at Brande and about five hundred a year. There was no capital. Wherever did he get the rest?'

'Did he never mention being in possession of any big sums? In the course of your recent talks, I mean.'

'No. He did talk about being independent of the family and not needing my money if we married again. I thought that meant that his formula would...'

'He had no formula, Mrs Dodd. He was trying to find one, but when he died, he'd been unsuccessful.'

'Poor Harry! He was trying so hard not to appear worthless, that he concocted a story...'

'I don't think so. He had some money from somewhere. The thing now is to find out where he got it.'

'I do hope it's nothing illicit... that he hadn't been defrauding anybody. I don't think he could. He was patently honest...'

Littlejohn sighed to think of Peg Boone and little Nancy, and how Dodd hadn't mentioned them to this woman who, in spite of all he'd done, still trusted him.

'He didn't bring any papers or books here in preparation for coming back to you, Mrs Dodd?'

'No. Did he leave a will?'

'I think so. He seems to have tried to do the right thing by Miss Nicholls. He left her the house and an annuity.'

'That will be all right. Where is the will?'

'With his solicitor, who, by the way, was murdered last night.'

Peter and his mother gasped.

'Another!'

'Yes. Did you know Mr Pharaoh?'

'Of course. He represented Harry in the divorce case. That was the only time I ever met him. Did you know him, Peter?'

'Yes. I met him several times with Dad. A very decent old buffer. But is this crime connected with my father's death?'

'I think so. And with your grandfather's. He's being cremated tomorrow, I gather.'

'Yes. Mother and I will be the only ones there, I suppose. The rest of the family have cast him off completely.' Mrs Dodd wrung her hands.

'I suppose the same person killed all three.'

'That's the inference. I think Mr Harry told his father something which incriminated a third party. Or, at least, which pointed the finger at the third party after Mr Harry Dodd's death. Mr Pharaoh must also have known it. It led, too, to the burning down of *Mon Abri*, the bungalow, this morning.'

'You didn't tell us that! How did it happen?'

'Arson, I think. Arson to get rid of some evidence which the criminal thought might be hidden in the house.'

'He must be mad.'

'Very frightened, Mrs Dodd. Very afraid something will lead us to him.'

Littlejohn left them to return to Helstonbury, calling on the way at the county police office at Helton. The same sergeant was on duty and he greeted the Inspector with a great show of deference.

He was a large, smooth man, with faithful, dog-like eyes. 'This is indeed a pleasure, sir. 'Ow can we 'elp?'

'You've been all over Gale Cottage, Sergeant?'

'Yes, sir. What 'ad you in mind?'

'You found no papers, no hiding-place with papers in it, no traces of information which the dead man might have possessed?'

'No, sir. The h'experts have been all over the place. Combed it over, as you might say. We're dealin' with a deep 'un, if I may be so bold as to say so. He did it well and cunnin'.'

'I agree. Well, let me know if anything turns up, Sergeant.'

'You can rely on that, sir…'

The Aching Man was closed when Littlejohn passed, but he knocked on the door and Sid Boone admitted him. Sid was a bit off-hand.

'I hope you don't think we had anythin' to do with all these crimes. We've just heard over the wireless that old Pharaoh's been done in, too. That can't have been us, either. We've good alibis.'

'You seem so keen on protesting your innocence, Sid, that I'll soon be thinking you committed all the murders.'

''Ere…'

'Is that the Inspector?'

It was Peg. She was dressed in a red corduroy costume and looked pale and drawn.

'Yes, it is. I called to see if you'd thought of anything that might help.'

'No…'

'The settlement Harry Dodd made; did he pay over by cheque?'

'No. Five-pound notes. It was a bit of a nuisance. There were such a lot of them.'

Sid sniggered.

'I, for one, don't mind countin' em. The more the merrier, when it's banknotes…'

'Was Mr Pharaoh there at the time?'

'Yes. It wasn't that Harry didn't trust me. It was that he asked Mr Pharaoh to look after me and Nancy if anything happened to him. Now I believe the lawyer's dead, too.'

'Yes. Shortly before he died, did Harry Dodd bring a box of papers here or did he bring some in his overcoat pocket?'

'Why, yes, he did. I remember. He said he'd been clearing up his things at his bungalow. He'd burned a pile of stuff but just brought away a lot of… what did he call them…? You know, the things you get when you buy or sell stocks and shares…'

'Contract Notes?'

'That would be it. I know he told us what they were. Didn't he, Sid?'

'S'right. The ones he got pinched in the raincoat, you mean?'

'That's it. He came with them in his pocket one day, Inspector, and hung his raincoat and hat on the peg there in the hall. When he went to get the papers, the coat had gone. Well, we couldn't think who'd taken it. You see, it was opening time and Harry had always hung his things there. Anybody could have taken the coat and not been seen. They didn't even need to go into one of the public rooms; the door was open and there was the coat. But we've never missed anything before. You get careless, don't you? We always thought it was a carrier who called for a drink and then went on and we never saw him again.'

'It looks to me as if you had a visit from the murderer. He must have been with or recognised Harry Dodd, found the Contract Notes in his pocket, and perhaps set about some fraud. But I thought Dodd wasn't wealthy?'

'He must have had money to give us the trust funds he did. And he always talked as if he'd never see me and Nancy want. I'm sure he was comfortably off.'

The child was calling her mother from upstairs, so the Inspector left them and went on his way.

At Helstonbury there was more news. Mr Pharaoh *had* been

murdered. That was definite, and the Lowestoft police were baffled by lack of clues and even motive.

'It's at this end, Judkin,' said Littlejohn. 'And by the way, is there some sort of society called the Free Fishers?'

Judkin's jaw dropped.

'What do you know of the Fishers?'

'Just that they sent Harry Dodd a wreath.'

'Yes. It's a local friendly society. Nearly a hundred years old.'

'What's their object? Insurance, or just nice cosy beer-parties?'

'Both, I'd say. There's a lot of common land outside the town with a mere in the middle of it, and the burghers of the town used to have free grazing and fishing on it. I guess when this friendly society started, the idea of the free fishers on the common appealed to them.'

'Was Harry Dodd likely to have been a member? He got a wreath from them and they called him "Brother".'

Judkin cleared his throat rather self-consciously.

'Well... To tell you the truth, I'm a member myself. I don't often go. Haven't time. It's a bit like Rotary, except that instead of being international, it's a gathering that belongs purely to our town. You have to be proposed and seconded, and it's composed mainly of shopkeepers and business men. They'd help you if you were in real trouble.'

'The puzzle to me was that on the funeral card at the cemetery they call him Brother Harry V Dodd. Do you have to give all your names when you join, like a legal document?'

'Of course you don't. I didn't give mine. My second name's Percy, if you'll keep it quiet. I don't look like a Percy, so I always omit it. In the Free Fishers, I'm inscribed as George Judkin, pure and simple.'

'That's what puzzles me. Have you a list of members?'

'Yes. It's somewhere in the desk. They publish a booklet every year with the list of those who've paid their subs. Rather cunning, that. If you're not in the book it means you've not paid up and you're sort of in semi-disgrace.'

Judkin rummaged in the drawers of his desk.

'Drane! Drane!'

'Yes, sir. Excuse me…'

'Where's my syllabus of the Free Fishers for this year?'

The polite constable asked again to be excused and took possession of his boss's desk. He found the paper-backed pamphlet at once.

Judkin ran his thumb down the list at the front.

'Yes. Here it is. Harry Dodd, *Mon Abri*, Brande. Paid.'

'Then why did somebody call him Harry V Dodd?'

Judkin shrugged his shoulders. Dear me! The piffling and fiddling these Scotland Yard chaps take over little inessential details!

'Who would be likely to send the wreath?'

'One of the stewards. Here they are among the officers.'

> *Charles Kingsley Cresswell*, Home Counties Bank, Brande.
> *Henry Hooper*, The Nurseries, Brande.
> *Wilfred Shepherd*, Palatine Cafe, Helstonbury.
> *Ishmael Lott*, 78 Sheep Street, Helstonbury.

Littlejohn consulted his notebook.

'Cresswell and Hooper seem to be two of Dodd's bosom pals. They spend the evenings with him at *The Bear* in Brande.'

'They're very keen on the Free Fishers. Probably they introduced Harry Dodd to the society.'

'And we also know Lott, the man who sells parrot seed. Who would be likely to send the wreath?'

'I couldn't say? Does it matter?'

Littlejohn smiled at Judkin.

'Just one of those little things…'

Cromwell looked across at the Inspector. He felt an inward

glow when he saw the glint in Littlejohn's eyes. It was usually there when the first faint scent of the quarry came his way.

'I wonder what he's at?' thought Cromwell.

'I'll see Cresswell and Hooper at *The Bear* tonight. Meanwhile it's interesting that Harry Dodd felt the same as you about his second name, Judkin. It was Villiers. He thought it sounded a bit too highfalutin and suppressed it when he could. He was hardly likely to use it at the Free Fishers, was he?'

'No. But that's not important, is it?'

'It may be. It's the only thing that's a bit queer in all this case. The Dodd family all have alibis, which, by the way, I'd like you to get checked, if you will. That puts the family out of it, if they're genuine. The Nicholls women and their Uncle Fred are hardly likely to have killed the goose that laid the golden eggs; so we can put them out of the first line. The Boones have alibis, as well, of a kind. Pharaoh's dead, and so is Walter Dodd. That leaves Harry's pals and Mrs Dodd without proper investigation and with possible motives. The pals at *The Bear* will probably be able to say they were all together when Harry left them, and Mrs Dodd says she was sick in bed. There we are. We've got to find some other trail.'

He passed across slips of paper bearing the family alibis and those of Peg and Sid Boone.

'Could your men just look into those?'

'Of course. They might break one or the other of them. Then you can bring in your big guns again.'

After evening dinner at *The Bear*, Littlejohn and Cromwell made their ways to the Snug, which they had already asked Mr Mallard to keep select for one evening and admit only the little gang who drank in the old days with Harry Dodd. Five men sat round the fire, their glasses on a table and on the mantelpiece, and they all looked up with challenging glances as the intruders entered. This was the way they cold-shouldered any strangers who tried to butt in on their little nightly party.

'The gentlemen from Scotland Yard, gents. H'Inspectors Littlejohn an' Cromwell,' announced Mr Mallard by way of introduction. Littlejohn's eye caught that of Cromwell, and he smiled faintly. Inspector Cromwell! Littlejohn wished it were true. His faithful hound had long deserved it.

They were cordially received, and the members of the gang bought them drinks.

'You're very welcome. Anybody tryin' to bring Harry's murderer to justice is a friend of ours,' said the one called Gambles. He was the village joiner and undertaker and a churchwarden. As such, he was the spokesman. A stocky, heavy fellow of around sixty. He had red-rimmed eyes, a large moustache and he did most of the talking. He had a habit of apologetically coughing behind his hand.

You couldn't mistake Shadwell, the garage man. He couldn't get the oil out of his fingernails and hands. A tall, spare man with a folded melancholy face and large nose. He hardly ever spoke. He liked hearing other people talk, and he thought Gambles was an oracle. He looked at the Scotland Yard men dubiously, as though his conscience might have been troubling him. He was the most honest and friendly man in Brande.

Henry and Charlie Hooper, a couple of bachelors, were little earthy men, almost alike. They had thin tanned faces, large moustaches and big horny hands from their work on the soil. They made a lot of money from growing tomatoes and chrysanthemums. They also did a comic turn at village concerts, in which Henry cracked jokes and Charlie was his stooge. In private life they looked anything but comedians.

And there was Cresswell, who managed the local bank, a sub-branch to the large office in Helstonbury. Cresswell had, after long being pursued by a wealthy customer, married her, and now he was independent and happy. He wondered why he'd struggled so long against Mrs Cresswell's blandishments. He was a medium-built, strong-looking man with a craggy face, and he wore tweeds and a cap, even to the office. His boss in Helstonbury objected to the horsy clothes during business, but Cresswell threatened to resign and take away his wife's large balances if his personal tastes weren't indulged, so no more was said.

Mr Gambles was obviously in the chair. The other three villagers held him in reverence, and Mr Cresswell was too comfortable to struggle for position.

'We'll 'elp to the utmost of our abilities. Won't we?'

There were murmurs of consent.

It was like an informal inquest. Even the casual Cresswell sat up and began to take notice.

'I've heard the story of how Harry Dodd left you all on the night he was murdered and went home. You were all here when it happened?'

Mr Gambles solemnly rose, walked to the fire, twisted a spill of paper and lit his pipe. He was heavy in the beam and walked like a large duck. He slowly ejected tobacco smoke.

'Yes. I appeared at the inquest and testified to same. Also the police took our h'alibis. We must have been all together when it happened. We'd stayed behind to settle a little argument.'

'Did Harry Dodd talk much about himself when you were all here sitting by the fire?'

Mr Gambles looked round to find if anybody wanted to answer, but they left him to it. The Hooper brothers had lit and were smoking small cheroots which filled the air with a rancid smell.

'Not about his private and personal affairs. We never pumped him about 'em. It would 'ave been unkind after what he'd gone through. We talked about what you might call the current events of the village and district. Crops, fishin', local deaths, scandal… Often enough, we'd jest sit quiet, smoking, enjoyin' the company at the end of the 'ard day's work.'

'What was Harry Dodd's real name? Henry or Harry?'

Nobody spoke. Mr Gambles seemed to think it was his duty to answer for them all.

'Harry, as far as we knew.'

'Had he a second name? This is a semi-official enquiry, you see, and my colleague will be taking notes.'

Cromwell put down his beer mug and pulled out his little black book to confirm it.

'Not that we'd know.'

They all grunted assent, and Cresswell rose to order some more drinks.

'Decent chap, Cresswell,' said Mr Gambles behind the bank man's back, as though somehow somebody had been doubting it.

'Are any of you members of the Free Fishers at Helstonbury?'

Henry Hooper gurgled with pleasure round his foul cheroot. He was happy to oblige.

'Yes. I am,' he said. 'So's Cresswell.'

'What am I?' said Cresswell, returning with more beer mugs on a tray.

'A member of the Free Fishers.'

'What of it?'

Littlejohn took his beer and passed along one to Cromwell. 'I saw you'd sent a wreath to the funeral today.'

Hooper beamed again.

'We always do. We didn't send a representative, though. With Harry's family havin' severed, so to speak, dimplomatic relationships, well...'

Henry Hooper lolled back in his seat and thrust his thumbs in his armpits. He was proud of his outburst at which Gambles gaped with astonishment. Charlie, his brother, prodded Henry in the ribs and giggled. There'd be something about dimplomatic relationships in their next lot of back-chat at the village concert!

'Who sent the wreath?'

'It'll o'be Lott's turn on duty. We always appoint four stewards annually, see? Then, one of them takes a week on duty and the rest off, we follow one another on weekly rotas. It's with the idea of dispensing necessary charity and doin' things like sendin' wreaths or letters of condolence. See what I mean? Cresswell and me are on this year, with two Helstonbury chaps called Lott and Shepherd.'

He took a great swig of beer to lubricate himself.

'Was Harry Dodd a friend of Lott's?'

Mr Gambles rushed in to take the lead once more.

'Not that we'd know. Lott's a funny little chap. Proper 'enpecked. His wife makes his life one long 'ell. He went bust and filed his petition many years ago, since when she's held the purse-strings and run the business. She seems to do well, but Ishmael gets little of it.'

'He minds the shop, does he, whilst she runs the firm?'

'Well, not exackly. He used to be in the shop all the time. But lately I've seen him runnin' round the countryside on their corn lorries. They buy a lot of produce from farms, you know. When Lott's father had the firm, it did well.'

'Did Harry Dodd ever talk about his money to you?'

Littlejohn looked round. They were all giving Cresswell his head as the banker of the party, but he was not impressed.

'He didn't bank with me. I think he kept his account at the Old Bank, Helstonbury. I'd cash him a cheque now and again, but nothing more.'

Shadwell started to make signs of wanting to speak. He looked excitedly round as though asking permission, and then gave tongue.

'Bit of a financier, was Harry...'

Nothing more came.

'Well?'

Mr Gambles sounded annoyed.

'Well? *'Ow?'*

'It's this way.' Mr Shadwell closed his eyes solemnly. 'He'd call at my place for petrol and talk like one of these big shots as makes money speculatin' in the city.'

'Well?'

It was like drawing blood from a stone. Mr Shadwell opened both eyes and looked annoyed at being rushed.

'Well… You fellows know I'm a bit short of ready for extendin' my premises. I earn a nice livin', but people keep sayin' I ought to put in a sort of showroom and lock-ups for people's cars as haven't garages of their own. I don't know… It's a bit risky, I reckon. You see there's not as much money about as there was, and what with people not buying cars and…'

Mr Gambles made swimming gestures.

'Hey, Shadwell. We don't want all the pros and antis about it. What the gentleman wants is, how was Harry Dodd like a financier? How was he, Shadwell? Tell us plain and simple.'

Shadwell looked hurt. His large Adam's apple rose and fell.

'I was tryin' to. I asked Harry what I'd better do. He was a knowledgeable sort, was Harry. I thought his advice 'ud be sound. He thought I ought to spread myself a bit. I asked 'ow. Build and get a mortgage, was what he said. But I said, no. My old dad had a mortgage on his farm all his life. Proper millstone, it were. Round 'is neck till he died. I don't hold with mortgages. Pay your way's my motter.'

Gambles rose, waddled to his friend, and caressed him on the shoulder to cool him down and show they all understood and sympathised.

'We agree, Shadwell. But wot's that to do with it? Tell the gentleman about 'Arry.'

'I was going to. When I told Harry I objected, like, to mortgages, on principle, he ups and says, speculate in the Stock Exchange, then. Speculate, he says. And he tells me there's money in it. In fact, he's made a packet himself. If I'd like to try, he could put me on a cert.'

Littlejohn looked at Cromwell and they exchanged eloquent glances.

So that was it! Harry Dodd made a bit on the side by playing the stock markets. They'd never thought of that! But this ran into thousands. He must have been lucky.

Gambles' eyes were wide open, and the two Hoopers looked at Shadwell in admiration.

'Mug's game unless you've got a packet to fall back on,' remarked Cresswell, who was secure in the speculating he did with his wife's capital, because there was plenty of it.

'Oh, I told Harry that, but he argued about it. Said he'd made a nice little pile. "I'd lend you a bit, Shadwell," he says, "because I got confidence in you, but I'll be wantin' ready cash any time now, so you have a try yourself." An' he gave me a list of things to put my money in for a rise in price. I never did, though, and I regret it, because from what I see in the papers now, Harry was right. They went up a lot after he told me about 'em. That's why I think Harry was quite a good financier.'

'How long's that since?'

'On and off over twelve months. Last time he tipped me some was about six weeks ago. I ought to have put money in 'em. But, I never had any luck. If I invested in 'em, they'd be sure to go down just because it's me.'

'Did you keep the lists?'

'Yes. I got 'em at home. I can pop over if you'd like to see them.'

'I would, very much.'

Shadwell rose like something projected from a spring. He was so anxious to help that he couldn't get home quickly enough.

'Good sort,' said Mr Gambles in his running commentary. 'Proper good sort, is Shadwell. No bisness man, though. Not a better man with his 'ands anywhere, but when it comes to bisness, he's like a child. Kingsley there does his books, don't you, Kingsley?'

Cresswell nodded agreement.

'Dodd was right. It's a good business, and a good man like Shadwell could double it if he'd extend. But he's afraid of laying out money. He's a family, you see, and he wants to do well by them. He won't risk a loss…'

Shadwell was back, panting from his efforts. He held in his oil-stained hand a number of bits of paper on which names of well-known shares, mainly industrials, were printed in pencil. Littlejohn eyed the printing closely.

'Who did this; you or Harry Dodd?'

'Dodd wrote 'em down. I'm usually mucked up with oil when he calls… or rather *did* call.'

He seemed to find it difficult to think of Harry Dodd never coming back to them.

The little party were watching with anxious admiration.

'May I keep these?'

'Of course. I won't want 'em. Stocks and shares is nothing in my line.'

Shadwell had withheld one slip. He evidently wanted to comment on it. He held it out to Littlejohn.

'That's the last he tipped me. Watch those, he told me. They'll fall, then rise again. And sure enough, they did. Only today they went up tuppence.'

Littlejohn looked at the piece of paper. Then he slapped his knee.

'A break at last!' he said.

The recommended investment was Freifontein Mines!

14

THE WATCHER UNDER THE LAMP

There was a hush in the Snug as Harry Dodd's friends waited for Littlejohn to speak again, but he put the slip of paper in his pocket without a word more about it.

'You all remember the road accident in which Dodd was involved. His friend, Comfort, was killed…'

Mr Gambles coughed behind his hand and sat up in his chair.

'We do. We was all very sorry for Harry about it. We knew, of course, that he was just taking his old dad for an airing. Willie Dodd had had the old chap shut up in an asylum, and Harry had made up his mind to get him out. Meanwhile, he gave his father as good a time as he could. That affair shook Harry…'

'Had he any idea who caused the accident?'

'No, but he said it was deliberate. The road was bad, and it was easy to make anybody skid. But Harry was frightened by it. "Somebody's got it in for me," he said. "I'd better set my affairs in order." That's how he took it.'

The rest nodded. 'Aye… That's it.'

'He had no idea…?'

'He said it was a saloon, and he couldn't make out who drove it. It was a grey saloon.'

'We can't seem to get any further than that. It's a mystery to me. Did any of you see any suspicious characters around?'

Nobody could help there, either. In fact, Harry Dodd hadn't taken any of them into his confidence. He'd just enjoyed their company over a glass of beer at *The Bear* in the evenings when he was bored with his women and wanted a change.

The clock in the bar struck eight, and simultaneously the telephone rang somewhere in the back of the pub. Mr Mallard appeared in the Snug looking very important.

'The Super of the 'Elstonbury police is wantin' a word, sir.'

It was Judkin on to tell him that Miss Jump had been through Mr Pharaoh's box at the bank and had found one or two items of interest. The original will seemed to have gone from the safe with other papers, but in the deed box was a copy. Dodd had left a number of interesting legacies, and a few of the papers referred to him as well.

'I can't talk over the phone. Are you free to come here?'

Excusing themselves, the two Scotland Yard men left in the police car for Helstonbury. The country road gradually grew more and more lined with suburban properties, passed the railway station, and then took on a drab, slummy appearance. The streets in this quarter were gas-lit, with workshops and tenements bordering the main road. Passing Lott's corn-stores, they observed a light coming through the grating of the cellar.

'Looks as if Ishmael's having an all-night session with his graphs. We'll park the car and then, if you'll wait for me at the police station, I'd just like to go back and have a little talk with Lott. I won't be long.'

From the car park, back in his tracks, Littlejohn walked the length of the better part of Sheep Street. It was well lit by electric sodium lamps. The shops were closed, but here and there the lights were full on, displaying their wares with illuminations controlled by time-switches. Through the empty, mesh-protected window of a large jeweller's, the great safe at the back of the shop with a spot-light trained on the door for the police to see. The red neon sign of the picture house, with one letter missing, blazed with diabolical radiance. EMP RE. The beery, hoarse voice of the man in a braided uniform assured the world that there were seats in all parts. A few people were going in and a few more coming out. The streets were almost deserted. Lights shone from the windows of hotels, in one of which you could see Freemasons moving about in evening dress. Somewhere, somebody was singing to the accompaniment of a tinny piano. "Because God made you mine…" And then a burst of applause. Groups of youths strolled about the streets, whistling after passing girls, boasting to one another, laughing coarsely. Far ahead, traffic lights monotonously changed from green to red and red to green, directing traffic that didn't exist.

About twenty yards before Lott's shop, the electric lighting ceased, and gas lamps took its place, their lights seeming dim and pale green beside the unearthly glow of the sodium filaments. There was a gas standard about three yards past the corn-stores. A man stood beneath it, smoking and spitting. He was tall and lean and wore a heavy, threadbare overcoat and a battered soft hat. You couldn't see his face, but in a circle round him were spent matches, fag ends, and dark disks about the size of a shilling from his incessant spitting. Without looking up, he turned his back as Littlejohn approached and remained with his face in the shadows. Beyond him, for some unknown reason, a small newsagent's shop, with toys, birthday cards, paper-backed novels with lewd pictures on the front, and a lot of other shadowy junk in the window, was still open, although there seemed nobody about to patronise it. The light showed through the cellar grating of Lott's shop. Littlejohn beat on the door with his fist. The glass panes in the panels had been covered by shutters bolted from within. The man under the lamp didn't even turn his head.

Footsteps in the shop, and then: 'Who is it?'

It was a woman's voice; the whining, harsh tones of Mrs Lott.

'Inspector Littlejohn, of the police. Is your husband in?'

There was a sound of a chain being unhooked and a lock turned. Mrs Lott stood in the gloom beyond, breathing heavily.

'He's not here. He's out at his Free Fishers. Anythin' I can do?'

She was very anxious to know Littlejohn's business. That's why she asked him in. He followed her to the stair-head and they descended into the cellar.

The bright naked bulb threw the contents into sharp relief. The desk, the filing cabinet, an iron safe in one corner, the grotesque graphs on the walls like the handiwork of some crazy modern artist. The desk was open, and two account books were spread on it.

'I was just doin' the books. My husband's no hand at figures.'

There was a cashbox, too, open, and revealing a lot of notes and coin. Mrs Lott hastily closed it and pushed it in one corner of the desk top. She had stuck the pen she was using in her hair and now removed it. She was wearing carpet slippers and her shoes stood beside the desk. She suffered badly from bunions and shed her shoes whenever she could. The naked light etched more sharply the lines of her thin, acute, mean face, with its small eyes too closely set together and her hooked, inquisitive nose.

'I called to ask your husband if he'd any contacts with Harry Dodd besides his weekly purchase of parrot seed. There was a light on as I passed, I thought I'd…'

'Of course…'

Even when she tried to be agreeable she couldn't keep the acid from her voice.

'You mean pore Mr Dodd that was murdered. What makes you think Mr Lott might have anything to do with him?'

She thrust out her neck like a hen drinking, the better to hear the answer.

'Your husband gets about on his lorries. I thought he might have heard some local gossip. Or then, they might have chatted when Dodd called every week.'

'I don't know of any friendship there. I would know, if there was any. My husband doesn't keep much from me…'

Littlejohn was sure of it. Every night when work was done and Lott got home with all his wife's parcels, the third degree would begin. Why was he late home? Who'd been in the shop? Why had they been and what had they said? She wouldn't rest until she knew it all.

Littlejohn looked at the walls.

'I'm quite intrigued by your husband's hobby. Those graphs of stocks and shares are very skilfully done…'

He cast his eyes round. Government stocks, tea, copper, tobacco… One of the graphs was very erratic. A series of acute V's connected by almost straight lines at the top, where they'd gone calm for a bit. At the side, in neat black printing, Buljone Tin Mines. Buljone… Littlejohn memorised it as an interesting freak. One day he'd look it up and see what caused all the ups and downs.

Mrs Lott was chattering all the time. Once started she didn't easily stop, and as she gathered momentum she grew more indiscreet.

'…Never was a business man. When his father left him this place, it was a little gold mine…'

Littlejohn, who'd been immersed in the stock exchange when the talk began, and had missed the start, assumed she was talking about Ishmael Lott.

'…Instead, he messed around speculating and drawing ups and downs in a book. Then he got to doin' them on the walls. You see all that… that's his day's work. Or was, till I found him somethin' better to do. He lost a fair bit, unbeknown to me, on his speculations, and neglected the shop and bought so badly for stock that he couldn't pay his creditors and had to go bankrupt. I paid his debts out of the bit I'd saved and what my mother left me, and now the shop's mine. He goes out with the lorries nearly every day. Throwin' and liftin' a few flour and corn sacks'll do him more good than stocks and shares. He still draws 'em on the walls, but in his own time now… at dinner time and sometimes in the evenin's after the shop's shut. Fat lot of good it's all done him. He's dyin' to get his hands on some money and try his luck, but *I* keep the cash and sign on the bank account. He's not makin' away with any more of the family money while I've got strength to stop him. He…'

'Your husband must have something about him, though. All this recording of stock exchange securities is a bit ingenious you know.'

Littlejohn had been busy eyeing the graphs and, having selected five of them, the fluctuations of which seemed very erratic, he was trying to make a note of their names without attracting Mrs Lott's attention. This was difficult, because she had eyes everywhere. Littlejohn, on the other hand, couldn't trust his memory for some of the names, in which, as one who never speculated for lack of funds with which to do it, he had never before had much interest. He took out his packet of cigarettes, and with a small pencil scribbled as the talk went on.

Amal. Brass Industries.
U. Ch. Belang.
Freifontein.
Assoc. Nick.
Ruritanian Conc. Oil.

'Oh, he's clever enough in his own silly way. You wouldn't think, to look at him, he was college educated, would you? His father made enough to bring Ishmael up like a gent. That's what's wrong. Big ideas and afraid to work…'

It was full-steam ahead on Mrs Lott's favourite topic of blackguarding her husband and complaining of her own sorry fate. Her eyes grew glazed as she warmed to the job, and Littlejohn was able to get on with his surreptitious scribbling on the cigarette packet without much trouble.

'...I'm here checking the books for the month. If I didn't, they'd be wrong. He'd have helped himself to the till. He knows what'll happen if he ever does. I'll leave him and, as I've got the money, he'll have to work... get a job and get his jacket off proper. He won't like that, so he behaves himself...'

She was venomous. Her hands on her hips, she took this opportunity of venting the spleen accumulated over years.

'So your husband never backs his fancy in the stock and share lines...?'

Mrs Lott almost spat.

'He'd better not try it...! It's his hobby, and as it is now, he plays it like playin' cards without money. That's as it's goin' to stay.'

'Does he keep his records in the filing cabinet?'

Littlejohn indicated the large metal contraption incongruously standing in the middle of the room with the rest of the old junk.

'Yes... It was what we took for a debt from a customer who went bankrupt. As soon as I heard he couldn't meet the account, I sent a lorry along and picked up that cabinet and a typewriter. "These'll do to be goin' on with," I sez. We sold the typewriter but kept the cabinet. Not that it's much use, and I'll sell it one of these days. We keep bills and things in it, and Lott has the top drawer for his silly fluctuations, as I call 'em...'

Littlejohn would have liked to see inside but didn't wish to cause any panic or domestic trouble for Ishmael.

'I'll be getting along, then, and call perhaps tomorrow. Thanks for wasting time on me...'

'Don't mention it. If there's anything you want to know, I'll tell Lott when he calls for me. He should be along pretty soon. Would you like to wait? I'm makin' some tea...'

She looked avid for more talk, but Littlejohn had had enough.

'Tomorrow will do, thanks.'

Outside, the lounger was still hanging about under the street lamp. He spat as Littlejohn closed the door, but his face was in the shade. The inspector strolled back to the police station.

Miss Jump had called and left behind a copy of Harry Dodd's will and an unsealed envelope, both taken from Mr Pharaoh's box at the bank.

Judkin and Cromwell were drinking tea again. Drane, with many apologies and polite noises, brought in a cup for Littlejohn.

'Sorry, sir. It's a bit dark-coloured and rather an old brew. But if you don't mind...'

'I don't mind, thanks...'

Judkin and Cromwell were both a bit excited by the papers left by Joan Jump. The copy of the will, unsigned, showed that Dodd had left all he had, after certain specific legacies, to Nancy when she reached twenty-one. Meanwhile Peg Boone got the income, but Pharaoh was trustee, so she couldn't handle the principal.

'That'll let the cat out of the bag good and proper. When this will's proved, the scandalmongers'll get busy, and poor Mrs Dodd will know the kind of man Harry really was. To say nothing of the Nicholls pair. The special legacies go to his pals. There's a thousand apiece to his five cronies at *The Bear*. He says how grateful he was for their company and friendship in his time of trouble and loneliness.'

Judkin paused.

'If I'd only known! I might have been a pal to him, as well.'

The envelope contained a list of securities and their values. Cromwell's lips moved as he slowly totted things up. 'Twenty to twenty-five thousand, all told, I reckon. Where did it all come from? He was supposed to be poor. Perhaps it was a final joke; leaving a lot of fancy legacies to all and sundry, and not a bean to meet them...'

Littlejohn removed his pipe thoughtfully.

'I'm not so sure. He found money from somewhere for Dorothy's annuity, and a lot more cash for Peg Boone's first instalment. There may be more somewhere. And, don't forget, that's only a copy of the first will. Dodd may have signed another. Pharaoh told me plainly that Harry Dodd was leaving everything to his wife. The new will might have been what whoever robbed Pharaoh's safe was after and may thus have been destroyed.'

Judkin held up a key.

'This was in Pharaoh's box. It's marked London Metro. Safe Deposit.' The label says, "Mr H Dodd". It looks as if he has a box there, as well. There might be cash in it. How can we get at it?'

'Through Pharaoh's executor.'

'Our Miss Jump,' Judkin chuckled. 'She's sole beneficiary, sole executrix, and everything else. Not that she doesn't deserve it. She's run that practice almost entirely since she started there. She's done all the work while the old man's gone sailing. It's all straight and above board. Their relations were strictly like father and daughter, and she's earned it. Good luck to her. She'll give us all the help she can, she says, and she'll be free from nine-thirty tomorrow to answer my questions…'

'Good… I've just been to Lott's shop. There's a fellow there propping up the lamp post outside, smoking and spitting, but doing little else…'

'Battersbee, that'll be. He lives in a house behind the shop, in a slum quarter. He's a bit of a bolshie. He has seven kids in a four-roomed house, and when he gets fed-up with them he goes in the street, watches the passers-by, thinks dark thoughts, and then turns in about eleven. He's told two or three of my men on the beat that he only gets peace in his spare time when he stands with his thoughts by the lamp…'

'You'd think he'd go and get drunk…'

'Drunk? Battersbee? Not likely. He's TT. He wants to be alone. He hates the world. One day he'll commit a crime. He'll either turn on the gas and kill his wife and family, or else hang himself on the lamp post.'

'I'm glad there's a proper explanation. I began to think he'd something to do with Harry Dodd.'

'Come, come, Littlejohn. Harry Dodd's getting on your nerves. Battersbee's just a harmless eccentric.'

Cromwell, who had been smiling to himself between puffs at his pipe, now burst into roars of laughter.

Judkin looked annoyed.

'What's bitin' you?' he said testily.

'I was just thinking of my father's brother, my Uncle Will. He left a will, leaving a lot of legacies here, there, and everywhere, appointed trustees, and formed trusts for the benefit of his nephews and nieces, including me...'

'Well...?'

'I hope Harry Dodd doesn't turn out like Uncle Will. He left three and eightpence halfpenny... Three and six was the balance of his old-age pension, and he'd a twopence-halfpenny stamp in his pocket that he'd taken off a prepaid letter...'

Cromwell gurgled round his pipe with delight. The sight of him and the thought of his Uncle Will made Littlejohn roar as well. The idea of Cromwell having an Uncle Will seemed funny in itself!

Judkin glared. His sense of humour wasn't his strong point at all and besides... A couple of Scotland Yard high-ups cackling like a pair of lads. It wasn't right.

'I'll bet he's hidden a packet in the Safe Deposit...'

'That's what they said about my Uncle Will. They said he'd hidden it somewhere, so they dug up the garden and searched all the mattresses...'

'Did they find anything?' Judkin asked it seriously, eager and carried away by confusing Dodd and Uncle Will!

The telephone bell interrupted the farce. It was Mrs Ishmael Lott. Had the police heard of anything happening to her husband? He hadn't arrived home and the Free Fishers' meeting had ended early. She'd rung up the secretary, and Lott had been gone more than an hour since but hadn't got home.

'He's never done that before. He's either gone out of his mind or else met with an accident.'

'Did the secretary say where he left him?'

'He said they left the *Duke of York*, where they meet, together, and that my husband parted with him to go to the shop and pick me up. I went shortly after Inspector Little… whatever's he called…? Left here. I couldn't wait all night for me husband to call for me. And now he seems to have vanished…'

'What was he wearing?'

With difficulty they wrung a description from the angry woman. She seemed more furious than anxious. How dared Ishmael Lott not turn in at a reasonable hour? How dared he disappear?

'I think he might have been drinkin' at the meetin' and, as like as not, he was a bit afraid to come home…' Judkin rang off at last.

'What do we do? Ring the hospitals and then put out a nation-wide call? I suppose it's something to do with Harry Dodd. To hell with Harry Dodd!'

'If I were you, I'd send somebody out to bring in Battersbee. If he was there when Lott arrived and found the shop closed, he'll perhaps be able to say what happened.'

'Good idea!'

In ten minutes the constable sent to get Battersbee, was back with his quarry. Battersbee was a pasty-faced, weedy man, with two or three days' growth of black beard, a long beak of a nose, and a face lined with bitterness and ill-health. He was tall, but stood half-bent, as though to straighten himself would tear his chest. He was still smoking, and now and then gave a hollow cough without removing his cigarette. He kept on his greasy slouch hat and blinked his black, button eyes at the light.

'What's the game?' he said. 'What's the meanin' of this? I've done nothin'. It's just another piece of officiousness… I'll…'

'Shut your mouth, Battersbee! Nobody's accused you of anything. We only want a bit of help...' Judkin evidently knew the requisite technique.

That suited Battersbee. A measure of confidence returned, and he started to be cocky.

'So that's it. You want something, do you? What about me? I want a hell of a lot! To start with, what about a cup of tea, coffee, or cocoa? I don't like being got out in the middle of the night. You're lucky I don't ask for a whisky and soda.'

The constable who'd brought him in also knew how to handle him.

'Shut your trap, Battersbee, and take off yer hat when you speak to police officials...'

Battersbee looked the burly bobby up and down, as though wondering whether or not to try conclusions with him. Then he took off his hat, revealing a long, narrow forehead, receding black hair, and a red line where the hat had bitten in his brow.

'Well... Get it over'

Littlejohn took a hand. He gave Battersbee a cigarette and lit it for him.

'Now, Mr Battersbee. You've been under the lamp by Lott's corn-stores all night, haven't you?'

'Nothing wrong with that? It's a free country... or is it?'

'You were there when I called over an hour ago, and you were there when I came out.'

'Yes. And I was there while you were inside, and when Lott called, too.'

'What do you mean?'

'While you were in, Lott turned up. "Evenin', Jim," he sez to me. "Still proppin' up the lamp?" "Yes," I sez. "More than you'll be doin' soon." When he asks what I mean, I tell him, see? I tell him the police are in with his missis.'

'How did you know me?'

'Wot, with your picture in the *Helstonbury Gazette* only this mornin'! I wanted to see old Lott squirm. And, by God, he did! He took to his heels and ran like 'ell...'

Battersbee laughed and coughed and spat at the thought of it.

'You should 'ave seen him...'

'Which way did he go?'

'He went to his garage behind, took out the light lorry, and drove off as if all 'ell was after 'im...'

They quickly got rid of Battersbee. They'd more to do than drag any more information from him.

'He's mixed up in Harry Dodd's death,' said Littlejohn, 'and he thinks we're on his trail and has bolted. We'd better send out a message to all police in the locality to stop and hold him.'

They hadn't to wait long.

At midnight the Lowestoft police telephoned. Ishmael Lott had tried to board Pharaoh's boat, the *Betsy Jane*, had been spotted by a dock policeman, had proved rough, and had been hit with a truncheon and put in the cells to cool off.

'We searched him,' said the officer at Lowestoft. 'He'd a bodybelt strapped round his waist with ten thousand in five-pound notes in it...'

15

THE TRAGEDY OF ISHMAEL LOTT

They were bringing Ishmael Lott back to Helstonbury from Lowestoft at noon, but before he arrived, Littlejohn had much to do. He spent the morning telephoning various London offices from the list of securities on his cigarette packet.

'Is that the registered office of the Amalgamated Brass Industries? Scotland Yard here...'

And so on, at the registrars, or their agents, of Belang, Freifontein, Associated Nickel...

'Have any shares in the name of Harry Dodd or of Ishmael Lott been registered with you?'

The same reply every time. They looked back for six years, as Littlejohn suggested, but there was nothing on their books.

Some of them got a bit fussy, too. Their books were confidential. Littlejohn's authority and persuasiveness, however, won in the end. The last on the list, Ruritanian Concentrated Oils Ltd, brought results. All the others had suggested that Harry Dodd might have speculated on margins and taken profit or loss without registering his shares at all. But he'd bought and registered a hundred Ruritanians; and so had Ishmael Lott.

'He held them three months, then sold. They cost about five

hundred pounds and he netted a cool five hundred on the deal. You see, the company was prospecting for new wells and struck it rich. Lucky he got out when he did. The dictator of Ruritania nationalised the oil three weeks after... Eh?'

'Were the transfers marked by a broker?'

'I'll have to ring you back. I'll try to find them. We're not really interested in Concentrated now they've been confiscated...'

An hour later the registrar was back. The stock had been bought through Everit, Byle and Co, Cornhill.

Everit, Byle and Co weren't very helpful at first. They didn't, they said, supply information about clients to strangers, especially over the telephone. The voice was a lazy, drawling one, but it was stung into activity when Littlejohn reminded it that Harry Dodd had been murdered, that the information was in the interests of justice, and that an official from Scotland Yard or the Public Prosecutor's Office would shortly be calling on Messrs Everit or Byle, or both of them...

Did the Inspector mind holding on till the drawling man got the ledger?

Yes. Mr Harry Dodd had, over six years, shown an uncanny insight into the ups and downs of the stock and share markets and had, in all, netted about five thousand a year in so doing. Now and then he'd lost, but on balance he must have made over twenty-five thousand pounds, all told. Mr Ishmael Lott? Yes; they'd worked together apparently. But Mr Lott had had a bad setback or two. Lost quite a packet on Persian Asbestos when the bottom fell out of them after the assassination of the chairman and vice-chairman at the general meeting in Tehran... Don't mention it. Always ready to help the police...

Mr Lott arrived on time in a police car. He was in poor shape. In his pugilistic effort to board the *Betsy Jane*, he'd lost one of his rabbit teeth and got himself a swollen lip. He also needed a shave. He looked like a shrimp beside the huge constable in charge of him. About five feet six or seven, with thin arms and legs. His trousers were braced too high and his ankles looked like drumsticks entering his shoes. His suit was too large for him, as though he'd shrunk in the night, or else that Mrs Lott had bought it for him, like a mother fitting up a growing boy and leaving room for him to fill it up.

As soon as he saw Littlejohn, Mr Lott rushed to him. The attendant constable lumbered after him and seized him by the coat collar.

''Ere…'

'I only wanted to appeal to the Inspector. He knows me. You know me, don't you, Inspector?'

'Of course I do. I want to talk to you about quite a lot of things.'

Mr Lott looked ready to break down.

'I don't feel like talking. I'm all mixed up. I can't collect my thoughts with all this crowd. Besides, they took my money. It's my own. I didn't steal it. I swear.'

'I know it's your own, Mr Lott. You'll get it back in due course.'

''E's got 'is receipt. What's 'e botherin' about?'

The guardian bobby sounded annoyed. It might have been a couple of pounds, instead of ten thousand, of which they'd relieved poor Lott.

'Have you had your lunch, Mr Lott?'

Judkin and the constable looked at Littlejohn as though he'd gone mad. Here was a little bloke who'd, as likely as not, murdered Harry Dodd and taken his money. And the Scotland Yard man was bothering about food!

'I don't feel hungry.'

'I'm not surprised!' muttered Judkin, eyeing the miserable little corn merchant.

'All the same, you'll have a bite with me. We can talk better.'

There was another room in the police station where Judkin dined as a rule. It smelled of soot, and a burst pipe in the winter had stained the ceiling. There must have been, at one time, huge pictures on the walls, for the paper was faded, leaving large rectangles the original colour. Somebody had worked a division sum in pencil in one of the rectangles, and another bore a grim warning: *Caution, gas pipe behind here*, with a break in the plaster to show that the message had been born of experience.

Drane, with many excuses and polite exclamations, brought food from the canteen.

'Get on with it, Mr Lott,' said Littlejohn. 'It'll make you feel better...'

In reply, Mr Lott carefully laid down his knife and fork, put his head in his hands, and burst into tears. His body heaved with his emotion and he choked with weeping.

'I'm sorry. I felt touched. I haven't a friend in the world since Harry Dodd died. Yore kindness just moved me, sir.'

'You see, Mr Lott, I know a good deal more about you than the others. I know exactly what you and Dodd did together, but you'll have to answer some questions before I can help you.'

'Anything, Inspector, anything...'

'Get on with your meal, then, sir, and we'll talk after it.'

Drane was too polite to express amazement when he saw Littlejohn and Lott smoking cigarettes together when the Inspector ordered coffee.

'And now, Mr Lott. Will you tell me what you were doing and where you were on the night Harry Dodd died?'

'You don't... I never... You don't mean I killed him?'

'That's the first question, and I want it settling before we go any further.'

'I didn't do it, Inspector. I was at home. My wife and daughter will tell you that. Yes, and my wife's cousin Abel from Exeter, who was staying with us at the time, can tell you. We were papering the sitting-room that night. My wife wanted it done, and what did Abel do but go and buy the paper and paste and start doing it. Got himself in a horrible mess with it. We 'ad to start all over again when I got in. Of course, my wife blamed it all on me, for not getting it done myself before Abel arrived. I can never do the right thing, you know.'

'Just give me Abel's address, will you?'

'Abel Birtwhistle, Itlldo, Parracombe Road, Exeter.' Littlejohn could imagine cousin Abel and his Itlldo! The Johnny Know-all, papering himself as well as the walls!

'And now, sir. You and Harry Dodd seem to have made quite a lot of money between you…'

Lott had been pale, but he now grew leaden. He looked like having a seizure.

'You didn't tell my missus, did you?'

'No.'

'For pity's sake don't. If she gets to know, I'll gas myself. I swear I will. That money's all there is between me and destruction. I can't stand it anymore.'

'Tell me about it.'

'About six years since, Dodd came in my shop for a budgerigar for his… for the woman he was livin' with at Brande. Then he started calling for bird seed for it. We got a bit chummy, and one day the talk turned to investments, and I showed him my graphs. He was quite took-up with 'em. So much so, that when I told him I did it for fun, and not profit, he said he'd like a proper try. It ended by him havin' a flutter. He was damn' good at finance. Shrewd, that's what Harry was. Do you know what he did? He made five hundred, cool, on his first deal, and he gave the profit to me. "That's a sort of royalty on your system, Lott," he says. "Now we'll start level. Five hundred apiece." I reckoned he made between twenty and thirty thousand on it, from start to finish. Mind you, he was lucky. Never knew anybody luckier. A fortnight after we'd bought Cornelian Stores, for instance, they sold out to Mammoths at three pounds for a ten-shilling share, and we'd bought at eleven and six…'

'And you, in your business deals, got to know Dodd's middle name?'

'Yes. What's that to do with it?'

'He never used it normally, but you put it on the card on the Free Fishers' wreath for his funeral.'

'Yes, I did, didn't I?'

He bared his rabbit teeth and smiled blankly.

There was a sudden commotion in the outer office. Mrs Lott had arrived, and her shrill voice could be heard demanding to see Lott.

'You've got 'im in there, I know. You can't stop me seein' him. I know my habeas corpus… I'll get my lawyer…'

'In heaven's name, don't let her get at me!' begged Lott.

'We're busy,' said Littlejohn to the sergeant, who entered with a red face. 'He can't be seen now.'

Lott crouched beneath the table as his wife passed the window of the room. He was terrified of her.

'I can't bear it… Dodd and I kept it secret. He put his cash in a safe deposit in London, because he didn't want his family to know. You see, they made him an allowance, although I understand he wasn't really entitled to it. If they'd got to know of his money, they might have stopped it. As for me… I kept it on me night and day. I had a belt with pockets in it. I was scared if I put it in a bank, or even hid it, *she'd* find out.'

'I see.'

Lott showed anger for the first time. He leapt to his feet and thumped his narrow chest.

'No, you don't see at all. Do you know I went to a public school and had two years at a University? Now look at me. Selling pints of peas and meal in a shop! My dad wanted me to go in the church. With a bit of luck I might have been a vicar somewhere now… or even a bishop. Instead, I put my wife in the family way before I married her. Her father kept a pub and she was at the bar. A crowd of us from college went there once on a spree. I drank too much, and next morning I found myself in bed with Emmeline. Her father was wanting to get her off his hands, and mine was a tartar for doing the right thing, and the way of transgressors was hard. They saw that we got married…'

Lott's eyes were wild, his hair dishevelled, and two bright hectic spots glowed on his cheeks.

'I hate her. And I hate the daughter I begot in my folly, because she's just like her mother. As soon as we were married, my wife took control. My father died, heartbroken, I reckon, not long after. What should have been the Rev Ishmael Lott started to deal in guinea-pigs, white mice and bird seed! I made a mess of it. I lost money and went bust. My wife, with money from her family, which she'd clung to like a leech, bought the shop from my creditors and I became her hireling, except that I didn't get wages; just spending money…'

He took three shillings and a few coppers from his pocket and flung them fiercely on the table.

'That's what I've got left till pay day tomorrow, when I draw twelve and six. The rest, she says, she keeps because I ought to be supporting her and her daughter.'

His face lit as he contemplated what was coming. He continued with a burst of enthusiasm.

'That's where Dodd and his help came in. I could never have laid my hands on enough to try out my stock exchange system. Harry found it for me. I lost quite a bit, though, through my own stupidity and eagerness to make money. Three times Harry got out just at the right time. I hung on and came a cropper. All the same, I made over ten thousand. I wanted fifteen and then I was going to vanish. I was going to leave Emmeline and her brat with the shop and go and live a life of peace and quiet on my own.'

'And then?'

'Last night, after the evening at the Free Fishers, which my wife let me join, by the way, because it was good for business, I called for her at the shop. Battersbee, a queer chap who spends his time hanging round the lamp near the shop every night, stopped me. "The police are in there with your wife, and they're turning the place upside down," he said. I panicked. I knew you were on the Dodd case and I thought you'd found out about our syndicate. I thought you'd told my wife. So I cleared out. The first thing I thought of was to get to sea. I could sail round to one of the northern ports, or even abroad, without being seen on the roads or the railway or buses. I know how you track people down these days. I went in the van to five miles from Lowestoft. Then I parked the van up a quiet lane and walked the rest. I'd seen in the paper about Pharaoh's boat being there, and now that he was dead, as likely as not idle. I knew which it was, because in the summer the Free Fishers took the kids to Lowestoft for a day's outing, and Pharaoh lent us the boat and his man for excursions. I went for the boat and ran right into a dock policeman. I was so desperate that I got rough, and he got rough, too… That's all.'

He looked at Littlejohn like a dog about to receive a beating.

'What'll happen to me? They won't take my money, will they? My wife needn't know, need she? Then, one day, I'll just slip off quietly and leave her. It'll be better that way. We hate one another.'

'If you get clear of the Dodd case, you'll probably be fined twenty shillings for trespass, and five pounds for violence to a policeman. I shan't tell your wife about the money; neither will the rest of the police. That's not our business…'

'Thank God!'

Ishmael Lott rose as he said it, and it was like a heartfelt prayer.

'There are one or two other things, though. Did you and Dodd spend a lot of time together?'

'Yes. Every Friday when he came shopping in town, and often on market days, Wednesdays, when he brought his women to the films. We went in the cellar and worked out our business and then laid the orders with the brokers.'

'Did he talk much about other things. For example, did he ever say what he wanted all the money for?'

'Obligations, as he called them. He said he'd enough to keep himself, but he had commitments.'

'What were they?'

Lott looked sheepish.

'He didn't tell me this. I found it out myself. You see, we have three lorries and a van which go all round the countryside and, well, you hear things, don't you? I go with one of the lorries three times a week. I pick up gossip...'

'Such as?'

'There's a woman at *The Aching Man*, for instance. Some of the farmers round there told me that Harry spent a lot of time there on and off. There's also a kid there, and her mother, the owner of the place, isn't married. I did hear you mightn't need to look farther than Harry Dodd to know who's her father. Dodd's been at *The Aching Man* more of late. It was said he might be planning to leave his two women in Brande and go and live with the Boones.'

'How do you know that?'

'We collect corn from farms round there. The farmers often spend a night drinking at *The Aching Man*. There's not much they miss.'

'Do you ever call there yourself?'

'I've been once or twice. We've stopped for bread and cheese and a pint on our rounds. It's a convenient spot and the limit of our territory. I've seen the girl, Peg Boone. She's a good-looker and no mistake. Can't say I blame Harry.'

He looked a bit furtively at Littlejohn, sneaking desire bred of long repression in his eyes.

'It's a well-known calling-place, then?'

'Yes. Harry isn't the only Dodd who's a customer. From what I hear, his son shares his admiration for Peg...'

'Wait! Which one is this?'

'The young 'un, Peter. It's one of his calling-places, too. I've seen his car there at night. We had a breakdown up there once and didn't get going till nearly eleven. My old woman nearly killed me when I got in. We stopped for a drink at *The Aching Man* on our way home. Young Dodd's car was there, but he wasn't in the public room. He'd be a special.'

'What kind of a car is it?'

'A little black MG, with a row of club badges on it. I'd know it anywhere.'

'Does young Peter come to Helstonbury a lot, then?'

'I've seen him around now and then. Perhaps he's been to see his dad, or Mr Pharaoh, who handled Dodd's affairs. I guess Peter looked after the family interests.'

'Did Harry ever mention to you going back to live with his divorced wife, or getting even with his family?'

'No. I should think that 'ud be the last thing Harry would do. He was very conscious of having done badly by them and was hardly likely to inflict himself on 'em again. He had affection for his wife and Peter, who, I must say, treated his dad quite decently, calling to see him when the rest of the family wouldn't recognise him. I never heard him mention going home again, though one time he did say he was fed up with the Brande set-up. Dorothy, he said, was too young for him and bored with him, and as for her mother… well… she just got on Harry's nerves.'

Lott rose anxiously.

'Is that all? Have I to go back to gaol, or what? I don't want bail. I'd rather be in prison than face my old woman after this. If they grant me bail, I'll go to a hotel.'

'They'll take you back now. Your case will be heard tomorrow most likely, before the magistrates, and finished with. Don't leave the neighbourhood until I say you can.'

'Very well. I'm much obliged to you, sir, for the kind and understanding way you've dealt with me. I'll not forget you for this.'

Ishmael Lott was taken back to Lowestoft to answer his petty charges next day. Fined and released, he was claimed by his wife as he left the court-house and taken home.

16

THE ACHING MAN AGAIN

On their way to *The Aching Man* again, Littlejohn and Cromwell called at the county asylum in search of Mr Glass, Walter Dodd's former friend and fellow inmate. Mr Glass was in his old place, gingerly weeding with a long hoe, the small patch of garden which he seemed to have made his own.

'Hello! Hello, Oliver!' he called to Cromwell, who whispered to his chief that Mr Glass had invented a nickname for him.

'Hello, Mr Glass. How's the garden coming on?'

'You've not come all this way to ask me that. What are you after now? Don't come too near me…'

'I just wanted to ask you something about when Walter Dodd came back from his motor trip… the one where they had the accident. Did he say anything about it?'

'As I said before, he hadn't anything to say. He was scared by what had happened. He seemed a bit mad with his son for the accident. As if Harry had done it all. As I said to him, "Walter," I sez, "Walter, you don't want to take on so. Harry wasn't to blame." But the old man kept on saying, "I can't believe that my own flesh and blood…" just like that he said it, as if he was talking to himself.'

'Is that all?' asked Littlejohn from the car where he had been listening to the talk.

'That's all, as God's my judge. Should there be anything more?'

'No. What you've told us is very useful. Thanks for your help.'

They left cigarettes and drove away quietly, Littlejohn grave and thoughtful, and Cromwell still puzzling out what Mr Glass had told them.

'Is there anything in it?'

'There may be quite a lot. It remains to be seen how things develop.'

The Aching Man was open. A few walkers and one or two lorry drivers were in the bar, drinking beer. Sid Boone was attending to them. He frowned as the detectives entered.

'You here again?' he said, coming round the counter and meeting Littlejohn and Cromwell on the threshold. 'I wish you'd get this affair finished and leave us alone. It's not good for the business always having police hangin' round the place.'

'Must be your guilty conscience, Sid,' answered Littlejohn. 'Nobody knows we're police.'

'Don't they? Some of these blokes can smell a copper miles off. What do you want this time?'

'Is your sister in?'

Peg was upstairs, and Sid crossed to the foot of the staircase and called.

'Peg! Friends of yours want to see you again.'

He left them standing there after she had answered she was coming. They could hear somebody moving about. Then a small rubber ball ran along the landing, struck the stairs and bounced slowly down, step by step, and rolled to Littlejohn's feet. It was followed by a small slip of a child as pretty as a picture.

Unlike her mother, Nancy was fair, with a crop of close-cut golden hair, china-blue eyes, a solemn oval face and a tiny, well-shaped mouth. Her ears were small, delicately made, and well set back, her brow was broad, and the hair grew to a small point over it, known colloquially as a widow's peak. She descended step by step, and Littlejohn gazed at her with astonished admiration. Cromwell, catching his chief's grave and kindly look, thought Littlejohn was reminded of his own child, the only one, who had died at about Nancy's age, and brought tragedy to an otherwise ideal union.

'Did you see my ball?'

Nancy looked up at Littlejohn, and he awoke from his reverie and picked it up.

'Are you Nancy?'

'Yes. Who are you?'

'My name's Littlejohn, Nancy.'

'Do you know Robin Hood...?'

The question remained unanswered, for Peg Boone appeared at the stair head, furiously watching the little meeting below.

'Nancy... What are you doing there? Haven't I told you never to go down there when the house is open. Come right back at once...'

She ran down and roughly hustled the child back upstairs and into what must have been a playroom again. The child tried to explain, but Peg did not listen. She hurried back to join the officers.

'She's not allowed downstairs while the place is open. I don't want her meeting our type of customers. It's bad enough her having to live on licensed premises, without mixing with all the rag-tag and bob-tail who come drinking here and mauling her...'

Her anger was slowly dying down, but somehow the intrusion of the child had made her uneasy.

'What can I do for you? I thought you'd finished with us.'

'So we have, Peg. Except for one thing. Did you know Harry Dodd had left you money in his will?'

'No. What's all this about?'

She was still uneasy. She didn't ask them inside but kept them standing in the dark hall.

'Harry Dodd's will has been lost or stolen, but a copy has been found. He left you quite a sum, from all accounts. Around twenty thousand pounds!'

They couldn't see her face plainly, but it was obvious from the way she recoiled that she'd had a shock.

'I don't believe it! He never told me about that. Why should he leave all that to me?'

Littlejohn shrugged his shoulders.

'Nancy, I guess, and, of course, if he was your lover and thought a lot about you...'

'Yes... That might be it. That would be it...'

She seemed doubtful and then suddenly emphasised it.

'Yes. That *would* be it.'

'Could we have a word in your private quarters? It's a bit public here.'

'Of course, if you've something on your mind.'

They went in the room where, a day or two since, they'd sat cosily by the fire. Now the fire was out, the embers were scattered about the hearth, the place was untidy. A bottle or two and a couple of dirty glasses on the table, an ash-tray full of fag-ends and ash. It felt cold and damp, and, unlike their previous conversation, the present interview was also cold and damp. Peg seemed to have lost her interest and vitality. A funny kind of reception for news of inheriting twenty thousand pounds. Peg looked quite glum and preoccupied about it.

'Do you know Peter Dodd, Harry's son?'

Cromwell looked up. He half expected another battle of wits and endurance, like the previous one between Littlejohn and Peg. But there was nothing of that kind. In fact, Littlejohn himself seemed preoccupied and unhappy about the whole affair.

'I may have met him. Harry never brought him here.'

'But he called here from time to time, all the same. His car used to stand outside some nights whilst he had a drink with you and Sid, or perhaps you alone, indoors. That's so, isn't it?'

'He was a customer. After all, he didn't live far away, and most people nearby pass and have a drink sometimes.'

'Do they, Peg? But Peter didn't only come for drinks, did he? He came to see you, too. Like father, like son. The pair of them were fond of you, weren't they?'

'No need to be offensive.'

'It's the truth, Peg. Did Peter know about Nancy?'

'I don't know. I never asked him.'

'That's not true, you know. Why keep trying to put me off, Peg? Why don't you tell the truth? Peter was in love with you as well as his father, wasn't he? Did he ever ask you to marry him?'

'You seem to know all about it. Why ask me?'

'Because I want to learn all I can about the late Harry Dodd. Was Peter his father's rival, then?'

'No, he wasn't. If you're thinking Peter wanted to do his father harm because of me, you're barking up the wrong tree. Peter was fond of his father. He was the only one of the family who stood by him. If you want to know, Peter did ask me to marry him. He did know about Nancy. He also knew his father was thinking of going back home and that Nancy might be an embarrassment. He tried to do the right thing. He asked me to marry him to right the wrong his father did, and make Nancy as near legitimate as we could, and give her a better home than this, with a proper father to look after her…'

Littlejohn removed his pipe.

'And what did you say, Peg?'

'I don't like your tone, Inspector. You sound as if you didn't believe me.'

'What did you say, Peg?'

'I said I'd think it over. Before I decided, Harry was killed.'

'And who killed Harry?'

'How should I know? I didn't. I've got an alibi… And I don't like this talk. I'm going about my business. I've plenty to do, if you haven't.'

'Have you seen Peter lately?'

'No. He's had no time, on account of family troubles. In any case, now that his dad's out of the way, Nancy won't be an embarrassment any more. Things might have changed.'

'That is so. Very well, Peg. If you've no more to tell us, we'll be on our way...'

They drove back to the outskirts of Cambridge, where Littlejohn wished to have another word with Mrs Harry Dodd. She was calmly doing needlework in a small morning-room when the Inspector entered.

'Good morning, Inspector. Won't you sit down...? This is my own little room. I work here when I've things to do, and I keep all my memories and mementos about me in it...'

There were framed photographs on the walls; a perfect picture-gallery of them. The children at various ages and one or two family groups, some of which included Harry Dodd, *paterfamilias* Harry, surrounded by his brood. Mrs Dodd seated, Harry standing by her side, Peter in arms and Winfield and his sister one at each end, with the whole ornamented by two large palms in huge plant-pots. Littlejohn crossed and examined them one by one. Although the Dodd children had grown into dark adults, and Winfield's hair had fallen out, leaving a bald dome, all of them were fair in childhood.

'Bonny children, weren't they, Mrs Dodd?' said the Inspector.

'Yes. They said they took after me. I was fair-haired before it went white. My husband was, of course, brown... a trifle gingery... None of them had his colouring. They went darker as they grew older. You'd hardly recognise any of them as the same people as those on the pictures, would you?'

'No. They've changed, madam. This, I take it, is Lady Hosea?'

'Cynthia; yes. She was such a pretty little thing. Now, I'm afraid, the strange life she leads with her husband has left its impress her features. She's got a vacant look. I've no doubt it's through listening to Bernard's eccentric twaddle. To be forever trying to make head or tail of his fantastic talk must give her that undecided, puzzled look she's assumed since they were married. He's a poet, you know, and has written quite a number of macabre stories for the reviews, which, I believe, are much appreciated in very select coteries...'

She spoke quietly and ironically, rather enjoying the thought of her comic son-in-law.

Littlejohn was fascinated by the photographs of Lady Hosea as a child. Mrs Dodd noticed it.

'Cynthia seems to have impressed you. She was a nice little thing. I shouldn't say it, but I have a picture of myself, a miniature, it is, and as a child she was the image of myself at that age.'

And Peg Boone's child was the image of Cynthia when she was Nancy's age!

In other words, although she was Harry Dodd's child, she resembled Mrs Dodd!

Littlejohn sat on a low chair on the opposite side of the fireplace from the old lady.

'Smoke your pipe, if you wish, Inspector. It makes me feel a tyrant seeing you hugging the cold bowl.'

'I'll be very pleased to, if you don't mind, Mrs Dodd.' He felt more at home with his pipe going.

'Now I'm quite sure you didn't call either to look at the family portrait gallery or to sit and smoke by the fire, Inspector. What is it that's worrying you?'

He was unhappy about it all. The serenity and kindness of Mrs Dodd, her gentle invulnerable way, her air of perfect breeding, all seemed so remote from the sordid murder of her late husband and the cowardly crime at Gale Cottage. He braced himself. It had to be said.

'Did you know, Mrs Dodd, of your late husband's connection with the Boones at *The Aching Man* public house on the Bath Road?'

'He did mention the place a time or two. There was a child

there he was sorry for. A sweet thing, he said, which oughtn't to be brought up in such surroundings…'

She looked at him steadily and he decided to avoid the final thrust as long as he could.

'By the way, your indisposition on the night your husband died… You know what caused it?'

'Yes. Peter made real coffee, instead of using the powder that agreed with me. It made the dog and me bilious. I had to go to bed.'

'Please don't think I'm suspicious of your behaviour, Mrs Dodd. Believe me, I only want to get a complete picture of what occurred in as many places as I can find, on the particular night. Now, you went to bed and your son, Peter, went to the doctor for some tablets?'

'Yes. I thought I'd a good supply by me, but the bottle was empty when Peter looked for it. He went round the corner to the doctor's for a fresh one.'

'What time would that be?'

'About nine… We had the coffee about eight and I was very seedy an hour later and went to bed.'

'And Peter hurried round the corner, got more medicine, and returned at once?'

'Very quickly… I fell asleep almost as soon as I got in bed, but it must only have been a short doze, for when next I woke, Peter was at the bedside with a couple of tablets and a glass of water for me. He apologised for being so long, he said. He'd gone right away in the car, but the doctor had some patients. The travelling clock at the bedside said nine forty-five, so he hadn't been unduly long away. I took the tablets, fell asleep, and by morning I was very much better.'

'I'm glad. One other thing, did your husband ever tell you he'd made a will?'

'We did talk of it the last time we met. He said if we came together again, he'd alter his will and leave all to me.'

'Did you need it, if you'll forgive my asking?'

'Not really. But I may as well tell you quite candidly that I've not much in the way of actual cash. Just after the war, the Sedgwick Engineering Company —my father was called Sedgwick — the Company was reorganised. With a view to avoiding considerable death duties on my death, a trust was formed of my shares. The beneficiaries under it were my three children and I enjoyed the income. Of course, had I needed any large sums, the trustees, my bankers, would have raised them, but my income is really in the nature of an annuity. Harry said that if he died, he'd like me to have such money as he had by him…'

'Do you know how much that was?'

'A few hundreds, I dare say. I didn't object. It was rather sweet and thoughtful of him.'

'It was over twenty thousand pounds!'

She was moved at last. She dropped the embroidery she was working, and her gentle hands fell in her lap.

'Impossible! The divorce almost beggared him, or so they told me.'

'It did at first. But Mr Dodd and a friend started to speculate on the Stock Exchange. His friend, a little corn merchant called Lott, had quite a flair for it, and your husband was rather good at finance himself. They made about five thousand pounds a year for many years.'

'You amaze me, Inspector! Where is all this money?'

'We don't know. We think it's in a strong box in a London safe deposit.'

'Incredible! No wonder he wanted to leave it to me. I fear I made light of his little savings. Poor Harry… Poor dear Harry.'

She wiped her eyes.

'Is Mr Peter in, madam?'

'No. He's gone to town to get his gun. It's being repaired, and the shooting season is here, you know.'

'I never enquired where Mr Peter worked. Is he in practice on his own, or…?'

'He's not doing anything at the moment. The war unsettled him. He was to have joined an old friend of ours, Tidmarsh, an old Cambridge firm, when he came from the army, but Mr Tidmarsh died whilst Peter was in North Africa and the firm was sold. They had no place for my son when he came home. He then tried starting a practice from scratch, but that fell through. He's not doing much just now but was talking the other day of finding a partnership somewhere. In fact, he has written to one or two solicitors who are seeking a junior man.'

'He has never married…?'

Mrs Dodd looked searchingly at Littlejohn.

'Oh, yes. He married. It was a war-time match. One of those quick, impulsive affairs. They hardly got on from the start and finally they separated. It's a pity, because he's still in love with her and she doesn't want him. She is living in London. A good business girl, who runs a dress shop in Mayfair. They were thrown together in London during the war and rather foolishly got entangled. Presumably she will divorce him one of these days on grounds of desertion…'

'Your doctor is Dr Macfarlane, did you say, Mrs Dodd?'

'No. My man is Dr Webb, but he lives some distance away. Peter called on Dr Macfarlane in his haste to get the tablets. He's got them there before. No; Macfarlane's not steady enough for me as a general rule. Too fond of the bottle.'

'Is he a friend of your son?'

'Yes. A lonely bachelor who lives with an old housekeeper and belongs to the same club as Peter in Cambridge.'

'They are clubmen, then?'

'It's a professional club. The Trevelyan… Peter lunches there when he's in town. He has a flat there, you know.'

'I mustn't take any more of your time, then, madam, but there's just one thing I must mention. It will be very painful for you, I've no doubt, but if we're to find your husband's murderer, this point must be raised...'

Mrs Dodd laid down her work and folded her hands in her lap.

'It sounds very serious, Inspector. What is it?'

The house was very still, and outside the room you could hear somebody, presumably the elderly maid, padding about on the thick carpet. The dog was asleep on a cushion and hadn't stirred since the Inspector arrived. The window overlooked the side of the house with a herbaceous border of withered plants and flowers, a dilapidated greenhouse, and some outbuildings badly in need of painting and repair. Mrs Dodd's capital was all locked up and it seemed, on the face of it, that the family didn't bother much about keeping the old home neat and trim. It was a pity Harry Dodd hadn't been able to come home and take matters in hand again.

Littlejohn filled and lit his pipe.

'Do you know much about the public house called *The Aching Man*, Mrs Dodd?'

'No, Inspector. Why should I?'

'I merely asked, because I wanted to tell you about the people there and some strange goings on.'

'Where is it exactly?'

'About three or four miles along the Bath Road after you leave the by-road leading to Gale Cottage.'

'I know it. I've passed it in the car, but I didn't know the name of it. How does the place enter into your affairs?'

'On the body of Mr Walter Dodd was a scrap of paper bearing the address of *The Aching Man*. We followed it up and there found a man, Sid Boone, running the place with his sister, Peg. Peg was a friend of your late husband.'

A look of amazement crossed Mrs Dodd's face, and, for the first time, she grew agitated.

'How did you discover...?'

'I insisted on knowing the connection between Mr Walter Dodd and the Boones. It came out that Mr Harry Dodd was their friend and, having taken his father from the asylum, he commended him to their care in case of need. One thing led to another, and we found your late husband was a frequent visitor there. He had known them a long time ago. As far back as when Peg, who is just past thirty, was a little girl.'

'Well?'

She was wide-eyed now, expecting the worst.

'There is a small child there; aged about four. Peg Boone told me who was the father...'

'No! No!'

It was as if Littlejohn had mentioned Harry Dodd's name already.

'Peg Boone said Harry Dodd was the father.'

'Not Harry! Not that! He *couldn't*. He wasn't that sort. That silly sordid little affair with Dorothy Nicholls; yes, in a moment perhaps of despair. A brief piece of stupidity, and then regrets. But not this. He surely would have told me when he wanted to come back home and settle with me again.'

'He talked of telling you, Peg Boone said. But she persuaded him not to do that. She said he would never get back home then, as you would never stand for it. Poor Harry Dodd even wanted to look after the child. He provided handsomely for Nancy; that's her name.'

'I can't believe it... This spoils all the happy thoughts I cherished even after Harry's death.'

She was too stricken to weep. Her face was set stony and pale.

'Peg Boone, she said, wanted your husband to return to his old life as a gentleman. She was ashamed that her child should live in a public house and be among such company. She wanted Nancy's father to be a gentleman. And that was her way of doing it. To persuade Harry Dodd to return to you.'

'It's a lie! She has made all this up. Some effort to get money… blackmail…'

Her eyes glowed as she found excuses, and then the light died again.

'But even then… even then, Harry must have been having an affair there. How else could she accuse him of being the father?'

'There might be an explanation. One occurs to me, but I've yet to test it and don't care to discuss it until after I've tried my theory.'

'Whatever shall I do if it's true? If the child is Harry's, someone ought to look after her, if she's living in such surroundings. Is she a nice child?'

'She is very sweet and has evidently been well brought up and properly cared for.'

'I could not possibly have anything to do with her, though…'

She was torn between her inclination and her duty.

'Please leave matters to me for the time being, Mrs Dodd. It may be more easily solved than we think. And now I must be going; I've much to do.'

'Thank you, Inspector, for being so candid and kind. Really, I don't know what I would have done without your understanding and sympathy in this sorry business.'

'I'll do what I can and let you know.'

'Meanwhile, I will not believe that Harry could do such a thing to me. Never! He was not that kind, and I believe that all will come right. His memory will be cleared.'

Littlejohn looked at her, and then at the pictures of the family groups on the walls.

'Yes. I believe you when you say Harry didn't betray you there. But, in clearing his name, we may have to cause you other distress and sorrow.'

'If my dear Harry's name is cleared and his memory unsullied, I can bear anything,' she said, and her face lit up with hope again.

17

HARRY DODD'S WILL

On the way back to Helstonbury, the detectives called on the Cambridge police, who had been checking the alibis in their own locality on behalf of Judkin. A polite Inspector informed them that those of the Dodd family, at least, seemed watertight, as well as those of the Boone pair.

'The county police went over Gale Cottage, too. We have the report here. There wasn't a single useful clue, except the piece of paper you found on the dead man; the address of *The Aching Man*. Whoever committed the crime made a nice clean job of it, sir.'

There was only one other calling place which intrigued Littlejohn. The Trevelyan Club, frequented by Peter Dodd and Dr Macfarlane, who had given him his alibi.

'Go in and see what you can find, Cromwell,' said Littlejohn. 'I'll sit outside and smoke my pipe and think the thing over.'

Cromwell left the car and mounted the steps of the club. It was housed in a large old mansion of the Queen Anne type, a magnificent survival of better times, the existence of which had been preserved by the fact that a number of gentlemen had bought it and started a club there about 1860. It was quiet and select and membership was strictly regulated. When Cromwell entered there was little going on. It was just before lunchtime and the rush hadn't started.

A uniformed flunkey was descending the dignified staircase. He cast a supercilious eye on the sergeant, who thereupon thrust his hands deep in his raincoat pockets and tried to look very official.

At the foot of the stairs a solemn precision timepiece with a large brass cylindrical pendulum, recorded 11.55; an important-looking barometer stood at *Fair*; and a notice on a baize-covered board announced that the main dining-room was undergoing decoration and that until further notice lunches would be served in the small assembly room. Pinned over the board a pair of chamois leather gloves awaited a claimant.

'Yes?'

The manservant raised enquiring, superior eyebrows. His breath smelled faintly of beer.

'I'd like to see the head steward, please.'

The man in uniform stooped, picked up a spent match, and carefully placed it in a large glass ash-tray.

'Sellin' somethin'?' he asked.

'No. Police.'

'Ho!'

He'd been in the force himself until he left on pension. He was a heavy, flat-footed sixteen-stoner, and had, during his five years of club life, absorbed many of the peculiarities of those he served. He was an insolent snob, but he knew when to climb down.

'Follow me... This way...'

They went into a small cubby-hole containing a desk and two cane chairs. It was an excuse for a room; you couldn't have whipped a cat round in it.

'Now, sir. You're not from the Cambridge force, if I may say so. One of the county lot?'

Cromwell drew himself up.

'Scotland Yard.'

The effect was comic. The man seemed to grow two inches less in height and girth. He might have been a criminal himself.

'I used ter be in the Midshire county police myself till I finished my time out,' he said humbly. 'I'm now 'ead steward here. Nice job.'

A young hall-boy thereupon intruded and thrust a cheeky face round the door, which you couldn't close properly if there were more than one in the headman's lair.

'Can you spare me a minute, Mr Ramsbottle?'

'No; I can't. I'm busy. Be off.'

He turned upon the interloper and showed that although he was humble before his betters, his underlings had better look out.

'But…'

'Be h'off!'

'Now, sir. What can I do for Scotland Yard? A rare thing seein' any of you gentlemen here. We've got a first-rate CID in Cambridge.'

'I know. I'm on the Dodd case in Helstonbury.'

Mr Ramsbottle whistled.

'Blimey! Are you now. How can I help?'

'If you're an ex-policeman, you can be discreet. Be discreet now, Mr Ramsbottle, and I'll be much obliged. You have a member called Macfarlane. Dr Macfarlane, I believe. What can you tell me about him?'

'Quite a lot, sir. He comes here regular. A bachelor, as finds our dinin'-room very convenient for his meals. He's a bit careful with his money. The only tip he ever gives is a bob to the staff fund at Christmas. He's a reg'lar old soak, if you ask me.'

'I *am* asking you, Mr Ramsbottle…'

'Excuse me, sir. The name's Ramsbottom. Wot you heard was an impertinent joke on the name made by the younger element of this club. I'll make that little twerp… if you'll excuse the term… sit up when you've gone. I'll give 'im his cards and be rid of 'im. You were sayin'?'

'Dr Macfarlane... Is he a reliable sort?'

'Pardon my curiosity, but is the medical gentleman h'implicated?'

'No. We're checking alibis.'

'Hu! He's all right. Undoubted integrity, except when he's drunk, which is h'offen the case these days. He's on whisky, and it doesn't take 'im long to get blotto... if you'll h'excuse the term... He'll come in here to 'is lunch after his mornin' visits is over, and then sit an' drink solid till three. Then he'll have a little nap and wake up sober as a judge, an' go and kill off a few more of his pore patients. Hu, hu, hu...'

He shook like a jelly at his own joke and clung to the desktop for support.

'Does he also get drunk in the evenings?'

'Sometimes, if there's a little celebration.'

Cromwell consulted his little black book and firmly intoned the date of Harry Dodd's murder.

'Would there be a little celebration on that date?'

Mr Ramsbottom repeated the date several times to himself in an effort to conjure up events from the past. Then he gave it up and turned to consult a large diary which he dragged from a drawer in the desk after a terrific struggle to open it.

'Why, yes. There was a hell of a binge... if you'll excuse the expression...'

'Hell of a binge... Don't mind the language; I can take anything. What sort of a binge?'

'A Scotch gatherin'. 'Aggis, pipers, some Scotch dancers, the whole ruddy shootin' match. Whisky was, on the only occasion I h'ever remember, flowin' like water, if you understand wot I mean...'

He licked his lips and drew in his breath savagely as he remembered it.

'Yes. The Micishire County Hem Ho, that is, the Medical H'Officer of 'Ealth, was leavin' for a better post. The medical faculty gave 'im a hearty farewell. They gave 'im a dinner, there was speeches and presentations to the departin' gent and his missus, and, to honour them, they bein' from over the border, in a manner o' speakin', they gave 'em a Scotch send-off...'

'Which included Dr Macfarlane?'

'Like 'ell it did, if you'll forgive the h'expression. The doc got a right skinful, if you'll...'

'I will. He was drunk when he left?'

'In a cab... tight as a drum, if...'

'At what time?'

'Eight o'clock or thereabouts. You see, it was what you might call the doctors' off-night. No surgery. That's why they fixed it that way. So's they could all come. I suppose they left the sick to die that night, if you see my meanin'... Hu, hu, hu...'

He jellied again and clung to the chair for support like a drowning man.

'Did you see Peter Dodd here that night?'

'Let me see... He wouldn't be at the party, mind you. Medical gents and wives only. Exceptin' the Mayor and Health Chairman... And maybe one or two others...'

'All right, Mr Ramsbottom. Peter Dodd. Was he about the place?'

'Sure to be. Always calls for a whisky and soda before goin' home to his maw. About seven-thirty he leaves...'

'Did he see the state Macfarlane was in?'

'Bound to. Mr Peter goes in the smoke-room which is approached through the lesser h'assembly 'all, in which the party was goin' on. Likely as not, he'd see an' hear it all, if he was so minded. Like as not, there'd be a few comments, like "Ole Macfarlane's under the table agen", and so on, etcetera... Catch the doctor missin' a chance of a free load o' whisky...'

'Thanks for your help, then, Mr Ramsbottom. You're a typical ex-member of the force. Observant and helpful...'

Mr Ramsbottom drew himself up and took a deep breath of pleasure.

'Honoured sir. Honoured, I'm sure. And now, if that's all, I'll jest have time to give that young whippersnapper the rounds of the kitchen and tell 'im to collect 'is cards before lunch is served. Proud to 'ave been able to assist Scotland Yard. Very proud indeed…'

He seized Cromwell's hand, pumped it up and down, drew himself up, saluted, and tried to click his heels, an operation which was a miserable failure and made him lose his balance.

'A bit of useful news,' said Cromwell, as he re-joined his chief. And he told him what Mr Ramsbottom had imparted. As he unfolded his story, he could see through the club window, the ex-policeman denouncing his insubordinate underling and handing him his insurance cards…

'I must call on Macfarlane and go over the alibi again later.'

On the way back to Helstonbury, they passed Mon *Abri*, now a blackened ruin. The Nicholls women, with the help of Uncle Fred, were raking among the ashes, trying to salvage as much as they could. Mrs Nicholls was examining the contents of a charred wardrobe, turning out water-sodden garments and scuffling, with them like an old-clothes woman. She had a pair of corsets in her hand. Uncle Fred, apparently driven off his head by the calamity, was trying on what looked like one of Harry Dodd's fishing hats, whilst Dorothy roared with laughter at the sight of it, much too large, sagging over his ears. There was a lunatic air hanging over the whole sorry scene.

'Any luck?' asked Judkin when they turned in at the police station. He seemed to think that a stroke of chance rather than hard work would solve the mystery.

Joan Jump had been to London and back and brought away Harry Dodd's box from the safe deposit. It contained his will, leaving all he had to Nancy, daughter of Peg Boone, and there was also in the box a certificate for £25,000 War Loan. Harry had evidently invested all his gains and had appointed Mr Pharaoh sole trustee to handle them after his death.

'Which now leaves Peg with a nice income to draw for Nancy,' said Judkin, who had been instructed to that effect by the efficient Miss Jump.

'We're getting warmer,' said Littlejohn.

'Meaning what?'

'I'll tell you after I've had a word with Miss Jump.'

They rang up the lawyer's office and soon Mr Pharaoh's pretty partner was in the police station.

'Yes,' she said. 'Mr Harry Dodd was going to make a new will. I've found Mr Pharaoh's diary, which was in his desk instead of the safe. He's jotted down the main heads there. With the exception of a few legacies to friends, all he had was to go to his wife on his return to her.'

'According to what Mr Pharaoh told me, that will was already made. It must have been stolen from the safe,' said Littlejohn.

'What about the kid, then?' asked Judkin anxiously. 'I've no doubt Harry Dodd had an idea of adopting her himself.'

'What! Ask his missus to adopt his own kid by another woman?'

'When I've put one or two more ideas before you, it might be easier to follow...'

'I hope so. I've kids of my own and I don't like to see this little girl banged around in a dirty business like this.'

'After the accident in which Comfort was killed, old Walter Dodd said to his mates in the asylum: "My own flesh and blood", and wouldn't explain what he meant by it. Both he and Harry Dodd were scared by that accident, quite apart from the shock. Harry wouldn't say anything about it in the Coroner's Court. Does Walter Dodd's remark throw any light on Harry's behaviour?'

'Walter must have been disgusted at his own flesh and blood, that is Harry, involving him in such a calamity.'

'No, no. He couldn't blame Harry, if Comfort was driving. Besides, Harry was scared as well. He said he'd have to set his affairs in order. Did he mean that he didn't expect to last long naturally, or did he mean *he'd have to change his will to save his life?*'

Light broke on Judkin's face like clouds clearing before the sun.

'He meant that somebody was out to kill him!'

'Go on. And old Walter's comment?'

'His own flesh and blood! One of the family was trying to murder them. Which of 'em. Willie? Winfield? Peter?'

'Let's go one further. I've seen Nancy at the Boone's place. She doesn't resemble Harry Dodd in the slightest. And Peg was wild when Nancy escaped from up in her nursery and came down and showed herself to me. She's the image, not of Harry Dodd, but of *Mrs* Harry Dodd. And also of Harry Dodd's daughter, Lady Hosea, when she was Nancy's age.'

'But how can she be like Mrs Dodd? Peg Boone's the mother, I suppose.'

'Yes. But Nancy's the daughter of one of Mrs Dodd's children, not of Harry. That's how she comes to resemble Mrs Dodd. Is it the fantastic Lady Hosea, or the cold and proper Winfield, in a moment of forgetfulness and passion? Hardly likely. There remains Peter Dodd. Nancy's Peter's daughter and Peter is, or was, a frequenter of *The Aching Man*.'

Judkin, who had been leaning forward intent in his chair, flopped back and relaxed.

'Got him! At last we've got him. But I'm surprised! Peter! Good Lord, we've let him have the run of the place because he's a lawyer. Do I feel a fool…?'

'Not so fast. We haven't got him yet, by a long chalk. There's plenty of motive, theoretically… He's broke and wants the cash his father made. Peter was always in and out of Pharaoh's office. He must have learned about the money and the new will when he was talking over the business of his father and mother coming together again. Harry was going to change his will. Once he did that, adopted Nancy, and gave his wife all he'd got, Peter would have to whistle for his share of the cash he hoped to get out of Peg. I wonder how far she went in persuading Peter to murder his father… And now I'd better go along to Cambridge again and have a word with Dr Macfarlane about that alibi. If it's watertight, it will put Peter Dodd in the clear. But you'd better put a man on finding Peter Dodd, Judkin, and tell him to keep an eye on him. One breath of suspicion that we're after him and he'll bolt.'

'It's as good as done,' answered the Superintendent, and he bellowed for Drane at the top of his voice to show how intent he was.

The Scotland Yard man left Judkin irritating himself by gazing through the front window at the workmen engaged in building the new police office over the way and who, as was their wont, had just downed tools to drink their hourly cans of tea.

This time Littlejohn and Cromwell had a police car apiece, for whilst Littlejohn was interviewing Macfarlane, Cromwell was to make his way to *The Aching Man* and carry out a double check on the Boone alibis.

'We can't be too sure. That pair may be in the murders just as deeply as we think Peter is.'

Dr Macfarlane lived in a large old house two blocks away from the Dodd residence. 'No Afternoon Surgery', stated, a card pinned over a corroded brass plate on which consultation hours had once been engraved and now, from much cleaning and later neglect, had worn away. Littlejohn rang the bell.

An elderly woman, presumably the housekeeper, eventually answered the door. She eyed Littlejohn up and down.

'No afternoon surgery,' she said acidly. 'Is it an urgent call?'

'It is. Will you kindly hand my card to the doctor, if he's in.'

She took the card and eyed it, holding it closely to her face, for she had cataracts coming.

'He's just having his lunch. He was out late.'

'I'll wait.'

She bade Littlejohn enter and showed him into the waiting-room. It was bare and poorly furnished, smelled short of air, and the odour of iodine hung about it. Cheap wooden chairs all around the walls, old prints hanging from the picture-moulding, a hatch through which medicines were dispensed and prescriptions handed, and a large old-fashioned gas-fire hiding the fireplace. The floor was covered in cheap linoleum.

Littlejohn waited for a good half-hour. Meanwhile, there was not a sound in the house. Then, a door opened somewhere in the hinterland, and footsteps sounded. The doctor stood at the door. He was a little, clean-shaven, chubby man with white hair brushed back from a fine forehead. His complexion was ruddy, and his large nose, netted with fine purple veins, told of his disposition. His blue eyes were pale and liquid and protruded behind round, rimless spectacles.

'Well, sir,' he said. 'You want to see me, I believe. Sorry to keep you. I was detained on a case, and you found me in the middle of lunch.'

His meal must have been mainly liquid, for he breathed a strong blast of whisky over Littlejohn as he shook his hand.

'Scotland Yard, eh? We don't often get you chaps down here. What can I do for you?'

'It's about Mr Peter Dodd, sir.'

The doctor began to look irritable.

'I don't see why I should keep being bothered like this. The local police have already been checking Peter's account of where he was on the night of his father's death. I told them he was here and gave the times.'

'I called to confirm that, Doctor.'

Dr Macfarlane drew out one of the cheap chairs and straddled it. He looked to be having a job to make ends meet, for his suit, though neat, was threadbare, and there was a patch on one of his shoes.

'Is my word not good enough?'

'This is a murder case, sir, and we have to be quite sure.'

'But you surely don't suspect Peter of killing his own dad, do you?'

'This is purely a formality, but what we hear has made this second visit essential...'

The doctor's loose mouth opened, and his watery eyes flashed.

'Whatever you've heard can give you no reason for doubting my word. I'm a well-known man locally, I'm respected, and if Scotland Yard think I'm a liar, the police of Cambridge don't. Now get it out of your system, Inspector, and let me return to work.'

'Is it true that you were drunk on the night of the crime, Doctor, and that Peter Dodd found you in no condition either to know the time or even dispense properly?'

Macfarlane sprang to his feet, knocking over the chair, and started to bluster. There was little conviction in his tone, however.

'Of all the blasted impertinence! Who told you that, and how is the story justified?'

'I must apologise, Doctor, for the blunt way in which I'm having to put it, but I am determined to get to the bottom of this alibi. Is it true that you were out celebrating the departure from Cambridge of a medical colleague, and that you drank so much that you were sent home in a cab? I'm not concerned with anything but how this affected the alibi.'

'I did go to the farewell dinner. I did drink along with the rest. There were several toasts and we drank them in alcohol, of course.'

'You drank rather freely, I gather...'

The man's will or pride must have been totally undermined by his habits, for he looked more like one rebuked than insulted.

'We had a good time together. But you mustn't get the impression that they picked me up from under the table afterwards and heaved me in a cab, like a sack of coal. No, sir. I got up and went downstairs under my own steam and got quite steadily in the taxi.'

'There was no surgery that night?'

'No. That's what I'm driving at. Even if I did take a little too much in view of the occasion, I was able to take a suitable antidote of which I know, when I got in, sleep for a while, and then wake refreshed. I'm telling you this at considerable cost to my personal pride, for the sake of Peter Dodd. What I told the local police was true in every detail.'

'May we just go through it again to refresh our memories, sir?'

'Of course. Waste of time, though. Come in my room…'

They went into the surgery together. A distempered room, badly in need of redecorating. A large desk with a green-shaded table lamp on it. Cases of instruments, optical cards, a couch for examinations… The usual paraphernalia of a doctor's office. The framed diplomas on the walls showed high qualifications. Doctor of Medicine, Master of Surgery. Books all over the place. Macfarlane was one of the best doctors in the neighbourhood if he'd only mastered his one weakness. He was a lonely man who'd kept a large family of sisters and his mother until it was too late to marry and have children of his own. They'd died one by one of complaints he couldn't cure, and here he was, on his own…

'Like a drink?'

'No thank you, sir. I'm on duty, you see.'

'Mind if I do? I haven't finished my meal… And now; this alibi, Inspector. I had just wakened from my nap at about nine o'clock when young Dodd rang the bell. Maggie, my housekeeper, let him in. His mother was a little upset after taking coffee. That was all. I'd previously given him some tablets for it, and he wanted some more, as the rest had been thrown away apparently. Dodd stayed about a quarter of an hour. I recollect giving him a drink and being unable to partake myself, because of the antidote I'd taken to my earlier potations. It doesn't do to drink again after it…'

'You're quite sure it was about nine o'clock, sir?'

'Positively certain. I looked at my wrist-watch when I heard the bell ring. It was exactly ten past nine. The clock in the hall and the electric one there on the mantelpiece were at the same time. I booked the case, too. Look here...'

He crossed to a cabinet, took out a card after shuffling rather unsteadily through them, and handed it to Littlejohn.

Mrs Dodd. Then the address and a previous date. An entry about biliousness and the remedy. The price had been half a guinea. This was repeated again on the date of Harry Dodd's murder. Not only that, but as if to justify the entry of a guinea, there was a pencil comment. 'Night... 9.30', presumably noting an extra charge for after hours.

'I gave him the tablets and we sat for a bit. Then I let him out. I can't budge from that. It's what I said at the start, and I repeat it emphatically. There's another, too, who'll reassure you, if you don't believe me...'

He rang the bell by the fireplace and the housekeeper entered, peering at her master to see what he wanted.

'Maggie... Do you remember letting in Mr Peter Dodd the other night?'

'Yes...'

'What night was it?'

'Your half day. Why?'

'Would you have any idea of what time he called, Maggie?'

'Between nine and a quarter past nine. I remember I was a bit mad about it, because I was just listening to the news before goin' to bed. It was somethin' about the Queen, God bless 'er, and I said to myself, "You'll have to wait... go on ringing..." and I let him ring again till I'd heard what it was.'

'Do you remember how long Mr Dodd was here?'

'I left you to let him out, as I was just off to my bed after the news. I heard the door bang about half-past nine... Why are you asking me this?'

'It's all right, Maggie. Just a bet we're having. That's all, thank you.'

The old woman left, mumbling to herself in disapproval.

'So you see, what I said was right. I ought to be very angry about all this, but I'm not. I don't like young Dodd and never have liked him. I wouldn't put it past him to kill his own father and mother if it suited him. He's a loafer who won't settle down to work in spite of his qualifications, he sponges on his mother, he's in debt up and down the place because he spends as if he earned a huge income, he's generally disliked at the club and in town as a man who thinks the world owes him a living and he owes it nothing in return. I was Harry Dodd's doctor once upon a time. I liked Harry. We'd a lot in common and spent much of our time together here, smoking. He was good company when one was lonely. But I'm sorry I can't help you lay the finger on Peter for murder. He was here till nine-thirty, and he could never have got to Brande in time for the crime, if what the papers say is true and it was committed at ten o'clock.'

'Thank you very much, Doctor. I'm not disappointed, if that's what you mean. Our only aim is to get the right man, not anybody we can pin it on. You've helped immensely, and I'm very grateful.'

So it wasn't Peter Dodd who killed his father after all. Littlejohn felt a bit weary and fed-up as he started out for the rendezvous with Cromwell. He thought of Judkin's remark, smiled and repeated it.

'To hell with Harry Dodd!'

Dr Macfarlane passed him in haste as he slowly made his way back to the main road. He must have set out immediately on his rounds after the Inspector left him.

He was driving a grey Letchworth saloon!

18

THE RELUCTANT SPONSORS

The county police had the assurances of two sponsors that Peg Boone had served them with drinks between nine-thirty and closing time of the night of Harry Dodd's death. These they regarded as firm enough support for her alibi. At the same time, both men had stated that Sid Boone was also about *The Aching Man*.

Cromwell had the two names in his black book.

Enoch Shoofoot, Crabtree Farm, Helton.
Samuel Macey, Maltkiln Farm, Norton St Michael.

From an ordnance map, Cromwell knew exactly where he was going to look for the pair of them.

Crabtree Farm was about two miles along a by-road off the main Bath Road. It was a prosperous looking place, standing well back from the highway, approached by a long, well-kept drive. The house was a clean black-and-white structure, with a spread of new outhouses and cowsheds behind it. A pedigree herd was grazing in the field nearby, and far behind the house itself stretched acres of well-farmed, good-looking land.

Cromwell drew up in the cobbled courtyard and got out of his car. His progress had apparently been observed since he turned into the drive, and a large, cross-grained-looking man emerged from the tiled dairy and approached him. He had not missed the police sign on the car and wondered what he had been doing wrong. He let Cromwell speak first.

'Good morning. Mr Shoofoot… Mr Enoch Shoofoot?'

'That's me.'

A vulgar man who had made a lot of money by skill at his job and ruthlessness in the markets, good or bad. He was gross and considerably overweight. His great bull neck emerged in folds from his shirt, on which he wore a tie without a collar. There was a cloth cap on his head and beneath it a heavy, round face, livid with satisfied appetites, thick-lipped, button-nosed, shifty eyed. His enormous hairy chest showed through the slit in his shirt, his trousers were a tight fit, with the two top buttons undone. He was without jacket, and a piece of material had been let in the back of his waistcoat to allow for expansion. His legs were so heavy that he stood with them wide apart, like a great tree with twin roots firmly holding it to its own soil.

'You were at *The Aching Man*, Mr Shoofoot, between the hours of seven-thirty and ten on the night of September 2nd?'

'Yes. What's wrong with that? A man can relax and have a drink when he likes, can't he? This is a free country, ain't it?'

His voice was deep and husky, and he started each sentence in a roar and ended up short of breath. He wasn't going to live much longer by the looks of him, he would die hard, and need an outsize coffin and a quick burial, thought Cromwell, eyeing him over.

'You stated to the county police that Miss Boone was on the premises all the time. I've just called to check that.'

Shoofoot's face contracted in a grimace like that of an angry gorilla.

'I've said what I've said. Call me a liar. Go on, call me a liar. I don't let anybody, police or not, call me a liar.'

'Nobody's trying to call you a liar. All I want is...'

'Peg Boone's a fine woman. Nobody's goin' to insult a friend of mine. Enoch Shoofoot stands by his friends, and Peg's a friend o' mine.'

The very mention of her name filled his eyes with lust. Doubtless half the good-looking women of the countryside, and a lot more plain ones, had suffered the pesterings of Shoofoot at one time or another.

'Nobody's insulting any friend of yours. I'm only after the truth.'

'Well, I've already told it to the police. You're wasting your time.'

A tall, shrivelled woman, limping about with the help of a stick, came to the door of the farmhouse. She looked unhappily in the direction of Shoofoot, shading her eyes with her hand. Presumably it was the farmer's wife, long-suffering and anxious about her husband's activities. A chubby land-girl crossed the yard carrying milking machinery, and in spite of his wife's and Cromwell's presence, Shoofoot's pig-eyes followed her retreating figure lecherously, whilst the girl, aware of their scrutiny, strutted self-consciously into the cowshed.

'What did you tell the other police? I've not got it quite clear.'

Shoofoot, knowing his own strength, eyed Cromwell bellicosely, whilst the sergeant, equally aware of his own boxing skill, met the stare.

'I can't be wasting time tellin' my tale over and over again. I said it once and I say it again, I was at *The Aching Man* all night, an' Peg Boone was there talking with me...'

He bellowed it for the benefit of his wife and all who cared to listen, and some pigs in a sty, hearing the familiar voice, thought it was feeding-time and started to squeal.

Cromwell knew that unless he tried trickery, he wasn't going to get much farther.

'That's not what Macey said, anyhow. He said...' Shoofoot thrust his face close to Cromwell's and snorted like somebody snoring.

'Macey? An' what did Macey say? Macey and me both agreed about our tale. What's he been sayin' since, the little...'

Shoofoot emitted a string of obscene oaths and turned more livid. He called Macey all the names he could lay his tongue to.

Cromwell waited till it had all died down.

'You and Macey agreed to say that Peg was in the bar all the time. Actually, she wasn't. For a full hour at least, Sid was looking after you...'

'Macey said that, did he? Next time I see the little perisher I'll break every bone in his body...'

He grew incoherent, swearing and roaring in his rage. His wife and the land-girl each appeared at their separate doors to find out what it was all about, and Mrs Shoofoot, seeing what must have been one of her rivals, turned upon the girl and waved her angrily to get on with her work. The girl, with a toss of the head, took no heed.

'Peg Boone persuaded you to say she was there all the time.' Cromwell reeled it off, intent on his improvisation and spurred on by the fact that each shot struck home.

'There's going to be trouble when all this tale is aired in court. I suppose you know what perjury means, Mr Shoofoot.'

'Any more of your bloody lip and I'll chuck you off the place. I only said what I did because the police were pesterin' a friend of mine. She was upstairs puttin' the child in bed. But what did the police try to twist it to? What the hell did they try to twist it to... eh?'

He grimaced and tried to whirl his arms around pugnaciously, but his flesh was so heavy that he couldn't raise them higher than his shoulders. He passed a huge paw over his slobbering lips.

'They tried to make out that she'd been out with some chap or other. They tried to blacken the poor girl's good name. When anybody tries to do that, police or no police, they've got Enoch Shoofoot to deal with, an' I'm a man as stands no messin'… Ask anybody…'

'She told you she was putting the child in bed between half-past nine and half-past ten, when you left the place, did she?'

'Never you mind what she asked me. A favour asked of Shoofoot by a friend of his is as good as done. Ask anybody…'

Mrs Shoofoot, anxious about her husband's excited state, thought fit to intervene.

'Dad,' she called from where she was standing. 'Don't get worked up, Dad. Remember what the doctor said about your blood pressure…'

A look of concentrated hatred flooded Shoofoot's eyes and face.

'Shut your trap! Who asked you to interfere…?'

'The doctor…'

'To 'ell with him! I don't need women and doctors to tell me what to do. And as for you…'

He turned his attentions back to Cromwell.

'As for you…'

He told the sergeant to clear off in unprintable language. '…Or else I'll set the dog on you…'

As if fully understanding the threat, a large sheep-dog with a most benign face emerged with a rattle of chains from his kennel, eyed Cromwell, and cheerfully wagged his tail. This added fuel to Shoofoot's obscenities and fury.

'Gerrout, or I'll chuck you out.'

He made as if to put his threat into action and held out his large hands to seize Cromwell. The sergeant backed a pace, drew himself up, and thrust the palm of his hand in Shoofoot's middle, just where his paunch emerged like a balloon from the unfastened top buttons of his trousers. The farmer grunted, lost his balance, staggered back a few paces, struggling to recover, his eyes goggling, his legs making backward figures of eight. He came to rest against a great heap of ripe manure, standing in its own drainings like a large pudding in a plate of golden gravy, slid down, and sat in the fluid. His roarings as he beat the air mingled with the starting of the engine of Cromwell's car, the shrieks of the land-girl, the alarmed screams of Mrs Shoofoot, and the cries of pigs and startled hens. To this hearty send-off, Cromwell steered his car through the yard gates and made off for Maltkiln Farm before Shoofoot could recover sufficiently to warn his fellow sponsor and liar of what had been said.

Macey's Maltkiln Farm was as miserable as Shoofoot's was prosperous. This state of affairs embittered Macey, who was religious, and thought that God had made a mistake in making the wicked Shoofoot to flourish, whilst he, a deacon, had a mortgage on his farm and received letters nearly every day from the bank about the state of his account. He was in the yard tinkering ineffectively with a broken old tractor when Cromwell drew up. The roadside gate which gave access to the farm path was askew and rickety, and the road beyond full of potholes and bordered by rusty wire. A few scrawny hens were picking and taking dust baths and flew cackling away from the car. The telephone bell was ringing…

A masterful-looking fat woman, with her sleeves rolled up to her elbows, appeared at the door. She had a man's cloth cap on her head.

'Sam! Sam! Wanted on th'phone. It's Enoch Shoofoot, and he's in a proper tear.'

Cromwell leapt from the car and stood between the master and his house.

'I want a word with you, sir. Urgent.'

He made it sound terribly important and fatal. Macey paused to make up his mind and then, taking the chance of letting down his neighbour a peg, called back to his wife.

'Tell 'im I'm in the fields and you'll get me to ring 'im when I come in. Well...? What are you waitin' for? Tell 'im...'

The woman glared and went indoors, and you could hear her passing on the message and arguing. Cromwell could see that she might return and warn Macey or give him a message passed on by Shoofoot.

'I can't talk here with all this noise. Let's take a turn along the path a minute or two.'

Sam Macey was a small, bandy-legged man, dressed like a jockey. He wore horsy tweeds, riding breeches, and dirty hobnailed boots. His thin neck projected from his collar like a snake, and his head was almost the same diameter, which gave it the look of a nail sticking out from his chest. The eyes were pouched and sly, the nose long and narrow, the lips fanatically thin and cruel. His ears stuck out like the handles of a vase. He regarded Cromwell suspiciously.

'Are you from the Ministry of Food or the Agricultural Committee?'

'No; the police.'

Mr Macey jumped. His was a queer dual personality. He felt on Sundays that the inspiration given by singing lusty hymns at chapel, of praying at length before the congregation, of listening to the outpourings of 'brothers' in the faith, would speed him on his way, honest, pure in heart, and of good repute for the remaining six days. But he always fell by the wayside. He fell almost as soon as he got out of the meetinghouse and saw the shapely, buxom bodies of the choir girls, or when some black-marketer shuffled a wad of banknotes under his nose, or when, by night, he stole the mushrooms from Shoofoot's fields, which, although not of the same parish, adjoined his own. Mr Macey wrestled on his knees against such attractions of the world and the flesh and was unhappy whether he lost or won. His mixed emotions had made him an easy prey of Shoofoot, who led him into black-market and just like a lamb to the slaughter. Mr

Shoofoot fascinated Mr Macey by his evil, drew him like a moth to flame, filled him with hatred, disgust and admiration.

'I haven't done anything…'

He protested so much that Cromwell was sure that here was some hidden jiggery-pokery. The pale blue, shifty eyes searched Cromwell's face, then fell.

'I wasn't suggesting you had, Mr Macey. There has, however, been a mistake about an alibi you gave Miss Boone at *The Aching Man*…'

Macey scowled.

'Who says so?'

'Mr Shoofoot.'

'Have you been talkin' to Shoofoot? What's he bin sayin'?'

'That you both said she was in the room all the time on the night the police were enquiring about, whereas, that wasn't quite exact, was it?'

Cromwell's voice was like silk.

They had walked a little distance along the lane leading back to the road. This farm was less prosperous than Shoofoot's, although the soil and situation seemed the same to a novice like Cromwell. The will and ruthlessness were lacking. The yard was dirty and untidy, many of the cow-sheds and store-houses were mere shanties, the house needed a coat of paint.

'I'll bet there's a whacking mortgage on it,' thought Cromwell to himself. He was right. Shoofoot held it, and one false step by Macey, and Sam would be out, Enoch would be in, and the two adjacent farms would become one large one.

Back at the farm, the telephone bell was ringing again.

'Tell me, what did Shoofoot say?'

Macey was panting and sweating with fear and anxiety.

'He said that Miss Boone was away an hour, putting the child to bed, and that you both agreed that you could count that as being as if she were with you down in the bar… That right?'

'Well… Yes and no. I'm not much of a drinker. We'd both been to market and sold some cattle. Some of the other farmers were there, and we all got talkin' together. Between half-past seven an' eight, that 'ud be. My car was in dock and Shoofoot had taken me with him in his car to the mart. Once we got in *The Achin' Man* he just wouldn't leave. Stayed till closin' time. I had to wait for 'im, else walk home. I got snoozin' by the fire, because a couple of glasses of beer always makes me sleepy, me not touchin' it as a rule...' He looked a bit pious and a smug note came in his voice.

'So you simply confirmed the tale Shoofoot told?'

'Yes. I'd no reason to doubt his word, and he spoke up for Peg Boone when the police called on him, and then phoned me and told me they were cumin' to ask me the same, and said I'd better say what he said was true...'

The pale eyes searched Cromwell's face again, like one waiting for judgment.

'Sam!'

It was Mrs Macey, hurrying towards them, waving her podgy arms, shouting like a town-crier.

'Sam! Mrs Shoofoot's ringin'...'

She ran to meet her husband, spurred on by urgency, her heavy legs hardly leaving the ground.

Macey looked rattled. Wherever he went, whatever he did, his wife was after him, calling for a full account, taking him to task, always on his heels.

'Can't I have even a minute to myself...?'

She was too excited to listen.

'Mrs Shoofoot's just been on the telephone. When Shoofoot couldn't get you... or you wouldn't answer him, he set off to come here. She said to try an' find you, because Shoofoot's in a tearin' rage and...'

'Well? Wot of it? I'm not afraid of Shoofoot.'

He said it without conviction, and his large Adam's apple moved anxiously up and down his windpipe.

Mrs Macey could hardly get it out.

'If Enoch Shoofoot comes 'is usual way, he'll meet Thunder... Thunder's out in foxholes field now...'

Macey jumped again, this time almost a foot in the air. Cromwell did not need to ask about Thunder, for his bellow was already on the air. Across two fields they could see the gigantic, gross figure of Shoofoot, making his way to Macey's farm. As they looked, Shoofoot realised what the bellow meant. He was in midfield and standing under a large oak in the hedge was a huge Hereford bull, working himself up for attack. He was pawing the ground and tossing his horns, limbering up for a chase.

Macey and Cromwell ran the same way, to the gate which led to the first field. By the gatepost stood a rake and a pitchfork. Macey seized the latter and Cromwell the former. There was a gate between Shoofoot and his rescuers. Both parties made for this. For all his bulk, Shoofoot could move. He covered the ground in great leaps and, as he became airborne after each jump, his legs made a pedalling motion. The bull came on his heels, breath emerging like two jets of steam from his flaming nostrils. Shoofoot started to zigzag, confusing the beast as best he could.

The gate between was wired instead of being held by a catch, and to save time, Macey and Cromwell climbed over it and, brandishing their weapons, thrust themselves between Shoofoot and Thunder. They fought a rearguard action back to the gate, which Shoofoot had now contrived to open, passed through it, and flung it to. The bull, chasing along the hedge, pawing the ground, trying to get at them, snorting and bellowing, was left to dissipate his energy, whilst Cromwell and Macey turned to Shoofoot.

Fear had spurred on the burly farmer; now it left him without support. He looked about him, recognising nothing and nobody. His limbs twitched, his face was running with sweat, his shirt soaked. He reeled to Macey, held out his hands, gripped the little farmer for a second, and then fell at his feet. He did not move again. They knelt beside him and turned him over. He was dead.

Later, Mr Sebastian Dommett found that Enoch Shoofoot died

from natural causes, but he was another victim of the Dodd case, and had he not been so handy making up an alibi for Peg Boone, he might, later that winter, have foreclosed and owned both Crabtree and Maltkiln.

Small wonder that the following Sunday, bright and early at the chapel, Sam Macey's thin tenor was heard above all the rest, shouting that God moved in a mysterious way His wonders to perform…

19

THE GREY CAR

Littlejohn accelerated, passed Macfarlane's car, and signalled him to stop. With an angry gesture, the doctor pulled to the kerb and called through the window.

'What is it now?'

'Park your car and join me in mine. There are one or two other questions I want to ask you.'

'I've told you all I know…'

Passers-by were beginning to take an interest in the exchange of comments coming from the two cars, and Macfarlane resignedly did as he was bidden.

'Get in and sit down, Doctor…'

Dr Macfarlane smelled strongly of drink and looked like turning awkward.

'Can't I be left in peace? There's no more I can say about young Dodd. What I told you was true.'

Littlejohn looked him in the eyes, and the doctor began to shift his gaze uneasily.

'I don't think it was, Doctor. What did Peter Dodd say he'd tell the police if you didn't give him an alibi?'

The by-road was almost deserted, but in the nearby highway

they were using a pneumatic drill which punctuated the conversation with tearing, drumming noises. Littlejohn raised the window.

During the pause, Macfarlane had tried to pull himself together without much success. Littlejohn's comment had evidently got him in a weak spot.

'Are you trying to threaten me, Inspector, because if you are…?'

'I only want the truth, Doctor.'

'You've had it.'

'Very well. Please lock your car. I want you to come with me to the police station?'

'Are you arresting me?'

'No. I want you to make answers to certain questions which the police will wish to put to you after I've told them what I think.'

'What *do* you think?'

Macfarlane's tone was truculent. He was trying to bluff it out.

Littlejohn took out his notebook and quoted the date of Comfort's death.

'Where were you in the afternoon that day, Doctor?'

'I can't say. It's so long ago. Most likely at the club. I'm going there now, when you'll allow me.'

There was a rasp in the voice. The doctor spoke quickly, and Littlejohn noticed beads of sweat appear on his upper lip.

'Mind if we have the window down? It's a bit hot in here.' Littlejohn apparently didn't hear. Instead, he lit his pipe. 'Are you trying to intimidate me?'

'Does the mention of the road from Helstonbury to Cold Kirby strike any note of remembrance? You'd been to Helstonbury and were giving Peter Dodd a lift home.'

'I can't remember.'

'You'd better try, Doctor. You were giving Peter Dodd a lift home. I don't know why you'd been to Helstonbury, but you were coming home and picked up Peter Dodd. You were drunk at the time and were unfit to be in charge of a car…'

'Who's told you that?'

'We know most of what has happened to Harry Dodd lately. We know that you were zigzagging across a bad road when you encountered a car in which Harry Dodd, his father, and a friend were taking a run. You skidded and, to avoid you, Comfort, the third party, who was driving the other car, also skidded, left the road and was killed in the accident. You drove on...'

Macfarlane was in great distress now. He'd removed his hat and was mopping his head.

'Can't you open the blasted window... I'm... I'm...'

'You drove on and left Comfort dying on the roadside. You... you, a doctor. Why did you do it?'

'Has Peter Dodd told you this?'

'Never mind. I want the truth.'

'Why haven't the police questioned me before? It's not right to try and trap me like this. If Peter Dodd's told them, I'll tell them he told me to drive on; the other car had righted itself.'

'You know very well the other car didn't right itself. Otherwise you wouldn't have driven away. Now, do we go to the police station to make a statement, or are you going to tell me what happened?'

Littlejohn, although apparently smoking his pipe contentedly, was himself feeling hot under the collar. This was a shot in the dark, a guess, stimulated by the doctor's grey car and Peter Dodd's apparent hold over Macfarlane.

'The police are still closely questioning all owners of grey Letchworth saloons in this county. They'll catch up with you. In fact, I shall report the matter to them. You'll have to tell a more convincing tale than the one you've told me. They'll array against you everybody you saw between Helstonbury and your surgery. What were you doing in Helstonbury?'

'I'd an old friend a patient at the infirmary. I went to operate. I wasn't drunk. I had a couple of drinks on an empty stomach. It was a hard operation and the patient didn't come through it. I was upset. I'm always upset when any patients of mine die.'

'I'm not denying that, Doctor. Where did you meet Dodd?'

'He asked me for a lift. He'd left his car to be decarbonised in Helstonbury and was waiting for a bus back. I told him to jump in.'

'...And you went off, careering all over the shop on a greasy road.'

'I wasn't drunk, I tell you. I wasn't well, and the whisky on an empty stomach made me giddy. I should have let Peter Dodd drive, but he'd had a drink as well.'

'A bright pair to be loose on the road with a car, weren't you? And you skidded and killed Comfort.'

'I didn't know till I read it in the paper. Peter Dodd called round and showed it to me. He said I'd better keep quiet, nobody would know.'

'Harry Dodd and his father saw you, and they saw Peter, too, which was a shock to them. They thought you deliberately ran them down. The old man was dumbfounded that his own flesh and blood should try it, and Harry Dodd suddenly realised that his son Peter might not be quite the loving boy Peter pretended to be. He expressed himself strongly, but he didn't betray either of you. He aroused the Coroner's suspicions by his fear and prevarication, but he didn't betray you.'

'Then Peter Dodd's told you? The swine! After all I did for him.'

'You were afraid to make a clean breast of what happened. You knew it would mean prison and disgrace.'

'I knew I couldn't undo what I'd done, and there seemed no sense in bringing disaster on myself. Well... I guess I'm for it now.'

'We don't exactly know that you *were* drunk, Doctor. You might simply have been driving to the public danger. You'll have to face the police. It may be manslaughter; it may be also drunken driving.

On the other hand, it may merely be dangerous driving. You'll have to take the risk. You cannot, as well, face perjury, which, if you persist in the tale Peter Dodd blackmailed you into telling, you'll have to repeat in court, and which will be proved false.'

'But I…'

'Peter Dodd told you that if you'd confirm his alibi, he'd keep quiet about the accident.'

'One good turn deserves another, is what he said.'

The doctor chuckled, a mirthless, choking noise.

'I'll kill him for this!'

'We'll look after Dodd. You tell me what happened. You'll have to give a signed statement later and, whatever happens, I'll have to ask you to accompany me and make a clean breast of the accident. If you tell me the truth about the alibi, I shall merely take you in to the police and say you wish to make a statement. There'll be no question of my arresting you, or even forcing you to come. I shall simply have given you a lift.'

'I can say I've just heard that I caused the accident…'

'That's up to you. You'd better tell the whole truth, because I may be asked about it later, and I shan't lie. But a voluntary statement will be regarded as very much in your favour.'

'Very well. Dodd asked me to help him out of a mess. He said he'd got himself in a jam with a married woman. I knew his propensities that way. He said he was with her at the time his father was killed. The police would be questioning him and, although he had an alibi, because he was with the woman at the time, there'd be a scandal if he made it public. I knew the woman and I knew what a hell of a row it would cause. So I agreed. He'd been at my place about nine o'clock and left right away with the tablets…'

'He deliberately gave his mother coffee… real coffee, which made her ill, so that he could get out on the excuse. He might even have drugged the coffee to make her sleep. From what she told me she was asleep when he arrived back with the medicine. He must have altered the clock at her bedside, too, because he called her attention to it, just to make her his extra stand-by.'

'You don't mean to tell me... Good God! You mean he killed his father and he wasn't with Monica Waters after all?'

'It looks very much like it. Who is Monica Waters?'

'She's the wife of one of his best friends. I didn't know Dodd's amours had extended that way, but he said so, rather shamefacedly. I've told you the truth. You'll do your best for me?'

Macfarlane now was a sorry sight. All his aplomb had gone. He looked years older; his frame even seemed to have shrunk.

'There's nothing I can do, Doctor. It's up to you now. Go and see your lawyer, tell him the whole tale about the accident, and the pair of you go to Cambridge and make a statement to the police. Who's your lawyer?'

'Aspinall...'

'The Dodd family lawyer?'

'Yes.'

'We'll go back to your place and you'd better ring him up. First, though, give me the address of Mrs Waters. I'd like to see her. I must be sure that Peter Dodd wasn't there, after all. What does her husband do?'

'He's a big steel man.'

'Indeed! You'd better drive your car home and I'll follow. By the way, your housekeeper confirmed Peter Dodd's alibi...' Littlejohn glared at Macfarlane, who winced.

'Maggie's been my nurse ever since I was born. She'd do anything for me. She's old and her wits are a bit woolly. I've told her the tale several times. She believes it absolutely. She believes whatever I say as though it were holy writ.'

'You ought to be damned well ashamed of yourself!'

'I am. Bitterly. But Dodd blackmailed me into it. If he'd...'

'Surely you had a way out. To go to the police and tell the truth.'

'But Monica would have been involved. I did it for her sake as much as Dodd's. I'm her doctor. I even brought her into the world. I attended when her two kids were born...'

'Didn't you check up with her?'

'How could I? Do you expect me to ring her up and ask if she was in bed with Peter Dodd on such and such a night?'

'Perhaps not. Peter Dodd knew you were very fond of her?'

'Of course. I'm known as a friend of both her and her husband, *and* of both sides of their family. I'm godfather to their youngest son.'

'And you believed Dodd, after all that! Is Monica Waters that sort?'

'I couldn't believe it. But knowing Peter's way with women...'

'Turn your car and drive home.'

'Don't question Maggie, will you? It would break her heart. She's all I've got of the happy old days now.'

'I'll not bother her. But you ought to have thought of all this before you involved her. Now, let's get going.' Back at the surgery, Littlejohn dialled the Waters home. A rough male voice answered.

'Wot is it?'

'Who's speaking?'

'Never you mind. What do you want?'

'This is Dr Macfarlane's surgery. Is Mrs Waters in?'

'No, she ain't, and that ain't the doctor...'

Littlejohn told Macfarlane to take the instrument and make sense of whoever was at the other end.

'Dr Macfarlane here. Who is it? Oh, it's you, Lecky. Is Mrs Waters in? I haven't seen her about lately, but I'd like a word with her.'

'The gardener,' mouthed Macfarlane to Littlejohn. Littlejohn took the telephone in his hand again. The rough voice was telling a long tale.

'I be in charge 'ere now. Got to be careful. Wrong 'uns rings up 'ouses to see if they's empty and then robs 'em. You see the Waterses is away. Gone abroad. Expected back next week.

Ameriker, they gone to. Mr Waters is on one o' them workin' parties as goes out to see how the Americans works. What good Mr Waters'll do, of dunno. He wun o' they capitalists, not a worker. Rum goin's on…'

'When did they go?'

'Eh? That you, Doctor? Your voice is different.'

Littlejohn signalled to Macfarlane to take the answer.

'They bin gone five weeks. All paid for, too. That's where the public money goes to. Waste! That's wot it is. We be taxed to pay for trips for the rich. But wait a bit. Our time'll come. The workers' time'll come…'

Macfarlane gently put the receiver back in its cradle.

'I didn't know that,' he said. 'I wish I had. I'd have rammed it down Dodd's throat. I hope they hang him. The little swine!'

'Better get on to Aspinall.'

Macfarlane dialled a number and asked for the lawyer. Littlejohn could hear a slow-speaking dry voice come on in reply. The doctor pressed earnestly for the lawyer to call on him immediately. There was some argument and then Macfarlane said he wanted Aspinall to pick him up and go with him to the police station. That seemed to clinch matters. A sharp exchange of words and the receiver at the other end clicked.

'I'd like a word with Aspinall in private before you tell him your tale, Doctor. You can arrange it?'

'Yes. You can talk to him in the surgery while I potter around.'

'I've heard a lot about Aspinall, but, strange to say, I've not yet met him.'

'He's a bit of a tartar. A bachelor, and worth a lot of money. In his younger days, he was in love with Mrs Harry Dodd, but she preferred Harry and turned Aspinall down. Aspinall was very bitter about it. He vented his spleen on Harry when the divorce blew up. He was mad that Harry should do such a thing, and then when the family pressed their mother into taking proceedings, he hounded poor Harry good and proper. Never gave him a chance.'

'He's still a friend of the family?'

'Of Mrs Dodd. He's her lawyer still. I don't think he's much time for the others. He never married.'

A sleek black car drew up at the front door of the house, and Littlejohn, watching from the window with Macfarlane, saw emerge with great difficulty a tall, military figure, with a strong aquiline face, a white moustache and a bad limp.

'Lost a leg in the first war. Wears a false one. It still troubles him, I believe, and gives him a lot of pain.'

Aspinall was limping up the drive. The drawn face spoke of pain or bitterness, the twist of the lips, the cold blue eyes, the lines between the nostrils and the mouth. The doorbell clanged. Maggie showed in the lawyer. Macfarlane introduced them.

'What's all this about? An arrest or something?'

The voice was dry with a whip crack in it. The eyes missed nothing and were set in heavy lids with wrinkles surrounding them. They never smiled.

'Inspector Littlejohn has given me some advice, and I want you to help me by your presence at the police station when I make a statement. I've been playing the fool, Cyril, and I look like being in trouble.'

'Is this an official visit, Littlejohn?'

'I'm here about the death of Harry Dodd, sir. The other matter doesn't really concern me, and I'd rather not be present when it's discussed. I shall naturally be on the side of the police in it; you'll be on the defendant's side. I did ask to meet you, sir, seeing you were coming.'

'Humph…'

'I'll leave you two alone for a minute…'

Macfarlane tactfully withdrew.

Littlejohn didn't beat about the bush.

'I'm here on the case of the Dodd murders, sir. I've heard you mentioned as the family lawyer, but, so far, we haven't met.'

Aspinall frowned. He hobbled to a chair, sat down with an

effort, his false limb stretched before him. Littlejohn could guess he'd had the leg removed almost to the hip.

'I'd better tell you right away, Littlejohn, that I'm Mrs Dodd's solicitor. I can't, therefore, be dragged into this matter. I may have to undertake the defence of one or other of the family, if Mrs Dodd asks me.'

'You judge that one of them may have a hand in Mr Dodd's death?'

'I judge nothing. I'm simply saying that I can't tell you anything that might incriminate all or any of the family.'

'You know Mr Peter Dodd, sir?'

'Yes.'

'I'll tell you, then, sir, that the reason I'm here is to check the alibi Mr Peter gave us for himself on the night his father died. Dr Macfarlane was to support it. The doctor tells quite a different tale. He will, at the police station, make a statement which will explain how and why Peter Dodd tried to make him a party to a false alibi…'

'And that's why you prefer to be away when it's done?'

'You'll understand when the doctor explains.'

'It's not surprising. Peter's a wrong 'un. I never liked him. He's been a great trouble, instead of a support, to his mother, although she dotes on him.'

'Why is Peter Dodd unemployed, sir?'

The lawyer's quick eyes met those of Littlejohn and seemed to probe right inside the Inspector's mind.

'Nobody wants him in his own profession. He was a junior partner in an old-fashioned firm in the city. He misapplied funds and joined up in the war in a hurry. The thing killed his senior partner. Mrs Dodd made good the defalcations.'

With a quick jerk Aspinall was on his feet and standing before the Inspector.

'You're not to use this in your case. I mean, it's not to appear on the record. I'm telling you because I want you to find out who killed Harry Dodd. I never liked Harry Dodd. He was a common fellow, who treated a superb woman badly and, at the time, I'd gladly have killed him myself, if I hadn't been civilised. But I believe Mrs Dodd hoped to find happiness in her declining years by joining her husband again. She told me, and I didn't approve. She wished it so, and her wish is my law. Instead, somebody killed Harry Dodd and spoiled everything for her. She still loved him. By God, I want whoever did it to suffer the extreme penalty. Who did it?'

'I don't know, sir. But I'll find out...'

'You'd better. Is young Peter involved?'

'Well... He's cooked himself an alibi which has broken down. I've got to see him about it. He says he was with a woman at the time and daren't bring her in. The woman he mentioned wasn't in England, so Mr Peter's going to have some explaining to do.'

'He's turned out a bad lot. Though to see him about, you'd think butter wouldn't melt in his mouth. He's living on his mother's bounty at present.'

'What happens on her death?'

'I'll tell you in confidence again, but mind you, don't dare divulge it. He gets an income for life from the estate. Mrs Dodd contends she found capital enough to put his embezzlement right and all he gets is a modest income... No capital sums, because he'd probably get through 'em quickly enough and turn to crime again...'

Aspinall paused.

'Turn to crime again, eh? Is that significant?'

'It may be, sir.'

Macfarlane was back.

'Am I a bit too soon?'

Aspinall shook hands with Littlejohn.

'Remember... All that was in confidence.'

'I'll respect it, sir.'

The doctor and lawyer went off together to Aspinall's office and then to the police.

Aspinall was a good lawyer. Macfarlane having nobody to testify against him, denied he was drunk and pleaded the state of the road. He got away with dangerous driving and a fine. His driving licence was suspended, and he had to walk and cycle to his patients for twelve months. He was lucky, because everyone who was present at the accident except himself and Peter Dodd was dead. And as for Peter Dodd... well...

20

CROMWELL DRAWS A BLANK

Cromwell and Littlejohn were due to meet in Cambridge at half-past four. It was a quarter to that hour when Cromwell drew up at *The Aching Man*. He had torn himself away from the tragic home of Enoch Shoofoot after doing all he could to help.

The Boone place was ominously quiet. One or two vehicles, mainly transport lorries, stood in front of the building. Inside, Sid Boone was leaning on the counter, blind drunk. His customers helped themselves from time to time and put the money in the till. At the sight of Cromwell, Sid straightened himself and addressed the assembled guests.

'To 'ell with police... Always 'angin' round places, spoilin' business, and keepin' customers away...'

He sniffed.

'Did any o' you fellers smell somethin'? Has the cat brought somethin' in... or is it a bluebottle in plain clothes that's buzzed around...?'

He reeled over to Cromwell.

'This is a respectable public 'ouse. I'm the landlord, and I can throw out anybody who's a nuishance. Gerrout… Gerrout… You're a public nuisance.'

Cromwell seized Sid by the V of his waistcoat and shook him like a rat. Sid's teeth rattled like a pair of castanets.

'Now, Sid. That's enough being offensive. Where's Peg?'

'In bed. She's not so well. You coppers 'as worried her stiff. She's sick. Can't see 'er.'

'Get her. This is serious.'

'Nothin's serious any more. You lot've spoiled it all. Here we were, the three of us. What do you do? You muck up the whole lot. We were 'appy till you came. Now what…?'

The customers began to look uneasy. They'd been taking a few free drinks at Sid's expense, and thought they'd better make themselves scarce before real trouble broke out. They shuffled off, trying to look as if they weren't interested.

Sid was making for another drink when Cromwell stopped him.

'You've had enough. Sit down.'

He pushed Sid in the middle of the waistcoat, and Sid slumped on the bench. His head lolled in drunken stupor. Cromwell seized a bottle of soda water from the counter and syphoned a shower bath of sparkling fluid over Sid's head and face. Sid's arms flailed and his eyes appeared wide and round through the jet of fizzing water.

'Gerroff… Stoppit… Whatyouthinyourat…?'

'Sober up, Sid. Sober up, or I'll give you another dose.'

'What's all this about? I ain't done nothin'…'

'You know Shoofoot and Macey…?'

'Oo?'

'You heard me. You and Peg persuaded them to give alibis to Peg on the night Harry Dodd was killed. Why?'

'I dunno nothin' about it. Count me out of Peg's business. She tells me nothin'…'

'Where is she?'

'I said she's in bed. She's sick.'

'Where's the kid?'

'Where you think she is? She's with her maw.'

'Get Peg down. This is important.'

'Go to 'ell. I'm not dishturbin' my sick sister for anybody...'

Cromwell thrust Sid aside and hurried to the foot of the stairs. There was dead silence above. He ran up two steps at a time.

The landing was dark and illuminated by the light from the bathroom at the end of the corridor, the door of which stood open, revealing an old-fashioned bath and an untidy interior with dirty towels and a bathrobe lying on the floor.

There were four other rooms on the corridor and Cromwell opened them one by one. The first looked like Sid's, a bare, untidy place, which could have done with the windows opening wide. It reeked of cheroots and stuffiness. Next, the child's room. Toys on the floor, a cot, Disney pictures on the walls, the whole neat and tidy. Cromwell went in. There was a wardrobe behind the door. The door of the wardrobe was open, revealing nothing but a little pinafore embroidered with rabbits. The rest of the clothes had gone.

In the next room, confusion. This must have been Peg's and smelled of scent and greasy face powder. The dressing-table was untidy with bottles of cosmetics and perfume. The bed was unmade, but Peg wasn't in it. The drawers of the chest and wardrobe were open and empty, the wardrobe rifled. Clothes scattered all over the place, as though Peg had been doing some sorting out.

Cromwell scuttered back along the passage and almost descended the stairs in a single bound.

Sid had been drinking again. He lolled over one of the marble tables, his eyes open, his mouth sagging, a picture of despair. Cromwell seized the soda-water bottle again. Sid leapt to his feet and faced him unsteadily. Cromwell might have been preparing to kill him in cold blood with a gun. He stretched out his hands in a terrified fending-off gesture.

'No… No… No more. I didn' do anythin'… It wasn' me… They lef' me… All alone… Nobody in the world now… All by myself… Don' shoot…'

Cromwell put down the bottle and seized Sid by his waistcoat V again. He shook him.

'Where are they?'

'I dunno… Lef' me for good. Nobody lef' in the world.'

'What happened?'

'I dunno…'

Cromwell picked up the syphon.

'Keep off… Don't shoot… I'll tell…'

Cromwell suddenly realised that Sid Boone hated water more than anything else in the world!

'Talk, then.'

'Somebody rang up. Peg got scared. Packed up and left.'

'*Who* rang up?'

'Shoofoot… I answered the phone. Said he wanted Peg. Told her somethin' that mus'ave been 'orrible. She took all the money an' all her things, sent for a taxi, and went off.'

'Did she take the kid?'

'Eh?'

'You heard. The kid.'

'I'll never see my li'l Nancy again. They've taken her away…'

At the sound of the word Nancy, the parrot suddenly roused herself in the next room.

'Nanceeeee! I want Nanceeee. Pretty Poll. Pretty Cora. I'm wild about Harry and Harry's wild about me. Harry Dodd. Where's Harry? I want Harry.'

A real mouthful, awful in its reminiscences of Harry Dodd and his times there in the past. Now they'd all gone and left Sid with only Cora, with her ghostly chatter, for company. Sid was blubbering with self-pity.

'What am I to do? I'm all on me own.'

He looked round at the dirty glasses, the empty beer bottles, the red corrugated metal caps. It seemed years since Littlejohn had talked about the red caps, and Peg had seemed so decent and co-operative.

'Who took the kid?'

'I dunno… Don't shoot… Put it down. I dunno who took 'er. A big car drove up and took her off. An old lady came and asked for Peg. Peg had just gone. Then she asks where Nancy is and I said gone, too. But jus' then Nancy came out lookin' for her maw. So the old lady takes her off without so much as a by-your-leave. I won't stand it. I'm Nancy's guardian now her maw's gone, an' I'm goin' to see my lawyer. Got to have her back. Don't want to be on my own.'

He blubbered again.

Three hikers walked in, looked around, and sat at a table. Their mouths fell when they saw Sid, tears running down his face, a bent fag in his mouth, which he was trying to light as well. Cromwell left them all together and drove off to meet Littlejohn. A policeman with a bicycle was standing at the crossroads which they'd arranged should be the rendezvous.

'Sergeant Cromwell, sir? Inspector Littlejohn left a message.'

He handed Cromwell a note scribbled on a sheet of a notebook:

> Meet you at Helstonbury Police Station.
> Meanwhile get report on movements of Peter Dodd from man put on his tail.
> On no account must Dodd be lost. Ask Miss Jump for as much as she knows about Peter Dodd.
> TL

'Where is the Inspector?'

'He met me here. I was just on patrol. It wasn't above five

minutes since. He'd been in Dr Macfarlane's and said he was going to see Mrs Dodd, but to give you the note.' Cromwell placed the note on the top of the car and scribbled a reply on the back.

Message received. Acting. Peg Boone's alibi faked. Peg Boone left for unknown destination.
Nancy taken away in car by 'old lady' — Mrs Dodd?
RC

'Could you take that for me to the Inspector at Mrs Dodd's home, please?'

'Yessir.'

The bobby flung himself on his bicycle and pedalled off as if all hell were at his heels.

21

THE PRODIGAL SON

There was a tension about the Dodd house when he arrived which Littlejohn had never felt before. As soon as the old maid greeted him on the threshold, he knew it and, when she led him in to Mrs Harry Dodd, it was intensified.

Mrs Dodd looked very much older. Her face was pinched and of a leaden pallor. The dog growled.

'Is Mr Peter in, madam?'

She sensed the loss of friendliness in Littlejohn's voice and looked hard at him.

'No. I don't know where he is.'

'Is he in town?'

'I can't say.'

It all seemed different. Littlejohn knew he wasn't welcome. To think of smoking his pipe here, as in days past, would have been taking a liberty.

'Relations seem to have changed between you and me, madam.'

He was at a loss how to start.

'I don't wish them to be. You have been a most helpful and considerate officer, Inspector. I don't wish you to think… to think…'

'To think, madam, that you're concealing something from me?'

Outwardly impassive, Mrs Dodd nevertheless showed signs of strain. Her thumbs moved across the insides of her fingers, like someone feeling material.

'What can I be concealing? I told you all I knew last time you called.'

'All you knew at the time. But you know a lot more now, madam. For instance, you know that the little girl at *The Aching Man* wasn't your husband's daughter. She's the daughter of your son, Peter.'

She grew rigid; then she relaxed and sat down.

'Sit down, Inspector Littlejohn. How did you find that out?'

'It's obvious, madam. The child resembles *you*; not your late husband. She's the child of one of your children, and the likely one, by elimination, is Mr Peter. Is he your favourite son?'

She stared hard at Littlejohn, trying to fathom how much he knew.

'I have no favourite son.'

'But Mr Peter was. He has since forfeited the right? But he's not yet lost your protection. He lost his rank as your favourite child after you discovered that he'd murdered his own father!'

She sprang to her feet and rang the bell.

'How dare you, Inspector ! My own son in his own home. How dare you accuse him of…'

She hesitated. The maid appeared at the door.

'You rang, Missisdodd…?'

'No. It was a mistake.'

She had recovered herself and found it might be dangerous to break off relations before hearing Littlejohn out.

'By what right are you accusing Peter?'

'We have a concrete case against him, madam. And he tried to build himself alibis, after his usual fashion of considering nobody but himself. I'm sorry, Mrs Dodd, but I must speak candidly. This is no time for mincing words.'

'I agree. But the alibis…?'

'I think you know, Mrs Dodd. If you don't think they were concocted to save him from accusations about *murder*, Mr Peter told you some other tale, a tale like he told Dr Macfarlane, who lied believing he was shielding the honour of a married woman.'

'I know nothing about such a tale. How did I give him an alibi?'

'He made you real coffee, instead of the harmless substitute. He made you ill to get an excuse to go out to the doctor's and to Brande. He could do it in half an hour in his fast little car. He returned, gave you the medicine, and convinced you he'd only been away a minute or two by altering the clock at your bedside. You said he called your attention to it. He blackmailed Dr Macfarlane into supporting him.'

She seemed utterly bewildered.

'Blackmail? How came that about?'

Littlejohn briefly told her of the road accident and the death of Comfort. She sat frozen with horror.

'Not other deaths? Not that!'

'Yes. Not only his father, but his grandfather and Mr Pharaoh. Once having killed, he took fright and, in trying to hide his tracks, he started to slaughter indiscriminately those who'd never done him any harm…'

'Stop! He wasn't alone, and he was always weak. I'm not saying he killed any of them, but please remember he was the weakest of us all, the one who, somehow, took after neither Harry nor me.'

'Why?'

'He always had a profligate streak in him. He was a bully and a coward at school… yes, you might as well know… and at the university he got a girl into trouble and brought great sorrow on us all. She tried to kill herself, and the baby died. Then we settled him, as we thought, in practice. He lived far beyond his income, took trust funds from his firm, and I had to make good his defalcations to the tune of over ten thousand pounds. Then he joined the forces, made a totally unsuitable marriage with a very nice girl, and treated her abominably.'

'And lastly... Peg Boone?'

'Yes.'

'How did his father take all this?'

'He stood by him to the end. I would have made Peter take his medicine for some of his tricks, but Harry excused him. When we paid up the defalcations, I cut Peter from my will. I created a trust to be quite sure he didn't touch any capital. I also made the trust income small enough to keep Peter working. I was very fond of him... once... But I didn't know about the child at *The Aching Man* until after you mentioned it. I asked Peter and I forced the truth out of him. We had drawn closer together, I thought, of late. He was the only one whom I told about his father and me remarrying. After Harry first wrote about the family Bible, Peter was the one I told I'd like to see Harry again, and he took me to meet him. I can't understand...'

She was bewildered and looked at Littlejohn, as if expecting an answer.

'He took you for the first meeting, little thinking that you and Mr Dodd both, in your hearts, wanted each other again. Do you think, if Peter had known you were likely to remarry, he'd have cooperated? Not likely, Mrs Dodd! He'd have done all he could to keep you apart. With you out of the picture, and nobody to leave his money to, Harry Dodd made a will bequeathing over twenty thousand pounds to his grandchild, the child of Peter and Peg Boone. With you back in the picture, he was going to alter his will and leave it all to you to disburse. Mr Pharaoh told Peter that, I've no doubt, because Peter was always in and out at Pharaoh's, supposed to be keeping in touch with family affairs. As soon as you and Harry Dodd decided to remarry, poor Harry Dodd was doomed.'

She broke down and wept, and Littlejohn left her in quiet with her grief. He stood at the window and looked out over the decaying outbuildings and the old trees and tried to imagine what it had all been like long ago.

'I got the truth out of Peter about the child. He had, it seems, been friendly there a long time, before his marriage, even. When he came back from the war, there was an affair and the child was born. He offered to marry Peg Boone when he was free, but she said until he got a steady job and enough to keep her and the child in decency and comfort, she wouldn't marry him. He was, and still is, mad about her. She is his evil genius, a girl who looks like a Botticelli angel and yet has been the downfall of us all!'

'In what way? You mean she egged him on to murder?'

'I don't admit he ever committed murder. He couldn't settle down for the madness in his blood about her. He was never away from the place after dark. He said he went after closing hours and stayed there all night, pretending he was at his flat.'

'He told his father about the child?'

'Yes. To borrow money from Harry… Peter, as you know, was at one time the only member of the family in touch with Harry… He went to his father, told him about the child and asked him for money to help bring her up decently. Harry went to see Nancy, and they took to each other right away. Harry was so delighted with her, Peter told me. She was his only grandchild. It gave him an interest in life and he took up with the man with a system of speculating on the Stock Exchange with a view to making money. He did so well that he was able to settle five thousand on the child.'

'I wonder where that money is now?'

'So do I…'

'Not only that, Mrs Dodd, he accumulated more money, hoping, perhaps, to get Nancy away to school and such like. He held it himself and in case of death, it was willed away to his grandchild. He was a fine man, Harry Dodd, and to save their own skins after his death, that pair, Peter and Peg, told the police that Nancy was Harry Dodd's child. That is what they'd come to and what they did to Harry Dodd!'

There was a pause. Each of them waited for the other to speak.

The clock raced on the mantelpiece, the dog on his cushion snored and kicked his legs about as he dreamed; somewhere outside a car backfired.

'I don't know whether or not Peg Boone was with Peter when Harry Dodd was killed. I'm sure, however, that she was his evil genius and engineered it all. I shall know before very long. My colleague is at *The Aching Man* now.'

Mrs Dodd looked hard at Littlejohn. The Inspector caught in her glance the first trace of cunning he had seen. He couldn't understand it.

'Do you know Peg Boone, Mrs Dodd?'

'No. But I know that Harry disliked her. Peter told me he tried to persuade his father to agree to their marriage, but Harry refused, nor would be find any money for it. He preferred an illegitimate grandchild to seeing his son and Peg Boone married.'

'I wondered... Have you seen your grandchild, little Nancy?'

'Where is this leading, Inspector? What I want to know is have you arrested Peter or is he likely to be arrested?'

'He is likely to be. So far, I haven't arrested him. I wanted to speak with you first. I wanted you to know how your husband was killed and by whom.'

'I still don't believe it!'

She wrung her hands.

'I think you know more than you'll tell. Did you, or did you not, know that Peter cheated you about the coffee and the clock on the night his father died?'

'Yes, I did. I knew that, normally, he would never be so stupid as to forget that I didn't take real coffee. I also knew that he'd moved the clock, presumably in altering the time. It wasn't in the same position on the bedside table as when I fell asleep. It was behind a photograph of my sister which is there, instead of in front. Furthermore, I know that he put sleeping tablets in the coffee… only a light dose to make sure my wits were dim enough not to scent the trick he was playing. I knew, because I gave the dog some of the coffee. He adores it. He always jumps up on my bed and sleeps at the foot, but, on that night, he fell asleep on the doormat as he entered, and he slept as I carried him to bed.'

'Did you tax your son with it all?'

'No. I thought he was up to some trick or other. In fact, I thought he'd got bored with my company and was anxious to get me to bed and leave him free to do as he liked.'

'You mean he'd go so far as to make you ill and drug you…?'

'You said yourself he thought of nobody but himself… You were right.'

Littlejohn was still uneasy about the atmosphere of the interview. With a little spasm of alarm he wondered if Mrs Dodd was hand in glove with Peter in murdering Harry. Suppose, after all, Harry had led her on and then let her down in the matter of marrying her again…? Or suppose she'd always cherished the idea of revenge…? He shook himself.

'You believe me when I say that your son made himself an alibi for the time when his father was killed?'

'It is difficult not to believe it now. But I know nothing of this case except the disjointed bits I've gathered in conversation with you. Suppose you tell me what happened.'

'It seems simple enough now, madam. It has eluded us for a long time, due to the fact that I simply couldn't believe that Peter could murder his father. It wasn't until I saw the little girl that I knew the truth. You already know that your husband had found his grandchild, was very fond of her, and wished to do his best for her. Of late, the two women he lived with at Brande had noticed his being restless and preoccupied. He spent a long time trying to discover a patent way of welding steel. At the same time, he also turned to the Stock Exchange. He'd met a man with a good system but no capital. So they formed a partnership which was a huge success.'

'Was it in London?'

'No. In Helstonbury. A little corn chandler called Lott. They made a fortune apiece, Harry Dodd provided their first capital. He did it for fun at first, I think. But after he found Nancy, he started in earnest.'

'And my husband was stimulated to do this by his love for his grandchild…?'

'I believe he was. He was an outcast from the rest of his family. Peter had no money and no job. Harry Dodd made up his mind that little illegitimate Nancy should not suffer, and she was his inspiration in this wild-cat money-making scheme which came off.'

The maid brought in tea things, but they didn't notice her. They were living again with Harry Dodd.

'Peter and Peg, who, I think, had the idea of telling Peter's father the sad tale of little Nancy, didn't know Harry would go as far as he did. They'd expected perhaps a hundred or two, because, after all, Peter knew his father only had his allowance as a remittance-man; a few hundreds. Instead of which, Harry Dodd went mad. A lonely, ageing man, bored with the two women fate had thrust on him, but whom, with characteristic simple sense of duty, he treated fairly… more than fairly… Bored, I say, he suddenly finds an interest on which he focuses all his powers; the child, Nancy. His grandchild takes to him and from then on, Harry can't do enough for her. He, metaphorically speaking, breaks the bank at Monte Carlo, gives Peg Boone a lump sum for Nancy, and lets her know, or tells Peter there's a lot more where that came from, invested and, in case Harry Dodd isn't there to dole it out, left to Nancy, or her trustee, Mr Pharaoh, in his will.'

'I never realised...'

'Nor did any of us when first we began on this case. There was Harry Dodd, divorced, living what appeared an aimless life with a couple of nondescript women, going every night to have a drink at *The Bear* in the village, with his cronies, loafing around, bored to death. That's as the world knew him. Actually, he had a purpose in life, and all his efforts were centred on achieving it. He went from strength to strength; he even planned to meet you again, leave his two women, and live a respectable and quiet life in his old home once more. The idea of Nancy started that, I believe. He wanted to give her a decent settled life away from the pub and her Uncle Sid... perhaps away from Peg. Once he thought you and he might adopt the kid and asked you about it.'

'He did. He didn't say it was Peter's... or his.'

'No. They kept it quiet between them. It might be that Peter didn't want it to get about for the sake of his reputation, or that Harry couldn't, as you say, bear the idea of Peter marrying Peg Boone, or that Peg was hoping to make a better catch and leave Peter in the lurch if a chance came. Be that as it may, Peter was her tool and she used him. She wanted to lay her hands on Harry Dodd's fortune. He wasn't in a hurry to hand it over. Probably he intended to look after the child's education and upbringing himself, and, if he died, Pharaoh would control the money. Then he suddenly had the idea of returning to you.'

'The family Bible incident was just a means of getting in touch again?'

'Perhaps. But Harry was so carried away that he had to have the Bible to put little Nancy's name in it as his first grandchild. Then he must have told Peg or Peter, who made him remove it. It didn't suit their purpose to have their plans rushed. They'd an eye on the money, I suppose. When Harry Dodd asked you about starting all over again and you agreed, it must have been a shock to that pair. Not only that, he told Pharaoh he was going to alter his will, leave his ready money to you, and most likely he mentioned Nancy and the matter of her living in the refined atmosphere of your home instead of at *The Aching Man*. Peter was always in and out of Pharaoh's. I think the old man rather liked him and regarded him as go-between and confidant about Dodd family matters. He might even have hoped he'd one day become his partner. When Peg and Peter learned of Harry's plans, they decided to work fast if they didn't want to lose a fortune. They killed Harry Dodd.'

Mrs Dodd covered her face with her hands.

'I can't believe it. And yet Peter seemed interested in his father, morbidly interested, after the time about which the child must have been introduced to her grandfather. Do you know, until then, Peter was on the side of Winfield and his sister in despising their father...'

'It didn't cost him much to kill his father. After all, Harry Dodd had gone away from home, disgraced his children, lived with a couple of poor-class women. In fact, I wouldn't be surprised if Peter didn't hate him, for, after all, if Harry Dodd had remained at home, the business might have done better under his practical eye than under Winfield's, and there would have been more money about.'

'That's true. Peter has complained.'

'We're forgetting something else, however. The other murders. You must remember that whilst Harry Dodd was uncertain of your reaction both to his returning to you and to adopting his grandchild, and hoped to persuade you in course of time, there was one person who had remained his loyal friend and in whom he confided. That was his father. William Dodd had put his father in a home, but Harry regularly called for him and took him out and gave him little treats and excursions. It was on one of such excursions that Dr Macfarlane, driving his car whilst drunk, ran them off the road and the driver was killed. Peter was in the doctor's car taking a lift. The doctor went on without stopping and left the driver of the damaged car to die in the ditch.

Peter used this event to blackmail the doctor into giving him an alibi…'

'You don't mean he…?'

'Peter knew his father and grandfather were in the car and yet he didn't stop to see if they were hurt. In fact, as things then were, it would have pleased him if they'd died.'

'You mean Grandpa Dodd knew about things, too.'

'In his pocket when we found him dead, he had the address of *The Aching Man*. Harry had given it to him as the home of his great-grandchild, and he must have called there, found Peter and upbraided him for his share in the accident. Perhaps he had tumbled to the idea of who Harry's killer might be, for Harry was bound to have confided in him about the money and what he was going to do with it.'

'Why?'

'Haven't we said that Grandpa Dodd was the only one of his flesh and blood he could talk to about anything intimate? As soon as the old man turned up at *The Aching Man*, his doom was sealed. It wouldn't have done to have him around talking and focusing suspicion on Peter and Peg.'

'But Pharaoh. Surely he did nothing wrong?'

'Pharaoh was a shrewd old bird. He seemed half asleep and to have all his heart in his boat, but he was a wily lawyer. He perhaps saw through Peter's scheme and talked a bit too much. He scared Peter into murdering him, too, and trying to make it look like an accident. Not only that, it made Peter aware for the first time that Harry might have left papers, some account of what he proposed to do in the way of altering his will, cutting Peter and Peg's interest away from them, and putting Nancy's money in your hands. Peter, with his father's blood on his hands, got scared lest papers or a diary left by Harry Dodd should betray him. He was first on the spot the day after the crime; he patiently put up with the women and Uncle Fred, who was their self-appointed lawyer, with that in view. And when he couldn't get anything, he robbed

Pharaoh's safe and then burned down Harry Dodd's bungalow in the hope of destroying the evidence. I do believe that Peter destroyed a new will, which was in Pharaoh's safe, and left the money to you. Only a copy was found. The original has vanished.'

'Why have you told me all this, Inspector?'

She stood up and looked him full in the eyes.

'Because you are the only person who could ease my mind about Peter. I have not had experience before of a son murdering his father. Such occurrences are a bit unusual. Of course, I mean, there might be a brawl and high words, and father and son might fight, but a cold, deliberately planned murder of this sort is rare in England. Abroad, sometimes, yes. At any rate, I've never made an arrest of this kind before. I wanted Peter's background. You've given it to me. He mustn't have regarded Harry Dodd as a father, except when he wanted something. Otherwise Harry Dodd was just another man and not a very desirable one to Peter, at that.'

Mrs Dodd's eye fell on the tea tray.

'The tea's cold. I'll ring for more…'

'Please don't. I must go now.'

But the maid had entered. She had Cromwell's note in her hand.

'Excuse me. May I read this message from my colleague, please?'

He read the hasty note in Cromwell's bold hand and screwed it up and threw it in the fire.

'I think, after all, I might have a cup of tea. That will do, Mrs Dodd. Don't bother to ring for more. I like it strong.'

She poured out a cup and handed it to him and passed the cake. They sat down. Nothing was said, except an odd exchange about the weather until they had laid down their cups.

'Is Nancy upstairs, Mrs Dodd? What have you done to her? She's very quiet.'

Littlejohn dropped it like a bombshell, and Mrs Dodd took a second or two to gather herself together.

'I… I… How did you know?'

'My colleague has been to *The Aching Man* and found the birds flown. Peg has gone and Sid, her brother, reports that Nancy went away with a lady…'

'She is upstairs, asleep. Her mother left her with Sid. I arrived to find the child heartbroken and weeping, and I took her and brought her here. She will live with me in future, and I will carry on the work my poor Harry Dodd set his hand to.'

'Peg must have got scared. We've been checking alibis more closely. The same applies to Peter. What have you done with Peg and Peter, Mrs Dodd?'

'I…? Why should I…?'

'What made you suddenly decide to visit *The Aching Man*?'

'*I* was interested in the child.'

'That will hardly do as an explanation why you brought her home with you. Peg would never have allowed it. You can't just go and steal a child like that. There was some other reason, and that reason was that Peter told you they were both in trouble…'

'The steward at the Trevelyan Club told him that the police had been there and had mentioned him and been particularly interested in Dr Macfarlane. He was terrified and said he was in trouble. I then accused him of killing his father. I told him that I knew all about his drugging my coffee, faking an alibi, and also that I knew about the child at *The Aching Man*. After you told me about her, I went there. Peg Boone doesn't know me. I left the car and walked half a mile. I put on tweeds and pretended I was staying in the vicinity. I saw Nancy on the stairhead, playing with a kitten. I thought how like my own daughter she was when my child was that age. I realised that she was Peter's child.'

'You faced Peter with it?'

'Yes. He asked me for money to get away. He was in trouble with the police, he said. I repeated that he was his father's murderer and he would get no help from me unless he made a clean breast of the whole thing. He told quite a simple story, in keeping with your own deductions, Inspector, except in one point. Peg, he said, stabbed my husband. Harry, it seems, asked them to give up Nancy and let us take her when we remarried. Peter said they would talk it over and let him have an answer the next night. They would meet just before ten outside *The Bear* in Brande. Harry could hardly have them in the inn with his friends there or invite them to *Mon Abri* (was it called?) to discuss a matter like that.'

'I follow...'

Mrs Dodd's cheeks grew flushed with emotion as she told her story.

'They met Harry and told him that if he'd hand over the money, which was to go to Nancy on his death, he could take her, and they'd renounce all right to her and go away. Peter, it seems, learned of the invested money from papers he found in his father's raincoat at the inn. Harry, who was naturally a hot-tempered man, flared up. He pointed out that the money was Nancy's, and nobody was going to get it from her on any pretext. He also, it seems, told Peg and Peter exactly what he thought of Peg in no uncertain language. Peter, who inherits his father's temper, insulted Harry. Now Harry was a stocky, strong man, who in his day had done a bit of boxing, and he thereupon started to chastise Peter like a naughty child. If Peg hadn't interfered it might have ended all right, but she tried to help Peter and caught a blow intended for him. She went mad at that, ran to the car, took out a bowie knife, which Peter always carried in the pocket... he had done some camping and it was really a kind of boyhood keepsake... and struck out at Harry. It was all over in a few minutes, some people were coming out of *The Bear*, and Harry told Peter to make himself scarce and he'd be all right. Peter said he walked steadily into the telephone box in the middle of the village and they drove off. Next morning news came that Harry was dead.'

'And Mr Walter Dodd...?'

'Called at *The Aching Man* and said that Harry had told him he was meeting Peg and Peter and going to agree to take Nancy. Grandfather knew the time they were due in Brande. His testimony would have hanged them. But Peg didn't tell Peter that, till Grandpa was dead. She had smothered him in his bed…'

'Did Peter mention Pharaoh?'

'Mr Pharaoh knew as much as Grandpa. Harry, elated at the thought of getting Nancy, told him triumphantly to get a deed of adoption ready and said he was meeting her parents at Brande that night. Mr Pharaoh must have been thinking things over. He sent for Peter from Lowestoft and told him he'd meet him on his boat. Peter said he went, and Mr Pharaoh was so abusive that he struck him, and he fell and cracked his head…'

Littlejohn smiled sadly.

'I can believe that Peter didn't kill his father or his grandfather. He can have credit for that until we catch up with him. But he murdered Pharaoh in cold blood. He told you a lie about that to win your sympathy. Mr Pharaoh was struck from behind, a hard, foul blow, and the murder was carefully made to look like an accident.'

Mrs Dodd rose to her feet.

'My son has done worse even than Cain. He has been responsible for his father's death and his grandfather's. In heat and fear such things may happen, and the woman who damned him might have done it. Mr Pharaoh was a harmless old man who was fond of Harry and made his life bearable at a time when everybody seemed against him. I can never forgive Peter for that. I promised him I wouldn't tell what he had done. I consider myself under no obligation to him. He is no son of mine. He and his woman left an hour before you arrived. I gave them a cheque for all the ready money I had, and I said I'd try to get more to them if they'd let me know later. I was sorry for Peter, who confessed like a wilful child, and said that, come what may, he'd have to stand by Peg Boone who was in it with him. He refused to leave without Peg

Boone. After all — he is my own flesh and blood! It seems he lied to me. He might even have killed his father himself.'

'Where did they go?'

'I don't know. That's the truth. They left with my cheque for two thousand pounds. It will overdraw my account, but the bank won't mind that. They had Peter's MG car and their suitcases and were going to the bank first and then on to heaven knows where...'

'May I use your telephone, please?'

He looked up the number of Mr Pharaoh's firm and soon was speaking to Miss Jump.

'Yes,' she said in reply to Littlejohn's question. 'Mr Peter Dodd asked me two days ago for a written permit to try out the *Betsy Jane*. I wrote one out. He said he might know a buyer...'

'Where is he?' asked Mrs Dodd.

'Probably somewhere out to sea by now, but not for long.' She walked into the hall with him and he took up his hat and gloves. Littlejohn gently reproached her.

'There is just one vital objection, Mrs Dodd, to our accepting Peter's story that he didn't think of murder when he set out with Peg to meet his father. The doctor's alibi was framed afterwards; the coffee was doctored *beforehand*. Why should he do that if he didn't anticipate needing an alibi?'

Mrs Dodd sighed. 'I asked him that,' she said. 'It wasn't for an alibi, but proved lucky for him, all the same. Peter had promised to stay in all night with me. Rather than concoct troublesome excuses to enable him to get out and meet Peg, he doctored the coffee to get me to bed. He was that way. The line of least resistance... always.'

'I quite understand, Mrs Dodd, that, as Peter's mother, you have felt justified in delaying us by withholding the truth until the very last minute. You hope thereby to give him a good start. But I'm afraid it will be no use...'

She pulled herself up and replied brokenly.

'I don't think I wish to give them a chance, now. But I pray God will destroy them in His own way before the law is called upon to do so…'

Her prayer was answered. Little, henpecked, rabbity Ishmael Lott was the chosen vessel of wrath!

22

THE END OF THE BETSY JANE

Mr Ishmael Lott arrived at his shop good and early on this particular day. He opened the front door, took down the shutters, rubbed his hands, and chuckled with glee. Then he descended to the cellar and began to behave even more strangely. From under a pile of sacks he took a large kitbag in which he began to rummage. He whistled between his little rabbit-teeth as he worked, his nose close to his job, like a foraging tapir.

A pair of boots, several lots of clean socks, a sweater, handkerchiefs, shaving tackle, toothbrush for his rabbit-teeth, an extra pair of flannel trousers... One by one he looked them over, counting them as he hissed his tuneless song. From the pockets of his raincoat he added to the contents of the bag some papers, a passport, a telescope, a copy of Culpepper's *Herbal* (for he believed in every man being his own physician), and, as if to bless the lot, a Testament. Carefully stowing everything with trembling fingers, he pulled on the rope of the sack, drew it tight, and swung it to feel its weight. Satisfied, he padded upstairs furtively, opened the back door, and unlocked the garage in the yard behind. A large corn lorry was standing there, ready loaded with sacks of meal. He'd arranged that the night before.

Ishmael, now humming like a bumble bee, carefully hid his kitbag under the meal sacks, gave them a pat of affection and reassurance, went back to his shop, and opened up. A quarter of an hour later his daughter, who closely resembled him, teeth and all, arrived, carrying her lunch in a bag and two lurid love tales with which to while away the time.

'What's the matter with you? You look feverish.'

She eyed her parent up and down.

Mr Lott gave her a crafty look and tried not to appear excited.

'I feel a bit chilly. It's gettin' colder. I'll be all right.'

'Are you goin' on the lorry today?'

'Yes.'

'Where to?'

Mr Lott would have ground his teeth with anger if they'd only met properly. As it was, he screwed up his face with distaste. His wife and his daughter couldn't leave him alone. Where? How? Why? When? It was sickening! Inside, he felt like laughing. Goodbye to all that today!

'We're goin' to Cambridge.'

'What are you takin'? Who are you deliverin' to?'

But Mr Lott was in the cellar, stuffing loose coin in his pocket, rummaging down the top of his trousers and under his shirt to make sure that the belt which contained a fortune was safely in place.

'Hrumph… He-he.'

He made little noises of pleasure.

At nine o'clock Bill Clarke, the lorry man, arrived.

Bill was a large, muscular man, brimming over with good health, blessed with a nice wife and three children, and in his spare time he was a pigeon flyer.

'Won a second in Saturday's race from Cherbourg,' he said to Lott's daughter as he entered the shop. Miss Lott raised her eyes from *Nights of Desire*, ogled Bill, and eyed him up and down with hungry admiration. Bill wasn't having any.

'Boss in?'

'In the cellar...'

Lott and Bill drove the lorry, but Mrs Lott had given strict instructions since the affair at Lowestoft that her husband hadn't to take the wheel again. They trundled along in silence for a while. They hadn't much in common. Bill talked a bit about his pigeons, and then they reached a farm where they had a couple of sacks of pig meal to deliver. They unloaded, and Ishmael Lott gave Bill the delivery note to take to the farmhouse for signature. When Bill had disappeared in the farm kitchen, Lott started the engine, drove through the gates a bit unsteadily, and reached the highway before his driver had realised he was gone. Keeping a steady twenty miles an hour, for Lott wasn't going to have trouble with the police on such a day, he took the road to the coast again, the same road he'd taken once before. The early morning air braced him and, as he reached the countryside, he accelerated and topped fifty. He kept it up steadily, following carefully prepared routes with the precision gained from long juggling with, figures on his graphs. He started to shout and sing to himself in a harsh, shrill tenor, without tune, first *Annie Laurie* and then, tiddly-om-pom-pom, the Gallop from *William Tell* which was just right for the rattle of the lorry.

He ate buns from a bag in his pocket, to keep off hunger, without slackening speed. He skirted Cambridge, struck the main road at Thetford and ran through Bungay and Beetles to within three miles of Lowestoft where, turning down a deserted by-lane, he parked the lorry. Ishmael Lott was like an insect with a set pattern of behaviour. On his last escapade he'd hidden the vehicle in exactly the same spot. He was unable to break habits once he'd formed them. He pretended as he did things a second or a third time, that this was the first time, and tried, in a fantastic way, to imagine that time had stood still between an event and its repetition later. He hated to think he was growing older, that Mrs Lott was stealing away by the imprisonment she imposed on him, the remaining active years of his life.

Mr Lott unearthed his kitbag, felt again at his waist to make sure the belt of money was safe, and danced a little jig. He wondered if, when he got to France, he might find a nice little girl to love and mind him, like the ones in *Bohemian Life* and *Madame Bovary*, which he'd bought for twopence on a book barrow, and which had stimulated him to make France his place of refuge. 'So long!' he said to the lorry. He read the name on the panel of the door. 'Isaac Lott & Son. Corn Merchants, Helstonbury, Mids.' For a brief moment, he thought kindly of his old dad and thought of himself as a parson. The Rev Ishmael Lott! He roared with laughter, swung his kitbag over his shoulder, and strode off to the main road.

It was nearly tea-time when Lott reached the quayside at Lowestoft. He made straight for a shop labelled 'Ephraim Conk, chandler. Est 1876.' There was nothing in the grimy windows, but when Lott opened the door, a smell of tar, paraffin and damp stone met him. The place was full of old junk. Anchors, chains, ropes of all sizes, oils, paint, riding lamps, oilskins… A little weasel of a man was sitting repairing a pair of boots. He grunted as he hacked the leather into the shape of a sole.

''E's down at the quay,' he said with difficulty, for his mouth was full of shoe nails.

'Is she ready?'

'Don't ask me…'

Mr Lott almost ran to the waterside and to a second-hand speedboat moored there. She badly wanted a coat of paint, and her brass was tarnished, but she was seaworthy, and her engine was in fine tune. A large mass of stooping hindquarters straightened itself and revealed a little fat man with staring eyes and a round, ruddy face.

'I was waitin' for yer. She's ready. All topped-up an' ready. Grub, petrol, ile, water, whisky… the whole bloody lot, as promised. Sure you can 'andle 'er? She's a rare turn o' speed when full out.'

Mr Lott flung his kitbag aboard, clumsily flung himself after it, and intimated to Mr Conk that his presence was no longer required.

'Awright. I'm off. Want me to give 'er a start...?'

He didn't wait for an answer, but cranked up the engine, which he'd already warmed up. Mr Lott in ecstasy threw his cloth cap over the side, took a yachting cap from his bag and slipped it jauntily on his head. It was a bit too large and, with his old grey suit, made him look like a shabby loafer instead of the owner of the boat, the name of which had once been painted on the stern, but had almost weathered away.

M RGAR T. LOW ST FT.

Without so much as a goodbye to Mr Conk, who had disembarked and stood eyeing him dubiously, Mr Lott, with a flourish, gently eased the boat from her moorings and began an uncertain course to the open sea. A few idlers watched him, laughing and commenting caustically among themselves on his navigation. There was little in the way of Mr Lott and the *Margaret*. Only a yacht rounding Penketh Point many miles to the north...

* * *

PETER DODD STOPPED his car opposite the Home Counties Bank. 'Wait here and I'll be back...' he said to Peg Boone and bounded out and through the great swing doors. Peg waited. Emotion, the quick sequence of events, and the faint stirrings of fear had left her numb. She hardly realised that she and Peter were on the run. He was back. 'Got it.'

He slid the car skilfully through the traffic and, as soon as the main stream of it thinned out, accelerated rapidly, keeping up a steady seventy, taking almost the same route as that along which Ishmael Lott was pursuing his lumbering, eager progress. Peter felt he didn't care as his foot trod the accelerator. If they came to grief, so much the worse. Bad luck had dogged him; a little more, and *finis* might be expected.

Peg Boone, who in her panic flight had thought only of herself and even abandoned her daughter, brooded as the miles passed. They had burned their boats! There could be no turning back. Henceforth their lives were together, and they held each other in the thrall of their wickedness and the secret they shared. She pressed her body closer to Peter's.

'Don't. I've no time now. Speed's what counts...'

He snarled it and she recoiled angrily.

In his pocket was the note Joan Jump had given him, authorising him to try out the *Betsy Jane*. Like hell he'd try her out! He planned to make for the French coast, provision the boat, and take on sufficient fuel for her auxiliary motor. Then it might mean France again, near the Spanish border, or Spain itself. Later, South America, and he'd have to find a job, because his mother's money wouldn't last forever.

The night before, he'd moved the boat from Lowestoft to Lumley's Cove, twenty miles to the North. A quiet little spot, three miles from anywhere. If the police started to watch the ports, they wouldn't think of Lumley's. The previous evening he had presented Miss Jump's note to Mr Caleb Conk, who had charge of the *Betsy Jane*. Caleb was the brother of Ephraim Conk, but they were not on speaking terms on account of a family schism about their Uncle Joe's will. Caleb, with enough money from Peter in his pocket to buy a barrel of ale, was not disposed to enquire very much about what he proposed to do with the boat. He knew Peter well.

'Have you brought your passport?' asked Peter of Peg abruptly.

'No. I never had one...'

He gave her one glance and she knew he despised her. She had bound him madly by her beauty and sensuality, tested them too far, and now...

Peter was in a dark mood. The monotony of the journey half hypnotised him. His mind worked as his body sat glued at the wheel. Since first he met Peg Boone, she had held him in bondage. The madness of desire, the pains of jealousy, the perpetual spurring of the wish to show her that, compared with other admirers, there was no limit to what he would do for her...

It was as if, for the first time, he was pausing to think in the wild career he and this woman had pursued since fate threw them together.

He remembered the night in the dark at Brande. His father had, on hearing his and Peg's proposal, slapped him across the mouth with the back of his hand. Peter hadn't hit back. He had felt like he had done when Harry Dodd chastised him as a boy. Then Peg Boone had butted in and...

In future he would be forever on the run, scratching for a living, honestly or dishonestly, a fugitive till the day he died. As the road flew past, he remembered the kindness of old Pharaoh, the man he'd killed to save his own neck. And his own flesh and blood Peg had killed to save hers...

Peter found he was thinking only of himself. In his mind's eye he was a solitary wanderer; Peg Boone had no part in it. They sat uneasily side by side. Peg was sure that as soon as this flight was over and they were settled quietly somewhere, safe alike from justice and curiosity, she could enchant him again and regain her hold over him. She smiled a lazy, voluptuous smile at her own thoughts and Peter caught it and his mood turned darker. He wished she were dead! From then on, his thoughts turned to death; not his own, but Peg's...

The *Betsy Jane* was at Lumley's waiting for them. Peter had spent a lot of time aboard her when old Pharaoh was alive. That made things worse. He'd been fond of the old man, but Pharaoh's straight accusation that either he or the Boones had killed Harry

Dodd… He couldn't let that pass. Especially when Pharaoh had tried to call a dock constable after Peter had haltingly endeavoured to explain…

Fifteen miles from Lowestoft, the road to Lumley's Cove showed almost like a cart-track, and Peter quickly turned left.

The way was through flat country, with ponds covered in reeds and drainage dykes cutting the fields. Birds rose, crying wildly as the car roared along. They passed between hedges, broken here and there by tumbledown gates; cattle looked up from their chewing at the thin grass. At length the hedges vanished, giving place to flat marshland through which the road ran like a causeway. There was nobody about and the only signs of life were the smoking chimneys of a distant farm. A sign pointing ahead indicated that in the holiday season trippers might sometimes visit the place. BEACH CAFE. TEAS. OPEN. They were nearing the coast. The tumbledown wooden shed advertised by the sign belied it, for it was closed down, the windows boarded, and the pot from the brick chimney lying broken on the threshold. The apology for a shore was really the estuary of a small river of brackish water flowing from the drains and ditches inland. The tide was in, and the *Betsy Jane*, forlorn and tied to a post, was bobbing in the wind.

Peter Dodd ran the car to the dilapidated hut, parked it inconspicuously, and got out. Peg Boone followed. They stood for a moment.

'What is it, Peter?'

She distrusted his mood, but thought he was contemplating turning back, whereas he was eager to be alone as soon as possible in the forthcoming adventure. He turned and looked back like one saying goodbye to something he didn't want to leave.

'Come on…'

They descended to the shore and Peter climbed aboard the *Betsy Jane*. It was as much as he could do to lend a hand to his companion to help her from the small stone jetty. This had at one time been a landing-place for pleasure boats, and the original owner of the now tumbledown bungalow cafe had erected a stone pier and bollard to enable fairly large craft to moor close in.

'Sit there...'

He indicated the tiller seat, and Peg obeyed without a word, giving him a questioning look. He cast off and started the auxiliary motor after an effort or two. The boat slid from the little harbour, down the estuary, and into the open sea...

Roe, the detective-sergeant detailed to keep Peter Dodd in sight, had followed the MG car, telephoning progress to headquarters along the way. His first news came from Thetford. Littlejohn received it from the Cambridge police.

'As we thought. He's heading for Lowestoft. He's planning a getaway in the *Betsy Jane*. Where he hopes to go, I can't think, but we've got to stop him...'

A fast car ran Littlejohn and Cromwell to Lowestoft. Roe and his companion in the police car had to stop and change a wheel twenty miles from Lowestoft, but they were quite easy about it.

'They've run right into the arms of the Lowestoft police. This road doesn't lead anywhere else...'

But the Lowestoft men arrived at the harbour to find the *Betsy Jane* missing. Mr Conk scratched his head in answer to their enquiries.

''E tuck 'er out last night and 'asn't come back yet. Guess he was wantin' to give 'er a proper run. Like as not, 'e's landed up at Lynn, I shouldn't be surprised...'

The local sergeant was annoyed by Mr Conk's flippancy. He regarded Caleb as a loafer, and his contempt for official questions irritated him.

'Rubbish! Dodd was back in Cambridge this morning. How can he be in Lynn? Have you been hiring her out on the side?'

Mr Conk was outraged. His face grew purple and he looked ready to burst.

'No, I 'aven't let 'er out on the QT. It's like the ruddy perlice to suggest sich a thing. If you'd get on with the job, stiddy theorisin'... The *Betsy Jane* ain't back, and I don't know nothin' o' where she is...'

'What's that...?'

The officer pointed to a small spot on the horizon, which in fact was Mr Ishmael Lott in search of France.

'A ruddy little fool as bought a motor-boat off my brother, Ephraim, and's takin' a 'oliday, by all account, tryin' to drown hisself coastin' around...'

Far out, Mr Lott was still pursuing an erratic course for what he thought was the Continent of Europe. He took from his bag a small brass telescope, drew out the segments, applied it to his eye, like a caricature of Lord Nelson, and searched ahead for the promised land. Suddenly he paused, shook his head, glued himself to the eyepiece again, and shouted aloud to nobody in particular. 'Hey... Hey... You mustn't... Hey...'

There was, ahead of him, a yacht which had rounded Penketh Point and, to the naked eye, looked like a graceful tiny toy. But in the lens of Mr Lott's telescope a grim drama was being revealed. One minute all was peaceful; the next two agitated figures were visible. One was a woman and the other a man. They were struggling, and the woman's hair had fallen and flowed over her shoulders as they fought. Mr Lott adjusted his telescope and got a clearer view. The man had the woman by the throat and was choking the life out of her. They rocked about and then, with a desperate heave, the man flung the girl from him. She reeled backwards, aided by the lurch of the boat, hit the water with a splash, and sank without a struggle.

Mr Lott tore his eye from his glass and looked around. At first, he had felt tempted to interfere, and then the consequences of such a rash act were fully borne upon him. He'd planned to make a show of sailing for Lynn. He'd told Mr Ephraim Conk he hoped to get there before dark, and Mr Conk had laughed. Once out of sight of land, however, he'd make for France and cheat them. In his tinpot way, he fancied France was just over the skyline. At all costs he mustn't become involved... And then a sight caught him which took his heart down to his boots. He was being followed by a fast launch which threw up a great feather in its wake. He screwed his glass in his eye with trembling hands. Police! He could see their uniforms plainly. Mrs Lott had found out and set them on his track! He forgot the boat ahead and its grim significance. He opened the throttle of the *Margaret* at full. She almost jumped out of the water and zigzagged her way ahead, now to Spain, now to Norway...

Peter Dodd, free from the encumbrance of his evil genius, altered course. Then he spotted the *Margaret*, making straight for him with corkscrew motions, her skipper waving him frantically aside, tinkering in the engine, rushing to the wheel, vainly trying to regain control.

Dodd yelled, Lott yelled, but somehow panic had reduced Ishmael to a series of crackpot movements which only added to the danger. His boat leapt like a torpedo in the direction of the *Betsy Jane*.

'Steer clear, you idiot!'

The pair of them recognised each other for a brief moment, and then, with all the wide ocean to go at, the *Margaret* hit the *Betsy Jane* full broadside. The yacht shook and heeled like a wounded bird, took a full wash of water and lay on her side. Peter Dodd, flung clear, floundered, rose, floundered again and sank. Ishmael Lott had no time to be bothered with him. He sat in his boat amid the wreckage, watching the water slowly rise in her and feeling her gently sinking beneath him. He couldn't swim. His wife and daughter seemed very dear and far away by now, and had he had anyone to offer it to, he would have unbelted his fortune and bartered it for a few more years of life. He said his prayers aloud in a whining voice and promised many things to the gods in exchange for rescue. His craft slid from under him as he wrestled with Providence, and he went down, yelling for help, flailing the air, swallowing water with every gulp and protest. He rose again, his thin arms beating the water. His yachting cap was still on his head. A boat-hook from the police launch caught his collar and hands were stretched out to him.

'I… I… He pushed 'er overboard… I didn't…'

'Yes, we know…'

But Mr Lott was unconscious and past hearing. He spewed water like a small hydrant as they pumped his lungs dry. The next day Mrs Lott and daughter arrived in Lowestoft to take him home in an ambulance.

''E must 'ave gone off 'is head. Mad!' said Mrs Lott when they told her. 'Stole 'is own lorry and lost his memory. I can't think wot's got in 'im…'

Mr Lott, dressed in somebody's flannels and sweater several sizes too large for him, smiling benignly, with his belt and its contents intact under his ill-fitting clothes, was turning over his next getaway. It included another boat from Lowestoft and a lorry parked in the same lane. His mind ran on tramlines and he couldn't get off them.

'Never saw such a modest chap as him,' said the male hospital orderly to his mate as he waved goodbye to Ishmael and his ambulance. 'He was half dead when they brought him in, but he wouldn't let us undress 'im. Kicked up a horrible row when we tried. We had to go out while he got off his wet things and put on a nightshirt. Same dressin' this mornin'. Clung to the bed and wouldn't start dressin' till we went out… No wonder, with a scraggy little body like his, he doesn't want to be seen naked…'

There was little more for Littlejohn and Cromwell to do, except attend the inquest. Peter Dodd's body was recovered almost at once on the scene of the accident. Peg Boone was washed ashore miles away, four days later.

'Harry Dodd at least got one wish. His little grand-daughter's in good hands and being brought up as he wanted. But what a cost! Five deaths which needn't have occurred but for that wicked woman. And to think that when I first met her, she seemed made of the right stuff. She could lie, improvise, and look like an angel at will…'

They were in the train on the way home, and Littlejohn seemed to be talking to himself.

'She took everybody in that way, from all accounts,' said Cromwell, ever eager to excuse his chief.

'All except Harry Dodd. That's why she killed him,' replied the Inspector.

They returned to Helstonbury again after the affair was cleared up. Judkin invited them down to the grand opening of his new police station. On that day, the Helstonbury force had a case which ended in the unsolved files. Mr Ishmael Lott, corn chandler, vanished from their midst and was never seen afterwards. His lorry was found parked in a lane near Lowestoft.

HALF-MAST FOR THE DEEMSTER

GEORGE BELLAIRS

1

HALF-MAST

"Any sign of land yet?"

The little man in a cloth cap and an overcoat several sizes too large for him regarded Littlejohn with pathetic dog-like eyes. His complexion was pale green, and he had only roused himself from his stupor in the hope of receiving some good news.

"I can't see anything…"

Littlejohn wasn't feeling very good himself. He had done a fair amount of sea travelling in his time; several trips to the Continent for holidays or to see officials at the Sûreté in Paris. Once he'd been over to New York to consult the FBI… But never anything like this! People said that on certain days you could see the Isle of Man from the mainland; now it seemed at the other end of the earth. This little man with his coat sleeves over his knuckles made retching noises, hurried to the rail of the ship, was met by a large wave, and retreated soaked to the skin. He didn't seem to mind…

"If I ever reach land, I'll never go to sea again…"

Archdeacon Caesar Kinrade, Vicar of Grenaby, in the Isle of Man, was the cause of it all.

"A friend of mine would like to have a talk with you," he had written. "And besides, if you don't pay me the promised visit before long, I will be too old to show you my beloved Isle. I am, as you know, eighty-three next birthday."

Mrs Littlejohn wasn't with him. Her sister, who had a Canon of the Church for a husband, and eight children, was moving again, this time to Comstock-in-the-Fen, and there was a vicarage with eleven bedrooms. With her ninth on the way and domestic help hard to get, the Canon's wife had sent the usual SOS to Hampstead…

It was the middle of September, and the weather on the mainland had been fine and bright. It had continued so across the Channel just long enough for an excellent lunch to be served, and thereupon the *Mona* had started to roll, then to pitch, and then both. Some of the passengers began to disappear down below; those who had been singing to the accompaniment of Sid Simmons and his Ten Hot Dogs, picked-up and broadcast over the ship's loud-speakers, had grown silent. Some lay on the floor and groaned; others were strewn all over the place. The timbers rolled under Littlejohn's feet; a blast of hot roast beef and cabbage rose from the dining-room and swept the deck. Littlejohn struggled to the top deck and looked out at the heaving water and the leaden sky.

"You ought to cross by boat," his wife had said. "It'll blow the cobwebs away…"

As he stood miserably peering ahead, the prospect slowly began to change. It was like the transformation scene at a pantomime, where the electricians by juggling with the lighting suddenly convert the devil's kitchen into the home of the fairy queen. The *Mona* was tossing in tortured gloom, but ahead the sun was shining on calm water, the sky was turning to blue, and, like a backcloth slowly illuminated by unseen floodlights, the Isle of Man with gentle green hills sweeping down to the sea, was stretched out before them.

The man in the big overcoat was at his elbow. He tapped Littlejohn's arm gaily. His complexion had changed to a rosy pink and the brandy he had absorbed rose abundantly on his breath.

"What did I tell you?" he said, as though he'd been a prophet of salvation all the way. "What did I tell you? There she is…"

He flapped his sleeve at the Island, like a conjurer who has performed a difficult trick. Having thus justified himself, he made off to the bar to celebrate. People were surging on deck smiling and congratulating one another as though the end of the world had somehow been deferred. As if to cheer them up still more, the *Mona* slid into calm water and blew a wild blast on her siren to those ashore, like a badly frightened cock which crows when danger is past. The echo from Douglas Head threw back the sound.

The man in the overcoat was back.

"What about a li'l drink?" he said to Littlejohn.

The holiday season was drawing to an end, but there was a good crowd waiting on the pier for the arrival of the boat, which glided comfortably into harbour and which, by an admirable piece of practised seamanship, the captain brought gently alongside in a matter of minutes. Someone waved to Littlejohn as he tried to catch the eye of a porter and get rid of his luggage.

The Rev Caesar Kinrade, Archdeacon of Man, was standing sturdily among a crowd of his friends, his shovel hat riding above the gallant white froth of his whiskers, his blue eyes sparkling. He wore his archidiaconal gaiters, too, but not like an immaculate prince of the Church; they looked utilitarian, like those of his forebears who, riding from parish to parish in the course of duty, found them more convenient on horseback than a cassock. The group round the parson all scrutinised Littlejohn with genial curiosity. The old man, with the native delight in tale-telling, had been treating them to the saga of how Littlejohn and he had between them solved the case of the man in dark glasses, and thus laid the foundation of a firm friendship.

Lying in ambush in the quayside carpark were Teddy Looney

and his chariot. The old touring car, looking like a cross between a charabanc and a hearse, had been spring-cleaned and the brass bonnet shone in the sun. Looney grinned and bared a gap in his teeth. He was pleased to see Littlejohn again and glad that the prompt arrival of the boat would get him safely home for milking time.

"Good day, Parson…"

"Now, Reverend! Good to put a sight on ye…"

"Nice day, Master Kinrade. And how's yourself …?"

It was like a royal procession to Teddy's rattletrap. Everybody knew Parson Kinrade, and everybody was glad to see him around.

The porter with Littlejohn's bags wouldn't be paid when he found the Inspector was a friend of the Archdeacon, and Littlejohn had to thrust five shillings in the man's pocket to ease his own conscience. The pair of them were almost hoisted into Teddy's tumbril by friendly hands and with a jerk the vehicle made a start. They ran alongside the old quay, bristling with the masts of tiny craft of all descriptions, dirty coasters busy unloading, trim yachts, timber boats from the Continent…

"Hullo, there, Parson…"

The good vicar of Grenaby shook his head at Littlejohn.

"I'll have to stop coming down to Douglas. They all get so excited to see me, and I get too excited, too, at seeing them. I'll be giving myself a stroke or something…"

The old car tossed round the bridge at the end of the quay and took to the country. Beneath the agitation of Teddy's conveyance, Littlejohn could still feel the roll of the deck he had endured for, it seemed, untold hours.

"Take the old road, Teddy…"

The car rattled through Port Soderick village, raced down Crogga Hill, turned on two wheels at the bottom, and snorted up the other side. They reached the top with difficulty and there stopped, for the contraption seemed to have caught fire. Dirty smoke oozed from under the bonnet, which Teddy opened to disclose a lot of dirty rags, smouldering with choking fumes.

"Forgot to take out me cleanin' cloths," he said, scattering them over the stone wall which skirted the road.

The parson, who hitherto had seemed half asleep, happy to let Littlejohn enjoy the scenery on the way in peace, suddenly roused himself.

"Let us out of this, Looney. We'll stretch our legs, and, if you can get going again, you can catch us up. Come on, Littlejohn, stir your stumps. I've something to show you..."

They strolled to an eminence in the road and the old man pointed in the direction of the sea.

"There! Did you ever see the likes of that?"

Difficult to believe the ocean had ever been rough, for now it stretched like a sheet of green glass as far as you could see. Between the road and the sea, undulating fields, divided by sod hedges, with gorse flaming on top of them and with clean white farmsteads dotted about them. Beyond, a long spit of land, like a granite spur, jutted out, with a ruined chapel and a fort at one side and a lighthouse on the other, and in the middle of the base of this triangle of rock, the towers of King William's College, in the old island capital of Castletown, rose strong and grey.

Parson Kinrade fished in the tails of his coat and brought out an old pipe, which he filled from a pewter tobacco-box, after telling Littlejohn to help himself. They leaned their elbows on the wall and smoked, and Looney who had drawn up beside them, knew better than disturb them.

"We've to call at Castletown," said the Archdeacon at length. "The court's sitting there today and I've promised we'll pick up the Deemster when it's finished... Know what a Deemster is?"

"A judge here, isn't he?"

"More than that, Littlejohn. A very ancient office... very ancient and stands in eminence next to that of the Governor of the Isle himself. In this small place, the Deemster's all His

Majesty's mainland judges rolled into one. Civil, Criminal, County Court, Quarter Sessions... All rolled into one. Judge of Appeal, too, against the decisions of his colleague, the other Deemster, when he sits with a judge from over the water to help him..."

"A busy man!"

"That's right. And before the laws were written or decisions recorded, he'd to remember the law... Breast Law it was then, as if cherished in his heart... They only take civil cases in Castletown now. First-Deemster Quantrell's sitting today. I'm calling to bring him with us for dinner at Grenaby. He wants to meet you. He's in trouble. Somebody's tried twice to murder him."

The parson dropped his last sentence like a bombshell and then was silent. It seemed impossible to think of murder in such a place. The birds were singing; the gulls were crying; a man, a woman and a sheep-dog climbed the road over the hill opposite and vanished; a small train puffed past in a cloud of steam and whistled; and, out at sea, a yacht with white sails spread, slid quietly round the granite spur of Langness and was gone.

Littlejohn pushed his hat on the back of his head, rubbed his chin, and smiled.

"My wife's last words were 'Keep out of mischief,'" he said. "By which she meant, I always seem to run into trouble if I go on holidays without her."

Parson Kinrade tapped his pipe on the wall.

"Oh, come now. I'm not intending this to be a busman's holiday. You're here because I wanted to see you again. But whilst you're with us, I thought you might perhaps help and advise a good man who's in trouble."

"Only my joke. Of course, I'll do anything you want. But aren't the local police good enough? They might take it to heart if—how do you say it?—if 'a fellah from over' started trying to teach them their business."

The vicar patted the moss on top of the wall and then turned his far-seeing eyes on the Inspector.

"This is only a little island, Littlejohn. News travels fast. They love a little gossip and the police aren't above joining in. Once it got abroad that somebody was out to murder a Deemster, where would he be? The law is above everybody else. It's safe and impregnable. Or that's the illusion that's to be created about it if people are to respect it. 'That's the man somebody's after murdering,' would think every malefactor brought before him. It just wouldn't do, Littlejohn. That's why Deemster Quantrell's told nobody but me and I said you were the man to share the secret and put it right in secret. Understand?"

"I understand. How did it happen?"

"Simply enough. His Honour drives his own car. The roads are good here and one tends to develop a fair turn of speed. Even Teddy there... The hills are pretty steep and there are bends and drops at the bottom of them. Fortunately the Deemster's steering went wrong too soon. It broke as he drove it out of his garage. Whoever'd sawn into it, did it a bit too much..."

"*Sawn* into it? Are you sure?"

"His Honour's no fool. In his young days, he mended his own motorbike and then his car. It was sawn, all right. He guessed then that somebody was up to no good. He kept it quiet for his wife's sake and, lest some local tittle-tattler should get talking, he sent for new parts and a mechanic from the mainland to fit them."

"But who could have wished to...?"

"That's just it. Who could? Deemster Quantrell's a member of a very old Manx family, always highly regarded, which has given to this land dozens of fine men; deemsters, doctors, lawyers, parsons. Everybody loves the Quantrells. And as for criminals he's sentenced...Do the mainland judges get murdered for their judgments? No, they don't. And any fierce sentences Deemster Quantrell ever gave were in the past, long ago. There hasn't been a murder trial here for untold years and most of the real bad criminals go across to the mainland and commit their evil deeds and get their just dues across the water…"

"What about the second attempt, sir?"

"Two bricks off a block of property being pulled down in Douglas. *Two*, I said. Like the barrels of a shot gun. Bang down comes one and misses His Honour's head by inches. Then another. And nobody up on the building, because it's dinner time for the men."

"Is he sure it was deliberately done?"

"No wind blowing; no children playing on the site. Just nobody about. Deemster Quantrell sent a policeman to look into it. He said he'd seen something fall down. He didn't tell the officer it had nearly fallen *on* him… That settled in his mind that somebody was out to give him trouble, to put it mildly…"

Littlejohn knocked out his pipe and shook his head.

"It looks like deliberate attempted murder. It's as well we're going to meet the Deemster. Maybe I can do something."

"I'm sure you can. Quietly, circumspectly, you'll put things right. We'll talk it over after dinner, and then you can decide what to do for the best. Well … I see Teddy's getting mad at the thought of his unmilked cows. Let's be getting along."

They followed the undulating road, with broad panoramas of hills and the sea until, with a quick turn, it joined the main highway to the village of Ballasalla, beyond which the view opened to reveal the ancient island capital of Castletown with its old granite castle standing like a bastion ahead of them. As they slowed down to pass the busy airport of Ronaldsway, the parson gripped Littlejohn's arm and pointed ahead.

On the topmost tower of Castle Rushen stood a flagstaff, and they were slowly hauling up the flag.

Teddy Looney turned in his seat.

"They seem to be celebratin', sir…"

"Wait!"

The limp flag had stopped half-mast, and a puff of wind caught it, revealing the emblem of the Island, three legs, in armour, and spurred, in gold on a red ground.

"Half-mast?"

"Hurry ahead, Looney," cried Parson Kinrade. "I hope it isn't, but it looks as if … as if …"

"Half-mast for the Deemster, sir?"

Littlejohn finished it for him, and they sat in silence until Looney braked at the roundabout leading to the by-pass road at Castletown.

"Go along into the town, Looney…"

But the parson needn't have said it. Standing at the junction was a policeman with a bicycle, who jumped with interest at the sight of Looney's car. He hurried across and held up his hand. He saluted smartly as he saw the Rev Caesar Kinrade.

"Afternoon, Archdeacon. The sergeant said I was to look out for you on your way back from Douglas, and say he'd like to see you, if you don't mind…"

"I was coming in any case … I promised to pick up the Deemster…"

The constable's face assumed a look of reverent awe, as though he were already marching in the funeral procession.

"The Deemster died half an hour since. That's what the sergeant said he wanted to see you for… And …"

The bobby turned to Littlejohn, gave him a look of admiration and fellow-feeling, and saluted again, a feat which required considerable contortion, because the officer's head was thrust through the open window of the car.

"And are you Inspector Littlejohn, sir, of Scotland Yard?"

He uttered Scotland Yard in tones a pilgrim would use of Mecca.

"Yes, Constable…"

"I was to bring you along, too."

"Why?" asked the parson curiously. "Nobody knows he's here… Or do they?"

The constable cleared his throat.

"Beggin' your pardon, Archdeacon, but I shouldn't be talkin' like this. The sergeant said to bring you right away… But they found a note the Deemster must have just started to write before he died. It said, 'My dear Inspector Littlejohn…' and then it finished. So the sergeant said you was to come as well, *if* you please…"

He flipped a thumb at Teddy Looney to indicate he had better be driving along and mounted his bicycle to escort them.

"Here, here," called the Archdeacon. "How did he die? Was he murdered…? Shot…? Stabbed…? What?"

He couldn't wait.

The constable looked at the ancient whiskers reproachfully.

"Oh, come, sir. Not that. He had a seizure in his room in the court. They found him dead when they went to call him after the lunch adjournment… They thought at first he was asleep…"

And to speed up progress, the bobby put on a spurt, pedalled ahead, and waved to Teddy Looney to get a move on.

Join the
GEORGE BELLAIRS
READERS' CLUB

And get your next George Bellairs Mystery free!

When you sign up, you'll receive:

1. A free classic Bellairs mystery, *Corpses in Enderby*;

2. Details of Bellairs' new publications and the opportunity to get copies in advance of publication; and,

3. The chance to win exclusive prizes in regular competitions.

Interested?

It takes less than a minute to join. Just go to

www.georgebellairs.com

to sign up, and your free eBook will be sent to you.

Printed in Great Britain
by Amazon